By Caite Dolan-Leach

Dead Letters
We Went to the Woods

We Went to the Woods

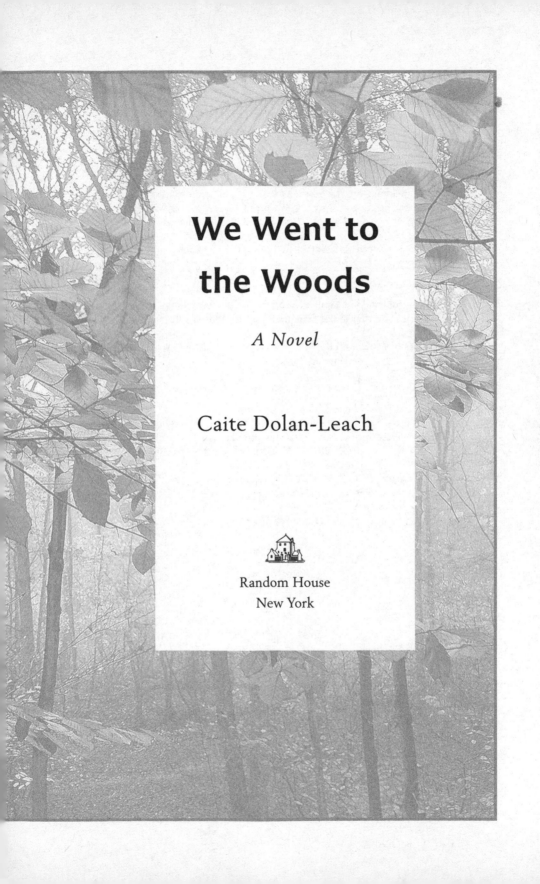

We Went to the Woods

A Novel

Caite Dolan-Leach

Random House
New York

Published in the United States by Random House, an imprint and division of Penguin Random House LLC, New York.

RANDOM HOUSE and the HOUSE colophon are registered trademarks of Penguin Random House LLC.

LIBRARY OF CONGRESS CATALOGING-IN-PUBLICATION DATA
Names: Dolan-Leach, Caite, author.
Title: We went to the woods : a novel / Caite Dolan-Leach.
Description: New York : Random House, [2019]
Identifiers: LCCN 2018042712 | ISBN 9780399588884 |
ISBN 9780399588891 (ebook)
Classification: LCC PS3604.O429 W4 2019 | DDC 813/.6—dc23
LC record available at https://lccn.loc.gov/2018042712

Printed in the United States of America on acid-free paper

randomhousebooks.com

2 4 6 8 9 7 5 3 1

First Edition

Design by Virginia Norey

Art from original photos by FreeImages.com and attributed as follows:
Title page / Pete Hellebrand; part titles: Winter / Troy Sherk, Spring / Sandy Yin,
Summer / Liviu J, Autumn / John Evans, 2nd Winter / Benjamin Earwicker.

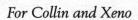

For Collin and Xeno

I went to the woods because I wished to live deliberately, to front only the essential facts of life, and see if I could not learn what it had to teach, and not, when I came to die, discover that I had not lived.

—HENRY DAVID THOREAU, *Walden*

In one word, Thoreau was a skulker. He did not wish virtue to go out of him among his fellow-men, but slunk into a corner to hoard it for himself. He left all for the sake of certain virtuous self-indulgences.

—ROBERT LOUIS STEVENSON, *Familiar Studies of Men and Books*

And what is wrong with their life? What on earth is less reprehensible than the life of the Levovs?

—PHILIP ROTH, *American Pastoral*

We Went to the Woods

I'm the wrong one to tell our story. I was the late arrival, the last on board, the self-effacing supplement to the lopsided structure of which Louisa and Beau were the main architects. If only it were Beau telling our tale, drawling his way through it, cigarillo dangling from his lips. Or Louisa, nattering on with her breakneck fluency. Best of all, maybe, Jack, with his sculpted insights, frank amazement, arms carving out a circumference of joy. Chloe could convince anyone that we were beautiful and right and noble to do what we did. Instead, of the five of us, I am the only one left. I was the least important, the watchful cipher who served only as an audience and an extra body, an afterthought. Maybe Beau knew that he would need someone outside their tight quadrilateral, to record and capture them, to witness—an extra point to make a pentagon. After all, he was the only one who knew the ending of the story we all thought we were writing together.

Today, I watched a squatter take a shit on the hill directly opposite my apartment window, and I thought of our composting toilet, the filth of five people, which we diligently shoveled, each in our turn. I wonder if she's still there, or whether she has abandoned our little failed paradise, leaving the basil to seed and the squash to rot back into the ground. I don't know what I hope for.

I am self-conscious here, feeling badly misplaced in Africa. Everyone talks about crime, obsessively. Every time I stretch my legs out to touch the sidewalk, I glance around, wondering who has noticed me, who has marked my body as a target. I leave my earrings, a gift from Chloe, at home, carry my effects in a ratty tote bag rather than in Jack's expensive backpack, which Louisa bequeathed to me before we parted. I do not want to advertise my privilege. I carry it around, ashamed of it and myself, lying about what I pay for airfare or computers or cheese. What to do about it? Give it back? I may as well try to give away my skin. I rub the now-smooth knuckles of my right hand, where my two missing fingers used to be, and think of those mislaid digits as twin ghosts.

Today is the anniversary. I will be hauntingly aware of it, an old delicious burden, all day, nursing it along, sipping from it as if from a hidden flask. It seems unreal, though, here in the sunlight. Today, those four people are just constructs. I came here as penance, but also partly to avoid experiencing another wintry March. So that I can separate myself from the person who feels that cold, heavy sky pulling downward on my skin. Here, in the sun, winter is impossible. And so they cannot be dead. No wintry roads and half-lit sunsets. No cults, no messy, complicated sex. No rabid convictions and desperate bids to defend them. One year since the failure of our (was it ours? or theirs? or maybe just his?) Experiment. One year since "the accident." By all appearances, I wake up, go to the townships, and halfheartedly teach English, but truly, I'm still awakening at dawn, sitting on the porch of the big cabin, sipping coffee in sleepy silence with the four of them. I put myself to sleep with a little pill, but I'm really watching the fire as Beau throws another log onto it, laughing at the taste of Jack's first appalling attempt at honey mead, watching Louisa's red hair mimic the flame, Chloe sidling up close like an adored cat and meeting a pair of lips. (Whose?) Our bodies twining together, separating, returning. I am still there with them, and I know that I will never really leave.

❧

Louisa called it apocalyptic provisioning, Jack called it the Grand Experiment, Chloe called it simply our homestead, and Beau never gave it a name. He didn't need to; he was certain enough of what we were doing that he didn't have to give it substance with clever words. It was real to him, in a way that we didn't fully grasp until it ended. I sought desperately for a clever title of my own but never mustered the courage to float my suggestions. Privately, I thought we could reasonably be called preppers, survivalists. We soon adopted Chloe's title in any case. Naturally.

We all secretly acknowledged that Louisa and Beau were the engineers of our experiment, though they insisted on maintaining the fiction that it had been engendered by the five of us. They had been talking about escaping the world, starting it over and doing it right, since tenth grade. But they claimed that it was only when we all came together that their project began to seem like a real possibility. We were the missing pieces, and nothing could begin until we were all united.

Supposedly.

Winter

Chapter 1

The day I met Louisa was not a good one. I woke early, as I had been doing since my ignominious homecoming, and, in spite of myself, reached for my phone. After everything that had happened on the show, I'd publicly tweeted an apology before shutting down my Facebook and Instagram and Twitter; all had become so toxic that just the sight of those little icons on my screen made my stomach flip with dread. My email, however, was still a miserable depository for the anger that could no longer be directed at my body or my social media. I opened it every morning despite the regularity with which threats and hatred found their way to me through the Internet.

This morning, there was just one new entry. I thought this might bode well for my day, even for my (shattered) future. Perhaps it signaled a downtick in the rage I had sparked? After all, how long could this group of strangers pursue me?

Today's email was not from the usual crowd of pissed-off spectators, however. I could typically disregard those messages as the words of (justifiably) frustrated but abstract strangers. This email was from Sara, my betrayed housemate, and she was calm and reasonable and direct, as ever. We hadn't communicated since she had publicly denounced me, and reading her words made me shudder with guilt. She couldn't forgive me, she said, but she needed to move on from what had happened and I should too. I threw up in the bathroom, clutching the cold tile of the floor and inhaling the ammoniac reek of piss, before I read the email again. Crouched on the shaggy blue shower mat, I looked at Sara's words again and again, and wished I could undo what I had done. I had replayed that disastrous interview so many times to myself, with so many eloquent justifications spun out soundlessly in the dark of my bedroom, rehearsed for an imagined audience. But this morning, reading her email, there was no denying that what I had done couldn't be excused. Whatever my delusions, I had badly fucked up.

During the last few months, I had developed a schedule to accommodate my desire to avoid my parents, with whom I was living. A disgraced baby bird returned to the nest. Though I sometimes woke while they were puttering around in their nearly silent morning routine of coffee and dry toast and backing vehicles out of the driveway to head drudgingly to work, I would lurk in my room until the sound of their two decrepit cars had faded. I listened to them talk at breakfast, in hushed tones about me and in glowing tones about my little brother, Ben, who was their success story, I supposed. Ben's friends, Ben's Future in Finance. Mackenzie's Failures.

After they headed off, I would go about my own dreary routine. Instead of swapping out sweatpants for something with a zipper, I would plunk myself down on the living room couch and flip open my laptop to begin my desperate daily hunt. Not a lot of jobs out there, however, for someone who had recently been publicly discredited. Occasionally, when I was particularly self-loathing, I would Google myself, which would remind me what my chances of employment really were.

I was an hour or two into my grim scavenging when my phone rang. I pounced on it, irrationally hoping that this might at last be the tug on the line, a fish, however tiny, that I could reel in. I swallowed and growled, to clear my throat, before answering in my very best professional voice.

"Hi, this is Mack Johnston," I said.

"Changed your name, huh? I know who you are. And what you did. I hope someone betrays your trust as—"

I jerked the phone away from my face, glancing briefly at the number before stabbing the red icon to end the call. I thought I'd successfully changed my number and hidden my tracks after fleeing Brooklyn, but clearly someone had ferreted out my details yet again. The knowledge of my continued visibility made me feel vulnerable, even sitting here, buoyed by low-budget Raymour & Flanigan and my mother's tacky throw pillows.

Thankfully, I had work today, a catering gig I'd had on and off since high school, and one of the few options for employment open to me. The money was better than nothing but would not allow me to move out of my parents' house; I was barely able to afford a meager shopping list and the occasional cup of coffee. I had no idea what I'd do when I could no longer defer my student loans. And I was still waiting to hear if there would be a lawsuit, of course.

I was grateful to go to work most days, because it meant leaving the house and escaping my sinister laptop. Because Ithaca is such a small town, I did occasionally find myself having to answer awkward questions about what I was currently doing and what my plans were, but I was grateful to be doing something, anything at all. If people knew what had happened to me—what I had done—they tactfully pretended not to. Even if most of my days felt useless, days where I came home with some cash felt like they hadn't been entirely wasted. This depressed me, this feeling that my life mattered only as it was measured out in paper dollars. But most things depressed me at the moment. At least it was harder to mope while up to my elbows in greasy dishwater or passing hors d'oeuvres to a roomful of strangers who were perfectly happy to ignore me. I was enjoying the invisibility of the food service worker.

Until the afternoon I worked a fundraiser and met Louisa.

The event was for the wealthy supporters of the Land Trust, a group of people committed to conservation on the lakefronts of the Finger Lakes. Their mission was to prevent development in natural environments all along the shores of our lake, and this little shindig was being held at the lab of ornithology, an architecturally impressive building set in the middle of a bird swamp. My antipathy towards the bulk of these catering events meant that I rarely paid attention to their purpose or their patrons, and I usually passed canapés listlessly, too busy wallowing in my own gloom to engage with anyone. I liked the idea of this party, though, which was being held either to raise money to protect a swath of lakeside nesting grounds for loons and other fowl or to celebrate having already raised the impressively large sum. It was a nice change of pace from bat mitzvahs held in temple basements or departmental parties where everyone wore the same expression of bored obligation and the grad students tried to knock back as much cheap albariño as they could manage.

While the ornithology lab was a beautiful building, it wasn't really set up for food service, and after I'd lugged several cocktail tables upstairs and schlepped in tablecloths from the vans, my calves were screaming. I lobbied my boss to be installed behind the bar, a task I preferred to passing apps; those who frequented the foldout table covered with rented linens and local wines were deeply appreciative of my services, while the same people impatiently swatted away the platters of crostini and tartlets. I poured hefty glugs of wine into the plastic cups of those who held them out, and leaned against the wall while various members of the Land Trust gave speeches and talked about the waterbirds and the woodlands that would now remain safe because of these millions of dollars. I felt very pleased that the loons would have their home preserved, but also a bit queasy at the vastness of the wealth being displayed. The room was very white.

At some point, a caption contest was announced, and the room tittered with pleasure. Buzzed folk love a competition. I've watched drunk parents at fancy birthdays play cornhole for two hours, never growing bored of chucking a beanbag into a box.

The drawing to be captioned was of a melting iceberg, upon which was perched a visibly nervous polar bear. The crowd was requested to provide a pithy caption, the most entertaining of which would secure its author a very extravagant gift basket.

I knew that I wasn't supposed to enter the competition. But I also knew that if I did, it would be extremely poor form for the organizers to exclude me; they could hardly reject my entry just because I was the Help. And I was skull-crackingly bored. So, in a moment of quiet at my bar station, I slunk over to the entry box, grabbed a Sharpie, and scribbled the first thing that had popped into my head, not looking around to see if anyone was observing my bold move. I felt seen, though, out of place in my all-black uniform and my clogs.

Back at the bar, I was tense. I craved invisibility, and yet I had just positioned myself for possible exposure, exactly as I had done last year in Brooklyn. I seemed to always battle between a conscious desire to stay hidden and a more sneaky desire for the spotlight. I tossed back a tumbler of wine when I thought no one was looking.

As the evening was drawing to a close, the competition winners were announced. Everyone was milling boozily around, eager for the results. The runner-up entries were embarrassing; they were silly and badly phrased, and bore the mark of people trying too hard to be funny. My heart began to thud as I realized what was about to happen.

"And the winner is—and I must say, they're a bit of a dark horse—but the winner is Mackenzie Johnston. Mackenzie, are you around? I understand she works with the caterers." Though some members of the crowd looked a teensy bit miffed, I could tell that others were visibly pleased at my win, and I felt chastened for my certainty of their class disapproval. I was sure that I had written "Mack" on my entry, not "Mackenzie"; the woman must have checked with my boss, who had always called me by my full name.

"Her caption was: 'But hey, at least gas prices are down!'" I walked up to the podium to accept my prize, my cheeks burning, and took my gift basket back to the kitchen, wishing I could go straight home. It had been a silly caption, and not at all clever, but there was something pleasurable about public recognition for something I had done well, rather than for my inadequacies.

My employers seemed amused, though it occurred to me that they maybe would have preferred if I'd asked permission. Everyone in the kitchen cooed over my bounty—coffee, biscuits, gift certificates. It really was a very nice gift basket.

"I'm just going to pop back to the bar and start packing it up," I said, to avoid any further conversation about my coup. I knew that my co-workers found me surly and standoffish. I didn't mind.

Someone had made off with at least two bottles of open wine (this always happened if the bar was left unsupervised), so I began tidying up the station, clearing away the used cups and corks and eyeballing the stragglers, who would remain within reach of the bar until all the visible alcohol had been definitively taken away.

"Nice work with the preening bourgeoisie," someone said to me, plunking an empty cup down on the bar. I looked up to see a redhead with wild corkscrew curls watching me, her cheeks flushed and her eyes squinting with entertainment. "Really pulled the rug out from under the Cornell intelligentsia."

"Well, that wasn't my intention," I said, sounding very prim.

"Good to take them down a peg. The savior complex in here gets to be a bit overbearing otherwise. Save the goslings, save the world."

"I can think of worse things."

"Oh, indeed. Everyone here's just a bit divorced from the lives of the other half," she said, helping herself to the last of a bottle of red wine.

"I would have thought *every*one attending this party would be . . . sort of upper-crust," I said, meeting her eyes. She had a spray of freckles across the bow of her nose. She laughed, tossing her head back.

"Touché. Though I am merely second-generation gentility. I'm here to supervise my father, who is a longtime supporter of the Trust. We were supposed to have a dinner date, but instead . . ." She waved around at the emptying room. "In any case, folk our age are unlikely to have the income to toss at ducklings and spiffy parties. Alas." Her tone was both flippant and self-aware, and I found it hard to get a read on her.

"Why do you think *I'm* here," I said flatly.

"To rub shoulders with the town's elite?" she asked.

I snorted. "For my student loans. Four hundred parties and I'll be free and clear."

"With or without interest?"

"Without." She nodded. I didn't know why I was revealing my debt situation to a stranger, but I found her compelling. And very odd.

"You're Mackenzie, right? Mackenzie Johnston?" she asked. I took a quick breath in alarm. Had she recognized me? Had she seen the show? But then I remembered that my name had been announced with my win.

"Mack. And you . . . ?"

"Louisa. Stein-Jackson. Oh Lord, there goes my doddering paterfamilias. I'd better collect him before he starts begging for scraps in the kitchen." Her eyes followed a round and redheaded man who was, indeed, headed towards the kitchen.

"Just three hundred and ninety-nine more to go, kiddo. Chin up!" Louisa launched herself away from the table and made for the door. Midway, she paused and turned. "Listen, I'm having some people over to my house in a few hours. Garden party. Wanna come?"

I met everyone later that night at Louisa's garden party, which, in winter, was not actually held in the garden. The jamboree was a way to combat the cabin fever that infects upstate New York in the tail months of winter, a claustrophobia that becomes almost desperate by April, when we are still likely to be subjected to late-season squalls. I felt like the plain cousin at some fabulous family gathering. They all looked like they were in costume: vintage tea dresses, white linen, a straw fedora. Having come straight from catering, I was clad in dreary black with a modest hem and neckline, sporting sensible clogs and hair that smelled vaguely of dishwasher. I did not look remotely festive. My feet hurt. I had brought a cheap bottle of local plonk—something called a Silenus Riesling—that even I knew was embarrassingly low-quality, but I currently had around seventy-five dollars in my bank account and owed my parents one hundred. Louisa graciously accepted it without too much of a raised eyebrow, and Chloe suggested adding it immediately to the rapidly diminishing punch bowl of Pimm's that sat on the table, a clever solution that would mask its raw bite. It was just the four of them, munching on Louisa's canapés and arguing.

"But don't you worry that conversations about sexual politics and assault have so diluted everything that we're in danger of completely denying women consent?" (Chloe.)

"Hands off that amuse-bouche, Jack! Such hunger, such boundless cupidity!" (Louisa.)

"Emerson could really be a tedious old windbag." (Beau.)

"I've been trying to make my own sourdough starter for weeks, and it is just, like, total and utter gloop. What do you think I'm doing wrong?" (Jack.)

"I'm really not sure that I'm interested in the essentializing nature of identity politics—" (Louisa.)

"Louisa! That's because you're white." (Chloe.)

"And rich." (Beau.)

"The original bourgeois socialist." (Jack.)

I reclined in the crook of Louisa's parlor, letting Chloe refill my cup and hand me delightful ginger-watercress morsels. She had a way of hooking my wrist with her fingers whenever she brought me something, a startling intimacy that made me drop my eyes each time. Louisa's hand rested on Chloe's hip in an almost proprietorial way, and Chloe always seemed to angle herself towards Louisa, resting her head on the redhead's shoulder. Beau, watchful as a wolf, followed them with his eyes.

I didn't understand yet what this triangle would come to mean to me, and how its geometry would drive me mad.

"Okay, but the way we live is grotesque," Jack was saying, arms swishing through the air. "Look at this. Almost none of the food we're eating came from within a hundred miles of here, and most of it's probably genetically engineered so that it can sit in a diesel-fueled truck for two weeks while it's being shipped from California. Where, I should add, it was picked by an exploited and underpaid workforce."

"I grew those tomatoes," Louisa said, pointing to the tomato chutney. "Though I'm not totally convinced they're safe to eat. Turns out there's industrial runoff everywhere here in Fall Creek. I added shit tons of vinegar and cooked it for about five hours, though."

"Tomatoes aside, you have to recognize there's something really, really wrong. I hate to throw around the word 'unsustainable'—"

"No, you don't," Beau said.

"No, I don't. This is fucking unsustainable."

"So when do we start the revolution?" Chloe asked.

"Yeah, yeah. Poke fun at me. I know you all agree." They all giggled and popped more treats into their mouths.

I was charmed. I'd spent my time since coming home making awkward conversation with my disillusioned folks and avoiding anyone I might know from high school, ashamed of my misdeeds and my extended career in food service. I was hungry for conversation, for people who played parts and overimbibed and told stories and knew one another too well.

"It just seems relatively apparent that the world's ending, is all," Jack reasserted.

"Haven't we always believed that, though? I mean, every generation? Humans are always convinced they will be the last generation," Louisa countered. "The Four Perpetual Horsemen of the Apocalypse."

"Sure, but other generations didn't literally have scientists telling them we probably won't live out the century," Jack said.

"No, they just had a Bible that said so, or a Mayan prophecy," Chloe pointed out.

"Or imminent atomic warfare," Beau added.

"But come on! We are definitely cruising towards the end times, guys," Jack said.

"Might be so," Beau agreed.

I drank quite a bit of Pimm's Cup, so I can't be perfectly certain, but

I don't think the Homestead was explicitly mentioned. Louisa and Beau were still mulling it over, tinkering with the idea and preparing to unveil their plan. Louisa, with her flair for theatricality, wanted to do it right, with the appropriate level of panache. She understood that we needed to fall in love with the idea, to be seduced by its romance.

Chapter 2

A week after the garden party, we went out to the Home-stead for the first time. The outing was shrouded in mystery, and we were all desperately curious to see whatever Louisa had percolating for us. She had been circumspect, and promised we would all discuss it together, once we saw it. I was the only one with my own vehicle, a rusty pickup that could fit three people but would soon regularly be deployed to transport all five of us, two riding on laps or quite illegally in the bed. It had belonged to my father and was yet another charity begrudgingly offered to me, along with my childhood bedroom and tense dinners of meatloaf and tuna casserole. I left my parents' house in the midst of a mild disagreement; I had failed to tell them that I was supping elsewhere that evening, and my mother had prepared baked ziti, apparently just for me. Though she said nothing, I could see her tight-lipped hurt, and my taciturn father had upbraided me as harshly as he knew how.

"This isn't a bed-and-breakfast, young lady. You're not on vacation, and it isn't your mother's job to make you special meals." I knew the subtext here was that this domestic situation was untenable. I was aware. Oh, was I aware. As I was mumbling my excuses, my phone rang, and assuming it was Louisa, wondering at my whereabouts or requesting that I fetch something for her, I answered.

"Hi there, bitch. I see you answered, you fucking coward—" I hung up as quickly as I could. The act of answering my phone in the middle of a family discussion didn't seem to endear me to my father.

"And that's another thing. You're on one of those devices every minute of every day. That's not how you're going to fix this situation you've created for yourself."

"Darling, I don't think we need to talk about this," my mother interjected. "I think Mackenzie has been through quite the ordeal."

"My mother lived through the Depression. I think Mackenzie should be able to handle this mess."

"Why don't we talk about it later? Mackenzie, honey, are you going to eat with some friends? I could make you a Tupper of ziti. . . ." At my father's expression, she abandoned the rest of her offer.

"No, no, we're eating at my friend's house. I'm sorry, Mommy, I didn't think you had anything planned. Next time I'll let you know in advance, it's just that Louisa—"

She put up a hand to stop me. "I'm glad you have some friends to support you. I think it's good that you're getting out of the house for a bit."

I bit back tears at her patience, at her bloody niceness.

"Thanks, Mommy." I gave her a quick peck on the cheek before darting for the door. In my coat pocket, I could feel my phone vibrating with another phone call. I ignored it.

For our grand arrival at the Homestead, Louisa had said she would borrow her dad's Volvo and she and Beau would meet us out there. We were given directions sketched out on a napkin, told to bring wine and fresh bread and arrive at five so that we could walk around while there was still some dimly glowing late-winter sun.

My little truck was not the best vehicle for snowy roads, but I'd learned to drive on the slushy surfaces of central New York, and we took it slow up the big hill out of the city. We drove ten miles out of town, onto dirt roads bordered by heaps of gray sludge that looked like they were desperately hoping to melt away. Even the snow seemed sick of winter. We finally turned down the last dirt road, the one that would bring us to our destination, and carefully veered into the driveway.

The Homestead was one hundred acres of mossy woodlands and neglected fields, five small cabins and one large one, a few sheds and semi-roofed structures in varying stages of dilapidation. It was twelve miles from the nearest commercial outpost, on a dirt road that, I would learn, threw up thick clouds of dust by the end of August and became deep gullies of frozen mud in late March and April. I discovered that in summer, a tall thicket of blackcaps hid the property from the road. Behind them, a grove of pine trees gave a false impression of grandeur as one came along the rugged drive, like a Yankee rejoinder to the magnolia-lined approaches of southern plantations. But soon the dark shade of the pines spit you out into the field, and you saw just ramshackle cabins and a plot of ground enclosed with chicken wire, flanked by more trees and a border of cleared land that had been reclaimed by goldenrod, wild raspberries, and tall grass. It didn't look impressive, and maybe it wasn't, but we were so very proud of it. It was our solution to the problem presented to us by the doomed world.

That day, we drove through the quiet pines, heavy with snow, the truck kicking up plumes of frozen gravel. The trees shrouded us from the world, and driving towards the Homestead felt like penetrating some wintry, dark fairy forest, thoroughly removed from reality. Which it was, of course. We made it that way. On that half-lit March day, it was easy to imagine it already a separate utopia, hidden away.

Jack and Chloe fell silent as we drove, peering excitedly out the windows. When I parked the truck, we tumbled out, gaping around us at the snow-covered clearing and the rustic compound of cabins. Smoke issued from the chimney of the largest, and Beau stepped out onto the deck, waving at us with a huge smile on his normally reserved face. We scampered through the snow, my hand-me-down L.L.Bean boots scuffing at the powder. Chloe flung herself up the steps and into Beau's arms.

"Is this it?"

"Naturally, you silly. Come inside." Beau gestured towards the door. We all lurched indoors, the cozy heat of the cabin stinging our cheeks and making my nose leak. Louisa was at the stove, and turned around at our entrance.

"Oh, you're here. Hoorah. What have you brought me?"

I mutely offered my tithe of a loaf of bread, and Chloe handed over the wine she had selected.

"How old is this timber?" Jack asked, arching his long, thin back to get a look at the joinery of the cabin walls.

"This cabin is the oldest, so at least a hundred years," Louisa answered, fondly rubbing one of the knotty beams as if it were a treasured pet. "Lovely, right?"

"You can't get wood like this anymore," Jack said appreciatively. "It's amazing."

"I think we should commence our little tour, no?" Beau prompted. "While there is still some light?"

"Right. Let me just pour out the hot toddies," Louisa said, fussing over something on the stove. "Don't bother unpacking yourselves," she ordered in Jack's direction. "We're going back outside." She thrust a thermos in his direction and readied her own arctic wear. We all stumbled back out into the cold. The temperature had dropped as the sun sank lower, now just glinting above the pine trees. We followed Beau's easy lope as he led us to the cabins.

"So, there are five individual cabins, and the big one."

"The big cabin has all the cooking supplies, and the biggest stove," Louisa said. Beau nudged open the door of a cabin. "They're all pretty much identical," she explained. Inside, the little dwellings were nest-like, a tidy, tight space. Each had a small Scandinavian woodstove, a small wooden table, and a chair. Though the roof wasn't high, a mezzanine level housed a mattress. Beneath the mezzanine were book-shelves. The cabins were about twelve by twelve.

And that was it. Unadorned, they were plain and shockingly simple. There was no clutter, nothing extra. And yet, while I can't fully explain it, I felt at home the minute we all crowded into that tiny space. Cross-ing the threshold felt correct. Louisa tugged the door shut behind her, and the five of us stood silently, booted feet rustling against the bare boards.

"It's a little home," Chloe said dreamily, echoing my thoughts. Jack chuckled.

"I was just thinking that." Louisa passed me the thermos, and I quaffed a deep slug of warmed and honeyed whiskey, letting the heat burn happily in my belly while I contemplated the simple window with slightly rippled panes of old glass. After the thermos had made its circuit, Beau stretched his arms out, as though to encompass all of us and the whole of the Homestead. His fingers brushed my shoulder.

"Shall we view the rest?"

We peeked into the other four cabins, walked the perimeter of what used to be (and soon would be again) the vegetable garden. There was a shed filled with rusted shovels and hoes, and two other rather ragged structures that looked more or less ready to topple over.

"I'm thinking a smokehouse and an herbarium, respectively," Louisa explained, if a bit optimistically. Beau bounced up and down on a springy door, beneath which was concealed a musty root cellar, frozen shut at present. We walked to the edge of the pond, a delicate skein of ice covering its surface.

"And the crowning glory," Beau said, leading us to the other side of the pond, near the border of the deepening woods. There, situated about fifty feet from the water, was what appeared to be a huge wine barrel. There seemed to be smoke pumping from a chimney at its rear.

"Is that what I think it is?" Jack wondered aloud.

"No way," Chloe gushed.

"What is it?" I asked.

"A sauna," they answered in tandem, Chloe dashing towards it with girlish bounce. My eyes widened appreciatively. I had been in a sauna exactly once, when I'd gone to the gym with a girl from college, a primped and stenciled-in WASP from Long Island who had treated me to a rather grueling day of self-maintenance in SoHo.

"But . . . it's a wine barrel," I said.

"Already airtight," Beau explained. "Perfect for a sauna." I reached the door of the hobbity structure to peer over Jack and Chloe's shoulders. It smelled woody and rich, and heat gusted into my chilled face.

"Was this actually used for wine?" Chloe asked. Beau nodded, grinning.

"Shit, that's awesome. Can we?" Jack asked.

"After dinner. It's not hot enough yet. It should be up to at least one-eighty," Louisa chided. "Shit, I left the stew on the stove. Let's go eat. It's too dark to walk the fields now anyway. We can do that in the morning." She led the way back to the big cabin, her breath puffing out in frozen clouds.

We ate Moroccan vegetable stew and seared lamb chops (for us carnivores—Jack and Chloe were both vegetarians), seated on the floor of the cabin and drinking Bordeaux from tin cups. The woodstove and the wine pinkened us all, and Louisa's rosy complexion was particularly aflame, a violent fuchsia that darkened as her lips did. We chattered about potential, our words filling the cabins with dried basil and hanging bulbs of garlic; we fluffed up down quilts and stoked the woodstove with pine to keep us warm in the long winters as we imagined a season here. Sitting cross-legged on the floor, sprawling across one another like a litter of puppies, we built a dock on the pond, we carved out new nooks in the root cellar, grew an acre of corn and learned how to grind it into meal. We were abuzz. We smoked a serious spliff. When the food was eaten and the dishes cleared away to a bucket near the stove (there was no running water) and the joint was all gone, we grew antsy and stripped naked, donning just our boots and our coats and dashing to the sauna. Self-conscious about my poky hips and narrow shanks, I kept my undies on, while everyone else cavorted nude. I marveled at their bodies: Louisa, pallor and blaze; Chloe, graceful lines and impossible symmetry; Beau, curved muscles and springy elegance; Jack, burnished down, long, strong legs, and a surprisingly large cock. I was thoroughly seduced—by their bodies, by the still forest surrounding us, by the homely hearth around which we sat roasting.

We ran through the snow, shrieking with glee and relying on the alcohol to insulate us from the cold until we reached our toasty sanctuary. We flung our coats on the hooks that lined the outside of the sauna and shucked off our boots as close to the door as we could, piling into the cylindrical jug, bumping up against one another's cold skin. Inside, we sweated and giggled and continued our speculations. Chloe wanted a piano. She could be wildly impractical in her desires for beauty, a fact Louisa was quick to point out, not without admiration. Bolstered by the general giddiness, I suggested an outdoor oven, a proposal met with coos of delight and general rhapsodies on the subject of wood-fired pizza. Jack resolved to standardize his haphazard beer-brewing methods and promised us regular offerings of stout. We dashed out into the snow whenever the heat grew unbearable, and finally, sweaty and thirsty, we trooped back to the house, thoroughly enchanted by our daydreams. Louisa unfurled blankets, pillows, and sleeping bags, Beau stoked the fire, and we collapsed on the bare floor, limbs akimbo.

Morning was the first dose of reality in our persistent and ongoing attempt to escape it. The fire had died in the night, and as I cracked my eyes open, I realized I could see my breath. The wooden floor was hard beneath my shoulder, and my arm had fallen asleep after I had been wedged against the wall, unable to turn over. I met Chloe's eyes as she poked her head up out of the nest, blond hair snarled fetchingly. She mirrored my expression of bleary suffering, then yawned. I was thirsty, but I couldn't quite remember how to acquire water; although the whiskey had been free-flowing, the other liquid of life required more effort. I seemed to remember Louisa coming in from outside with a jug, but then it might have contained snow, placed on the stove for melting. Chloe stealthily stood up and crept outside. When I joined her, the three-headed body beneath the blankets stirred, and soon we were all up and grumbling in rather close proximity. The stove was revived, a pot of coffee was brewed semi-successfully, and after a rushed and brutal trip to the "facilities" outside, I felt better.

In the light of day, we were a little more sedate, less grandiose, and less blithely confident in our rugged abilities. We were stiff and cold, thirsty, and bashful about our absurd projects. Beau alone seemed undaunted; it was he who finally shattered the inertia that had us lounging on the floor with empty mugs.

"Hey, you kids. Let's go for a little walk." We lurched to our feet and returned outdoors, the fresh air bracing and harsh. Chloe wryly pointed to our messy trail of footprints, coiling towards and around the sauna, and Beau led us on a path into the woods. The sun barely penetrated the boughed pyramids that grew up around us, and none of us spoke, not wanting to drown out the crunch of snow as we trudged deeper. We had walked for what seemed like an hour, but was certainly less, when Beau stopped, pointing to a half-concealed NO TRESPASSING sign that hung askew from a lone fence post. Squinting closer, I saw other posts driven into the ground, and here and there a limp strand of barbed wire joining them together in a bedraggled border.

"This is the property line," he explained. "Everything from the road to here is part of the property."

"Who owns that?" Jack asked, pointing across the barbed wire to the forest beyond, identical to the one in which we stood, but made foreign and sinister by its belonging to someone else.

"Local farmer. Owns about two hundred acres, most rented to the huge agribusiness assholes that farm most of the land around here," Louisa spat out. "GE corn. They haven't 'developed' this part of the property yet, but they will. Tried to buy the whole parcel off my dad. Thank God he's a stubborn hippie." We walked the edge of the property line, curling back towards the cabins. The sun was getting higher but still barely visible through the trees. Louisa pointed out two deer-hunting stands up in the trees, explained that there were deer, pheasants, rabbits, and wild turkeys on this property. We walked through a cleared field that had once been planted with alfalfa and now lay fallow. The fresh air cleared my head, and I began to regain the almost deranged sense of well-being I'd felt the night before. This was good land, I could feel it.

We walked for nearly two hours, Louisa and Beau guiding us around and pointing out hidden details—you can find mushrooms in this woodland; there are always pink lady's slippers here in the summer; wild strawberries grow between these two fields; all those worrying-looking weeds are actually wild raspberries and blackcaps. Finally, we stood back near the cabins, the sun nearly as high as it would get in the sky, the drip of melting ice and snow audible.

"Welcome home," Beau said simply.

From the first, Beau treated the land as though it belonged every bit as much to him as it did to Louisa. He was comfortably proprietorial, the self-assured heir before the benefactor has passed on. His assumed ownership seemed natural, though, and we all grew to feel in some measure as he did about the Homestead: it was ours. The names on the deed were just so much legalese, symptomatic of the flawed system we railed against, and we believed our cooperative cultivation of the property served to undermine the network of global capital we resented and mistrusted.

But my own sense of belonging took several months. After that first chilly evening out in the country, we were like unlanded peasants bewitched by the promise of future rootedness. I can't remember if we ever really articulated the plan, whether there was a moment when Louisa sat us down and said, in her quick and authoritative schoolmarm voice: "Listen, we all babble on and on about everything we see that's terribly, hauntingly wrong with the world, and here in front of us we have a chance to try out something else, to counterpropose. Let's quit our bitching and see if we can't do better." Either way, we never needed her to say it. I'd like to think it was a meeting of minds, that we found our way to one another and knew, in a moment of kismet, what we were destined to do together.

We thought homemade pickles and working for ourselves under the broad, open sky would save us. We really did. Everything was so irredeemably fucked-up and horrifying that the only answer seemed to be self-sufficiency, homegrown zucchini and big crocks of sauerkraut. We knew we were being idealistic, utopian even, but we didn't care. What were the alternatives? Wait for the icecaps to melt, for the workers' revolution, for the government to do something about the future that was so clearly evaporating before our eyes? Better to try something, even if that something involved composting toilets and bathing in the murky cow pond. We thought we had a responsibility to take action because of our privileged vantage point, to lead our misguided cohort away from Whole Foods and Apple to a compostable, probiotic future. The Homestead was five answers to a dilemma that needed billions of responses, but we could hardly make things worse, right?

Absurdly, we thought we were a we. We thought it was ignorance and shortsightedness that blinded everyone else to a self-evident reality. But what we didn't know was that our collective reality would blind us even more.

Chapter 3

I don't know whether Louisa's certainty and charisma alone would have been sufficient to draw me in. I was hungry for a way out of my sabotaged life, but ultimately, I was practical. Would I have thrown my lot in with them without the promise of something so prosaic as sex? Though I like to think of my motivations as high-minded, I'm not sure that accounts for how quickly I converted. I suppose there was the difficulty of my ulterior motives, which I had yet to acknowledge to myself—it would be many more months before I would really examine the possibility that I had bound myself to these people because of what had come before. In the beginning, I felt simple desire. If there is such a thing.

After our first visit to the Homestead, it was safe to say I was infatuated. It had been such a long time since I had felt close to anyone, had felt anything like a sense of community, and I found myself craving that sensation. I wanted to fold myself into a chair and watch these strange new people talk in their brusque shorthand about the vagaries of corporate America. After meeting them just a few times, I missed them. Had I been more worldly, I would have perhaps recognized my preoccupation as a crush. As it was, I just craved them.

After finishing another dull shift of catering (an event on campus, listless pasta salad under fluorescent lights while everyone stared at the clock and waited for the day to end), I found myself, without excuse, lurking by the café where Beau and Chloe worked. I couldn't justify being there with anything other than the truth: that I hoped to get a glimpse of one of them. I was evidently smitten; this boldness would have usually been unthinkable for me. I strolled through the hall; their restaurant was located inside a larger building, a former school, and there were other shops I could ostensibly be patronizing, were I asked to explain my presence.

My heart sank on seeing the dimmed lights; the café was obviously closed. I caught sight of myself in a mirror and cringed—what was I doing here? My hair looked flat, and my eyes darted unattractively with anticipation. I had just turned on my heels, preparing to flee, when I collided with Beau, who was walking around the corner with a bus bin.

"Young Mack," he said, clearly unruffled. I couldn't say the same for myself.

"Um, hi. Sorry. I didn't mean to— I mean, I was—"

"Look at you," he said simply, holding eye contact. "You look so pink and alive." I imagine this comment did nothing but deepen my complexion.

"It's cold out," I said, stupidly.

"You always seem to be just arriving from somewhere. Some adventure." Beau settled the bin more sturdily on his hip and looked at me with frank interest. How could he possibly find me interesting? Adventure? I'd just come from working an extremely tedious departmental meeting and was almost shaking with boredom and the desire to make something of myself.

"Well, actually, I was hoping to find some more adventure," I said. I prayed that I sounded saucy.

"Oh my. Did you have anything in mind?"

"Mack!" I heard. Turning around, I saw Chloe. She wore an outfit almost identical to mine (simple pencil skirt, clogs, T-shirt—the uniform of food service) and yet she somehow looked composed and elegant. I felt frumpy.

"Oh hi," I said.

She folded me into a quick hug. "What a nice surprise. What brings you out this way?"

"Mack was going to invite us on an adventure," Beau said, quirking one eyebrow at me.

"Oh, really?" Chloe said. "Well, that's hard to turn down. Where are we venturing?" She tugged the elastic from her fine blond hair and it tumbled over her shoulders.

"I, uh. It's not quite dark yet. I thought maybe we could walk. To the waterfall," I added. This was not much of an adventure, but my mind was blank. Obviously, I had come with no plan other than low-key stalking. Beau and Chloe looked at each other, and both smiled in what seemed like approval.

"We're running late with the cleanup today," Chloe explained, with another glance at Beau whose meaning I couldn't quite decode. "We'll be done in just a few minutes. Wait for us?" she asked, as though it would somehow be putting me out, as though I hadn't come here desperate for a sighting of them. She led me to a chair where I could wait, and I absently fiddled with my phone, trying to look as though I could entertain myself. I made a show of not watching them hungrily, even when Beau approached me. I glanced up in faux surprise.

"Hey, follow me," Beau said with a cock of his head. I did not need to be asked again. I trailed him downstairs, into the bowels of the restaurant. I watched where my clogged feet landed, the uneven tip of the staircase making me dread a klutzy fall. Beau carried a large mixing bowl under his arm, and as he walked he slotted it away on a shelf without really looking: the muscle memory of an oft-repeated movement. He continued into another room and opened the steel door of a walk-in. He gestured me inside with a subtle bow, and I flinched at the cold air. Once inside, we were pressed close to each other, and I could smell his skin and his low-bunned hair, tangy with sweat and food and him.

"Um," I said.

"Close your eyes," he said.

"Um," I repeated.

"Don't worry. This isn't some corny pickup from a romance novel," he said, chuckling. "It's just a nice surprise for a nice girl." I looked at him, then obediently closed my eyes. "Okay, open your mouth."

"I thought you said this *wasn't* a pickup line," I protested, though I still didn't open my eyes.

"Trust, wee Mack." He waited for me to open up, which I did, though I hoped my face conveyed that I wasn't falling for this. (I was.) I could feel his fingers near the edges of my lips, pausing before he popped something into my mouth. I had expected a cliché, a strawberry or whipped cream, maybe, but my mouth was filled suddenly with something solid, heavy. I bit into the sides of the tiny cold ball, feeling a familiar, satisfying crunch, letting the taste of butter run over my tongue.

"Is that . . . ?" I asked mumbling around the treat.

"Chocolate chip cookie dough," he said. I opened my eyes to see him grinning at me, warm pleasure on his face because of my own pleased expression. He popped a ball of dough into his own mouth.

"It reminds me of my mom," I said. "And of my mom worrying about salmonella. Your mom didn't have a paranoia about raw eggs?" I asked, savoring the last chocolate chip melting in my mouth.

"My mom didn't ever bake me cookies," he said brusquely and held open the door of the walk-in. I regretted having mentioned his mother.

"Hang on," he said, leaning against the open door, barring my exit. He held my forearm with his hand, the calluses of his fingers hot and dry against my skin. The warmth of the kitchen and the cold of the walk-in collided, and I shivered, caught in the strange slipstream. "Don't tell Chloe about that, okay?"

"What, about the walk-in?" In the throes of my delusional crush, I thought he didn't want me to tell anyone about this odd moment of intimacy, the way he had stood so close to me while I shut my eyes and opened my mouth so willingly.

"About the cookie dough," he said. I must have looked puzzled.

"Chloe's the one who makes it. It drives her nuts when it all disappears before she can bake it. If she knows it was me, she'll fucking kill me," Beau added, smiling goofily.

"Ah. Your secret will die with me then." Silly as it was, I was thrilled to share it with him.

The waterfall towards which we were headed was at least a mile from the café, and the wind churned spindrifts of snow up into our faces and down into my clogs. It was too cold to qualify as brisk, but it could, I supposed, legitimately be called bracing. We walked quickly, noses tucked into jackets and hands into pockets, making conversation only occasionally. Chloe sidled closer to me to get warm, and I was shocked with pleasure when she hooked my arm in hers, as I had seen her do with Louisa. We stamped our feet in time, laughing at how cold we were and how foolish we were to be outside.

"I don't know, you warm-blooded creatures," Beau said. "It's too damn cold for this nonsense." He nevertheless seemed exhilarated, and at some point, he raced ahead in a fleet-footed scamper that Chloe and I didn't even try to match. He disappeared onto the playground that bordered a school and we lost sight of him among the uprights of the jungle gym, his graceful body slinking through the monkey bars and behind a slide. We forged ahead, and Beau chucked snowballs at us from behind his childish parapets.

"Such a boy," Chloe said, though she smiled. We snaked through the quiet streets of Fall Creek, avoiding the slushy patches of partially melted snow where salt had been chucked onto the sidewalk. Everyone was inside their cozy houses; I wondered if they watched us from behind frosted windows, envious of our youth, our camaraderie.

We turned right off the pavement, careening down a small, steep hill. In my clogs, I slid and cartwheeled my arms; Beau and Chloe each caught one, and we barreled down at a pace just too fast to be safe. The waterfall was tucked back in the woods, down a short foot trail about a hundred yards long, but we could already hear the boom of water surging over the frozen lip of the gorge. As we drew nearer, our cheeks were coated in an icy film of spray. My eyelids flinched. I could feel freezing moisture collecting in my hair.

Standing before the waterfall, I found it hard not to feel overwhelmed: by the cold, by the sight of such casual natural power, by the pleasure of being with these two people. The waterfall was wide, and the water moved with clout over the stony lip of the gorge. Perched on the slick rocks near the edge of the angry pool, we huddled together, and Beau turned his back to the waterfall briefly to shield us with his body and coat, tipping his forehead into first Chloe's, then mine. It was tender, and felt more significant than just the tap of two skulls in the cold. There was care in the gesture that belied the carelessness he often projected.

"What's that?" Chloe interrupted, lifting her arm to point up at the waterfall. Her movement broke the warm sphere we had created with our bodies, and Beau turned to look, briefly obscuring my vision. When I took a step forward, I saw what she'd seen. A figure stood at the top of the falls. Or, rather, it didn't stand but clung to an unsteady-looking tree near the edge; there was too much water for anyone to stand in the gorge itself. I couldn't tell from here whether it was male or female, but the form looked slight and fragile.

"Fuck," said Beau. "That is not at all good. Do one of you gals have a cellphone?" I would learn that although Beau owned a cell, he rarely had it with him. His voice was even, and he seemed unworried by this situation, even as my heart rate climbed.

"Do you think they're trying to jump?" I asked as I fumbled for my device. My hands were stiff from the cold. When I tried to unlock my screen, the phone wouldn't recognize my touch; it was heat-sensitive, after all, and my fingers were bloodless.

"Either way, they're in trouble. Let me call," Beau said, taking the phone from me. He was quickly on the line with what I assumed was a 911 operator.

"We're at Ithaca Falls, and it seems as though someone is either trapped or trying to jump from the falls," Beau explained, his voice neutral. Chloe stared blankly ahead, unable to take her eyes from the body above us. It wasn't such a high drop, and whoever was up there seemed so close, as though we could almost get to them, if we really wanted to.

"Stay there!" Beau called up, but with the roar of the water, he probably wasn't audible to anyone but us and the emergency operator. The figure moved, either deliberately or because the snow and slush beneath their feet were eroding; the intention was hard to read. I imagined the panic on this stranger's face. "Yes, I'll stay on the line," Beau answered. "But I'd get here real quick. This might not take too long." We stood, the three of us, staring up at the top of the falls.

"There's no way they're up there by accident," Chloe said, her teeth chattering.

"I tend to agree," Beau said. He moved a few steps closer to the bank of the pool beneath the waterfall. It was roiling with the precipitation and snowmelt that had come swelling through the gorge, and a heavy, brownish film clung to the driftwood that had washed up on the bank. Beau was carefully choosing stones to get closer to the edge. There was no way he could climb up the side of the waterfall, though; the rocks were smooth from millennia of erosion and covered in ice. Beau seemed to realize the futility of trying to make his way upward, but he still called out to the figure. I could barely make out his words. It sounded like a name, like he was calling for this person. But that couldn't be, surely.

And then, they jumped. One moment the body was standing at the top of the gorge, and the next, it was gone, suddenly subsumed by the violent roil of water at the base of the falls. It was whitewater and wrath there, and we could see nothing but the power of the water. Beau made a move to go into the pool, but Chloe clung to his arm. Although my instincts were slower, I grabbed his other arm, pulling him back. Beau didn't fight us; he was a practical man.

"That water is freezing," I said. "And there's zero chance you can swim to the other side. Just wait. If they pop back up . . ." I didn't finish my sentence as we all hoped for the body to reappear. There was nothing. Seconds ticked on, and I began to count them. Beau seemed to remember that he held my phone, and he put it back up to his mouth to say, "They jumped. Send an ambulance." He handed the phone back to me without meeting my eyes, continuing to stare at the spot where a human being had vanished.

We huddled on a log, shivering, as the paramedics and cops arrived. Chloe had said nothing since the jump, and Beau and I answered questions. The cops seemed unruffled; clearly this wasn't their first waterfall suicide—probably not even the first of the season. These deaths were a regular occurrence in Ithaca, and many of the other, steeper gorges and bridges had protective nets to ensnare jumpers. The cops wanted to confirm that this had, indeed, been intentional.

"I can't think what else they would have been doing up there," I said. "Not exactly a good day for a hike." The cops nodded in agreement and wrote down my words. After the questions, the three of us continued to wait, even though we were all shaking now. None of us acknowledged it, but we were still waiting for a body, for someone to surface in the water. Not alive; we understood that. But for the finality of reappearance, a phoenix gone wrong. Beau, who had begun to fidget, ushered us away from the cops, and we slunk away without asking for permission.

We stumbled back up the trail, realizing we had a lengthy walk back to town ahead of us. Chloe was shivering, and I had long since stopped feeling my fingers and toes.

"I don't know about you ladies, but I'd like a drink," Beau said, and I smiled at him gratefully, able only to nod my head. He steered us across the road and towards the bar that sat there, a townie dive that looked warm and inviting. I staggered along, my numb feet stubbing gracelessly against gray slush. I wished my feelings were as numb. I was jumpy, as though that inexplicable death would follow us three in the dipping light. I wanted to take Chloe's arm—or, rather, I wanted her to take mine, as she had just an hour earlier—only she seemed shut down, lost in her own head. I tried to catch her eye, but she kept her face shrouded in the hood of her parka.

There was a handful of committed day drinkers perched at the bar, but the rest of the space was largely empty. The lighting was pleasantly dim, just the pale neon of ads for domestic beers. I've since had the chance to admire the neutrality of the affect produced by dive bars— the generic coziness created by crap music and anonymous men in trucker hats, which obscures and soothes. That day, though, was one of my first entrées into such adult escapes from sadness. We were so young. Beau strode up to the bartender.

"Do you think you could fix us up three hot toddies?" he asked. The bartender nodded and returned to his boozy labors. Chloe and I headed for the back room, leaving Beau to wait for the drinks. We sat in a booth, sandwiched next to each other. I started to remove some of my layers, hoping to let the warm air in, but Chloe just sat, staring at the sticky table.

"Hey, are you okay?" I asked her with a nudge.

"Honestly, Mack? I don't know," she said. I thought she might be crying.

"You don't have to be."

"Good." She sniffled. Beau slid into the booth across from us, holding the handles of three mugs filled with hot ocher liquid. I claimed mine and Chloe's. I tried to think of something to say, to craft something comforting we could cling to, but I had nothing. There was no narrative for the death we'd just seen. Had we witnessed the end of someone's life? Could my own end just as quickly, and without purpose?

"There's no reason for it," I said aloud. "It's just so fucking pointless." Chloe nodded her head vigorously.

"His life—or hers—it ended that way—and for what?" She took a deep slug of her toddy.

"Is death meant to have meaning?" Beau asked. "Most people don't die for a reason. They die because their time is up."

"His time wasn't up!" Chloe protested.

"Well, evidently it was," Beau said with a shrug.

"His *life* must have meant something," I suggested. "Surely it did to the people who loved him."

"He was probably just some college kid, depressed over midsemester grades or something even more meaningless," Chloe said, a hitch in her throat. "We've all been there. It's so easy to imagine yourself into that headspace, that kind of . . . desperation. He was just too young to see how unimportant it was. Would be."

"Who decides what's important?" Beau asked. "If she were a suicide bomber, would she have died with more purpose?"

"No!" I said, irritated. Though I noticed how Beau had switched the gender—did he, somehow, know that the jumper was a woman? *Had* he called out a name? I scrutinized his face, not yet used to its impenetrability. Was this the first time I searched his features for information, to see only his wide green eyes, the plump lower lip that pouted out when he was amused or thoughtful? If it was the first time, it certainly wouldn't be the last.

"Well, I wonder," Beau answered. "Maybe that was for her to decide."

Chapter 4

Though we felt we could dispense with formality among the five of us, the Homestead did not technically belong to us, and we were forced to acknowledge this inconvenient fact before the others reneged on their leases and we all traded in our party frocks for overalls. I was very reluctant to whisper even a word of this to my parents, they of the infinite capacity for disappointment. I had no intention of revealing to them even a shred of our burgeoning plot until it was more or less officially settled. And to settle it, we had to convince a lawyer.

Thankfully, Rudolph Stein was not a stern figure of justice rigidly hewing to the letter of the law. He was a rotund creature of mirth and a great lover of after-dinner liqueurs. His absurd ginger curls spiraled from his balding pate much more frizzily than did Louisa's, and his pale skin was latticed with visible veins. He was really a lot of fun to have around, especially when he was moved to argue. We resolved to formally ask him for use of the estate, even though Louisa had assured us that no one would mind if we just moved in. The idea of this made me skittish, and I was very relieved when it was Beau who insisted that we treat it with some ceremony and a degree of legal authority. We had Mr. Stein come for dinner one night. His second wife and her kids, Louisa's stepsiblings, were left at home.

He was late, and I was on edge, worriedly sipping at my glass of Chianti and feeling like a penniless pauper asking a member of the landed gentry for his beautiful daughter's hand. I had no qualifications for this. I had a degree in anthropology, for Chrissakes. I needn't have worried. About Rudolph, that is.

He arrived eventually, jolly, his round belly quivering as he tugged on his striped suspenders and boomed cheerfully at everyone. The day had been warm, a glimmer of spring, and he arrived on Louisa's porch just as the diminishing icicles were refreezing for the night.

"Beauregard! Good man, nice to see you." He slapped Beau on the back. Beau smiled coyly. They liked each other.

"Daddy! You're here!" Little Louisa scooted in from the kitchen, pink-faced from leaning over the steaming risotto. She gave her father two quick pecks on his vein-besmirched jowls, tugging affectionately on his gingery goatee. "Wine?" She was already fluttering back to the kitchen for a glass, ever the hostess.

"Of course. And introductions!" Rudy gestured to the three of us, lurking around the living room. "Strangers! How exciting. Almost never happens around here." He stuck his hand out first to Chloe, who leaned in and shook it, introducing herself with one of her most winning smiles. Jack, taking up more space than he needed to, shouldered forward next.

"I'm Jack Schumann," he explained, pumping the moist hand offered to him rather too many times. I was last, and more or less swallowed my own introduction along with another glug of wine, hoping to be soon forgotten. As usual, I got my wish.

Over Louisa's Swiss chard and Gorgonzola risotto, we laid out our plan, oscillating between mature practicality and (hopefully) endearingly youthful enthusiasm. We were young and healthy and realistic about the amount of work we were facing, and articulate about why we felt it was a better option for us than slaving away as baristas and scullery maids. Honestly, Rudy didn't take much convincing. His description of his once-upon-a-time summer of roughing it out on the

Homestead filled him with bucolic nostalgia, and he understood all too well our desperation to eat things we had harvested ourselves. He seemed to agree with our political motivations, nebulous as they were, and even commended us on rejecting "the system of underpaid labor that exploits workers, and to which your well-educated and creative generation is falling tragically prey."

"You know, they used to call this part of the world the Burned-Over District. This area was rife with religious movements, people who believed the Rapture was about to happen any second. Intense part of the world. And, of course, back in the seventies we had our share of communes and all that. Seems like everyone was dropping out and signing up for free love. In fact," he said, settling in for a lecture the way only professional talkers do, "the man credited with coining the term 'free love' has some connection with this property. Some defectors from a commune he helped found lived here, for a while. At least that's what I was told. I've always had a fondness for heady idealists. Right, Lou?" Because of his teasing tone, we all glanced at Louisa, who was blushing.

"I hadn't told them about my namesake, Daddy," she said, evidently hoping for a change in subject.

"But you're named after one of the best!" Rudy said. We waited expectantly.

"Louisa May Alcott," she continued reluctantly. "Her father began a utopian commune too. It didn't last long, but Louisa May got some decent material out of it." She shrugged.

"Always loved people who are willing to attempt the impossible, however destined for failure they are!" Rudy boomed. Perhaps we should have heard the omen in this comment. He then waxed enthusiastically about the sun-ripened tomatoes we would pluck and devour. Before Louisa had even brought out the (slightly collapsed) tiramisu, he had agreed that we should lease all one hundred acres for a three-year period at the rate of fifty dollars per annum, ten dollars to be contributed by each of us for the first year's rent. He chortled in amusement as Louisa sketched out a simple lease agreement on her phone, and, laughing, he accepted the handful of cash we thrust into his fingers.

"So it's a done deal! Excellent. I will be expecting some of your delicious strawberry jam, little one, before the summer is out."

"Not in the lease agreement!" Louisa giggled and got up to fish around in her cupboard for port.

Among the five of us, we were reluctant to be so official. There was some discussion of a charter, or a manifesto. Chloe mentioned the "Roommate Rules" that passive-aggressively dictated chores and quiet hours in her co-op up on South Hill, but we all soon rejected this as puerile.

"If we can't agree on whose turn it is to do the dishes through reasoned conversation, then we have no business doing this," Louisa said, ending that discussion, as she ended so many, with sheer authority. Jack wanted a document of core principles and shared beliefs, a statement of purpose; he wanted to put everything in words, to tease out all ambiguity and make every stance explicit. Jack could be very literal-minded. But Beau quietly objected until Jack stopped insisting. I wanted something else—anything I could use to demonstrate to my parents that I was not cracking up or joining a cult, preferably proof of 501(c)(3) status and a payroll stub proving at least a minimal income. In the end, we settled on nothing except a vague verbal agreement to be honest and forthcoming with one another. I guess we should have put it in writing.

Telecommunications were another stumbling block. Beau advocated for being totally off-grid: no cellphones, no TV, no Internet. This appealed to me deeply, for obvious reasons; I would be completely cut off from the nastiness of my emails and voicemail. No one balked at the TV interdiction (we couldn't remember the last time any of us had switched on a television), but Louisa insisted that she needed the Internet to work (she was doing freelance editing and copywriting for some online publication—not that she really needed the money).

"Look," Louisa said. "We're not doing this out of some half-baked spiritual notion of cutting ourselves off from the world and finding ourselves in nature. We're not fucking Thoreau. We just want to be more in control of what we put in our bodies, how we spend our days and lives."

"Closer to the means of production?" Jack offered.

"Sure."

"We absolutely can't give money to one of those huge communications corporations," Beau insisted. We agreed.

Chloe expressed little preference (we didn't yet realize how completely cut off from the world she was; she continued to conceal her worrying isolation for months), and Jack agreed with Beau. I halfheartedly advocated for Beau's Luddite position, but I didn't want to draw too much attention to myself. In the end, Louisa won out, naturally, and we began the long and frustrating process of trying to get Wi-Fi access in a remote rural location that had no electricity, without involving Verizon or Comcast. As it eventually turned out, that was impossible without running electricity to one of the cabins, and we ended up using our cellphones as hot spots whenever we needed the Web. We charged our phones in my truck and plugged in our laptops whenever we went to town, sometimes sitting in the café and watching Beau and Chloe work, sometimes purloining electricity and Internet access from the corporations we otherwise eschewed.

We all felt it was best to stay without electricity, as both a romantic and a practical gesture. We liked the idea of getting up with the sun. And it would have been a headache to have it installed, not to mention expensive. Solar panels were similarly rejected; the price tag was prohibitive. Louisa bit her lower lip whenever it came up; I knew she wanted solar power, and could have paid for it, but refrained from insulting or alienating us with a show of her largesse. The tedium of dealing with powered-down phones and laptops soon became routine, as all inconveniences do. Chloe said that it was almost like a practice, to remind ourselves that electricity came at a cost.

Plumbing was more contentious. No one was especially excited at the notion of shoveling their own shit, but we similarly rejected the possibility of installing a full-blown leach field, a luxury that would have cost in the neighborhood of fifteen grand. For me, this was an astronomical sum and therefore a purely hypothetical question. Louisa tactfully suggested asking her dad to invest, but none of us was very keen on this. We agreed that if two years from now we still wanted running hot water and toilets that flushed, we would work out the financing then. The unspoken *if* was "if we are still living at the Homestead," but queerly, no one said it. We decided on a composting toilet in a freestanding outhouse to be communally emptied in rotation. A simple pump that worked off the well near the big cabin provided potable water, and in the summer we would use rain catchment bags that spent the day baking in the sun for showers. We could also bathe in the swampy pond, as long as we used the right kind of soap and shampoo. We were confident in our ability to rough it once we moved in full-time that first summer, and we felt sure that we would work out all the other little kinks in no time at all. Ha.

Until we were better situated, we were mostly reliant on the pond; the well provided some drinking water, but severe droughts had brought the water table dangerously low, and the well ran dry regularly. Beau informed us it wasn't nearly deep enough—"Maybe in the nineteenth century, my dears, but altogether too shallow for our twenty-first-century woes." The pump was similarly unreliable, and froze or broke pretty often. While the advisability of drinking pond water seemed iffy to me, we boiled it each evening, and so far had yet to unearth evidence that we were gulping down parasites and other treacherous organisms. The bathing arrangements were currently rustic: you could heat a bucket of water and perform ablutions in your cabin, spattering the floor with moisture, or, when it wasn't frozen, you could use the outdoor shower for a frigid, though more thorough, engagement with hygiene. I had tried the outdoor shower exactly once and discovered that my constitution was not sufficiently hardy. Since we weren't yet formally moved in, we still had other bathing options at our homes, but there were days of manual labor that demanded at least a cursory wash before reentering the world.

Chloe and I were alone at the Homestead one afternoon—Jack and Louisa were acquiring some equipment, and Beau was at work. We'd been painstakingly sinking postholes so that the garden could be protected from critters once it was up and flourishing. We were hot, our sweatshirts soggy, and I desperately wanted a shower before we broke for dinner. Chloe lowered her nose into the neck of her shirt and made an eloquent expression of disgust before smiling at me.

"We are filthy creatures," she acknowledged. "Shall we try to clean ourselves up?"

"Ugh, but we'll freeze."

"Let's light up the sauna. We can have a quick dousing and then warm up in the barrel." This seemed sensible, if not downright pleasurable, and we stoked the fire in the cylindrical structure and set about preparing our "shower."

The pond had been frozen since our first visit to the Homestead, and we had either broken open the crackling ice at the bank or ventured farther out to an ice hole into which we could dip our buckets. The weather had been bitterly cold this whole week, and the ice was frozen solid for a good ten or fifteen feet from the bank; we would have to walk out on the ice to get the buckets of water we needed. This process always made me nervous, but Chloe slid confidently out onto the slippery surface, delicately stamping a boot into the ice every few feet to test its solidity. She cracked a skein of surface ice off the hole we'd been using and gingerly lowered a bucket, grinning at me while I stood reluctantly on the shore. She trundled back to me with the first bucket, which we emptied into the basin on top of the woodstove. We both tramped back to the pond to repeat this several more times, each with our own bucket. We skated across the surface, goofing off slightly while we hauled water up from below.

When I heard the first crack of the ice beneath my feet, it elicited an overwhelming neurochemical response unlike anything I had ever experienced. I was closest to the hole, Chloe just a few feet behind me. I could hear the gunshot sounds of ice moving, changing its mind. We froze, paralyzed with panic as the ice began to shift. We had gotten cocky, I realized, after our first few forays. I had stopped testing each step, had grown complacent.

"Get down and spread your weight," Chloe said, right before the ice collapsed beneath her and she shot down into a chilly fissure. I leapt forward, hoping to grab her before she disappeared, and in my hurry, I sprang off my back foot, cracking the ice underneath me. The surface of the pond began to fragment, turning into a slushy ice floe in what seemed an impossible matter of seconds. My boots were pulling me deeper, and though I clawed at the splintering edges of the ice, there was no purchase, just cold handfuls of icebergs. I splashed into the freezing water, my chest immediately constricting. My heart banged and hurt, and I remembered dimly that cardiac arrest was common if you fell into water this cold. I flailed around, looking for Chloe and panicking. *Mack, you must. You must keep your head clear.* I felt sluggish. How long had I been in the water? Ten seconds? Twenty? I wasn't sure I could breathe. I slid deeper into the water, and the weight of my sweatshirt tugged me off the precarious shelf to which I had been clinging.

Under the ice, I felt oddly lucid. Opening my eyes, I could see the light just a few inches above my face. The rest of the pond was obscure, and, out of some old childish instinct, I didn't dare confront the darkness. I kept my eyes aimed towards the surface. I could hear Chloe thrashing nearby, and I thought perhaps she was saying my name. Even as my brain started to panic without oxygen, I thought, ever so briefly, of the human being whose death we had observed—it was one thing to watch someone's body plunge into icy water and a wholly different experience when it happened to you. Was this what his—or her—final moments had been like? Brutal shock, a racing heart, and then recognition that you will never take another breath again?

My winter boots pulled me downward, and my feet abruptly sank into the silt of the bottom. The pond was only six feet deep or so where I had gone in, and though my legs felt numb and unspeakably heavy, I kicked against the bottom. For a hallucinatory moment, the mud held me down, and I felt certain that some pond goblin was clinging to my soles, a cranky naiad unwilling to let me return above. Then my boots released from the mud with a sucking squelch of resistance, and I shot back up to the surface. My forehead smacked against an ice chip, but, thankfully, the solid ice on which we had so recently stood was now entirely disrupted, and I didn't have to battle my way back to my point of ingress into the water.

"Mack!" I heard Chloe say behind me. Swirling around and grasping for any floating object, I saw her plowing her way towards me. She seemed nearly able to stand on the bottom; she was several inches taller than me. I sank again, and as the water again poured icily down my neck and into my sweatshirt, Chloe grabbed my arm and pulled, much harder than her delicate frame would suggest possible. We both flopped gracelessly towards the shore, breaking up the remaining ice in our desperate bid to get out of the water. I tripped up the bank, panting, and Chloe and I collapsed, shuddering, on our backs on the cold ground. Her lips were blue.

"Fuck me. Fuck." I wasn't sure if it was Chloe or me speaking. I reached out my hand, which I couldn't feel, and groped for her. Grasping her sodden arm, I squeezed, a vague acknowledgment of our survival.

"We have to get up," I managed to chatter. Though we were out of the water, I realized that we were in no way out of danger. I rolled onto my belly and forced myself up onto my knees, giving Chloe a shove. We both managed to drag ourselves upright.

"The sauna," Chloe croaked, and we stumbled towards it, clinging to each other. My legs felt not like my own. We reached the door, grabbed the handle (made from a deer's antler), and tripped inside, feeling the hot draft of woody air. Though the sauna wasn't quite up to temp yet, it was still at least one hundred degrees inside, and the heat stung my skin. With numbed fingers, we tore at bootlaces and ripped off saturated socks. Each item of clothing hit the sauna floor with a sloppy slap. Our frantic striptease lasted just seconds as we peeled off every freezing layer. Thankfully, we had put fluffy towels in the sauna to heat up, and, naked, we swaddled ourselves in them, wrapping them around our shoulders and shivering fiercely, trying to get closer to the stove. I was reminded of being a little girl, cold from the bath during icy winters when we couldn't afford to turn up the heat. My mother would rub my shoulders and arms through the towel to dry me, and the gesture was one of pure coziness and care. Unthinkingly, I reached across the sauna to do the same to Chloe, and she purred in delight as I scrubbed her skin with the dry, hot cotton. She reached out with the edge of her towel and began to tousle my hair dry, flicking droplets from my split ends onto the woodstove, which spit and sizzled. I could see her golden body through the opening in the towel, the sloping curve of her abdomen and the dainty bend of one breast. Her hip bone was the only sharpness I could find, a knob of definition against the bow of her belly. She pulled me in closer to dry the nape of my neck, and I couldn't help reaching out, my chilled forearm seeking the already warm center of her body. We folded in on each other, our two towels now forming a tepee of warmth, and I leaned my forehead against her clavicle, feeling the pulse of her blood there. Still moving, thank God.

"We could have died," I said dumbly.

"It was so incredibly stupid," she agreed. "What a fucking dumb way to die." I snorted into the skin just above her breast, which made her giggle.

"We didn't think. Careless." We shivered in relief, laughing at our foolishness. My nose nestled against the skin where her chest met her arm.

"Did you think of them too?" she asked. "In the water?"

"The jumper?"

She nodded.

"Yeah. It's a cold death."

She shivered against me. "Let's maybe not mention it to the others," she said, after a pause.

"What? Why?" I was surprised; I was already imagining the tale as a fireside story. The terror was still too fresh for me to think of it as funny, but I knew that when I warmed up and my adrenaline settled, I would see the humor of our thoughtlessness, and the providence that had allowed us to walk away. Chloe seemed to be considering her words.

"I sometimes feel like they—like they think of me as helpless. Damsel in distress," she added. "I know I don't have Louisa's fierceness or Beau's, I don't know, stoicism. Or even your stubbornness." She smiled, and again I was surprised. I tended not to consider myself stubborn. "I have to dredge my resources up elsewhere. I couldn't stand for them to think me foolish. Helpless. I think they think of me, sometimes, as just a beautiful rag doll."

"Oh," I said. I realized that I, too, felt vulnerable, as though I also had something to prove to our intrepid companions. I liked that Chloe was telling me this, entrusting me with this insecurity of hers. "Well, we're not helpless. We got ourselves out of the pond."

"Luck," Chloe said with a shrug. "If we'd been another ten feet out, we'd be dead." This unsettling assessment struck me hard, and I again felt the weak-kneed relief of having simply survived.

"Okay. Let's not tell them," I agreed. She nodded, pulling me closer. I was happy to share a secret with her. So many secrets, even in those early days. I felt her mouth close gently on my earlobe; I shuddered, and not because of the cold.

"Well, there is an upshot to our misadventure," she murmured.

"Oh?" I said, distracted.

"At least we're clean." I laughed, and she slithered her arm fiercely around my waist.

Chapter 5

We moved in on April 1. I had informed my parents a few days earlier that I was moving to a farming co-op nearly twenty miles away to hoe rows of beans and sit around the campfire talking radical anarchist politics. I did not tell them I was more or less in love with the four people with whom I would be undertaking this excellent little project, that only one of us had serious farming experience, or that we had virtually no money. I reassured them that I would be keeping up with my job, earning my pittance. I would have email. I would invite them over for dinner as soon as we had the place organized. They volunteered to help me move in, but I didn't want them to see the Homestead as it looked now, with deep ruts of mud piled high and the cabins drooping under the weight of melting snow. As I was packing up a modest suitcase (jeans, books, and, optimistically, my prettiest underthings), they lurked anxiously in the doorway.

"But what about your student loans, sweetheart?" my dad murmured.

"I'll still be working and earning some money." I didn't tell them that Louisa nearly had me and Chloe convinced that defaulting on our loans was the right solution; we would be free of the debt while saying a simultaneous "fuck you" to privatized loans and the credit-rating system. I knew this to be an irrevocable choice (much like getting into debt in the first place, really, though the permanence of that decision had been deliberately obscured while I was making it), and I was therefore hesitant. And frankly, it was easy for Louisa to talk.

I'd made plans to pick up Chloe; though I was running late, I knew that she would still be sitting in a heap of clothes, helplessly trying to decide what to bring and what to give away, so I felt only a little rushed. Still, I had no desire to drag out this scene with my poor parents. For months they had been hinting that I should seek full-time employment and an apartment of my own ("There are some temp jobs in town, sweetheart—you could try that until you get on your feet?"), but they were visibly unenthusiastic about the solution I had arrived at.

"And car insurance? How will you keep up with that if you're, uh, farming all the time?" My father, ever the bourgeois, stuck to the money.

"We're all contributing to the insurance and the gas. And the inevitable repairs." I smiled brightly. "Really, we'll only be using it once a week for runs into town."

"Do you think this is such a smart move, after what happened the last time you decided to get involved in some little experiment?" my father pointed out bluntly.

I flinched. "This is different. There won't be any cameras this time. We're off-grid."

"When you say 'self-sufficient,' hon, what does that mean? Are you going to, I don't know, make your own flour and things?" My mother wrinkled her nose adorably; I knew she had been Googling madly, trying to see if this was something all the kids were trying.

"We've given ourselves a small budget for the first few months, until we're really producing. To buy things like flour, lentils, meat. We're mostly going to rely on barter once we're up and running, for anything we can't grow. There are lots of small farms willing to trade for the basics." At least, Beau knew of two, and we figured we'd soon find more. "We've bought some supplies from local growers with greenhouses for the next few weeks, and by June, we should have some food of our own." This was wildly optimistic, but the most intricate agricultural enterprise either of my parents had engaged in was managing the houseplants in the living room, so I thought they probably wouldn't call me out.

"Sweetie, it's just, you know, I looked up a little bit about what you're trying. Homesteads, intentional communities, and all that. And I mean, I don't want to sound like a worried parent, but I just, I read about this other commune or whatever you call it and they sounded like really bad news."

"What do you mean, Mom? Like, historically?"

"No, this was recent! They were news items. Somewhere out in Hector, there was this group that started off a real successful farm co-op, but then, I guess, they became . . . well, I hate to say it, sweetie, but it sounded like some really creepy stuff. *Sex* stuff." She pronounced the word in a hushed voice, as though someone might be listening.

I snorted. "Mom, don't worry about it. We won't get involved in any creepy sex stuff."

"It just seemed . . . I don't know what I Googled exactly, but aren't you going to be in Hector?"

"Mom, it's fine. I'll be okay. I'll email you tomorrow, I'll send photos, this is a good thing, I love you," I reassured them, schlepping my suitcase through the carpeted halls of the modest single-story house I had grown up in. My dad insisted on dragging my suitcase to the truck; my mother hovered, tears in her eyes, and insisted I take a bag of groceries. I finally accepted, unable to tell her that we wouldn't eat anything she'd given me because it was all processed, and none of it was locally produced. Were we ridiculous? Yes, I suppose. As I put the pickup in drive, my mother made a final salvo:

"Just—just try not to let it get out of hand this time, Mackenzie? Have better judgment?" I rolled my eyes, but nodded. Surely my judgment could hardly be worse?

I waved from the truck and backed out of the drive, fleeing the manicured lawn and the grim town of Lansing, gunning for South Hill as fast as my little Ford could go.

Chloe lived pretty high up on Hudson Street, within walking distance of campus, and I had a hard time finding parking. Her house was essentially a tenement, a collapsing building filled to the brim with artsy Ithaca College students who had nearly enough money to pay their exorbitant tuition but not quite enough to live in a legally zoned building with more than one bathroom. As depressing as I found living at home, Chloe's grim building was worse. I located her upstairs in her dark, boxy room, dithering. An hour later, after much hemming and hawing and unpacking and repacking, we were wrestling her suitcase into the bed of my truck. Then we were driving out of town, headed to the Homestead, stomachs aflutter with excitement and panic. We drove silently, taking the back roads up the hill and climbing into the country.

The other three were there when we arrived, scrubbing out the stuffy cabins, which had stood uninhabited for decades. It was a chilly day, and I prayed desperately that it wouldn't snow. We'd begged some cured wood from a neighbor, enough to keep us from freezing for a couple of weeks of less-than-balmy temperatures, but we would need to hoard our fuel in case spring came late.

Having agreed on who would take which cabins ahead of time, our task today was to make our little huts habitable before launching into the daunting farm work. Louisa was the first one we saw, standing in front of her dwelling with a kerchief tied over her curls, wearing a turtleneck and worker's gloves and staring in consternation at the cabin's grubby floor. She came skipping over to us as we pulled up. The ground was soggy and treacherous.

"Oh, we're all here! Goody. The cabins are appalling. Come!" She led us to a ragged shed that was untidily crammed with various tools. A glance at a serious hatchet and a jagged, rusty hoe gave me a spooked pause. They looked like props from a horror film. "Brooms, mop." She pointed. "I borrowed a bucket and some cleaning supplies from my dad, just until this place is habitable." By agreement, we'd decided not to buy anything yet, so this seemed like a necessary workaround. The windows were filthy and needed Windex, even if said product was produced by an evil multinational. Another concession in a lifetime of them. The five mattresses that sat wrapped in plastic on a tarp were an indispensable gift from Rudy, along with the cleaning supplies, delivered earlier.

I remember that first day in stark detail; many of the others stretch out in identical visions, endless sessions of digging in the dirt and collapsing, legless with fatigue, into a hammock. That first day, though, I had yet to spend a night in my own little cabin, which felt at first so blessedly private and cozily flanked by friends, before I began to lie awake, unable to close my eyes, feeling alone and isolated and listening for sounds outside—clues to what was happening nearby. That day, everything was imagined and imaginable, and I fantasized about folding myself up into a fluffy bed, possibly with someone else, waking with the sunrise to harvest beans. The bare walls and floor of the cabin could be host to infinite scenes, moments of intensity and perfection that would justify this decision I was making. Had made. I tackled cobwebs and scrubbed corners and polished the magnificent old wood of my floor in a happy daydream.

After a few hours of cleaning, we helped each other schlep the strangely dense mattresses into each cabin in pairs. Beau easily lifted a corner, I less easily lifted another, and we stumbled into his cabin and hoisted the mattress up onto the boards of the mezzanine, then did the same in my own. Our eyes met as the palliasse slipped into place, and I couldn't look away.

Reader, I wanted him. I knew it in a second of perfect clarity: *Oh, this is lust.* Maybe I should have left right then, taken the keys to my Ford and headed home to Lansing to lick my wounds. I knew that Beau didn't want me, that I probably didn't have the stomach to compete with Louisa. But I wasn't capable of leaving. Standing there, gazing at Beau's coy smile, quirked almost knowingly, I was transfixed. I would stay on the Homestead until it was finished. Whatever "it" was.

Chapter 6

With the equinox a scant fortnight behind us when we'd
arrived, the sun was setting later each evening, and as early twilight
crept across bare fields, we hastened to stoke our meager fires, batten
down the windows, and think about tucking ourselves in for the night.
I made my bed with sheets that still smelled like my home (a sudden
flash of the basement, of my mother clearing the lint trap), fluffed my
down comforter, and engaged the stove. I made sure my door was shut
tight and bounced to the big cabin for our evening meal.

Recognizing that we couldn't avoid eating and hadn't yet grown
much, we had procured some start-up materials from local farms and
producers, most of whom Beau and Louisa knew personally. It is difficult to begin without borrowing. Our pantry was stocked with a huge
bag of local flour, cornmeal, and oats. We would buy eggs from a neighbor until we got the chickens laying (which would occur, presumably,
at some point after we acquired the chickens). A few bricks of hard
cheese lurked on a shelf, a precious commodity. Louisa had a stash of
sweet potatoes from last year, when she had halfheartedly planted a
few semi-successful winter crops. Chloe had brought some chutneys
and sauces she had received as a gift from a local CSA. People loved
giving things to Chloe, though she didn't seem to realize this was out
of the ordinary. She loved gifting as well. We five trooped out to the

pantry to see what we could make for dinner, and to stare covetously at our goods.

"When I was little, I liked to play this game," Chloe explained. "Basically, all my stuffed animals and doll-things would provision themselves for the winter. What I liked was making lists and being certain of a season of bounty."

"Born to live off the land," Jack said, with a charmed smile. We continued to contemplate the shelves of our pantry, which looked pretty good, considering that we hadn't dirtied a fingernail yet.

"Sweet potato frittata?" Chloe suggested.

"We'll use up all our eggs and not have any for the rest of the week," Louisa said dismissively. "What about pasta?" she countered. We deferred, naturally. She was a tyrant in the kitchen, and it seemed wise to let her plan the menu.

Alcohol was a concern. We all liked to drink, though in different degrees of depth and frequency. Beau was in the process of constructing a basic still and concocting some type of grain alcohol, but it wouldn't be ready for a while yet. Jack was going to make beer and mead. Our temporary solution was barter with a local winemaker named Bartoletti, a friend of Rudy Stein's and an occasionally whimsical fellow. He thought our little project was "downright admirable" and had a lot of sympathy for our thirst. We'd offered a share of veggies delivered weekly to his house once the season was in full swing, and he'd advanced us five whole cases of wine that had gone unlabeled during bottling last year and were subsequently unsalable. We had no idea what we'd be drinking, but it seemed like an excellent deal to us. We were also hoping to arrange similar trades once we had something more to offer.

Our first evening, we uncorked some reddish wine while Louisa rolled out pasta using another bottle. Beau went outside to the now-working pump and filled a pot with water, which he set up to boil on top of the woodstove, then went back to bring in a jug of drinking water. It was slightly sulfurous and a little earthy-tasting, but it was cold and came straight from the ground. We later splurged on a filter, which helped with the taste; I kept hoping I would grow to love it but never did. We giggled and sipped wine out of Ball jars, and after dinner dispersed to our cabins with full bellies. My cabin was blazingly warm, and I tugged on my long underwear with languorous happiness, wondering what everyone was doing in their own little rooms. I snuggled into my mattress and fell asleep to the sound of coyotes calling to one another nearby, a tight-knit little pack that hung together even in the late-winter night.

I had assumed that Louisa and Beau were a couple because of their intense, evident intimacy, and probably because of Beau's habit of fondly leaning over and biting her on the nape of the neck in a possessive chomp that just about broke my heart each time.

We were loafing aimlessly in the big cabin the first evening I saw him do it to Chloe. Seated on the floor, on an old rug of Louisa's, we were playing some foolish game. Pictionary perhaps, or charades? Duck, duck, goose? Discussing, in any case, the provenance of some of our seeds.

"Did you know Monsanto controls, like, ninety-eight percent of the food that's grown commercially in the U.S.?" Jack was looking slightly pink with rage. He had a tendency to repeat his arguments, in an attempt to perfect them; we'd heard this complaint before, and knew that he would segue into a rant about subsidized corn farming.

"Preaching to the choir, Jacky boy," Beau said, leaning casually back on his elbows. His long body stretched out catlike, all in black. He was seated between Jack and Chloe. Chloe leaned her head against his shoulder, the motion so confidently physical, like all her gestures.

"Yeah, but even we're not immune from ingesting all that shit. You can't just order up seeds from a catalog, because they're most likely Monsanto. That company is evil." Jack was getting all fidgety, as he did when he had an ideological bone to pick, his sandy hair sticking up. Pretty soon he would accidentally knock something over.

"Let's destroy the fuckers!" Chloe said, pumping her fist in the air and wrinkling her nose.

"You," Beau said very simply, and leaned down to bite her neck in his playful, rather erotic way. I froze, completely unsure of what was happening. I looked at Louisa, expecting her to erupt, but she was suddenly studying her drink, as was Jack. My eyes widened as Chloe nuzzled a little closer, twisting sinuously. It wasn't a kiss, but there was something distinctly sexual in the arch of her back, the curl of his neck, and I realized I had misunderstood Chloe and Beau quite drastically.

"Well, someone really should do something about those criminals," Jack said, awkwardly trying to fill the silence. There was a long pause before Beau answered.

"Maybe somebody will."

It should be noted that I knew next to nothing about farming. I grew up in a rural community, true, but the largest industry in our part of town was probably the coal-fired power plant that sat belching smoke on the eastern shore of Cayuga Lake. My parents cultivated an obnoxiously green lawn, which my father managed with manic intensity, perching on his riding mower with a cheap beer clenched in his fist at least three times a week. My mom grew geraniums. We purchased corn on the cob from roadside stands in the late summer and sometimes bought tomatoes from the Amish. My knowledge of a potato involved only the final product, none of its interim stages or states of being. I was a total rube, swept along by enthusiasm and desire. My misadventures in Brooklyn had been informative about making kombucha and bathtub mozzarella, but I had no idea how to milk a cow, and fermented tea wasn't our first priority.

Louisa and Beau were cagey about the work they'd done around the Homestead during the last year, for reasons that eventually became transparent; we were all meant to feel equally crucial to the success of this little enterprise, and it was supposed to have germinated only once we were all assembled. The two of them concealed the fact that they'd been thinking of doing this for a long time—partly, I surmised, so that we wouldn't feel like we were just laboring bodies put to work on their land, like hungry sharecroppers, tugging at the coattails of their vision. The preservation of this illusion was manipulative and self-serving, sure, but I also think they genuinely wanted us to feel at home, invested and indispensable. They couldn't do it without us, and they knew it. We'd learn about the year before eventually, but the work those two had done before our arrival seemed at the time just like good forethought.

Louisa had waged a bloody crusade against the burdock that plagued our vegetable garden, digging up the tenacious weeds with a fervor that bordered on manic; her eyes glowed with a fury as she buried her pitchfork deep into the earth, uprooting viney underground filaments that were sometimes as thick as her forearm. This campaign would continue into the spring, and the sight of the gritty fronds of a nascent burdock continued to provoke fits of disbelieving rage in her—each leaf that doggedly popped up sent Louisa flying out to the vegetable patch to tug it out. She took it personally. Jack wanted to try eating it, but Louisa forbade it, having taken an almost religious umbrage at the crop.

Only Jack knew enough about farming to understand that some previous prescient groundwork had been accomplished; Chloe and I accepted the early arrival of ramps and scallions just a month after our arrival as naturally occurring. We threw ourselves into tilling deep furrows into the garden, putting in seed potatoes, along with carrots and beans. Jack was in charge of irrigation, and managed a network of trenches and raised beds that still remains opaque to me.

We spent days repairing the sheds and patching up the cabins; Chloe had volunteered with Habitat for Humanity and had some basic knowledge of woodworking and tools. Beau spent long, solitary afternoons out in the woods locating deadfall and breaking it into more manageable chunks, which we would later take turns splitting. As the owner of our one road-worthy vehicle, I was the unofficial admiral of our small flotilla; I presided over an antique tractor, two bicycles, and my own rusting truck. Towards the end of the afternoon I would head through the woods on the wheezy tractor, making painstaking headway to where Beau waited, sweaty and with blistered palms, and we would fling dismembered trees onto the ratty hay wagon while I tried not to make a fool of myself.

Soon, things were tentatively, bravely budding, and we prayed that the frost would stay away. The remnants of an informal orchard still stood in one of the clearings, and we hoped the trees might eventually fruit. On one warmish day when the buds were beginning to look blowsy, Louisa led us beneath the trees for a picnic and read aloud, with Chloe, some of the more hilarious segments of Emerson's *Essays*. The sunlight and smells of incipient summer drove us bonkers after the gray of the previous season, the accumulated gray of a lifetime of these upstate winters.

Beau turned his face skyward, adopting a moony expression.

"What are you doing?" Louisa asked, flopping onto his belly and propping her elbows on his rib cage, abandoning the book. This posture didn't look comfortable for either of them, but Beau neither complained nor shifted to dislodge her.

"Contemplating nature with my transparent eyeball," he said, with such sincerity that I couldn't help a snort. He really meant it.

"Indeed," Louisa said, rolling her own eyeballs.

"I think I'll stick with Thoreau," Jack announced. "He's much less self-serious. And less, I don't know, spiritual. He's a practical fellow, our Henry David."

"Agreed," Beau said. "He worries about how many nails you need, not whether divinity is present in each of them."

"Well, divinity is present in these nails," Chloe said, grabbing one finger each from Jack and Beau and kissing the tips. Both were somewhat grubby, but she seemed not to mind. She lay between them, all three on their backs. I sat at everyone's heads, a heap of wildflowers in my lap. "That's the kind of mysticism I'm interested in," she clarified. "What keeps each of your souls alive, and what connects all of ours."

"Well, isn't that obvious?" Beau said slowly. "We're connected by desire." I raised one eyebrow. This was very direct, for Beau, and I was curious where he was headed. "We desire a different world, a better life for ourselves. To discover something real, beautiful."

"We want to learn how to live," Jack corrected. "We believe we've maybe found an answer. At least, we're trying it out."

"Together," Chloe added. "We're trying together. That's what keeps us here. This is something we have to do, all of us."

"I dunno, kids. Seems a little hi-falootin' to me," Louisa said, adopting her faux country accent. "I'm just here for the tomatoes."

"Lou, don't be that way," Chloe chastised, extending her leg across Beau's shins to poke Louisa with her bare big toe. "You always want to avoid anything about what we feel, anything that alludes to the existence of feelings. Desire *is* part of this." She waved around us, indicating the entire homestead.

"Maybe I just don't feel like talking about it as some sort of group problem," Louisa said, sitting up. "My feelings are my own, and I don't always want to discuss them, Chloe." Though Louisa directed this comment at her, she didn't meet Chloe's eyes. I felt like there was a subtextual conversation taking place, perhaps one they'd had more than once.

Beau tilted his head back to look at me, his familiar features inverted. His grin looked odd upside down. "Mack, you're the most sensible person here." I blushed, as I did whenever he paid me a compliment. "What do you think? Of our collective endeavor?" he asked.

I paused, though I'd already been formulating what to say, if asked. "I think we all have our own motivations. And they don't need to perfectly align. So much of what goes wrong in other communal-living scenarios is an attempt to force everyone to feel the same way, to, I don't know, worship the same thing. Maybe Jack cares most about the environment, and Louisa cares most about anti-capitalism. And, Beau, you share those opinions, but what you want is the good life. None of that conflicts, so why should you try for absolute agreement? We can all have what we want."

"See?" Beau said, smiling at Louisa. "I told you she's incredibly reasonable."

I bobbed my head to hide my pleased smile. "Not only that," I said. "But I'm very talented." I held up the garland I'd been crafting. "Who wants it?"

"I do," Jack said, instantly springing to his feet. He knelt before me and I crowned him with a wreath of dandelions and forsythia.

"Lovely," Chloe said. "And one for Beau?" she asked, pointing to the other circlet in my lap. I laid this on his head, and he, too, stood. Looking both comical and elegant, he beamed at Jack, and shifted his weight in a clear indication that he meant to play, the same way a puppy will crouch down and wag his tail in invitation. Jack correctly interpreted his mischievous expression and tore off into the field, scampering through the brush with an equine gallop. Beau followed, and we watched them dance, playing an unnamed game. They looked like satyrs, romping carefree in the grass.

"Testosterone," Louisa said, shaking her head and rolling her eyes. Chloe huffed in irritation.

"Why do you do that?" she asked. "Turn everything lovely into some sort of ironic critique?"

"I don't do that."

"You do. It's as though you can't bear to say you enjoy something. To admit what you want."

Louisa said nothing, tugging up a handful of grass. She didn't look up.

I wasn't sure what their particular beef was about, but it definitely seemed ongoing. A cool breeze ruffled my sleeves, and I felt a drop of rain. The drops began to intensify, and Beau yapped a throaty howl of pleasure from the other side of the clearing. His voice and body were suffused with joy. I felt lifeless in comparison, as though every moment of passion I'd ever felt was nothing like his ecstasy at simply being alive then. I wanted to feel something intensely.

We stood up, hurrying for the big cabin, Louisa and Chloe quickly forgetting their spat and racing arm in arm, knees knocking together. Jack and Beau followed with their long-legged lope. I slowed as I neared the steps, wanting to feel something for just a moment longer, and shaking with each cold drop. Could I learn to live? The clouds opened up and I let them drench me. The intensity I wanted seemed close, attainable—the chill I felt out here and the coziness I would feel inside, with them? Was that what I hoped for? The distance between two feelings? Beau turned around on the porch and looked at me as though he knew exactly what I was waiting for. He cocked his head, as though to ask: *Alone in the rain, feeling the potential of what's to come, or here, inside with me?* I skipped through the puddle accumulating near the steps and through the door. Chloe was already starting a fire.

Chapter 7

Morel season dawned on us in chilly spring, and we fell
upon the mossy ground in a porcine frenzy. Trillium appeared first,
heralding the arrival of the fungi. We snuffled out the precious little
nubbins, their sulcus cortexes winking up from the warming earth, and
we dragged them home in little net bags, letting their spores scatter as
we brought them to Louisa in her kitchen, where she verified each
one, ensuring they were not the poisonous false morels. Our woods
seemed to be unusually blessed, and without other produce, we committed ourselves to truffling about beneath the trees. We cooked up a
beastly amount: morel "risotto" (Louisa lamented the lack of local va-
rieties of Arborio rice, alas), morel and chèvre crostini, morel omelets,
morels and garlic on pasta. Jack desperately wanted to make a morel
pizza with some of the mozzarella he'd sourced from a nearby cheese-
maker, but we didn't have an oven yet, a project we meant to get
around to eventually. When we were sick of morels and had dried a
bunch more, we went off to trade them for cornmeal, oats, early spring
greens, and some new seedlings. We met some of the neighbors, who
didn't seem especially covetous of the little fungi, but they took pity
on us and gave some cheese in exchange. I'm sure they thought we
would starve to death.

With the warming weather came the time to invest some money.

We needed chicken wire for the coop, not to mention some chickens. We needed more seedlings than had already been started, to supplement our rather pitiful crop, which Chloe had been lining up on the windowsills. And we wanted that wood-fired oven, damn it.

We had some tools, and we were able to scavenge more from the local ReUse center, along with big cast-iron pots and pans that were perfect for the job of prepping big vats of rustic food. We had compost from Louisa's old apartment, with a backup supply from Rudy's house if we fell short. Chloe had brought a few tarps that she had liberated from backstage at an Ithaca College drama production.

We were settling in. Since the weather was still too cold for our catchment bags and outdoor showers, we were basically just putting a big tub of water in the sauna and sudsing ourselves off whenever we grew too gross from the manual labor of hoeing up the nearly five-thousand-square-foot garden that was to sustain us. We built up beds and carved out troughs, sowed early seeds for next spring. We wondered if we needed a greenhouse.

Because I was new to the group, I didn't know much about the others' habits and assumed that those first few months were typical of their behavior. For example: Chloe hated waking up early. She was miserable in the early morning, a shadow of her usual glowing self; this made farming a singularly weird profession for her to take up. She would mulch the squash beds listlessly until the sun was warmly and fully up in the sky, seemingly unable to say a word or emerge out of herself until midmorning. Louisa drank too much, but seemed hell-bent on proving that it didn't affect her the next day, and subsequently flung around dirt with alarming vigor after every overindulgence in wine, sweating it out. Jack sang tunelessly while he worked, smiling as he walked the rows or went to check the neglected apple trees for blight. Sometimes I would catch him grinning giddily at a slug or a crocus, in private communion with God knows what reveries.

I'd learned that Beau was prone to mysterious disappearances; anyone who knew him noticed his sudden absence from a gathering or his coy refusal to reveal where he'd been earlier that morning. He did this on the Homestead, too, naturally, but often returned with a loaf of bread from the baker two miles away, or news that he'd found what looked like a huge patch of early strawberry leaves in the clearing due west of the big cabin. But sometimes his disappearances had no apparent explanation, leaving Louisa in a repressed but seething froth of annoyance if he missed mealtimes. We all figured he must be out roaming the back forty, seeking mushrooms and wild garlic to heap on our picnic table (recently constructed by Chloe in the clearing) with the self-satisfied smile of a provider. We tolerated this behavior, I suppose, because we let Beau get away with so much. Embarrassing though it is to admit, I think we revered him somewhat: his enigmatic pauses, his feline grace, the sharpness of his mind. He was rarely challenged, and his absences were considered par for the course—his unavailability making him all the more appealing.

In April, I was out walking near the end of the drive, picking a small bouquet of forsythia blossoms (woody branches prickly in my hand, yellow blooms almost too much) when I saw Beau hop out of a genuine hippie VW van, painted with the predictable sunflowers and cornstalks. From the sound of the engine and the stenciled embellishments, I speculated that it was probably run on either corn or sunflower oil. Squinting, I watched him wave goodbye to a young woman with a deep tan and a tower of brownish dreadlocks. She had some sort of tattoo on her firm, sinewy shoulder. She lurked at the edge of the driveway as though not wanting to come down it, and she seemed to glance towards the cabins from time to time as she talked to Beau. He grinned at me when he saw me in the drive, my arms filled with yellow branches and the mammalian buds of late-blooming pussy willows. He was wearing black today (indeed, his white outfits were trotted out for festive occasions, due to their impracticality, and he wore only those two unambiguous shades). He lit up one of his cigarillos.

"Who's this?" I asked, trying not to sound shrilly jealous. Though I couldn't have known what her presence would come to mean, I must have felt some presentiment that Fennel would drive a wedge into our lives.

"Oh, just some ladies headed from town out this direction. They were nice enough to give me a lift and save me a long bike ride." He gave a careless shrug and began to turn me down the drive, leaving the "ladies" behind him. Something about his nonchalance made me wonder if he didn't want me to properly meet them for some reason. But when he linked his arm with my own, my whole body became suffused with blood, and I followed him, as I had followed him out into the country.

When Louisa appeared striding down the driveway in front of us, though, Beau stiffened.

"Hey," he said, too casually.

"Hi, Beau. Been hanging over at the Collective?" she asked, with an edge that could only mean trouble.

"Just socializing with our neighbors."

Louisa raised a hand to her forehead to look towards the road. "That you, Fennel?" she called. "Why didn't you come up the drive to say hi?" This comment was laced with too much friendliness; it came across as sarcastic. The dreadlocked woman paused warily before replying.

"Hey, Louisa. We were just headed home," Fennel said.

"Oh, really? You're not just, I don't know, afraid to come up and say howdy? After everything? Thought maybe it would be, I don't know, awkward?"

"Look, I know you're upset about what happened—what you think happened—"

"I know exactly what happened, Fennel. And so do you. But he's gone, right? Matthew's back in California?"

"He was just as upset as you were—"

"I really doubt that," Louisa interrupted. "Skipped town like the last time, though, I guess. Wouldn't do to have someone else suggesting that he's a creep, abusing his power."

Fennel said nothing.

"I'm sure we'll be seeing each other around," Louisa said brightly, looping her arm in Beau's and spinning around to march back up the drive. Without turning around, she called over her shoulder: "You all just stay out of trouble, you hear?"

As we walked up the drive together, it occurred to me that Beau's bike had been in the yard all day, and he could never have planned to bike home.

Each of us observed the nocturnal comings and goings from each of our cabins with a deep and abiding interest, though we all feigned indifference. I would sit in my chair, wrapped in my downy duvet, peering out my window and pathetically trying to get a glimpse of who was headed to which cabin, who would share which bed. Though we all typically retired tactfully to our own cabins at the end of the evening, this was merely a formal ritual, enacted to preserve some unspoken illusion of celibacy. I don't know why we bothered, as there was a reshuffling of sleeping arrangements almost every evening, with very few real attempts at dissimulation. After cleaning up from a meal in the big cabin, we would bid one another good evening and slink to our own cabins, still slightly cold in the spring damp. Each of the five cabins would light up with a candle or a little kerosene lamp, and you could sense the evening bedding-down taking place. Soon, Beau's or Chloe's candle would migrate outdoors to the dull glow of a new windowsill.

The first few times I saw it, I assumed it was a last-minute privy trip and dismissed the wandering light. But soon I started to notice that Beau's light wouldn't return to his own cabin, and would instead venture to Louisa's or Chloe's. Chloe's lamp would disappear, usually to Louisa's cabin, less frequently to Beau's. If Louisa's candle moved, she was headed not to anyone's cabin but, rather, to some outdoor spot, where she would soon be joined by one or two other candles. She entertained visitors in her cabin, but I don't think she ever visited someone else's.

Naturally, I writhed with jealousy. I lay there imagining Beau's shiny dark hair bent over Louisa's pale breast, or Chloe's wide, sweet mouth meeting Beau's in the darkness. My little cabin became the site of racking fantasies about the pale limbs a few dozen yards away. They twined together and multiplied from four to eight to twelve and sometimes, when I felt truly dejected and excluded, to sixteen, with Jack's lanky legs and tawny arms tossed in for good measure, to reinforce my sense of outsideness. Riveted by this nightly procession, I sat glued to my window, crouching low so my moony face wouldn't appear in the telltale glass, hoping to witness I don't know what. Consummation, the verification of my anxiety, a rosy, taut nipple pressed to the glass? I watched Jack's door with hawk eyes, certain that he, too, was slipping out for these torrid trysts but was, alone of the four, attempting discretion. I never saw his candle waver, however, and I believe he lacked the subterfuge to pretend; he was a terrible liar, his face too revealing, his spirit too open. I would have been grateful had Louisa or Beau or Chloe concealed their evening peripatetics, but I consoled myself by pretending that I would rather know than remain ignorant.

A more mature human, consumed by jealousy and unrequited lust, would have voiced her frustrations. What prevented me from waylaying Beau in the orchard grove and colliding with his sinewy trunk against the unyielding one of a tree? From bending down to graze Chloe's lips while we sat on a blanket shelling peas, slowly stretching her supple dancer's frame alongside my own? I even, on certain occasions, thought of Louisa, stripped in her white bed, her skin a dusky pink, beckoning for me to come and join her. But action is not something that has ever come easily to me; I wait for others' decisiveness, not choosing for myself. Never recognizing that my passivity, too, is a choice.

Jack alone did not appear in these tortured waking dreams, and I think it was simply because he seemed more available and, therefore, less desirable. In an unfortunate personality quirk (one I think I share with more than a few other folks), I find myself pretty uninterested in anyone who might remotely be interested in me or who is not actively pursuing another object of their desire. Jack wasn't actually less lovely than the others. His smile was the biggest and the most genuine, his laugh full and wild, his broad face open and alive and without deceit. His arms were as thick as Beau's and his waist as narrow; he was even perhaps an inch or two taller. Of the four of them, he was certainly the one who tortured me the least, and for that reason alone he would have been the best match. I knew this, lying there and working myself into an unreciprocated lather. And yet.

By day, the night-born tensions were frequently evident. Louisa was hotheaded and prone to sulks, and after nights when Beau and Chloe had found their way together in the dark, Louisa would take herself off to the woodpile to attack the logs with a petulant fury, leaving us to fret in the vegetable plot. Jack and Beau seemed oblivious to these funks, but Chloe would stare off towards Louisa, then finally, after some internal regulator ticked down, decide that she couldn't take it anymore and would scamper after her with some present of water or apples. Louisa would return pacified, and Chloe would inevitably join Louisa later that night.

When Beau visited Louisa, Chloe would opt for careful friendliness the next day. She loathed conflict, and went out of her way to ensure peaceful relations. She wouldn't be the one to bring this little ménage à trois to an inevitable head, no sirree. Louisa would try to ignore this gallant display of sportsmanship, but eventually she couldn't help planting an affectionate kiss on the bridge of Chloe's nose.

Beau alone seemed completely unaffected by whatever took place. It didn't matter to him who spent the evening with whom; he remained slyly pleased with himself no matter what. This enraged Louisa most of all.

Spring

Chapter 8

Louisa and I were out hunting morels, though it was grow-ing late in the season for it, and it was unlikely that we would find any more. Still, there we were in the woods, scanning the mulchy ground at the base of old trees for the subtle furl of mushroom, indistinguishable from a dead leaf except for a faint intuitive tickle that told you: Wait! Look again! Louisa was cranky that day; I'd watched Beau's candle join Chloe's last night after we'd supped on bean stew and drunk a bottle of something Chloe had decided was malbec. Louisa had headed to the woods earlier that morning without speaking to either of them, just handing over their coffee with blank huffiness before grabbing a sweater and tugging on her mud boots. I'd tagged along, not certain if I was wanted but desiring the quiet of the forest.

"So do you miss New York, Mack?" Louisa asked me as we stepped into a particularly picturesque clearing, gingerly avoiding the ferns and mayapple that grew on the fringes of sunlight. The birdsong and whisper of leaves were absurdly lovely, almost a parody of pastoral beauty.

"Oh yes, I daydream about the traffic at Union Square." Louisa knew that I had dropped out of grad school, but I had yet to share the rest of my story with her. Of course, I was sure that even a little Internet sleuthing would produce some YouTube videos, but I felt protected by our disconnectedness and abysmally poor reception. For the first time in months, I was able to separate myself from what had happened on *The Millennial Experiment*. There were distinct echoes with the Homestead, of course, yet I found that I liked that echo.

"You know what I mean," Louisa continued. "We small-town girls work hard to get out, get to the big city. Don't you ever feel a little weird to have run straight back here, in shame?"

I thought I heard something in her tone, an implication that she knew more of my departure from Brooklyn than I had disclosed. The thought brooked a wave of panic. I hedged uncomfortably, not ready to tell my story. I would tell her, tell them all, eventually; but I couldn't just now. I hoped my skittishness didn't show.

"Yeah, of course. I can't really help feeling like leaving the city was a type of defeat, you know. My last night there, while I was packing up and getting ready to head home, head upstate, I was singing the Sinatra song. 'If you can make it there, you'll make it anywhere,'" I crooned. "The reverse implication being, of course, that if you *don't* make it there . . ."

"Indeed. But isn't that just so much poppycock that we're fed? Like"—she paused and tried, unsuccessfully, to line her words up with Frankie:—"'If you successfully conform to our values of teleological progress by getting a paid job at a huge corporation, you'll make it anywhere!'" She shrugged. "And then we're taught to feel shame, to self-enforce this notion of success and internalize it when it doesn't work out. Which, of course, it can't, because there are too many college graduates overqualified for the remaining handful of desirable jobs."

"Well, we all hope we're the special ones."

"And then we get labeled 'the entitlement generation'! Like, yeah, I worked my ass off through my adolescence to ace the SATs so I could go a hundred grand into debt at an elite institution that I was told from birth was my destiny, and now am I maybe entitled to an entry-level position at the same global corporation that will ensure I have no breathable air by 2050? And maybe healthcare? Pretty please?"

"Well, I'm the idiot who bought into it. I let my parents project their fantasies onto me without ever considering if that was good for the world. Or even what I wanted," I said, crouching down to seize what looked like a morel but turned out to be a ball of dirt.

"It wasn't just you."

"And I think my parents are ashamed to tell people what I'm doing now. As though trying to learn how to feed myself is somehow beneath me. Beneath them."

"It's fucking ridiculous," she concurred.

"At least your parents—or your dad, at any rate, believes in what you're doing," I said. I felt I had to point out that she was impossibly privileged to be handed not just a free pass on the generational-expectations front but also the land on which to give her version of the future a whirl.

"Ha," she snorted. "Of course he supports me. He would support literally anything I tried, even becoming a Republican. He's symptomatic of the bizarre American parent who believes that their child really is flawless."

"Could be worse," I pointed out.

"Maybe. But now we have a generation of kids who don't especially *want* to go work in the salt mines because Mommy and Daddy said they were unique and they could be whatever they wanted. Explains why so many of us are just genuinely bummed over what paths we have open for us. Not exactly the ballerina/astronaut future we were told was within our grasp as wee tykes."

"I didn't even think I was being particularly ambitious." I paused. "What about your mom?" Louisa rarely mentioned her.

"Oh, she's desperately committed to the rat race," she said. "An eighties feminist who thought the only way she could beat the patriarchy was by joining it. She's a partner at a law firm in the city. A cold, brilliant, driven woman." She smirked bitterly. "I think she was relieved when Dad wanted to keep me. Her protestations were feeble."

"Well, your dad is pretty great."

"Maybe Beau is the lucky one," she said halfheartedly, though it seemed immediately as though she wanted to take it back.

"How, um, how did they die?"

"Overdose."

"Jesus, both of them?"

"Well, his dad might actually still be alive somewhere, but he's probably dead. He was a drug addict, and Cindy threw him out when Beau was still real little. She OD'd when he was fourteen." She shrugged, familiar with this tragedy. I couldn't believe I hadn't known. Had it been intentional? "Supposedly just an accident," Louisa said, sensing my morbid curiosity. "Beau found her. I feel the whole experience explains his strong self-destructive streak, though."

"Jesus." I inhaled the sharp foresty smells and felt briefly grateful for my own timid parents. They disapproved of me, sure, and made me feel profoundly incompetent, but the idea of my tiny mother doing something so damaging was more or less unthinkable. "And you and Beau? Were you guys, uh, together then?"

"I think Beau and I have never really been together," Louisa said lightly, and strode ahead with a tug of her chin, clearly intending to leave me behind.

On a cool morning, Jack, Beau, and I rose early to clear some brush from the far end of the orchard. We were hoping to plant some young apple trees, though the commitment to the future that this investment implied made me, at least, a little twitchy; would we be here in five, ten years to see them fruit? Like all mornings when I knew I would spend time with Beau, I changed into multiple outfits, gazing down at myself with dissatisfaction. I pinned back my straight, thin hair, which had been cut into a rather impractical length—a straggly bob, making it impossible to properly put up out of the way—and finally settled on a pair of jeans that at least partially concealed the straight angle of my hips and my complete lack of anything approaching luscious curves. Jack finally interrupted my dithering by knocking on my cabin door, offering a thermos of coffee and a chatty recitation of his dreams from the night before. Beau fell in beside us as we loped off towards the undertended fruit trees, silent and thoughtful. We startled a clutch of rabbits from their hiding place in the brush, and they scattered into a frantic fan, scampering off in terror.

"The bravery of minks and muskrats. And rabbits," I said, and Jack and Beau smiled at me appreciatively.

The weeds we were planning to eradicate were tall and dense, even at this time of year, and we all had thick gloves to protect our hands from the bite and itch of the foliage. Though I was slight and not nearly as strong as the boys, I liked these days with a hoe in my hand more than the slushy, inclement hours spent scrubbing pots or sorting through seeds inside. For the first time, my sticklike arms had a swell of muscle, and my abs were solid, compact. I liked the sweat, the bruise of color that rose up on my skin from the cold air and the exertion. I liked to watch Beau swing mechanically through his steady strokes, sometimes tying a bandanna around his forehead to keep the sweat from dripping into his eyes. Maybe most of all, I liked seeing our progress, how I started at the beginning of the day with a huge heap of unchopped wood or untilled earth and forced my body to defeat it with incremental trials and defiances.

We attacked the brown foliage, a thicket of tall grass, hops, and old vines. Within minutes, I was pink and damp; we all looked at each other, acknowledging that this would be a long day. I paused every ninety seconds or so to readjust my gloves and take a deep breath. After an hour, I was worried that my arms wouldn't be able to lift the hoe much longer, and I resorted to tugging determinedly on the vines, ripping them loose, and hurling them over my head, into a pile we would later burn. Burdock caught at my clothes, leaving itchy little hangers-on that I would have to tear from the fabric that evening, burr by infuriating burr. I let some of my rage—at my debt, my decisions, myself—do the work. At some point I noticed Beau watching me, and risked a glance at him: his mouth was curled in a smile, one eyebrow slightly raised.

"You look very determined there, Mack," he said, and I blushed.

"No point dragging it out," I mumbled self-consciously.

"You're that desperate to finish and leave us?" Beau asked, maintaining eye contact. I shook my head.

"Shit, guys, look at this," Jack said, bending from his long waist to poke at some rotted wood and what looked like old roofing tiles. Using our hoes, we nudged some of the moldy timber aside, and Beau and Jack tore back the vines to reveal a small collapsed structure.

"Do you think it was another cabin?" I asked.

"It seems smaller than our cabins," Jack mused. "Could be a storage shed or something. Obviously hasn't been used in a while."

"I'd guess outhouse," Beau suggested. "Maybe we shouldn't disturb it," he added with a smile. But Jack was already flinging aside boards and planks with his gangly force, achieving results with fervor rather than precision. A broken chair soon came into view, along with a bucket and a container filled with some badly rusted nails. The next layer produced an axe head, an old saw, and a large shard of glass. As we shifted a window frame, trying to avoid jagged nails and splinters, we all glimpsed something menacing made of steel. In surprise, I almost dropped the crumbling wood I held.

"Jesus, is that what I think it is?" Jack asked. Beau stooped to investigate, then held up a steel animal trap that was rusted but fully intact. Its fiercely toothsome jaws were fused together, and a crawling sensation raised goosebumps on my forearm as I imagined feet or fingers clamped within. What creatures had died caught in this industrial maw?

"Spooky," Jack said succinctly. Beau tossed it to the side, into a grassy clearing. I instinctively gave it a wide berth, even though the trigger had long since been tripped.

"There's a box here," Beau said, shoving at the debris. "Help me drag it free." He and Jack pulled at the metal container, pinned beneath some of the collapsed roof. I felt strangely anxious. My fretful mother had raised me to be unadventurous, to let things be, and confronted with this unopened box, my urge was to leave it, to walk away from this doomed storage shed and clear some more space on the other side of the orchard instead. Beau and Jack had no such concern. They immediately sprang open the lid on the chest, revealing a stack of yellowing pages, bound in leather and still beautifully emblazoned on their covers.

"Oh, you must be joking!" cooed Jack, lifting out a volume of Plato's *Republic*. "This is too perfect." The books were in remarkably good condition; maybe the box had been airtight, or the roof had protected it from the elements? They looked old.

"Where did these come from?" I asked, still hanging back slightly.

"We'll have to go home and ask Louisa. There have been some other folks who've lived out here on this land," Beau explained. "Rudy told her about some of them—she'll know."

"Should we bring all of these back now?" Jack seemed eager, his curious, insatiable mind already moving away from brush clearing to the pleasure of pawing through a stack of decomposing books.

"Let's try to wrap up here first," Beau said. "We can bring them home when we stop for lunch."

Around the lunch table, Louisa lifted out copies of *Walden*, Walt Whitman, Emily Dickinson, and, to her extreme delight, *Transcendental Wild Oats*. Upon the discovery of this last text, she let out a girlish shriek of glee and began excitedly to flip through the pages, which threatened to disintegrate in her hands.

"This is amazing! These must have belonged to that guy who started a utopian commune before the turn of the century. My dad did a whole bunch of research on them when he spent the summer out here. The whole group sounded mad as a bag of cats, but he said they made a go of it, and probably started the orchard. I guess their leader wrote a few semi-religious tracts. There's an archive of his shit at Syracuse University, I think."

"I remember your dad mentioned something. What happened to them?" Chloe asked.

"I forget. I think eventually they got bored and merged with a bigger commune, closer to Canada. Or died? I'll ask him if he remembers."

We finished lunch with Louisa reading Dickinson poems at random, until Beau beseeched her to knock it off. She did, though she looked hurt. A sprinkle of rain threatened the books, and we bustled inside, bringing the remains of lunch with us.

"Oh, nearly forgot," Beau said to Louisa, ignoring her sulk. "I have a present for you." He ducked outside and came back in, damply, with the steel trap. Chloe recoiled, but Louisa cooed excitedly, forgetting her hurt feelings.

"What on earth?" She reached out her hands to accept Beau's creepy offering, and she fondled it thoughtfully. "This is amazing. Do you know what I think this is? I think it's an Oneida fur trap. A Newhouse."

"From the Oneida Community?" Beau asked.

"The very same," Louisa confirmed. "This is how they made their first fortune."

"Who's this now?" Jack asked, inspecting the trap more closely.

"They were a utopian community not too far from here. Dad thinks our utopians started off there, sometime in the mid- or late nineteenth century. They were basically communists, though they adopted some other more unorthodox practices. Like a version of polygamy." Beau's eyebrows quirked up, and he coughed. "Anyway, they're fascinating because even though they were utopian communists, they built their entire community on this really cruel, industrial product. Fur traps."

"That's fucking terrible," Chloe, our confirmed vegetarian, said.

"It was, rather. They later transitioned to silverware, but it all started with these things. It turned into this really successful capitalist enterprise."

"The irony," said Beau.

"This must be a hundred and fifty years old, at least. It's amazing."

"Louisa, it's fucking awful! We should bury it or something," Chloe said.

"Nope. I love it. I think it's also an important reminder," Louisa countered. "I think we should keep it as a way to remember that trying to live the good life can be fucking complicated." She moved over to one of the kitchen walls, where a nail protruded from the old wood. She dangled the fur trap from the nail, right by the stove. "There. Perfect."

"*Et in Arcadia ego*," Beau said. Louisa grinned at him.

"Exactly."

As we finished and cleared our plates, I offered to tidy up, explaining that my arms were wretchedly sore after our archaeological mission of the morning. Chloe and Louisa were going to take over clearing, and Beau and Jack planned to start erecting the chicken coop. We'd just acquired some coop fencing, and we wanted to get a few hens soon.

Alone in the big cabin, I scraped food into our compost bin and put dishes into the buckets I would use to wash them outside. I wiped down all the surfaces of the kitchen and swept. Only Chloe and I seemed particularly concerned about cleanliness, and I viewed my days on kitchen duty as an opportunity to combat the entropy permitted by our three other comrades. I was also feeling lazy and not particularly excited to retrieve my hoe—I had a blossoming blister at the base of my thumb—and was experiencing post-meal grogginess. I boiled some water for nettle tea, which I would deliver to everyone after it steeped, and rummaged deeper into the chest of books. Our new library. I took each book out and spread them all on the table, admiring their antique type and the almost miraculous quality of the pages; they were yellow and delicate and the bindings were separating, but they could still be read, albeit gently. The box *must* have been airtight, or at least mostly immune to the weather.

The last thing I pulled from the chest wasn't a traditionally published book. It had an unembellished leather cover, and the lettering on the inside read, "Mr. William Fulsome." The pages in this manuscript were in slightly better shape than the other books, in spite of the leather binding, fastened with two leather thongs. The pages were lined with minute handwritten script that had faded to brown against the yellowed pages. I understood, not even considering it, that I would keep this book a secret. Another.

From the diary of William Fulsome

Early Spring:

Our flight from Oneida was a hurried affair, conducted under cover of darkness, and with a strong sense of sin and guilt. Sulfur and brimstone in our nostrils as we fled. In truth, I feel we are in fact leaving behind the sinful, those who have extended the practice of complex marriage beyond its original purview. Could Monogamy and One True Marriage be closer to true Spiritual Honesty? I feel that I may breathe easier, and finally speak my mind now that we have left, to begin again. To, once more, attempt Perfection.

If Mutual Criticism remains essential to our journey and Spiritual Health, then I must in good conscience criticize myself as much as my peers, and I have found myself lacking. Not only do I question the premise of Complex Marriage, but so, too, the manner in which our young people are initiated into it. What happened to that young girl . . . May all men of Virtue and Spirituality be called upon to confront their own conscience, and to act in accordance with its needs and instruction!

Even simply to call Elizabeth <u>my wife</u> seems luxurious and foreign, after so many long months of hiding our attachment. We have feigned mutual indifference to satisfy the elders' distaste for exclusive relations, but I have felt this burdensome subterfuge increasingly unnecessary. Complex Marriage being one of the foundational sentiments and beliefs of our old community, I recognize how our exclusive attachment (redolent, perhaps, of more

traditional monogamous couplings) could threaten the elders'
programme of Community Building. In that community, how
closely did we observe the openings and closings of doors! Each
bedroom opened into the common room, where all passed their time
talking and sewing. In this manner, no exclusive attachment could
be unobserved. However, I am still not entirely certain that my love
for Elizabeth is incompatible with the overall aims and ambitions of
that glorious Project. Indeed, we have been engaged in nightly
Communication these past three years, often unobserved, ever since
Elizabeth was herself deemed ready to join the Community at the
age of fifteen. My virtuous Elizabeth! May I deserve her.

With trepidation we set out on our own, joined by a few friends
in our attempt to achieve our own Self-Reliance. This plot of land,
unworked and untended as it is, is a welcome gift and an unlooked-
for bounty—today, I awakened to the frost-tipped grass with
such an overflowing of Gratitude that I was unable to speak for
moments. In just a few short days, we have rehabilitated the modest
living structures in which we will dwell, and cleared a field of rocks.
The physical labor has hardened my hands but opened my heart,
and I have not felt my conscience so lightened in what seem to me
years. I listen to Elizabeth smooring the fire, and to the sounds of
squirrels up on our newly thatched roof and I feel at peace, with
myself, my God, and my home.

Spring:

Just a few short weeks have so transformed our home (and, indeed,
our very souls!) that I scarce know where to begin in my chronicle.
But such a project as this needs the steady hand of a true and honest
scribe, and it has been my intent to faithfully record our Experi-
ment, so as to avoid and prevent the tragedies and failures that
besmirched our previous attempts. I am determined that the perni-

cious, immoral blight which befell my uncle's community shall not
touch us here, and to ensure our authentic and open discourse, I
shall endeavor not to dismiss or conceal my failings out of Vanity.
Rather, I shall write them down, for my wife, Elizabeth, and for any
who come after us to read and reflect upon my imperfections.

The planting and tilling is most back-breaking work, and our
dwellings are rudimentary. We will have to work doggedly to prepare ourselves for the long cold of winter, but I have faith in our
determination and ability. Daily, my wife astonishes me in her
Strength and Capability. Truly, she is a helpmeet sent to me by our
Lord, to help us achieve our more perfect Society.

Brother Jeremiah's wife, Annabelle, is, like Elizabeth, a mother of
two small children, and they find themselves in such similar circumstances that I wonder at my wife's reticence. Her avoidance of
young Mary is perhaps more understandable, though no less un-
lucky; Mary's refusal to speak since she joined us in our departure
from Oneida has been a source of great concern and some consternation. I realize that her childhood within the Community was
not easy, and that she found herself most disastrously paired with
Elijah, who has since been excommunicated for his regular failure to
adhere to our practice of Male Continence. Truly, she should never
have been encouraged in that Communication, and I fear I will
never forgive my uncle for his part in making that decision. I cannot help but feel, however, that once removed from that harmful
union, Mary might find her way once again to Language and
Friendship, and perhaps even to Trust. I speak with her daily, and
encourage her to speak and share with me whatever has so destroyed
her Faith in men. She now looks at me with the Fear and Unease she
held for Elijah, and as I try to soothe her, she further withdraws.

I will ask Elizabeth to speak more to Mary, and will encourage
both Jeremiah and Annabelle to reassure her. But how I would love
to hear her voice, emitted from that sweet, bow-lipped mouth!

Late Spring:

My most recent trip to town for provisions turned unpleasant. We are here in the North, surrounded entirely by those who supported Abolition, and I was consequently shocked to overhear three gentle-men in a public house detail their support for the most horrific practice of Slavery in these United States! These reprehensible Snowflakes held forth for some time, girding their unconscionable Opinion with a most dubious appeal to Science.

I gathered my courage to confront them. Though, unlike my uncle, I am no orator, I have been well educated. These callous in-terlocutors had no interest in reasoned conversation, however, and immediately launched ad hominem attacks, casting aspersions on my own Character, and that of my Family! The local opinion of our former fellows in Oneida seems to be as it was in Hamilton: that we are godless men who have profaned Christ. I was called a Bigamist and many worse things. One man even accused me of being a fol-lower of Joseph Smith, who, I understand, lived in this area some decades ago. I am reluctant to defend the practices of my former brethren, but it wounded me to hear them slandered so, by such ignorant creatures.

This encounter has left me to doubt, and to wonder: What is the good of our Project if we cannot alter the Evils of the outside world? Is it enough to find and create our own Utopia when Society itself remains so profoundly unjust? How dare we dream of Perfection from the safety of our quiet homestead, safe in the luxury of know-ing ourselves able to withdraw and support ourselves with other means? My old companion Henry David confronted these anxieties, refusing to pay his taxes while that money would go to a govern-ment that enforced Slavery . . . but does this not seem too small a gesture, too timid a response to the horror of that institution?

But then, how can one small group of committed individuals hope to alter a whole Society bent on Injustice?

Chapter 9

"Where's Beau?" Louisa asked testily. We had deposited a fresh batch of early spring greens on the table, gleaned from another farm in exchange for some eggs; the chickens had arrived a few weeks earlier, and two had begun to lay already. We wanted to raise chicks, but we had gotten conflicting answers on when we could begin the project. We had a rooster, in any case, who had been terrorizing us, as roosters do, whenever we had to go into the fully enclosed chicken yard, or when, invariably, he escaped.

Deferring to our neighbor's assessment, we had buried the fence three or four feet deep in the ground, to keep out coyotes and foxes, then tented the whole arrangement with additional yards of chicken coop wire to fend off the hawks. So far we had managed to keep all our fowl safe, but the fucking rooster somehow managed to get loose at least once a week; sometimes he intimidated and bullied whoever came to the coop until he was able to escape, but at least once he had just sauntered up to the big cabin, where he had charged anyone who walked out the door. Predictably, he woke us with the dawn. Chloe, in an uncharacteristic display of irritation and resentment, had begun to mutter "Goddamn fucking rooster" every time she heard or saw him, and had torn out a recipe for coq au vin from an old Julia Child cookbook and posted it prominently in the big cabin. She disliked his disruptive nature, his commitment to discord. To her, the greatest crime was promoting disharmony. Only Beau seemed not to mind the cantankerous bird, and referred to him as "that excellent rooster fellow." This may have been just to irritate Chloe, but in my less generous moments, I speculated that he appreciated Rooster's preening, undaunted masculinity.

The minute the chickens began to lay, Louisa insisted that we set aside as many eggs as we could for barter; we would each be allowed one per week, but we needed everything else to bring to neighbors or farmers' markets in exchange for early summer vegetables. This exchange served two purposes. We were able to vary our diet, which for the last month had consisted of fiddleheads, ramps, rhubarb, and whatever bread Chloe could make with our dwindling supply of flour. We'd relied on our storage of legumes (oh God, the endless lentils!) to supplement these few fresh ingredients, but I was deeply excited to eat something that wasn't green or beige. In addition to our dietary needs, though, we also needed information.

And so we went to the market and visited other farms and CSAs, asking questions and trying to keep track of where to plant the squash and whether eggshells really were great for the compost. And we brought anything we could use to trade. Firewood turned out to be a useful commodity, and the back eighty acres or so of the Homestead were mostly untouched woodlands, filled with hardwoods that had stood for a hundred years. At first we felt horror at the prospect of chopping down trees, but Jack pointed out that they were a terrific renewable resource, and after agreeing to replant each year, we stopped feeling guilty. We borrowed a chain saw and felled some of the larger trees, then split the trunks and limbs into logs and stacked them under tarps to stay dry and start curing. There was also plenty of deadfall to haul in, so we were able to keep our cull of the old wood modest. We knew we would need several cords at least for our own needs that winter, and Beau insisted on setting aside most of what he thought we'd burn during the cold months before we began to use the wood as trade.

One day in June, Chloe, Beau, and I had brought two dozen care-fully hoarded eggs to the farmers' market, along with the first quart of painfully harvested wild strawberries. We'd also dragged along giant armfuls of rhubarb, without any real expectation that anyone would be interested; at the Homestead, rhubarb grew as vigorously and fast as a voracious weed, and an entire patch of ground was overrun with the big, leafy pink-and-green plants. Still, not everyone had such a bounty of it, and it looked like we were going to be able to trade our goods with some friends of Beau's who had a stand at the market.

The wiry dreadlocked girl smiled at the sight of Beau. I recognized her and her friend, a tiny human with gorgeous skin, as the same girls who had dropped Beau off at the Homestead, and they spoke with an easy familiarity that suggested they had spent some time with him. He leaned casually against the sturdy wood of their stand while Chloe and I lurked, arms laden, a few steps behind him.

"Girls, meet the other girls," Beau said by way of introduction.

"Chloe," she said, with a curtsy-like bob.

"Hi, I'm Mack Johnston."

"I'm Fennel," the dreadlocked girl answered, looking irritated. "We're part of the commune on the other side of the hill. West Hill Collective." She stopped and squinted more closely at me. "Mack John-ston? Wait, are you the Mackenzie Johnston from *The Millennial Ex-periment? That* Mack Johnston? What a catastrophe that was!"

"Fennel!" her friend said, giving her arm a remonstrative rap. "If she were, it wouldn't exactly be polite to bring it up, no?" she mumbled under her breath.

"I suppose," Fennel answered with a shrug. She didn't seem to feel chastened or embarrassed. My heart was racing at the possibility of being outed, right here; how dare she ask like that? But really, I rea-soned, it was a miracle no one had mentioned it before now. Beau and Chloe had almost certainly heard. I ducked my head to hide my guilty eyes but was spared having to say something as Fennel immediately turned her attention back to Beau. They continued their negotiations until a deal was struck. I felt that Fennel was unnecessarily generous with the arrangement; the West Hill Collective apparently had a great greenhouse, and they were even seeing early tomatoes. She gave us three "to bread and fry," she explained, as though the words "fried green tomatoes" couldn't possibly mean anything to us. We also walked away with spring greens, some fresh herbs, a handful of aged sausages, and a prize bottle of homemade applejack. I knew Louisa would be delighted with our daily haul, but I sensed that she wouldn't love its provenance—her irritation at Beau's frequent absences seemed related to this gaggle of green-thumbed women. When Beau announced that the "West Hill girls" could bring him home in their van at the end of market, I felt that my anxieties were maybe not so far-fetched.

"It's the least I can do, after all these treats," Beau explained. "I'll help them unload the van, and I can walk home later."

"Always walking, you." Fennel smirked. I felt outraged at the intimacy this implied, as though she knew him and his habits well enough to comment on them. Glancing at each other, Chloe and I piled into my truck to drive back out to the Homestead, toting fresh supplies but minus Beau.

Louisa's reaction was restrained but clearly annoyed; when any one of us didn't sit down at her table for meals, she became personally affronted, and when it was Beau, the most frequent offender, she was downright seething. I always thought she wanted to cultivate in her own demeanor a version of Beau's mysteriousness, to mimic his maddening ability to conceal his thoughts and feelings. But with her, it always came across as sulking. After learning that Beau would get a ride back to Hector with some of his other friends, Louisa sniffed.

"Fennel, I presume?"

I nodded.

"That fucking girl," she said. Louisa then asked pointedly what we had brought her, since we'd failed to bring back Beau. I let Chloe catalog our items, while I searched for clean glasses for the applejack. Louisa's broody expression and fiery eyebrows made me nervous, and after pouring glasses for her and Chloe, I slipped outside with a glass for Jack, who was pacing the length of the remaining garden space, apparently in an effort to determine what else we could still plant. His fore-head was rumpled in thought, and he periodically spun around to glance up at the sun, performing calisthenics presumably meant to help him calculate some abstruse agricultural cipher.

"Happy hour," I said, shoving aside the awkward gate that allowed us access to the garden. We'd put up eight-foot stakes strung with more chicken wire, to keep the deer out of the veggies. The garden still looked meager at this time of year, but Jack was excited about it, talk-ing with his arms, shoulders, and torso in enthusiastic terms about what we could expect it to yield. I handed him the applejack, which he drank in one swallow before shaking his head in surprise.

"What the hell is that?" He scowled at the glass, then at me, as though we had both intentionally conspired to fool him.

"Applejack."

"I thought it was apple cider," he said accusatorially.

"I think that's how it starts. But then I think you freeze it, and keep saving the really boozy bits." I hadn't listened too carefully to Fennel's explanation, but that seemed like the gist of it.

"Hmmm. Interesting. Makes sense." Jack stared at the glass again. "Maybe I could try something similar with my beers. . . ."

"I'm not sure, Jack—"

"No, no, no, I'm sure you're right. Still, interesting idea. Concen-trates the alcohol . . ." I watched him as he contemplated this, and knew that he was engaging in the millennia-long human occupation of concocting things that fuck you up. We were still breathlessly antici-pating his early batch of mead, and Beau had rigged up a kooky still back in the woods for producing some hard stuff. Louisa had criticized the practicality of its location, but I suspected that Beau was secretly aspiring to imitate a Prohibition-era bootlegger.

"I didn't see Beau come home with you," Jack said, letting his arm and glass fall to his side as he gazed out on the garden.

"He caught a ride home with some friends."

"Huh. Is that where he goes when he just disappears like he does?"

"I have no idea. Probably sometimes." The idea of Beau lurking around someone else's campfire made me cranky in a way I couldn't fully justify. Certainly, I had the smallest claim on him out of everyone, and my jealousy made me feel foolish.

"Is Louisa pissed?" Jack asked, a mischievous grin on his face. He really was a terrible gossip.

"Of course. Though she's pretending to be distant and unaffected."

"Ha! Of course she is. And you left poor Chloe to deal with her alone?"

"Chloe is the only one she won't snap at," I said with a shrug.

"True. Those two have . . . a special rapport," Jack said. I squinted at him, seeking any sort of subtext or innuendo, but he seemed to mean nothing by his statement. Could he possibly be oblivious to the nocturnal game of musical mattresses? I had assumed he knew, had followed the moving candlelight with the same intensity I did, but suddenly I wondered if his innocent good-naturedness was actually born out of ignorance.

"We should go in, regardless. Louisa will want us to wash the greens we brought. Shame you're a vegetable—we got sausage," I bragged.

"Wow, red-letter day. Maybe I'll try it. I've been curious about the whole carnivore situation, lately." We ambled back to the big cabin, and I watched the gloaming settle over the Homestead, intensifying the grays and purples of spring. I leaned my head on Jack's shoulder, and thought: *This*.

That night, I peered through my window for hours, waiting for the appearance of Beau's moving flame (it was for Beau that I pined the most, and his light that I watched for in the dark). I observed Chloe's little gas lamp traveling to Louisa's cabin, where it didn't remain long before dancing back to her own. When the lights weren't moving, I stared at my walls, and at the parade of stinkbugs, restlessly in search of whatever their spiny bodies craved. Finally, I slumped up the ladder to sleep, miffed.

A sound at my cabin door rattled me awake, and I sat bolt upright, nearly knocking my head on the ceiling. I was momentarily disoriented; for half a second, on waking, I thought I was still in my parents' house, in my drab little room with wall-to-wall carpet. The scratching persisted, and I flailed around wildly for my little lamp. In the flat darkness, I was afraid of knocking it off its hook and breaking it, though, so I slid from my covers and down to the floor, blind. As I crept towards my door, the only possibility I considered was that it was Beau outside, asking to be let inside. I can only assume now that this was the desperate wish fulfillment of someone still asleep, since the scenario seemed unlikely. I didn't pause for a moment to further consider what might actually be lurking out there in the dark.

Which is why I was completely unprepared for something large and hairy to launch itself past me and into my cabin. In the absence of light, I could only hear some sort of hefty panting, and smell that this was an animal, inside my cabin with me. Toenails clicked on the wood floor, and I shuddered, a primal response harkening back to the cave. I thought about defending my home for only a fraction of a second before I flung myself out of my door, leaving the hellbeast to ransack and ruin as it would.

I ran directly to Louisa's cabin, sure that she would know what to do. She blearily opened the door, annoyed, and I quickly took in her crumpled curls and white nightgown. The moon was bright enough that I could see her clearly.

"Jesus, what?" she said.

"There's a—thing! In my cabin!"

"Sweetie, are you sure you're not having a nightmare?" Hands on hips, she could not have sounded more condescending.

"NoI'mnothavingafuckingnightmare," I hissed. "There's a fucking animal in my house!"

"Right. Okay, okay, not ideal. Do you . . . did Beau come home?"

"I don't think so."

"Fuck." Louisa yawned broadly, and I felt a surge of frustration that I wasn't being taken seriously. Everyone here thought I was nothing, just some meek, mousy extra pair of hands. With a truck.

"What's going on?" Chloe called from her stoop. She wore nothing but a delicate kimono, belted round her waist with a silk scarf.

"Mack has an infestation," Louisa answered. "We should get our pitchforks, I guess." She waved a sleepy arm.

"No Beau, right? I'll wake Jack!" Chloe scampered barefoot from her cabin to pound on Jack's door. Louisa ducked back inside to grab a thick sweater. I thought it might be Beau's. She also carried a walking stick that Beau had brought her from one of his surveying expeditions deep into the woods. Jack joined us, dressed in his skivvies and a ratty T-shirt, holding a shovel. We four advanced on my little home.

On the stoop, we paused to listen. For one chilling instant, I heard nothing, and began to feel the crippling humiliation of a little girl who has summoned her parents for the monster under her bed, said creature having conveniently vanished at the appearance of others. But then there came the clicking of toenails, and the distinct sound of something growling softly in the back of its throat.

"Fuck," Louisa said. "I thought you meant, like, a squirrel or something."

"Maybe it's a raccoon?" Chloe offered.

"Or a possum?" countered Jack. I shuddered. I hated possums. Everyone did. They were fantastically creepy. The idea of it in my bed, or pacing the boards that I had so happily trod these past weeks, gave me a frisson of the willies. The growl intensified.

"Where the fuck is Beau?" asked Jack, expressing the thought we were all too proud to make explicit. This was a job for him.

"Not here," Louisa answered. "Right, it could be a coyote, I guess. Which means it likely won't want to have much to do with us. I bet once we open this door, it just takes off."

"Right," I answered. "But then why did it come inside in the first place?" No one answered. Instead, Louisa purposefully hopped up the steps, flung the door open, and leapt back, walking stick held comically aloft, preparing to brain whatever creature wandered out.

Nothing did, immediately, and we all stared anxiously at my darkened door. Then inside we could see a shape, moving and massive. Chloe let out a small whimper. I concurred. A giant, toothy head emerged from my cabin, and we all stepped back in alarm.

Out onto my stoop came a giant, shaggy wolf. Or at least that's what he appeared to be. He was nearly as tall as I was, a hirsute primordial critter panting casually on my porch. His eyes were reddish brown, and followed each of us as we instinctively tried to protect ourselves.

"Bloody fucking hell," said Louisa, breathless. I was trying to decide whether to turn and run (was I faster than Louisa? Jack would certainly outpace us all, Jesus, I was the smallest and would definitely be the easiest prey oh God) when the hound yawned conspicuously and lowered himself into a downward dog. His tail wagged, and he loped easily off the stoop. None of us moved, and I fought panic as he came over and sniffed each of us, tail still flapping.

"You know, I think he's friendly," Chloe said finally. I extended my hand, palm outstretched, the way I had always greeted my uncle's rottweiler, and the dog good-naturedly sniffed at it before delicately taking my fingers in his mouth. His rump wiggled in pleasure, and I ran my hand up the side of his face, giving his hairy ears a scratch. He panted and rolled his head into my armpit. It was a strange feeling, like giving a pony a rub, but the dog seemed perfectly happy with my efforts.

"Do we have any sausage left?" I asked.

"You're going to give that—thing—sausage?" Louisa asked incredulously.

"I think he's hungry. He must have smelled food in my cabin."

"Yeah. He smelled *you*."

"Look, if he wanted to eat any of us, he probably would have tried already," I explained. "He's definitely been domesticated. Probably some kind of wolfhound."

"Well, maybe he should go back to whoever domesticated him," Louisa suggested. She glanced nervously around. "Seriously, could his people be out here in the woods?"

This gave me a jolt—were the dog's owners skulking about, just out of sight, watching us? I felt around his neck, searching for a collar, but encountered only a burr tangled in his fur. Surely someone wouldn't allow their pet to romp around the wilderness unidentified. I began to relax. He trusted me, I felt it.

"We'd hear them, if they were nearby," I said, giving him a solid scritch.

"Unless they were trying not to be heard," Louisa countered, scanning the tree line for glowing human eyes. "Hello? Has anyone out there lost their wolf?" she called into the woods. We heard only the swoop of pine boughs in the wind.

"He doesn't have a collar, and he's grubby as hell. I think he's a stray. Come, pup. I'll get you something to eat." I patted the side of my leg, though this seemed like an inappropriate gesture for a dog of his size; I should have patted my shoulder. When I strode towards the big cabin, the huge creature followed, tongue out. The three humans trailed behind, Jack and Chloe amused, Louisa still uncertain, and they watched as I fixed up a bowl of lentils and sausage from the scraps of dinner that had been left sitting on the stove. The dog waited patiently at the door, clearly trying to demonstrate his good-boy status. I put the bowl down in front of him, and he happily fell on it, devouring it within seconds before returning to a sit and looking at me expectantly.

I let him sleep in my cabin that night. For the first time since arriving at the Homestead, I didn't watch for any candles from my window.

Beau returned home to a frosty welcome and an equally frosty bowl of oatmeal. He seemed not to notice the temperature of either greeting or meal, and nuzzled Louisa fondly on the side of her neck as we sat around the picnic table in the middle of our cluster of cabins. We'd agreed to give up coffee, since it wasn't local, and were instead sipping hot water laced with honey. The doggo had disappeared after I'd let him out this morning, and we were all waiting to see if he would return. Chloe had regaled Beau with the tale of the nighttime intruder, and he had chuckled in delight at the picture she painted.

"And where is this mystery hound?" he asked. We all shrugged, and then he startled us by erupting into a long, wolfish howl that first Chloe, then Jack, and finally Louisa and I joined, until we were all cackling foolishly around the table.

The mystery hound returned late that afternoon, as we were all collapsing sweatily near the garden, ready to call it a day. From his jaws limply dangled a rabbit, whose ears flopped from side to side as the dog trotted powerfully towards us. He dropped the bunny near me before sitting back on his huge haunches. Chloe made a little mew of distress, but Beau looked impressed.

"You. You are a good mutt," he said approvingly, patting the dog on the head.

"Sweet dog," I concurred. "What a sweet boy." I gave him the tiny nub of carrot I had just tugged from the garden in order to gauge its growth, and the dog chomped it happily. I glanced over at Louisa, who was eyeing the rabbit. "Well, chef? What's for dinner?" I asked teasingly. She stood, considering.

"Rabbit stew," she answered finally. "I don't think I'll kill us all with tularemia as long as I cook the shit out of it. But one of you is cleaning that damn animal."

"Dog or rabbit?" Beau asked.

"Both," she said, heading towards the big cabin.

Chapter 10

Beau threw the party without telling us. We'd been plan-
ning a shindig since April, when the unremitting gray and gloom of the
winter had begun to lift off the Homestead and our living arrangements began to look less ramshackle and more charming and rustic, at
least to our eyes. I desperately wanted to reassure my parents that I
was not in a cult, not addicted to drugs, and not starving to death in the
wilderness. My handful of visits home had not entirely convinced
them; always thin, I now had the wiry springiness of an acrobat or a
jockey, and my hair had grown out unevenly and ragged. I hoped they
could see the happy glow of my unusually tanned skin or appreciate
the pride I felt in displaying the calluses on my hands, but my mother
merely pursed her lips and encouraged me to eat another plate of
baked ziti. My father, uncharacteristically, had given me a hundred
dollars when I had climbed back into the cab of my truck after my first
visit, no doubt urged out onto the icy driveway by my mother, who'd
watched from the kitchen window. Their disappointment had been so
palpable that I'd wanted to race around the lake and towards the next
one, home.

We'd all discussed having an open house to show off the Homestead—to parents, friends, and Beau and Chloe's coworkers from the

café. We wanted everyone to see the tidy cabins, our fortress-like chicken coop, the garden that promised infinite cucumbers. Chloe had even gone as far as making another long table (from little more than salvaged wood, nails, and a stack of sandpaper) for guests to dine on outside, and Jack had hauled in a dozen stumps left from the wood splitting to provide seating around it. We'd said May, but here May was, and we had yet to organize anything.

So when Beau appeared in the driveway with the colorful VW and another pickup truck, out of which spilled around ten people none of us knew, we all temporarily bristled. I didn't want to come across as someone who needed to plan things, some uptight suburban house-wife with no spontaneity, but my first thought was that he could have at least given us a heads-up. Of course, I would never open my mouth to actually disagree; I always retreated.

I saw Fennel first; she was wearing loose harem pants and a ragged sweatshirt that was now an indiscriminate gray, whatever its previous hue had been. Her dreadlocks were twisted into a towering beehive that defied gravity, and she wore what looked like old military-issue boots. Her cohort was dressed in a mélange of Carhartt overalls, ragged jeans, Tevas with socks. They were carefully androgynous.

At the sound of the vehicles, Louisa and Chloe emerged from the kitchen. Jack was in the second clearing, a distance away, sowing alfalfa (we wanted a goat and, eventually, a cow), and I wished for his easy social abilities. He was unfailingly friendly and welcoming to everyone, immediately interested in their story, ambitions, plans. And, of course, their vegetable gardens. The dog, whom we had named Argos, stuck close to my side—he seemed to be completely bored by the visitors—and I turned to him.

"Go get Jack, buddy. Go find Jack!" I had no idea if this would work, but I watched Argos race off with a satisfying elegance, headed towards the woods.

Chloe had ambled off the stoop of the big cabin and was coming to introduce herself, while Louisa lingered where she was, apron tied around the country-style dress she often changed into in the evenings. Under her arm, she carried a copy of *The Settlement Cook Book*, one of her favorite sources for old-time recipes.

"Hey, you," Beau said, giving me a quick kiss on the cheek and sliding a hand around my back. I was a little sweaty, and feared that he would notice, but also couldn't help leaning into the touch. "You remember Fennel?" I nodded, shook hands, and let myself be introduced to three or four of her friends, whose names I promptly forgot. The rest of our visitors had straggled off to inspect the orchard and cluck approvingly at our coop.

Louisa had joined us, after giving Beau a fairly demonstrative kiss on the side of the mouth.

"Howdy, Fennel," she said coolly only after her possessive smooch. "Long time no see."

"Not because of me," Fennel responded. "I've been waiting for an invitation out here for ages."

"You know what it takes to get things up and running. All is well at the Collective?"

"Even better than the last time you were there," Fennel said. Louisa pursed her lips and then tersely asked whether everyone would like to stay to dinner. Given the armfuls of food and bottles that were emerging from the VW, this seemed like a given, but Louisa made it sound like a formal invitation.

"Well, come, let's see what we can throw together," she said to Fennel, who had no choice then but to follow her into the big cabin. I knew that Louisa would be happiest giving Fennel orders around the kitchen, and from Beau's smirk, I could tell he knew it too.

"Introduce me to some more of your friends?" I asked, hoping I sounded coy and appealing. I very much liked the idea of being introduced by him, next to him. He waved to a dark-haired girl who wore a wildly patterned caftan and cowboy boots and who, unlike most of the other women, had a deliberate smudge of black eyeliner on each eye.

"Mack, meet Zelda," Beau murmured, steering me towards the girl. Her gaze was intense, and I tripped a little before extending my hand. She took it with an amused smile.

"Mack, huh?" One eyebrow quirked upward and she looked as though she was waiting for me to say something. The silence was too lengthy to not mean something, but when I didn't respond, she just shrugged with an amused, knowing smile. "Well, fancy that. You're the little scribbler." I looked at Beau, puzzled. Had he noticed me with my notebook, jotting down thoughts? "Because you're always keeping track of things, writing things down. A grand chronicler of past and present!"

"Oh, hardly. I just don't remember things unless I write them down. I . . . guess I keep a sort of almanac."

"But the almanac is the future, sweetheart. Do you do fortunes?" She stuck her hand out, showing me her palm. "What's in store for me, Cassandra?" Unthinkingly, I took her hand before realizing I lacked the panache to fake my way through a faux fortune-telling.

"Nothing good if you don't take it easy," Beau admonished, in the funny scolding tone he liked to use. He stroked her forearm, and I noticed the track marks that scored her skin.

"Fiddle-dee-dee! Tomorrow is another day, Beauregard Hull. Come, help me fetch the wine. I took it from the familial cellars!" She grabbed Beau and tugged him towards the VW, and he complied quite happily.

"Her family runs a vineyard," Chloe said, having appeared next to me. "Actually, I guess she runs the vineyard, technically. She and her twin used to come to the café pretty often. I think that's where Beau met her, but I'm not sure."

"She has a twin?"

"Uptight pain in the ass. Took off to Europe, what, two years ago? Zelda's been something of a loose cannon ever since."

"Is the wine any good?" I asked.

"Not very. But it's local, so Jack won't be able to complain." She smiled at me, her cornflower eyes full of fun and her wispy hair blown across her face. Looking at Chloe could be almost painful. "And at least they didn't come empty-handed. Beau once brought Fennel over to my co-op in Ithaca, and not only did she bring absolutely nothing, she sat giving me instructions on what she could and couldn't eat while I cooked her dinner."

"I've no doubt Louisa is returning the favor right now," I answered, and she grinned happily.

"Come, it's a party! Let's find Jack!" she said. Jack, as it turned out, had returned from the future alfalfa field, whether because Argos had successfully fetched him or because he had heard the ruckus from the crew's arrival. He was very contentedly showing someone his mead-making operation, a process that was supposedly nearing completion, and that he fussed over neurotically every day.

"Don't you get annoyed, obsessing over it like that?" Louisa had asked one day. "I mean, Jesus, come on already, let's just drink it."

"I think I get a lot of the satisfaction out of thinking and overthinking," he had mused. "Part of the pleasure, for me, is to obsess."

"You *do* do that with everything."

"I process things with my head. I like to think about things, analyze."

"Yes, everyone knows how charming overthinking is as a personality trait," Louisa had said.

"Well, you process everything with your mouth," Jack had sniped back, an observation that was apt enough to silence the barbed round of mutual criticism. Louisa *did* process with her mouth: eating, drinking, tasting, kissing, talking. It was how she interpreted the world.

I watched Beau and Zelda muscle a case of wine out of the van and felt a giddy pleasure at the sight. We'd been careful not to consume too much of our bartered booze; at first, it had seemed so bountiful, but we'd realized that between the five of us, it wouldn't last nearly as long as we wanted it to. Tonight, at least, we would feast and raise our cups.

After delivering all the food to Louisa in the kitchen, Beau offered to lead everyone on a tour of the Homestead, whereupon Fennel was able to escape Louisa's reign and join the expedition. She met us outside, and Argos bounded up to her. Drawing back from the beast, she looked at him distastefully.

"Oh, this dog," she said. "Um, hi." She patted his giant head awkwardly.

"Do you know him?" I asked, both worried and curious. I did want to know where my buddy had come from, but I feared having to return him if he did indeed already have a family.

Fennel gave me a quick glance. "He hung around the Collective for a while. I think whoever owned him is long gone, though."

"Do you know who owned him? Where they are?"

"No, I can't really remember. We had a bunch of early initiates who didn't work out, some visitors. I'm not sure if he belonged to one of them." This struck me as odd—surely the presence of such a sizable domesticated animal in your home would be memorable. But Fennel was a strange bird. And she seemed unwilling to discuss it further with me; she struck out ahead to join Beau at the head of our tour.

I knew that the West Hill Collective was a pretty well-established farm—there had been a group of people living there and developing the property for at least five years, possibly longer—and I was sure that these newcomers would snort at our pathetic efforts. Instead, everyone cooed over our work, pointed out potential spots for cultivating mushrooms or adding another root cellar. They gave us tips on how to keep the bugs down in the garden and what sort of feed we could use for the chickens (basically anything, as it turned out—Louisa would be annoyed that we'd spent money buying chicken feed). Someone lengthily expounded on the benefits of raising pigs, and Chloe's mouth rumpled in faint disgust when he described butchering them in the autumn. Beau looked elated, the country gentleman playing host at his rural seat. He beamed with satisfaction.

Louisa rang the dinner bell (she had a literal bell that she'd hung outside the door of the big cabin) and we all swooped towards her. A tablecloth was produced, dishes were carried out, bottles uncorked. We didn't have enough plates and cups, but many of our guests seemed to travel with sporks and dishes of their own, unclipped from carabiners hanging off belt loops. I ate my salad from a coffee cup, and drank wine from another. It was bright and puckery, and made my teeth feel red. But it was wine, and it was a gift, and even though Beau was seated between Fennel and Louisa, I was happy, content.

"I mean, frankly, it's people like us who have the responsibility to try to make a more ethical life," one of the young men expounded. He had a raucous beard and wore a Carhartt beanie.

"People like us?" Zelda said. "What the fuck does that mean?"

"I mean people who have education and some . . . economic flexibility. If we don't try to undermine freewheeling capitalist expansion, then who can be expected to do it?"

"So you're saying our position of privilege makes its own ethical demands?" Chloe asked.

"In a sense. I mean, it seems pretty obvious that we need to change trajectory or we're all going to die in a freak tsunami."

"Or go out in a fiery blaze," countered Zelda.

"Or as victims of a GMO accident."

"Or deliberate conspiracy."

We giggled as we all offered up our own doomsday plots, ranging from zombie apocalypse to government takeover to chemical warfare.

"What do you guys have in your bug-out bag?" the bearded young man asked us, though he directed the question at Beau.

"Our what?" said Louisa.

"Your bug-out bag. For your various SHTF scenarios." Louisa just stared at him blankly. "Shit hits the fan? Your go bag?"

"Ignore Jesse," said Fennel. "He's a prepper."

"And you can bet I'll be saving your asses when the zombies do show up," Jesse retorted. "I mean seriously, you guys can't think this is going to end well."

"This?" Chloe said.

"Civilization! Late-stage capitalism. Radical global wealth inequality. Corporate control of government—"

"Yes, yes, we all watch CNN, buddy," Zelda interrupted. "Actually, that's a lie. None of us have TVs. We're all perfectly aware of our situation. But we're not actually going to change the world, any of us. We may as well just take out mortgages and keep buying and get to the end of this tragic little pickle we've gotten ourselves in. Rome is burning—pour me more wine!"

"So you're an accelerationist," Jack accused.

"Live fast, die young." Zelda hoisted her cup in a salute, while Jesse shook his head in dismay.

"Well, thank God we don't all share your opinion. I mean, what are we all even doing out here, then?"

"We are . . . living the good life," Beau said.

"Reclaiming the means of production?" Fennel asked, leaning in.

"Beau tends to think of our quest as more philosophical than political," Louisa explained. "An Epicurean pursuit of enjoyment, an Emersonian emphasis on self-reliance . . ." She waved her hand to indicate all the rest of Beau's personal philosophy.

"Do you all feel that way?" asked Fennel, grilling us. I buried my face in my coffee cup, not wanting to be put on the spot. When I was being honest with myself, I knew that my reasons were probably neither philosophical nor political. I felt sheepish in this crowd of people committed to changing the world; how to say that I wanted only to find out what I was meant to do with my life?

"Some of us have general Marxist tendencies," Louisa explained, happy to speak for us. "Obviously, we all have issues with capitalism as a whole, and we're trying to carve out a space in which we can live better, ethically and politically."

"Conservation is key. Totally clutch," Jack added. He was a bit drunk already, his nose flushed and his eyes glassy.

"But you own this property," Fennel accused. "You're basically a feudal landowner."

"I think that's something of a stretch," said Louisa. "We don't collect rent. We don't have tenants."

"Oh, don't you?" Fennel asked archly, looking deliberately at Chloe and me. "I must have been confused."

"Yes, I think you were," Louisa said.

"We want to eat good meals, shared around this table. We want to not be confined by heteronormative ideas of sex, family, and partnership," Chloe said, coming to Louisa's defense. "Not to mention that we want to avoid being wage slaves for the rest of our lives."

"Don't you all realize how absolutely fucking ridiculous you sound?" Zelda asked. "We are a bunch of relatively well-off white kids—'cept you, Natasha, beg your pardon—most of us with advanced degrees and tolerant families. You want to fucking bolshevize the nation?" She cackled. "I mean, take all this hippie-dippie back-to-the-land bullshit to the ghetto! See how the poor oppressed masses like your suggestion that they learn to live on cabbages and turnips they grow themselves."

"I think you'd be surprised, Zelda," Fennel said primly. "I think the exploited working class would be the most enthusiastic about learning how to avoid further exploitation by the ruling class. They're not animals. They're capable of rational thought."

"I'd like to state for the record that I did not call people from the ghetto 'animals.' That's all you, Fennel."

"I feel like we're losing some intersectionality here—" Natasha began, but Fennel interrupted her.

"Give it up, Zelda. You're not even part of the Collective. You sit there judging from your private estate and your little business. *I* wake up and live every day with the rhythm of the sun. *We're* actually committed to living with the earth. You're more privileged than any of us here."

"Probably right, Fen-Fen. And with that, I think I'll take à walk around the pond. Do enjoy the wine, though," Zelda added, gesturing to the bounty she had uncorked on our table. "As long as you don't personally pay for the spoils of capitalism, your hands are clean." She stood up and walked away from the table, weaving slightly. The sun was setting, and she disappeared into the gloom near the pond. We all sat awkwardly, not sure what to say.

"She's fun," Louisa said finally.

"She's just a bit wild," Jesse said.

"And drunk," Fennel added nastily.

"I'm going to go talk to her. And maybe give Wyatt a quick heads-up," Jesse said, getting up from the table. "Her boyfriend," he explained.

"More like her keeper," Fennel snarked. I nibbled uncomfortably at my salad, spearing a piece of chèvre soaked in vinegar.

"Anyone for seconds?" Louisa asked. "There's more in the kitchen."

"Everything was delicious. Thank you guys so much," Natasha said.

"Our pleasure!" Louisa replied, and she and Chloe stood to begin clearing. Natasha and one of the other visiting boys rose to help.

"You guys could become more involved in local issues, if you wanted," I overheard Fennel saying to Beau. "You started to be, last year. I mean, I get your concern that we can't change the whole world."

"You don't accept that, though," Beau said, smiling.

"No." She laughed. "But we can definitely change how things work around here, in our county. On our lake."

"Mack!" Louisa's voice called from the cabin. "Can you do that thing you do with the cream?"

I sighed and stood, press-ganged into whipping a bowl of cream with an antique manual beater.

In the kitchen, Louisa scraped plates with an irritated intensity, while Chloe hovered nearby, ready to defuse her.

"I mean, it's not like we all need to have identical motivations," Louisa mumbled at one point. I knew Fennel was pissing her off, and I got the feeling that Zelda hadn't overly endeared herself.

"You know what matters to all of us. You don't have to let her hijack our vision," Chloe agreed. I spun the wheel of the rickety beater in the big bowl of fresh cream someone from the Collective had brought over. Apparently they had a cow. We had a tiny heap of strawberries left. But we would have to wash all the dishes in order to serve everyone. I heard a playful shriek from outside, and laughter. I listened hard for Beau, but his quiet chuckle was engulfed by the general sounds of bacchanal.

"Ignore Fennel," Natasha said on one of her trips inside with more dishes. "She likes to play at being the radical because her family is nice and conventional and middle-class. She likes to make a point."

"She likes to be self-righteous," Louisa mumbled.

Natasha smiled. "That, too, sometimes. As you know damn well,

Louisa." Natasha gave her a pat on the shoulder, and I wondered if she was referring to something in particular.

When we returned outside with the dessert, it was full dark, and we had to fetch our little oil lamps and the handful of beeswax candles we had traded for at the farmers' market.

"Do you guys have a bee colony yet?" Jesse asked Chloe. She shook her head. "If you want, I could show you how to set one up and get some honey going. It's not too late yet."

"That would be amazing!" Chloe said, genuinely excited. She'd wanted to start a beehive all along, but the notion had been shelved until we were more established. She liked the idea of the beekeeper's suit.

"Speaking of insects, have y'all noticed the ticks? We're already crawling with them," Jesse said.

"I pulled a few off the dog this morning," I answered.

"There's your damned apocalypse for you," Beau said. "We'll all go down in a swarming mass of deer ticks, bodies slurped dry by their little grasping mouths, the whole of the earth overrun by vast colonies of sucking bugs."

I continued to sip on my red wine, even though it contrasted unpleasantly with the sweetness of the cream and the strawberries. My head was swimmy, and I felt happily disembodied. I'd never been entirely at home in my own skin; sometimes looking in the mirror produced a terrifying sense of otherness as I failed to recognize myself in the sharp accumulation of angles and bones. I found myself explaining this, suddenly, to Fennel, who was sitting next to me.

"It's like, I look at my rib cage and think, *That can't be me. That just isn't me.* I try and, like, avoid my reflection. The antithesis of Narcissus!" I giggled tipsily at my own rhyme.

"Body dysmorphia is a real thing, Mackenzie." I flinched at her use of my full name. "A few years ago, I got rid of every mirror in my house and decided not to look at my own reflection for a year. It was amazing. I stopped worrying about how my body looked, I stopped wearing makeup, I grew these dreads. . . ." She fondly patted her immense pile of hair. "Seriously. We overinvest in our appearance to such an extent that we actually become unable to recognize ourselves. This totally gendered alienation." She sounded like she had made this speech a few times, and I noticed that she was drinking hot water, not wine.

"You don't drink?" I asked slushily.

"I just don't like feeling as though I'm not myself, you know. Being out of control can be, I don't know, a little unattractive."

I opened my mouth to point out that we had just been discussing ways of distancing oneself from the pressure to be attractive, but I had no wish to argue or debate. Louisa would have seized on this point and pushed it until Fennel broke, but I wanted no brokenness. I wanted harmony, and agreement and cooperation. I wanted this night, these people, this piece of land! I was drunk.

Before I realized what I was saying, I was suggesting that we light up the sauna. Beau heard my suggestion and latched onto it enthusiastically. Chloe, ever the self-designated fire maker, leapt up to fetch kindling and flame. Beau followed her, and I watched for a moment, ready to be jealous, before realizing that I was actually content, not envious. I had suggested something, and it was a good idea. I fought a wave of alarm at the thought of what Louisa would say, then decided she probably wouldn't get terribly mad at me. It occasionally felt like I was so invisible that even my errors were somehow not my own.

Hearing a splash, I realized that the inevitable skinny-dipping had begun. I had wandered towards the pond and started to undress before I recalled the state of the pond these days: on top of being still frigidly cold, it was murky and dark, and we hadn't had the chance to get control of the algae situation. Frankly, we weren't sure if there was even an organic, natural way to do this. The water smelled dank and musty, and given our lack of hot showers, I knew my hair would smell of it for days. And in all honesty, there was something about that pond that simply felt wrong. Since the little mishap Chloe and I had had on the ice, the pond had made me nervous. Like it was out to get me. I slid my bra straps back up my shoulders and turned to head away from the pond, encountering Natasha, who had stripped off her shirt and pants and stood in front of me in bra and underwear.

"I was just rethinking," I explained. "It's a little scuzzy in there. And my hair . . ." I trailed off.

"Oh, I don't go under," Natasha said, patting her tight, dark curls. "But I do love to swim. Gotta destroy the stereotypes."

"Oh."

"Look, you don't have to worry about Fennel," she reassured me.

"Okay . . . ?"

"She won't tell anyone. About you, I mean. She shouldn't have mentioned it that day, when we met. It was really cruel of her. I can't imagine that any of what happened was easy on you." She knew. She and Fennel both. I felt a swoop of terror at the thought. I had tried so hard to run, to get away, only to find myself cornered by a dark pond, my shame stripped bare and undeniable.

"I, uh, don't really like to talk about it," I mumbled. "It's still . . . I mean, it's sort of ongoing. I get a lot of emails."

"Seriously? Fucking people. I'm sorry. You were just . . . I'm sure you were just trying to do the right thing. I read your interview, on *Slate*. After everything aired."

"I asked them to take it down. The comment section got out of hand really quickly, and now I'm just . . . trying to move on."

"That makes total sense. And like I said, Fennel won't mention it again. She has to work on her social sensitivity, if you know what I mean."

"Okay, thanks," I said, ducking my head. "Honestly, I'm surprised you guys even bothered to stream it."

"We hardly ever do. But we watched it at the library on my iPad," Natasha said, smiling. "Fennel couldn't resist the premise. You know she grew up in Queens? Before she moved out to the Collective, she was trying to get an urban farm going in Astoria, and it just got so frustrating in the city."

"Don't I know it," I agreed. "Anyway, I have to tidy up a bit. Have a nice swim, though." I moved off into the cooling grass, forcing myself to focus on the feel of it between my toes as I tried to hide myself in darkness.

Collecting the rest of the dishes, I thought I would bring them to the big cabin and get the cleanup started, hoping to please Louisa before she learned that our guests would be staying a little longer. After a certain point, I knew, she would abandon her role as the Lady of the House and would bum a cigarette or start an argument, but probably not until the dishes were cleared. I stumbled around in the dark, looking for our remaining teacups.

"Fuck," I said as I tripped over something immense. I sat down on the ground too hard, bruising my tailbone. "The fuck."

"Merf," said Jack.

"Jesus, Jack. Did you think this was a good spot to nap?" I rose shakily to my feet.

"Muuuufffff," Jack answered.

"Bloody hell." I poked him in the rib cage, where he was normally very ticklish, but he barely squirmed in response. "Buddy, get the fuck up," I said. His eyes fluttered prettily open, and I was struck by their blueness, paler than Chloe's. Jack's, though, were distinctly glazed at the moment.

"So glad it's you. Mack. You're . . . great."

"Yes, I am. And you're going to like me even more tomorrow." I grabbed his arm and gave him a pull. He rose biddably, if not gracefully, and toddled unsteadily next to me. I hooked his elbow with my own and began to pick my way across the uneven ground towards his cabin. Given my own lack of sobriety, our itinerary was not entirely direct, but I finally led him up the steps to his cabin and tugged him inside. Jack seemed uninterested in climbing up to his mezzanine mattress without me, however.

"Walk me home safe, Mack," he said, eyes not fully open. "Almost there."

"Yes, we are. And once you're there, you'll be very happy. Up you go, Jack." I nudged him towards his ladder, though suspecting that this ascent might be a little ambitious in his condition. I wondered how I would make it up into my own bed later. I could, of course, just stay here. . . . I rejected the idea quickly. That wasn't what I wanted. I continued to encourage Jack towards his bed until he finally slumped bonelessly onto the floor, his back propped up against the wall. I shrugged. He'd wake up in a few hours and creep beneath his blankets when he was good and ready. Still, I filled a glass with water from the stoneware pitcher—we each kept one in our cabins—and left it nearby, though not so close that his long limbs could destroy it. It would be very dark in his cabin when he woke up. But there was nothing I could do about that.

Back outside, I could still hear the sounds of people cavorting in the pond. A light mist had settled over the ground, as it often did on spring nights when the day had been warm but the earth was still cold from the long winter. The pond must be fucking frigid. I looked up at the sky, but the fog obscured most of the stars, and all but a faint shine of the moon. Unsure what to do with myself, I toddled towards the sauna, hoping to find Beau and Chloe. Or both.

I continued to walk around the pond, treading carefully so that I wouldn't make too much noise.

I found Chloe blowing on the fire in the sauna, looking annoyed.

"It won't get hot," she complained. "Jack must have brought us damp kindling or something."

I knew that Beau had been responsible for kindling the last week, and I was pretty sure she knew it too. But Beau somehow always managed to be blameless.

"Here, I'll blow," I offered, and took her place by the stove, cupping my hands around my mouth in a makeshift, inadequate bellows.

"You're a good egg, Mack," she said, and kissed my forehead. I looked in her eyes and tried to pretend that what I saw there was for me. Then Beau stood in the doorway, holding paper and some very small pieces of kindling.

"Hullo, girls," he said with a smile. "Can I help?"

"Give me that," Chloe said, reaching for his materials. "We're not all going to fit in here, you know."

"We can snuggle up," Beau suggested. My heart raced. This made my head throb and my belly swoop alarmingly.

"I'm just going to poke my head outside," I said, feeling nauseous. I ducked through the doorway just in time, racing into the field next to the sauna before my stomach emptied itself into the tall grass. The scorch of bad red wine burned my nostrils. I hoped desperately that I'd made it far enough into the grass to go unnoticed, and that no evidence would be visible in the morning. Queasy and full of shame, I crept slowly back to my cabin. When I saw Fennel heading towards the sauna, I briefly wished I could rally, but recognizing my weakness, I instead scuttled home, tail betwixt legs, to make the journey up into bed that Jack had failed to manage earlier.

Later that night, I awakened to the sound of shrieking. Ramrod straight in my narrow bed, I listened to the panicked screams. I knew I should fling off my covers and saunter into the night, full of derring-do, ready to rescue whoever was so clearly being eviscerated on my doorstep. But I lay immobile, stricken with an undeniable terror I hadn't felt since childhood: that absolute certainty that there is something beneath your bed and that the instant you stretch your bare toes to the ground, it will seize you and drag you off to some darker place. I fought the temptation to pull the covers over my head.

I listened to the screams for a lengthy thirty seconds, waiting for death, mine or the stranger's. But the screams grew less and less human, until I realized I was listening to the sound of an animal, caught in mortal terror and signaling its anguish. I wondered how I could have mistaken those cries for human. The panicked keening continued, so high and so desperate. I almost grew used to it. Abruptly, it stopped, and I fell almost immediately back into unconsciousness.

The next morning, I found two rabbits dead on my stoop.

Chapter 11

Chloe was out in the wildflower field with Jesse, learning how to start a hive. If she hadn't been so far back, we might never have noticed what was going on near the property line, and Louisa might not have taken up her standard. And maybe then things wouldn't have ended the way they did. But because Jesse recommended a quiet spot filled with pollen and far from any human disturbances, they walked through the woods to the flower field to install the hive. I think Chloe relished the idea of having her own project, of being able to creep all the way back there to do something useful by herself. I was mindful of what she had said the day we fell in the pond: that she disliked being perceived as helpless. Since then, I had watched her carve out space for herself, assert herself in dozens of small ways, even as she became lost in each of our worries and tasks.

The field itself was exquisitely pretty, flanked by pine trees and old oaks. At one point it had been cleared and cultivated, but it had sat fallow long enough to return to tall grass and flowers. Over the next few months, it would be filled with goldenrod, asters, black-eyed Susans, and milkweed (this last useful more for the monarchs than the bees, though no doubt the bees would deign to sup on those gooey pods). Jesse said it was perfect.

After they'd put in their panels and settled the new colony, they

decided to walk to the property line at the end of the next clearing to
look for more strawberries or see if they could spot a raspberry bram-
ble, or even a place to harvest wild garlic or mushrooms.

But when they broke through the tree line that separated this flower
field from the next one, Chloe's jaw dropped. The field was meant to
be fallow—it was where we thought we might plant hay if we ever got
a cow—but it had been plowed into neat furrows. Jesse dropped to his
knees and buried his hands in the earth, even though it smelled of
manure, and inspected the tiny seedlings that had just started to poke
through the topsoil.

"Corn," he said. "Is this yours?" Chloe shook her head emphatically.
We had a few rows of corn in the vegetable garden and were hoping to
add a whole secondary plot of it in the next few weeks, so we could
make cornmeal in the autumn. We definitely hadn't planted an entire
field of it on the property line. "Then it's probably cow corn, not sweet.
And you need to find out who your neighbors are. I'm betting this shit
is not organic."

Chloe bore the news back to Louisa, who was immediately outraged.

"Goddamn it, it's the Larsons," she explained. "They're a big agribusiness and own half of this county. They lease the rest of it and cram
every acre with GMO crops and pesticides." She immediately trooped
out to the field with Chloe, and came back even more enraged. "They've
crossed the property line! They're planting on *my* fucking property.
This is illegal. We're going to sue the hell out of them." None of us
could really object that she'd called it her land. It was, after all.

After a quick phone call to Rudy, Louisa was a measure calmer, but
still obviously inclined to crusade. She had found a cause, and I could
tell that she had no intention of dropping it, or chalking it up to neighborly inconvenience. She was sure that the Larsons were on her land,
and not only did they have no right, they were corrupting the water
table that fed her farm. Jack finally convinced her to just let it be until
Rudy got to the bottom of things, and she agreed, reluctantly. I could

tell by the glances she kept giving Beau, though, that she wasn't ready to let it slide.

We were making progress. The veggies looked promising, the chickens were all laying, the lilacs were starting to bloom. It was warm enough, finally, for us to remove our tattered sweaters when we tilled the garden or cleared another plot. We'd acquired three young apple trees from a local orchard, and though they wouldn't fruit for years, just watching them leaf out made me happy. We got a goat! Beau and Chloe had returned home with him after a visit to a farmer in Trumansburg; he was a raucous, dark young male who kicked his legs and tried to get in the vegetable garden.

"What will we do with him?" Louisa asked, looking at the goggle-eyed creature skeptically. She had lobbied ardently for a goat, but had evidently wanted a female. "We obviously can't milk him."

"We'll get a female soon. This guy was the only one old Rob was willing to part with," Beau said, patting the goat on the head. The goat responded by giving him a vicious poke in the side.

"I wonder why," Louisa said drily. "What will we name him? Black Phillip?"

"I already named him," Chloe answered. "Ferdinand."

"Isn't that a bull?" Jack asked. "From a children's book?"

"Really?" Chloe said with a frown. "I was sure he was a goat."

"A pacifist bull," Jack answered, shaking his head. "But maybe his name can be . . . aspirational." We watched as Ferdinand bucked off, kicking up his haunches and prancing through our yard, bent on destruction.

"He looks like Black Phillip," Beau mused. "I think that's what I'll call him."

"Please don't," Chloe said.

"Wouldst thou like to live deliciously?" Beau asked.

While I was happy to expand our menagerie, Argos was the animal that meant something to me. We'd begun to hunt together.

After Argos's arrival, Beau had been the one to suggest I try hunting. He hunted deer and turkey in the autumn, but in spring, our carnivorous intake had been limited to what we could barter for. He sized up Argos one morning as the dog was assiduously stalking squirrels and chipmunks near the tree line. Argos would hunker down and creep, cheetah-like, until he was between the unsuspecting rodent and the safety of a tree before launching himself into a powerful spring. Most of the time he struck out, but eventually he returned, proud, with a squirrel dangling from his mouth. Beau and I were sitting in the clearing, taking turns with a butter churn—and, so far, having limited success; Natasha had shown us how to do it, but we lacked either skill or sufficient patience.

"Well, aren't you a clever pup," Beau said when Argos pranced towards us with the unappetizing scrap of drool-soaked gray fur poking from his jaws. "You're clearly a self-reliant guy."

"He brought me two rabbits the other night," I said. "I thought someone was being murdered."

"Rabbits, hmm?" Beau mused. "Have you thought about hunting them?"

"I've never been hunting in my life," I said.

"He'll do most of the work. You'll just have to train him to bring you his prey. Looks like he already does it instinctively. But maybe you can nail some of them yourself. If you clip something in the leg, he'll definitely be able to do the rest for you."

"Clip them with what?"

Beau looked at me like I was simple.

"A gun, silly." He stood up. "Bring that churn with you." He led me over to one of the storage sheds that we'd repaired in our first weeks. It had a log propped in front of the door to keep larger critters from getting in. Inside were mostly hand-me-down rakes and a couple of rusty shovels, but Beau maneuvered towards the corner.

"We've got a couple of options here. For small-game hunting, you're going to want the rifle, this little twenty-two here. It won't do much, but if you learn to aim, you should be able to help out the professional over there." He handed me the length of metal, and I held it by its smooth wood stock. It was light and easy to handle. "You'll want to do target practice, see if you're any good with that," he said.

"What about that one?" I asked, pointing to another gun visible in the corner.

"That's a shotgun. There wouldn't be much rabbit left for you if you went out with that."

"Why do we have it?"

"So far, only to put down a rabid raccoon. I found it staggering around in the daytime a few months back and we couldn't risk letting it go. Had to shoot the poor little guy." I shivered. I was glad I hadn't been present for that execution.

"This one's for hunting deer," Beau said, handing me a heavier rifle. "Belonged to my father, of all things. Pretty decent once you get used to the kick. Louisa refuses to touch it, ever since it bonked her in the shoulder. She had a bruise for two weeks." He chuckled. "She's a warrior, but she's no good with guns." He hung both the rifle and the shotgun back on the wall. "Ammunition is on the shelf right there," he said, pointing to a row of boxes directly above the weapons. Looking at the ammo, I saw the butt of a handgun. Knowing nothing about guns, I couldn't identify it, but it didn't seem like something you would go hunting with. Beau saw my eyes linger on the pistol.

"You don't have to worry about that one. You won't ever need to touch it," he said.

"We sure have a lot of firepower out here," I said, trying to conceal the uneasiness I suddenly felt. Guns made me nervous; I hadn't grown up with them, and in my mind they would forever be linked to news bulletins about mass shootings.

"Ha. You should see what Jesse has stashed at the Collective. Preppers have a whole other idea of what's a reasonable amount of armament. We've just got the country basics here."

"Land of the free," I said, smiling. He grinned back.

"C'mon. I'll show you how to shoot that thing so you can bring me home some dinner."

Since that day, Argos and I had only tried for rabbits. I wasn't sure he was particularly suited to catch anything else—big as he was, I doubted he could bring down a deer, even though the thought of venison for the winter was deeply tempting. Still, he was excellent at snagging the little bunnies as they raced obliviously through the underbrush, and I again wondered where he had come from and who had trained him. I loved our afternoons out in the woods, me crouching low to listen for him as he hunted ahead of me. We soon learned where the skittish cottontails lurked and we'd finally gotten the barbecue shipshape and were experimenting with smoked rabbit. We were careful with the bunnies, inspecting them for parasites and cooking them until we were sure they were safe—after some research, Louisa had decided they were about as safe to eat as anything else, and though I had my doubts, I liked hunting too much to question her. I ate sparingly of the meat, anyway.

I was saving all the skins, salted and stretched on my porch, planning to make a rug for my cabin when I had enough. Jack and Chloe had each taken tiny bites of carnivorous temptation when Louisa had barbecued two rabbits one evening when we were out of stew supplies. Our diets were still so limited that being a vegetarian didn't make enormous sense, though Chloe in particular seemed to feel guilty and disgusted. Still, as Jack had acknowledged, we were hardly supporting the factory farming industry or endangering ourselves by consuming undisclosed antibiotics. He would not last as a vegetarian much longer. I knew that we would eventually kill a chicken, though, and I felt sure Chloe wouldn't be able to partake. Even I would have misgivings. Maybe it would be better to barter a chicken from someone else.

Louisa saved the rabbit skulls and lined them up on the windowsill in the kitchen, near the bear trap. She boiled their bones for broth.

Though it was satisfying as fuck to see our crops succeed, and to watch the fruiting and spurting of life, I began to feel restless, devoid of something essential that had made me *me*. Without the anchor of my PhD program and my research, I felt unmoored, as though the days somehow lacked real heft because they didn't serve a larger function. Of course they did, really, I would reason with myself: What more purpose could there be than self-sufficiency, a radical remaking of the world? But I couldn't distance myself from the niggling impression that it mattered less because I was not documenting it adequately.

Because I'd so badly bungled my last case study, I was obviously reluctant to embark on a similar process here; after the failure of *The Millennial Experiment* and my subsequent abandonment of my dissertation, I was not in a hurry to reboot my academic aspirations. Formal anthropology held nothing for me any longer (I was certain), but I found I still cared about the social concerns that had preoccupied me as a grad student and still felt compelled to chronicle what happened around me. I took to jotting down impressionistic sketches and bugging Jack and Louisa for more detailed descriptions of their recipes and alchemical experiments. I mused, lengthily, on the importance of our work, and waited for some more profound inspiration to arise, something that would allow me to spin all of this into the perfect text, the oeuvre that would redeem me. This translated into a lot of rambling through the fields and forests, mumbling arcanely to myself and pausing to document, in a small notebook or with my phone, the bustle of grubs under a rock or the persistent natter of an errant woodpecker.

One afternoon in high spring, I returned home from a fruitless romp through the woods to find two unfamiliar vehicles parked in the still-drying mud near the cabins. Argos barked gruffly a few times, though not with any particular agenda; while a surprisingly efficient hunter, he was a lousy guard dog, always willing to poke his sweet wet snout into the armpit of any visitors. He careened off towards Louisa's cabin and stopped in front of the open door.

The lilacs were in full bloom, and I was nearly as giddy as the bees with the sunlight and incipient warmth. The morning glories were already retreating from the onslaught of daylight, and I had stared rapturously at the peonies' violent waxing, composing goofy rhymes like some feckless Romantic infatuated with nature. Spring had turned my head, and I was in the mood for picnics and hikes. Not Louisa's machinations.

I poked my head inside her cabin door to see her, Rudy, and a stranger, all peering intently at a sheaf of papers.

"The property line is clearly marked here, on the far side of the field in question," Rudy was saying, stabbing emphatically at the documents before him. "That's a fairly simple matter to establish legally, given that we hold the records."

"You're absolutely sure that's where your property ends?" the stranger asked, brow furrowed.

"You can see it right here on the map!"

"Even if that weren't the case," Louisa interjected, "could we argue that their use of pesticides is, I don't know, somehow affecting our adjoining fields?"

"That would be tricky," Rudy explained. "I can see why no one would want to establish a legal precedent for something like that. It would make it impossible for any non-organic farmer to grow next to an organic farm."

"Exactly!" Louisa crowed. "Look, we share the same water table. If they're using pesticides and God knows what else, it runs off directly into our irrigation, into our ditches. Ultimately into our land. It precludes our ability to make our own decision on whether or not to farm organically. Surely there has to be something there?"

Rudy frowned thoughtfully and rubbed his chin.

"Mack!" Louisa said, spotting me. "Hey. You remember my dad, Rudy?" She waved in his direction. "And this is—damn, I'm sorry, what's your name again?"

"Ryan," the stranger answered.

"This is Ryan. He works with the cooperative extension—you know, at Cornell—and he's going to do some tests on the groundwater and soil out here."

"Is this about the field out behind the hives?" I asked.

"Yes, this is about the fucking Larsons," she answered, her expression darkening. "They think we'll just ignore them or, I don't know, not even notice. They think they own this whole fucking county, and I'm not going to let them just get away with this."

"Louisa, we need to be smart about this. There's no point in running off half-cocked—"

"I'm not half-cocked!" Louisa snapped. "This is our land, and we've made a commitment to use it sustainably. What they're doing is unacceptable!"

"Agreed. Of course I'll help you," Rudy reassured her. "Why do you think I'm here? I just— We're going to get the information we need."

"Okay, good, I just want us all to be on the same page," Louisa said, smiling too brightly. "Are we ready? Shall we hike out back?"

"Let me grab my kit from the car," Ryan said, looking relieved for an excuse to duck out for a moment. Louisa swung towards me.

"Wanna come, Mack? You're not too busy right now?"

"The rabbits are all in hiding today. Sure, I'll come," I said.

"Great, the more the merrier! And it can't hurt to have an extra witness, if we need one!"

At this comment by Louisa, Rudy looked like he was tempted to say something, or correct her, but he stopped short.

Ryan returned with a bag and we set off into the woods, walking along the trail that had begun to emerge from our frequent excursions farther onto the property. Argos sped merrily ahead of us, periodically loping back to rub his bristly fur against my abdomen, just to verify that I was still coming at my disappointingly human pace. The ground still squelched from the spring rain. But I glimpsed the mayapples and ferns poking up from the layer of half-rotted leaves on the woodland floor and felt another seasonal frisson. Louisa and Rudy talked intently as Ryan and I trudged behind, unsure what to say to each other.

We emerged into the flower field, passed Chloe's hives (I was gratified to hear the manic thrum of a colony gearing up for the season), and walked through the break of creaking pines to the next field.

"You're right, Lou, I'm pretty sure this is our land," Rudy said with a shake of the head. "Unbelievable! I cannot believe the nerve of Chuck Larson." He crouched down, getting impressively low on his substantial haunches. "Corn, you say." He squinted at the furrows stretching out across the whole field, gripping a fistful of soil. "Right, Ryan, this is where you get to work."

"Absolutely, Mr. Stein. Let me just get a few things out. . . ." Ryan tossed his things onto the ground and began his preparations.

"I mean, this is definitely illegal, right?" Louisa huddled conspiratorially with her father.

"Pretty damn sure. I haven't signed anything that leases them the land, so they're essentially squatting here."

"And pumping our land full of toxic chemicals." Louisa kicked at the ground.

"I've finished up here," Ryan announced after a few minutes, packing away his things. "I'll take some samples of the soil in your vegetable garden, and from the irrigation ditch near the road, when we get back."

"Good. Let's head home, then." Louisa led us back through the woods to the Homestead. I could see the cogs working in her head, the plotting growing ever more complex and serious.

We found Chloe and Jack sitting at the picnic table in front of the big cabin, drinking from one of Jack's jugs of honey mead.

"Hallo, the house!" Louisa called, racing towards them. "We return from our mission, bearing confirmation of the nefarious goings-on of our neighbors."

"You were right? It *is* on our property?" Chloe asked eagerly.

"It sure is." Rudy nodded. "We're looking into it."

"And we've tested the ground and the water, thanks to our pal here from the cooperative extension."

"You work at the Coop?" Jack asked. "I've got a friend who works over there—her name is Becca. You know her?"

"Yup, she works in the food education program, right? With the kids?"

"That's her. Jack," Jack said, extending a hand.

"Ryan," Ryan responded, doing likewise.

"Hey, Ryan, would you like a jam jar of honey mead?" Chloe asked, smiling at him. I could tell from his expression that he was not terribly invested in the honey mead but he wouldn't mind a little more time with Chloe.

"I probably shouldn't . . . but as long as it's a small, uh, jar," he said, bobbing his head. "Thanks, yeah."

"And what about me, young lady? Will you so neglect your elders?" Rudy asked, feigning offense.

"Never. Certainly not when our elders are our benefactors," Chloe answered, skirting the table gracefully and giving Rudy a peck on his pink cheek. "I'll bring you a *large* jar."

"That's a good girl," Rudy said. Remarkably, he managed to avoid making this sound lascivious, which it definitely would have coming from almost anyone else.

"Has anyone seen Beau?" Louisa asked, scanning the clearing, one hand shading her eyes. Having already done the same thing, I knew that Beau wasn't just lurking at the far end of the pond or driving in more stakes for the fence he was building around the edge of the orchard.

"Haven't seen him all morning," Jack answered.

"Or last night," Chloe answered rather casually. I thought this was probably an unnecessary detail.

"I'll try his cellphone," Louisa said. "I want to give him an update."

"It's off," Chloe said.

Louisa said nothing.

"I'll be right back," Chloe promised. "Got to grab cups for our guests." She breezed off towards the big cabin after smiling widely at Ryan and Rudy.

Louisa held her cellphone in her palm, her brow knitted in irritation.

Ryan stayed for a while, and Rudy stayed even longer. The lengthening spring day faded slowly, and the temperature dropped. We scampered to our cabins to gather sweaters and gloves—all but Jack, who merely draped one of Louisa's scarves around his shoulders.

"I can't stand to put that winter coat on one more time," he explained. "I'd rather freeze."

We were all desperately sick of the cold, desperate to put away long johns and extra socks and frolic outside without boots. I wondered darkly, though: If this was how we felt after just a couple of months on the Homestead, how would we feel by this time next year?

Beau returned later that evening, just as Ryan was heading off—Chloe walked him to his truck. We saw a flash of headlights at the end of the drive, and Beau sauntered up. Louisa's lips were still pursed and silent, and she said nothing until Ryan had pulled onto the road. Jack clapped Beau on the back and recounted the afternoon's adventures, clearly unaware of the tension.

"Will you help me build a fire?" Chloe asked after a few minutes, trying to draw Beau away from the crowd. It was the wrong move.

"Actually, could you come help me with dinner?" Louisa asked him curtly. "I could use a strong, capable pair of arms." Her cheeks were worryingly pink, a shade that signified either serious tipsiness or fury. Judging from his expression, Rudy knew this look all too well.

"Sure, Lou-my-dear," Beau answered, unconcerned. Louisa spun and headed towards the cabin, Beau following at his own smooth pace.

Once the door of the cabin had shut, Rudy whistled.

"What did that poor boy do?" he asked.

"He failed to report for duty," I answered. "Been AWOL. And General Louisa likes to keep track of our whereabouts."

Rudy chortled heartily. "She can be a domineering thing, can't she?" he said, though with a tinge of pride. "She's like her mother that way—always the boss."

"What's her mom like?" Chloe asked. "She never really talks about her."

"High-powered lawyer. High-strung. High-maintenance," Rudy said. "But brilliant. Capable. A little cold."

"I think Louisa tends to run warm," Chloe answered, smiling. From the big cabin we could hear her voice, though not her words. In the brief pauses between her irritated exclamations, I could imagine Beau's responses: "You don't own me, you know" or "You're being foolish, you" or "Does it really matter where I go?" Chloe sighed. The conflict set her on edge, and I could see her trying to determine whether she should go involve herself in the squabble.

"Well, perhaps I should head off," Rudy said. "I, for one, don't want to get in the middle of that."

"You should come say goodbye, though!" Chloe said. "Louisa will probably want to set up a time to come to your office, make a plan of some kind."

"I expect you're right." Rudy sighed. He shifted his bulk from the picnic table, moving ponderously in preparation for bidding farewell to his offspring. He and Chloe lumbered off towards the cabin while Jack and I sat with our mugs.

"Think anything will come of this crusade of Louisa's?" Jack finally asked.

"I really don't know. I guess it would be nice, if it worked out. It's hard changing the world one potato at a time."

Jack snorted.

Everyone emerged from the warm light of the cabin then, Rudy chuckling and boisterous. Chloe walked him to his car, as she'd done with Ryan, though now that it was dark this was a necessary courtesy. I hoped he hadn't had too much of Jack's mead. Once Rudy had hoisted himself into his seat with a bit of puffing and a dangerous-looking teeter, Chloe scampered back to us, and we five stood waving him off.

"Come, sweet girl," Beau finally said to Louisa, draping an arm around her shoulders. "Don't be mad. I've been making a surprise for you, and I think you'll like it. Don't get huffy."

Louisa glanced at him sidelong, but I could see from her crossed arms that she was softening.

"Let's celebrate the new spring," he continued. "Drink some wine and tell a campfire story." He leaned down to kiss her, looming over her.

She met his eyes, finally, and I could tell he had won.

"You too," he said to Chloe, giving her a kiss as well. "And you." He moved on to Jack, who looked surprised but not at all unwilling, and Beau held his cheeks and gave him a sound, lengthy kiss on his mouth. Jack looked a little dazed. And when Beau bent to give me his own kiss, I knew why.

"What's for dinner?"

"Pasta with garlic and arugula and that 'Parmesan' Beau obtained for us," Louisa said. "But it's too fucking cold out here. Let's go inside."

Summer

From the diary of William Fulsome

Summer:

Today, Tragedy has visited our modest enterprise. Though we all dwell in close proximity with Death, and hold the promise of Life Everlasting close in our breast, the loss of a child cannot but elicit the depths of Grief in any feeling person. And for a mother to lose a treasured son!

Annabelle's wailing has not abated since we found the body of young Josiah in the pond this morning; she has keened and shrieked with a fervor that makes me fear for her mind, if not her very health. Her Suffering fills us all, and there is no one among us who has not walked around carrying the Grief of this loss from this dark morning's sun to its disappearance over the Horizon. Initially, she was unwilling to relinquish the boy's lifeless body, but instead clutched at it in her cabin, brushing its hair and stroking its face. I left her to her mourning with a shiver of Horror.

We suspect that poor Josiah awakened before his parents, and crept down to the pond, whether for sustenance or amusement we will never know. Being scarcely three years old, he was not yet a strong swimmer, and, finding himself entangled in the pond weeds, he only succeeded in thrashing deeper into the water, where he met his End. I pray to God that his dying was merciful and brief. I have no doubt that his young, untarnished soul will be accepted into Paradise by our just and loving Lord.

For the sake of her living child, I hope that Annabelle can find a way to live with this loss, and continue in this undertaking with us.

The cost of our Venture feels heavy today, I am afraid. Living here, off the land, we are ever aware that death lurks at the edges of each long winter, each careless mistake. And yet, we hold out hope for the promise of a more perfect Afterlife, a balm to salve the pain of Loss.

But perhaps there is a sliver of Promise to be found in this horror; Mary approached Annabelle in her Vigil and, leaning down to her, whispered something in her ear. Annabelle shortly thereafter deigned to let Jeremiah take his son from her, and remove him to the stable, where Elizabeth has been helping to prepare him for Burial. These were the first words Mary has uttered since she broke with Elijah. After, she met my eyes and, for the first time, smiled at me. I could not interpret her Expression, but it felt to me like an invitation: to help her return to herself. Let me be worthy and able to help her.

Tomorrow morning we will bury the boy, and Life, however cruelly, will return to its normal routines.

$\backsim$

We are awash with Bounty. Our gardens overflow with food, and my own heart with Gratitude. I suspect that I will at any moment turn into a tomato or squash, which seem to grace our table morning, noon, and night. Praise God for this Life, and this land, and the gift that is my family and friends! We are blessed.

Money is sparse, however, and I have "borrowed" from our friend Thoreau: I have not paid the county taxes which were due last month. Though I was in no way afraid of this demonstration of Civil Disobedience, I couldn't help but feel Trepidation as the bailiff summoned me to the jail. How would my small Flock fare without me?

In the end, I passed only a few evenings in the jailhouse; Jeremiah was able to collect the necessary funds to pay our fine. He seemed angered, however, by my actions, despite my efforts to elucidate my motivations. At home, I discovered that Elizabeth shared his irrita-

tion. They do not understand our dilemma: How to subsist here, on our own property, while also undertaking a comprehensive Project of Social Change. I lay awake at nights grappling with these two horns, unable to reconcile the two Duties.

Annabelle is once again with child; while I try not to judge Brother Jeremiah, we had agreed to continue our practice of Male Continence here, so as to spare our wives the complications and difficulty of Labor until we might be better settled. Still, it is not for me to judge my Friend, especially when he has made this paradise a reality through his Generosity. Annabelle's last pregnancy was difficult, and I pray that this one is less arduous. After the loss of her child, though, I cannot begrudge her another.

I continue to fear for Mary and her Soul; some days it is as though she is truly Lost to us. Her continued silence unnerves the children, and while we have all tried to draw her into conversation, she refuses all but the most basic gestures. She has a way of gazing into one's eyes in these moments of frustration, and I will confess to several instances of Impassioned Discourse—anything to make her speak a word, to speak to me! I cannot help but feel that she is asking something of me, that these baleful stares and long moments of intensity are her manner of requesting my aid and my protection. She must feel so Alone, a single woman here amidst two families. I have yearned to make her feel truly a part of our family, and, if we were still within the Community, I would have asked her for an Interview, perhaps to put her mind at rest that she is truly wanted here. But I must banish such thoughts instantly; we have forsaken Complex Marriage. Mary will have to come to me in a traditional manner, and convey her wishes in language, even while it might be more expedient to converse in the wordless and sacred manner in which a man and a woman may Communicate. I could prevail upon her to come to me . . . but no, I shall wait for her to approach.

❧

Ah, Mary! An angel of Goodness and Beauty. How grateful I am to have her here. Surely, with her by my side, we will be ready for the Resurrection. And how Grateful I am that she has opened herself to me.

Elizabeth seems not herself, but I suspect this is because of our daughter's sickliness of late; she fears for the child, as do I. Our lives seem wholly bounded by our preparation for Winter, the need to put aside enough food for the season of snow that lies ahead. I trust that once the cans are in the pantry and the vegetables in the cellar, Elizabeth will once more be merry, and join me in our room for an Interview.

The households seem to crumble without firm Authority, a single voice that serves to remind each and every member what needs to be done. I find myself forced into the role of Patriarch; with the three women seemingly distracted by matters of the heart and the hearth, it is essential that there be a voice of Reason which commands us all to do God's work and prepare for the coming season of cold. Poor shepherd though I am, I am best equipped to Lead.

Chapter 12

Summer arrived suddenly, as it often does. One morning, instead of seeing the glimmers of frost on the grass, you wake up and it's already warm outside. The lilacs look wilted, browned at the edges. By midday, you're sweating. The dandelions erupt.

The sun seemed to loosen the tension that had been burgeoning between Louisa and Beau, and Jack was seemingly walking on air, measuring his delicate buds and saplings what seemed like every other hour, crouching down in the field to see if his bean shoots had emerged. He deliberated every morning when it would be safe to move his tomato seedlings into the ground. Louisa was also particularly invested in this delicate question of timing, as tomatoes were, she claimed, her spirit animal. Chloe sang and trilled on a flute she had borrowed from a friend and was teaching herself to play. At the moment, she favored spritely Celtic airs. Beau took long walks around the edges of the property, his sharp eyes always hunting for something edible, new, or beautiful. He brought us each posies of wildflowers: pink lady's slippers, mayapples, lupine, ferns. Chloe, not realizing what they were, strung a garland of wild hops around the pillars of her cabin, and Jack decided to experiment with them, mumbling something about wet-hopped ale, jotting down notes in the pad he kept with him. He spent a day constructing trellises in the small clearing behind his cabin, and Louisa looked annoyed until Chloe explained what it was for. Louisa was in favor of anything that could supplement her larder.

In the midst of our large-scale political concerns (it was the summer of the 2016 primaries), Louisa amplified her efforts to put an end to her neighbor's farming. She had convinced Rudy to file some petitions, and something that I vaguely understood to be a cease-and-desist order had been issued to the Larsons. Beau pointed out that this rather clearly identified us as hostile, and I mumbled something similar about fences and neighbors, but Louisa was uninterested in our objections.

"I want them to know that I know what they're up to! They're counting on complacency—so much of this world is! They think we'll just roll over and let them fuck us in the ass with *Citizens United*. Shop at Target and be good worker bees. Fuck that. And fuck Chuck Larson."

I would frequently mouth this inevitable tagline whenever she concluded a rant; once, Beau saw me do it and burst out laughing. I was absurdly pleased.

"Fuck Chuck Larson" had become her mantra, and she spent a significant percentage of her time fretting about Larson's comings and goings. She installed herself in an old deer stand at the edge of the field and logged spraying times, fertilizing days, number of people who came and went. She took pictures of the property, tractors, and employees. Whenever a person or equipment encroached on what she believed to be her land, she came barreling out of the tree brandishing some document or other, apoplectically berating whosoever dared to trundle into her world. She had heated conversations on the phone with Rudy and the unfortunate lawyer he had saddled the case with, supposedly on the grounds that he was more experienced in property law and environmental issues. I once even overheard Louisa on the phone with her mother. It was a clipped, uncomfortable conversation, and I could tell that Louisa was trying to elicit her support, if not her legal expertise. But from her taut mouth and the uneasy way she paced around her cabin, I suspected that Ms. Jackson was not especially forthcoming with either, and was also coming up short on maternal indulgence and sympathy.

"More or less what I expected," Louisa answered curtly when I asked her what her mother had said. She seemed disinclined to talk any further about it. Personally, I felt it was probably good for Louisa to have a dash of cold water thrown on her machinations, but I certainly didn't want to volunteer for the job. I'll confess to some cowardice, even, in that I would sometimes let her pressure me into accompanying her on her "reconnaissance missions." Though I refused to confront the burly older men who drove the Larsons' tractors, I did take pictures of Louisa doing so, holding up her legal documents like some sort of medieval sword, prepared to vanquish these environmental desecrators. Yet again, I was complicit in my passivity.

While Jack joined in with Louisa's invective quite enthusiastically—citing court cases he had read about on his weekly excursions to both the public and the Cornell libraries, where he would happily prowl the stacks for hours—Chloe and Beau distanced themselves. Chloe because she hated the conflict, and Beau for indeterminate reasons that seemed related to his general desire for secrecy. I got the impression that he felt that Louisa's blatant, provocative campaign was simply bad warfare. This made me nervous, but I was loath to bring it up to anyone, least of all Louisa. A decision I deeply regret. But perhaps part of me longed for the chaos too.

The morning of the fire, we were drinking an unpleasant mustard tea (yet another Jackian experimentation); it had been concocted from foraged herbs and greens and tasted basically like boiled dandelions. Dandelions, in fact, may have featured prominently in the recipe that day; "Jack's Tea" was different every morning.

It was warm outside, so we sat clustered around the picnic table, making a list of what needed to be accomplished that day, as well as during the rest of the week. Jack liked to break everything down into short-term and long-term goals, and he had an elaborate, color-coded key of tasks, partly in his head, partly transcribed in what we now thought of as the Homestead Almanac, our little log of this first year's successes and failures. Jack, the founder of said publication, was the primary author and custodian, but we all undertook to make the occasional contribution. The sight of this journal invariably made me think guiltily of the notebook and the growing compendium of my own project, hidden in my cabin, hoarded there for my own nighttime subterfuge. I had yet to (and in fact would not, during my tenure at the Homestead) show it to anyone—the pleasure of that little text, and the possibilities it afforded me, was a private one.

The evening before, I had watched the nocturnal migration of the gaslights, swirling in one of their usual constellations. At one point, I had noted that all three cabins were dark, and, as though fooled by a magician's three-cup trick, I realized that I had lost track of where the respective marbles had ended up. I considered my inattention a good sign for my mental health, and I was prepared to call it a night when I saw a figure, presumably Beau, slink back to his cabin. The light stayed on for a minute or two before the Homestead again went completely dark. I had set a box near the wall so Argos could leap more easily in and out of the mezzanine bed, and he had long since tucked himself in. After Beau's return, I slunk up to bed, shoving Argos's long legs out of the way to clear a nook for myself.

That morning, we sat sipping "tea," still in our pajamas (Chloe slinky in her kimono, naturally), arguing over who would have to clear brambles and weeds and shake things up with the composting toilet. We were all eager to harvest some salad greens. Argos was pacing around the table, occasionally plopping his large head in my lap in search of an absent scratch or a forgotten crumb. Normally he sat flopped in the dust at our feet, but I didn't register his antsiness until I smelled smoke.

Louisa and Chloe seemed to sense it the same moment I did, and Louisa leapt up from the table to race into the big cabin, where she was cooking porridge with berries on the stovetop.

"I better not have burned that fucking pan," I heard her cry as she dashed up the steps. But she appeared only a moment later with a puzzled expression. "Stove's fine in here," she said from the steps. In a primal gesture, we all simultaneously lifted our snouts into the air to sniff. Fire.

"It's too wet for a forest fire," Jack said, if somewhat uncertainly. This seemed true, though; we'd had plenty of spring showers, rejoicing each time.

"Everyone check your cabins," Louisa snapped, clearing the stairs in a quick jump. We all dashed to make sure our lamps hadn't fallen over or our mattresses spontaneously combusted. We reappeared at the same time, shaking our heads.

"Look," Chloe said, pointing. "Over there. Smoke." We all turned to follow where her finger gestured, behind the back field.

"You don't think—if those fucking Larsons did *any*thing back there, I'll sue them for this whole damn county!" Louisa cried, rushing back to her cabin for her duck boots. We all set off at a jog, rushing through the woods. Argos outstripped us all, racing ahead only to circle back and collect us periodically. The back field was roughly half a mile away, and we reached it after a few minutes, me and Jack light-footed in the lead.

"Holy fuck," I said.

"Jesus," Jack said. We stood staring as the others arrived, Louisa panting and red-faced.

"Fuck me," she said, staring at the flames. The Larsons' massive tractor billowed smoke and fire, a sooty plume stretching up from the cab and rising above the tree line. As we watched, the windshield exploded outward from the heat.

"We need to go," Beau said evenly. He tugged at Louisa's elbow, and she allowed herself to be steered away—but only for a few yards. Her head snapped back to stare at the fire; she seemed to be transfixed by the inferno.

"Should we call the fire department?" Chloe suggested anxiously. "I mean, couldn't this start a forest fire?"

"The ground and the wood are wet," Beau answered, pointing at a muddy footprint in illustration. "It'll keep for a few minutes. Let's get back to the cabins." He seemed to want distance between us and the fire, whereas Louisa clearly wanted to stay and watch the blaze.

"Serves those assholes right," she spat, her face splitting into a worrisome grin. "For once they might have a sense of what their industry costs."

"Who do you think did it?" Chloe asked, looking around.

"*They* probably did it so they could claim it was us," Louisa insisted, gesticulating wildly at the vehicle. "Frame us and take the insurance."

"Frame us, Louisa? Listen to yourself," Jack said.

"To make us look unhinged! Then they can undercut us if—when—the lawsuit gets to court. Say we harassed them."

"Some people might say that even without the arson," I muttered.

"Do you have any idea how much a tractor like that costs?" Jack asked. "That is a hell of a price to pay for one field and a neighborly dispute. Insurance probably won't settle if it looks intentional."

"One tractor means nothing to them! They know what they stand to lose if our lawsuit succeeds. They'll use our strategy of being persistent against us, claiming that we're overly invested"—I could see the gears of her mind turning, her legal breeding evident in her quick assessment of the opposing side—"and they'll say that we've gone outside the law. Those fuckers will get away with it, and their insurance will pay for it!"

There was a desperate, grasping quality in Louisa's argument, and I could see that she didn't really believe her accusation at all. Which raised a question: Why was she bothering? If she knew it wasn't the Larsons, that meant she had some inkling of who *had* set the fire. I watched her twitchy face and wondered what she might be capable of.

"Well, whoever did this couldn't have done it too long ago," Beau pointed out. "This fire certainly hasn't been going all night."

Beau had remained silent during Louisa's incoherent rant, but his desire to get away from the field and its wreckage was evident. The fire had probably been lit as we were waking, putting the kettle on to boil. The arsonist was probably not that far away from us. I whirled around, certain that we were being watched from the deer stand, from the woods. The birds were quiet, and I tugged down the sleeves of my suddenly inadequate T-shirt. Surely Beau wouldn't? But I believed that he was capable of erratic, reckless choices. Would he dare? Would he do it for Louisa? But he'd been with us all morning. Almost conspicuously so.

"We need to get back home immediately. Someone could show up here any second," Louisa said curtly. "Come on. We need to call my lawyer."

She was on the phone with Rudy before we reached the Homestead, informing him of the basics in clipped tones. I knew she must be anxious, because normally she would be overly informative, would use too many words. But she was being very careful to say only what she knew and was trying not to speculate. Already coaching herself as a witness.

"He says if we call the cops, it will look less suspicious," she said immediately upon hanging up. "Especially since we likely left footprints. He also says the insurance company will almost definitely investigate, and we should probably plan on a criminal investigation." We all flinched.

"But we didn't do it," Chloe said. There was an uneasy silence.

"Obviously," Louisa said after a pause. "Unless somebody would like to confess?" She looked us each square in the eye. No one said anything. Unsurprisingly. I gazed around at my friends but could glean nothing from their expressions. Even Jack's guileless face looked shut down. "Okay, next question," she went on. "Anyone have any contact with the Larsons that we aren't aware of? Run-ins on the road? Words that could be taken out of context?" We all shook our heads mutely. "Right. Okay. We're going to come under the most scrutiny, so everyone has to be totally clear on what's happened. We were trying to bring a lawsuit against them. We had every reason to think we would get what we wanted by legal means. We would never, under any circumstances, take matters into our own hands." I half-expected her to ask us to recite these lines back to her, but we all just nodded diligently. I wondered what my parents would say if I added convicted arsonist to my list of disgraces.

"Okay, if we're ready, I'm calling the cops."

I remember giving my statement, clipped and restricted to the facts. I was overly circumspect in my attempts not to incriminate anyone— I didn't know whether I suspected we had somehow been involved or I was just scared. The cops finished with me quickly; my unassuming looks and quiet voice once again worked in my favor. They spoke to Louisa the longest, predictably. Rudy appeared while the police were still jotting down notes, and I couldn't help wondering if his presence somehow made us appear guilty. And of course I couldn't help wondering whether we—or one of us—was. I thought of Beau's light, flickering on at strange times during the night. I thought of Louisa's intense psychological fixation on the Larsons' field. Of Chloe's willingness to play along with any fantasy, her eagerness to start any fire. Of Jack's impulsivity, his failure to recognize the permanence of choices, of how silly he could get when he was stoned. I sat on the steps of my cabin and stroked Argos's grimy head whenever he strolled up to me, pausing in his patrol. Too anxious to continue monitoring the true-crime scene unfurling on my own little piece of paradise, I eventually fetched my gloves and went to go tear up burdock from the edges of the garden, dousing the ragged ground with vinegar when I had finished wrenching them from the ground. Dripping with sweat, I watched the two cops pile into their patrol car and drive off, leaving the Homestead quiet and worried.

We were all on edge for the rest of the day. Rudy left, making us promise not to give further statements and not to go anywhere near the back field. Chloe disappeared into her cabin, I assumed to lie down, wearing that glassy expression that so worried me. Jack turned over the compost with an intense fervor. Beau disappeared, naturally. I wandered listlessly from the garden to the soggy woodland patch where Jack's mushroom spores were under cultivation, unable to remember what was on today's short-term list. I wanted to sequester myself to work on my project, poring over my notes and flipping through the library books I had surreptitiously borrowed. I was getting off on my own secrecy.

Wandering through the orchard, I found Louisa in a tree, draped over a branch like a languorous monkey. Her elbow was pillowed on a ragged book. With her chin hovering above the curled, chipped pages, she read aloud, without looking at me:

> *I am enamour'd of growing out-doors,*
> *Of men that live among cattle or taste of the ocean or woods,*
> *Of the builders and steerers of ships and the wielders of axes*
> *and mauls, and the drivers of horses,*
> *I can eat and sleep with them week in and week out.*
>
> *What is commonest, cheapest, nearest, easiest, is Me,*
> *Me going in for my chances, spending for vast returns,*
> *Adorning myself to bestow myself on the first that will take me,*
> *Not asking the sky to come down to my good will,*
> *Scattering it freely forever.*

"'Song of Myself,'" I said, hoisting myself up into the branches of the apple tree to perch in a jagged crook near her. I had to tilt my hips and slot them into the rough Y of the branches, so that I listed towards the trunk.

"Sometimes I worry that we're asking the sky to come down to us," she said, chin now propped on the book, eyes gazing at the Homestead, or something farther off.

"Well, we're asking capitalism to shove off and let us re-create our own small-scale agrarian society," I pointed out. "It's not the sky, but it might as well be."

"I understand that we're probably destined for failure. That the world and the culture we live in have a vested interest in us failing, because for us to succeed would mean that there's an alternative. But. But." Louisa righted herself on the branch to turn her head towards me. "But don't we have to try? Isn't it somehow our obligation?"

"Obviously, we all believe that," I said. "Why else would we agree to eat quinoa with fiddleheads for a solid month straight? And drink that awful mead of Jack's?"

"Ugh, what I wouldn't give for a *real* beer!" Louisa laughed. "We all agree on sacrificing something; we all believe we can *do* something. But what if this isn't the way to do it? Maybe we should all be politicians. Writing political manifestos. You should maybe start your own publication. I don't know."

"Or we could all just become rabid consumers. Vote for the crazies. Push capitalism to the edge of revolution and give it a final shove over."

She smiled again. "It does have its appeal, doesn't it? Fuck our liberalism, our environmentalism, our lukewarm socialism. Nothing will change until the death knell of the system is sounded!"

"Sounds a hell of a lot easier than stockpiling enough potatoes and sauerkraut for the winter," I said.

"It does. But maybe not the 'commonest, cheapest, nearest,' et cetera."

"No. Probably not."

Her brow wrinkled and she turned away from me again. "And didn't I just adorn myself for the first person who would take me?" she said softly. I wanted to answer, but as she slid down from the tree, her voice sharpened: "And didn't you?"

Chapter 13

That evening, Chloe and Beau declared that we needed to play. I expected Louisa to protest, but even she relented in the face of the edgy gloom that had settled over the Homestead. We were worried—we felt as though our young, desperate experiment had been violently encroached upon, and I could see it cracking us open. A bacchanal seemed ideal. How simple and easy and nice it would be to lose ourselves in food and wine and chatter. With renewed vigor, we leapt into action, pulling down dried herbs from their racks in the kitchen, tugging up scallions from the garden, counting our bottles of booze and budgeting them for the party. Chloe and Louisa tugged me off to Louisa's cabin to primp, and I watched breathlessly as Chloe tried on all of our clothes, looking effortless and beautiful in everything she put on. Louisa donned only her own things, out of deference to those wild cheeks and round curves. She settled into an Edwardian-style black gown that nearly reached her ankles and pulled her bright tumble of curls into a springy beehive. Chloe kept switching between a delicate blue item and a simple floral prairie dress.

"The blue reminds me of Isadora Duncan," she said wistfully, twisting her hips so that the chiffon switched daintily in fluttering ripples. I thought of a nightgown I had been given as a little girl, and remembered spinning manically to watch the skirt billow out princess-style.

The thing had probably been extremely flammable. (Sweatshop crap, madeinChina, notsustainablyproduced.) Chloe seemed to bask in that childish grace without any of the ambivalence I had felt then; I had thought myself to be an impostor, a mawkish interloper in the world of princesses. Not she, not Chloe. She leapt and did a series of pirouettes, arabesques, neat pas de bourrée. Louisa gazed at her appraisingly.

"You do look worthy of the Great Astaire. But you remember how Duncan died," she chided. "The other dress won't tear or get caught in the brambles. Better to look like Laurey *before* her big dance scene." At my quizzical expression, Chloe explained: "*Oklahoma.*"

"That's supposed to clarify?"

"It's a musical." Louisa waved my question away, not wanting to explain her allusion. She had a strangely comprehensive knowledge of musical theater. ("It was the only thing my mother could think of to do with me when I visited her in New York," she had explained once. I had been led to believe that those visits were fairly uncommon, but Louisa could name every song on the *Breakfast on Broadway* radio program, which aired for an hour on a local radio station every Sunday. I suspected that there might be more to this, but I had yet to do enough snooping to get to the bottom of her extensive knowledge.)

"Mack? What do you think?" Chloe asked, zipping up the flowery peasant dress. Naturally, she looked lovely in that too.

"They're both delightful, but Louisa is probably right. You know we'll end up dragging wood for a bonfire or running around in the dark."

Chloe sighed. "You're right, of course." She turned to me. "And what are we going to do with you?" I looked down at myself, startled. I was wearing leggings and a button-down flannel shirt. My one concession to the festive occasion had been to trade my Timberlands for a pair of cheap flats that had remained untouched in the corner since my arrival at the Homestead. Even those seemed inadvisable, since there were still patches of mud to be squelched through.

"You look like you do every day," Louisa chastised, always unafraid to be blunt. "Come now, we don't want to seem like a bunch of country mice in front of Beau's ridiculous friends."

I suddenly understood. "You mean Fennel, in particular, I assume?" I said.

Louisa glanced briefly away, but then looked back at me. "Yeah, Little Miss No-Mirror. If you're going to adorn yourself—and let's make no mistake, we all do, one way or the other, even Fennel—you may as well own it." She turned back to the mirror and defiantly swept on black eyeliner in a wing that traced the crease and crinkle of her eye. Chloe came behind me and tugged my hair from its usual position, then twisted it into a tight knot at the back of my skull. She pulled her fingers through my fine, dirty blond tresses, which were always a little dingy these days, given the nature of our bathing arrangements. Fanning my hair out on my shoulders, she pursed her lips.

"I think it should go."

"What?"

"Your hair," she said.

"What?" I yelped, instinctively pulling my head away from her.

"Hmm. She's right," Louisa concurred. "You haven't got the volume for long hair, anyway. But you've got cheekbones and a cute little chin. Off with it."

"You guys, my hair hasn't been shorter than this since second grade," I protested. "Besides, I need to be able to tie it out of my face. For work!"

"Not if it's so short that it's not in your face," Chloe reasoned.

"But everyone has long hair!" I whined.

"Not Jack," Louisa pointed out. "Come to think of it, he could use a haircut too."

"Where are your little scissors, Lou?" Chloe asked. She turned to rummage on Louisa's table, cluttered with books and trinkets. Of all of us, Louisa had most thoroughly filled her small cabin. It resembled a boudoir, crammed as it was with scarves and delicate objets.

"Here, you better do it," Louisa said to Chloe, producing the scissors. "You have an artist's eye."

"Guys, I can't have short hair!" I protested, even as Louisa nudged me into the chair and found a scarf to drape around my shoulders.

Chloe stood behind me, shears in hand, and held up a chunk of my hair, which did look admittedly lank. She gazed at my eyes, reflected to her in Louisa's mirror.

"Do you want to do this, Mack?" she asked seriously. I looked back at her, and felt my resolution fade. She wouldn't cut without my consent, she meant that—but she was nudging me in the direction she wanted to go. I trusted Chloe, though. I took a deep breath, giving myself over to her.

"Fine. Do it. It's just hair."

"It always grows back," Louisa said cheerfully from the bed, where she had sprawled to watch my cropping.

Half an hour later, I emerged from Louisa's cabin. I felt both dazed and utterly wired, as though every sound and shard of light was strangely magnified. I didn't know whether to cry or leap into the air.

"Shit!" Jack exclaimed when he saw me, vaguely heading in the direction of my own cabin. "You—your hair!"

"You better not say anything critical about it or I'll start crying," I said honestly. I reached up to brush the nape of my neck.

"No! I mean, you look like someone else! You look incredible!"

"Shucks, thanks," I said. "Quite the compliment."

"I didn't mean it that way. It's just—you look pretty amazing, Mack."

I sighed, but I couldn't help smiling a little. "Thanks, Jack," I said, and continued to my cabin, to take stock.

I examined myself in my own, much smaller mirror once I got inside. Jack was right. I did look like a different person. Gone were my dull strands. They were now clipped close, framing my face in sharp little angles across my forehead and in front of my ears. My cheekbones *did* jut out more, my chin more pointed and feisty. I actually rather liked the shape of my neck. In addition to the changes made to my coif, Chloe had given me subtle swoops of black eyeliner at the edges of my eyes and a coat of her reddest lipstick. She had also made me exchange my flannel shirt for a lightweight striped sweater.

"There. You look like Jean Seberg," she pronounced. This was apparently a good thing.

I sat studying myself for a few minutes longer before mustering the courage to venture back outside. I was afraid of how Beau would react, that he would see me and think me foolish or vain. Or perhaps no more fuckable than before.

But Beau wasn't outside. Louisa was spreading tablecloths and a picnic blanket. Jack was testing his various batches of mead and apple-jack, to see which was "showing best." Chloe was humming brightly and plucking at her ukulele, tuning it up. Ferdinand bleated loudly from his pen in contribution. "A Pastoral Scene."

"Where's Beau?" I asked, joining Louisa to help her set dishes out on the porch of the big cabin.

"He's gone to collect the party," she explained. "They'll be back soon. Hey, you don't want to invite anyone, do you?" The question surprised me.

"Um, no, probably not." I felt I should make some excuse for why I had no friends beyond these four people I spent every day with. But I had none.

"Mack," Louisa said, her voice dropping. "Listen, I've wanted to talk to you about something." Her tone made me shiver.

"Uh, okay. What's up?"

"I've been meaning to bring it up for a while. But I was sort of hoping you'd talk about it first."

"Talk about what?" I asked, though I had a fairly good idea.

"About what happened before you came here. With the *Experiment*. About why you're here."

"I'm here for the same reasons as you guys," I insisted.

"I don't doubt that—don't worry," she said, placing her hand on my forearm in a manner that was meant to be reassuring but that instead made me flinch. "But I watched the show."

"They edited it to make it look worse than it was," I mumbled, ducking my head and wanting badly to run away.

"So I assumed. Why . . . why didn't you ever talk to me about it? Or to Beau?"

"Does Beau know about this?" My heart sank.

"I asked him if he knew, yeah. You know Beau, though. He didn't seem to care at all. Not that I care," she said swiftly. "I just—I wish you'd felt like you could talk about it. I kept waiting for you to mention something—"

"Look, the whole point was that I wanted to put it behind me. I left New York under some nasty circumstances, and I just didn't want—to keep revisiting it, all the time. Trying to defend myself for having done something really stupid. Something wrong."

"Mistakes," Louisa said with a shrug. "Bygones. You think we all haven't done some really questionable things?"

I narrowed my eyes at her. "Well, you don't seem to be advertising them, either."

"Point taken. Look, I just wanted to clear the air. I've been feeling weird, aware that I know but you don't know that I know, and I keep asking leading questions and whatnot. . . . Just, it's out there." She pushed her hands away from her body, as though shoving her knowledge of what I'd done back at me.

"Okay," I said, then bit my lip. "Do Jack and Chloe know?"

"I haven't said anything to them. But you do know that all you have to do is a bit of Googling."

"But I'm Mack now," I whispered.

"It's not such a huge leap from Mackenzie to Mack, doll," Louisa said. Though I don't think she intended to be unkind, her comment revealed how naïve she thought me, how apparent my shame was.

"And voilà, there's Beau," Louisa said, speaking as though this conversation had never taken place and pointing at my truck turning up the driveway. At some point, Beau had stopped asking if he could take my truck. I found it very difficult to get annoyed with him.

Beau's friends tumbled from the vehicle, like some traveling gypsy horde bringing merriment and strangeness. I spotted Fennel's dreadlocks—she had been sitting in the middle of the truck cab, snuggled up to Beau. In a second truck close behind them, I could see the dark snarl of hair that belonged to that girl Zelda. There was a thin, frizzily curled blonde, and one of the guys I recognized from the last visit—Jesse? And the glowing girl I had seen the first time with Fennel, Natasha. A motorcycle pulled in behind them, and two men hopped off, one with a long blond ponytail, the other with a shaved head and marvelous cheekbones. I recalled the freshly visible curve of my bare neck and felt absurdly shy. Screwing my courage to the sticking place, I advanced to welcome Beau's guests. Our guests. This was my place too.

As I approached, Chloe came scampering from the big cabin and raced over to Jesse, excited to report on the development of her bees. His face lit up when he saw her, and he didn't even acknowledge my presence as Chloe rapturously began regaling him with the blow-by-blow of her hives. Beau came forward with his hand extended, and for an exhilarating, giddy moment, I realized he was about to introduce himself. To me. When he drew close enough to see my face, his eyes widened, and I couldn't help but beam in pleasure at his surprise.

"My, my. My *Mack*. Look at you!" he said, delighted, and scooped me up in a spinning hug that left me breathless. "You've been busy," he whispered coyly into my neck before turning back. "Do I need to do some introductions? You remember everyone from the West Hill crew?"

I nodded in reply. "Except for you," I said, reaching my hand towards the thin blonde. "I don't think you were here last time?"

"I'm Kayla. Richardson," she said. There was something a little glazed about her expression.

"Mack. You grow up around here? I know a couple of Richardsons."

"Watkins Glen."

"I went to Lansing. Did you have a brother? Who played baseball?"

"That's Kyle. Jock asshole." Her words were slow, as though she were chewing on marbles.

"I remember him. He was the nemesis of our star player. Andy Reed."

"I don't really remember," Kayla said. "Kyle used to talk about sports all the time. But now he's fat, so he doesn't bring it up."

Zelda snorted. "You can be a mean little bitch," she said fondly to

Kayla, and gave her a kiss that was brief but firmly on the mouth. "I've brought more wine," she announced. "But I should probably deliver it to your fearless leader." She leaned towards me and stroked my shorn skull. "It's enchanting. Very nouvelle vague. You're fetching as fuck. Right!" She hoisted the case of wine a little higher on her hip. "The fiery redhead is at the helm of her ship, I assume?" Without waiting for an answer, Zelda strode off towards the big cabin, Kayla following dutifully behind her, toting a canvas bag with a loaf of bread poking from the top. I joined Beau and Fennel, who were unloading other supplies from the back of the truck.

"I don't know why you invited her," Fennel was saying. "She and that Kayla girl only come to West Hill because Sy is their hookup. And we've been trying to vote Sy out for at least six months."

"Why can't you?" Beau asked.

"It's in our membership bylaws. It's why we're so careful about inviting new members to join. Once they've finished their provisional membership, they have a stake in the Collective and it's really difficult to remove them from the consensus decision-making."

"People change," Beau pointed out.

"Yeah, no shit. I want to amend our community agreement to include a clause about drug use," Fennel said.

"Or illegal activity?" Beau asked. Fennel glanced at him in warning.

"It just doesn't seem practical to not be able to remove members who are jeopardizing the entire project with their personal decisions. The weed was one thing, and we were all in agreement that that was actually a useful member contribution. Well, mostly. Obviously, I don't smoke. Though there was some income. But this is totally something else now."

"You have a formal agreement? At West Hill?" I chimed in. Beau had been, as ever, rather vague about how his friends ran things, and I was desperately curious about their process.

Since my discovery of the notebook, I'd been researching intentional communities and reading extensively about some examples; I'd read about Twin Oaks and the Shakers. I had chuckled over the Alcotts' Fruitlands, imagining Louisa's namesake growing up in the feck-less shambles of that utopia. I was most interested in the Oneida Community, though—our local incarnation of communal life and free love. My research had made me feel that the Homestead might benefit from something a little more rigorously determined. I'd brought it up once with Louisa while we were breaking up topsoil to plant some greens.

"I mean, we're not really that formal, are we?" Louisa had said casu-ally. "Sure, if we make this work for a couple years then, yeah, we should probably consider expanding. And defining what our priorities are and all that. But I mean, for us, we're friends who are experiment-ing. We're not going to go all fucking EcoVillage overnight. Or turn into the Collective."

I nodded. "I know—that's not necessarily what I mean. It's just, in-tentional communities usually have a stated intention," I said timidly.

Louisa looked at me, amused. "Mack, don't you think the endless conversations we have about what we're doing out here qualify as our intentions? Do you think we need to put it all down in writing?"

"That's not what I was saying," I stammered, and then I backed out of the conversation as quickly as I could.

"You like to write everything down," she said, patting me on the hand.

"We've got a formal process for agreeing on new members," Fennel explained to me now, tugging bags from the truck. "We all have to agree at a committee meeting to accept a potential new member for the provisional stay. We usually have to meet someone several times before we even get to that step. I mean, these are people you have to spend years of your life with. Make decisions with. As much as we'd all like to be free spirits about it, there's too much risk."

"And if you do vote someone in?" I asked.

"They stay for six months, so we can all get a feel for whether or not they're a good fit. Then we vote again, to accept them as permanent members who have a share in the Collective."

"Meaning what, exactly?" I pushed.

"Meaning they own a piece of the property we all live on. That their investments and improvements to that property will be acknowledged in the event that they want to leave the Collective at some point."

"Who owns the property?" I asked. Fennel dropped her chin and wouldn't look at Beau. For whatever reason, this question seemed to create tension between them. Beau cleared his throat.

"His name's Matthew" was all he said, heading back to the truck for the rest of the supplies. Everyone congregated near the picnic table. Dusk was falling, and I could feel the cool air on my ankles; I still wore my flats. Fennel launched into further explanations about the minutiae of decision-making chez Collective, but she was interrupted.

"Knock it off, Fennulia! We're all bored with hearing about your rigorous attempts at direct democracy," Zelda cried, walking up to us with bottles under each of her arms. Jesse, the bearded fellow, stood with her, holding bottles of his own and a small wooden box. He set the box down on the picnic table; it was decorated with the image of a wild satyr, painted in the style of an Italian fresco. "I do declare a moratorium," Zelda pronounced. "Jess, uncork the goods, will you?"

Jesse obliged. Louisa appeared at Zelda's elbow, and they winked at each other. Clearly, they had bonded in the kitchen.

"Gather round, friends!" Louisa called. Everyone clustered around the picnic table in response, clamoring to see what sort of feast she'd been preparing for us. But there was no food, none of her usual hectic cornucopia. Instead, Louisa flipped open the lid of the wooden box, revealing withered brown nubs of organic matter. "We're going to eat a little differently tonight," she explained. "Everyone, grab a mushroom. But just one, for now."

"Compliments of our friend Sy," Zelda said, with a wide smirk at Fennel.

"I don't think I *need* one of those," Fennel announced to the general public, hands on her hips. Zelda continued to stare at her while she popped one of the dried mushrooms into her painted maw. Louisa did the same, then blew a kiss at Beau, who followed suit.

I was among the last to claim my little spore. I'd never done any hallucinogens; I had, in fact, smoked limited amounts of weed and done Molly, or whatever the kids are calling it, exactly once, with my Long Island friend from college. She had dragged me to a sweaty club (near Long Beach, I think), and we had danced with manic delight until she had puked outside and left me to call a cab alone; it had cost me twenty dollars to get back to the LIRR, and I'd had to wait, shivering on the platform, until the morning's first train arrived. All in all, the idea of taking any more psychoactive substances made me nervous. But I solidly did not want to be in Fennel's camp, and so when I saw Chloe pluck a button from the box and consider it briefly before shrugging and swallowing it down, I did the same without further reflection.

Zelda poured some wine, though when I leaned in to accept a Ball jar filled with red, she held on to it momentarily.

"Careful with this, sweet pea. You're about to get fairly nauseous, and puking up red wine can really spoil the mood if you're not used to it. Go slow."

I nodded, too nervous to feel insulted by any implied condescension. Had she maybe noticed my delicate tummy last time? I took a tiny sip of the sour red and couldn't help making a face.

"Also, this shit is terrible," Zelda acknowledged, tossing back her glass with a slightly unhinged grin. I watched as she careened off to collide with Louisa, who giggled and caught her. Zelda leaned into her shoulder and whispered something in her ear that made Louisa blush an even deeper hue of rose. Zelda fished a phone out of a deep pocket and handed it to Kayla before tilting in towards Louisa to give her a hearty smack on the cheek. Louisa stared back straight at the phone's camera, eyes blazing.

I was certain the mushrooms hadn't worked, and it seemed like I had taken them hours ago. But as I turned around, I began to feel the early stirrings of something foreign cruising through my neurochemicals. I was afraid of feeling sick, yet excited by the possibility of tripping. I could feel the solstice drawing closer, could feel the earth rising up to greet us as we all surged towards the peak of the growing season.

I imagined my feet sprouting tiny tendrils and burrowing farther into our fields as the seeds we'd planted heaved upward—me settling into this ground, into my place, as the crops I'd sown found me and Beau and Louisa and Jack and Chloe. I watched Chloe leap in her prairie dress and imagined her turning into a willowy tree that would live here at the Homestead forever. I was definitely starting to trip. But this awareness didn't undo the feeling of rightness, of genuine belonging.

Jack appeared at my shoulder and tugged me towards the picnic blanket, a strangely domestic space in the midst of this wild. The border of forest loomed dark around us, and the quilt that lay on the ground became a home, a fortress for us. I collapsed, giggling, onto it, laughing harder as Jack tumbled down next to me, long limbs folding in on themselves like those of a puppet.

"Jack-in-the-box," I said, and magically, Jack looked at me and knew exactly what I meant. He saw his own body moving downward as though someone had pressed a button to turn his bones to jam, and he crumpled into a tiny compressed space. He saw me seeing him see it and he laughed, and I knew I was understood. "Now I see the secret of the making of the best persons! It is to grow outside and eat and sleep with the earth," I informed Jack gravely. "That's the secret."

"Mack, your brain," Jack said, and reached out to touch my short hair. He stroked it as though he were actually stroking the pleated organ beneath it.

"Meh. It's never done me that much good," I said. "These hands, though. Maybe they're the secret."

"No, Mack, no, it's your mind. It's your mind that is . . ." Jack rubbed my hair again, shooting static across my scalp.

"I'm tired of it—I want to leave it behind and go trotting through life without it. With a different one."

"That is the saddest thing I've ever heard," Jack said, musing. "The idea that you don't feel like you have a home inside your own head. That breaks my heart."

"We all just want to be free," I said, trying to pretend that what he'd said hadn't struck some horrifying chord.

"I would give anything to be inside that brain for just one evening," Jack said. "To see the way it works, to watch how you think."

"Well, I suppose that's the purpose of language, no? If I'm doing it right, you should be able to see how I think."

"Jesus. Yes."

"But that doesn't mean I don't want to escape from it sometimes. Escape from myself. Escape from language." Impulsively, I leapt up from the blanket. "Maybe I can." I caught Beau's eye; I realized he had been hovering at the edge of the blanket the whole time, listening to our exchange. *Let it catch me, if it can*, I said, possibly to myself, possibly out loud. I kicked off my flats and sprinted across the clearing, heading straight for the woods. I thought I could hear footsteps behind me, but I couldn't be sure, or determine who they belonged to. I ran as though I could outrun myself, as though I could leave language behind.

In the woods, I began to consider whether my flight was maybe a stoned fancy that would prove to be extremely embarrassing, if not physically disfiguring. Though the forest floor, with its carpet of old leaves, was surprisingly soft, I still stabbed my feet with a twig or rock every few steps, feeling the ground come up to meet me as I streaked thoughtlessly through the trees. The branches snagged at my sweater, and in frustration, I tore it off, leaving it hanging from a tree branch, absently reminding myself that I should return to find it later, since it wasn't mine. I now wore just a simple black tank top and leggings, and I knew I should feel cold, but my skin was roasting. Another branch scratched at my arm, and the pain felt exactly right. So much better to run through these woods, my woods, letting the trees, rather than some garment made in a Southeast Asian sweatshop, touch my skin! I may have hollered these words into the darkness. I stopped listening for footsteps, just flung myself onward, loving the feel of my burning lungs.

Suddenly, I spilled out into a clearing. I didn't recognize it. The moon was up now, and I could see a field stretched out before me. A single pine tree stood in the center. I froze, unable to run farther. I watched with horror as a creature moved at the edge of the field, approaching with a distinctly inhuman gallop. It leapt up and down, and as it neared me I saw horns against the sky. It was a hybrid beast that wanted me. The god Pan, here in our Arcadia. I turned to run, but I couldn't—was I now a nymph, turning into a reed? I tried to scream and made only some strangled cry that echoed into the field. Finally, I shut my eyes and turned my head towards the moon.

"Enough with your barbaric yawping," Beau said firmly, and my eyelids snapped open. How did he know Whitman was on my mind? Because he knew me!

"The goat. It's Pan. I'm a nymph. Or a dryad," I said.

"You are indeed. Shoo, Black Phillip," he said to the god Pan, and pulled me close to him. I should have been afraid to breathe, afraid to say anything to him, but we were both different now, I could tell. Running through the woods had changed us. I put my hand to his cheek and craned my neck back to kiss him, very gently.

"You. You are faster than you look," he said simply.

"Mm-hmm," I agreed, kissing him again. This time I bit his lip—not savagely, but not exactly delicately. "You never would have caught me unless I wanted you to."

"I'm glad you did."

"For now." I snaked my hands around his hips and leaned backward, collapsing into the grass, pulling Beau down on top of me. I felt his hips grind his weight into me, and I coiled one leg around him, clinging to his rib cage. I let him kiss me a moment or two longer before I pushed his shoulders back and rolled on top of him. Straddling his middle, I looked down at him, at his familiar jaw and the jut of his lip, which I had memorized so many months ago. His eyes were dark, and the expression in them made me smile. Like he was overcome. I peeled off my tank top and felt my skin ripple, could feel the moon shining behind me. I imagined what I looked like, my short hair and hard nipples rimmed by the light.

We tugged each other's clothes off until we were both naked. The wild weeds scratched at my skin, but I didn't mind, and at long last, I fucked Beau senseless in the clearing, thinking of how much we would grow and change.

We must have dozed off temporarily, as impossible as it seemed with the mushrooms coursing through my system. I had the sensation of having momentarily left my body—perhaps achieving what I had just fantasized about with Jack. I sat up, wondering if I would be able to locate all my clothes, then wondering if I would mind wandering back to the Homestead naked. I currently felt I would not.

"Hey, you," Beau said softly next to me. "That was fun."

"Yes sir, it was," I agreed, leaning down to give him another kiss before springing up. "I'm still feeling a little flighty."

"Oh, really?" Beau grinned at me mischievously. "Three-second head start."

I shrieked and dashed towards the pine tree in the center of the field. Now my fleet-footedness seemed to have deserted me. Or perhaps I wanted to be caught. In any case, after a moment or two of giddy prancing, Beau gathered me up in his arms and swung me around easily.

"You're so tiny," he murmured, and for once I felt not like some stunted, underdeveloped creature but more like something spritely, unearthly. We grappled, naked in the middle of the field, until I heard a soft braying noise.

"Pan!" I said again. "He's back."

"Let's find him—maybe he has something to say," Beau said, and I couldn't tell whether he was mocking me or dead serious. We began to race across the field, looking for the god.

"Goat!" I called, and tried to imitate his hearty bleat. Beau chuckled and did the same. I was giggling at his interpretation when I nearly slammed into Jack.

"There you are. I called for you in the woods, and you kept talking back, answering me," Jack said. "We're getting naked now?"

I burst out laughing anew. Sweet Jack. "I love you, Jack," I said earnestly, and curved up to give him a kiss. I drew him towards me and grabbed Beau's wrist. We stood, the two of them towering above me. I kissed Beau, then Jack, then Beau, drawing them closer with each kiss until all three pairs of lips met in the middle. I leaned back to watch them, tormented and turned on at once.

"Now I'm fucking freezing and I'd like to find my undies," I finally said.

"Treasure hunt!" Jack answered happily, breaking the kiss, and we grabbed each other's hands and raced back towards where I thought Beau and I had left our things. Ferdinand bleated again, and we saw him shuffling around the little circle of our clothing. He'd gotten a corner of Beau's black shirt, and we wrestled it away from him, leaving in his mouth a ragged tithe to the deity. I dressed, wondering why I felt so unself-conscious, but delirious with the feeling. We gave Ferdinand a fond nuzzle and tried to convince him to come back to the Homestead with us. In goaty fashion, though, he stubbornly headed off towards something of more caprine interest. Jack was chattering happily, covering a lot of intellectual ground very quickly. I smiled at him, then at Beau. My boys.

We had been much closer to the Homestead than I had thought, and we rejoined the party with no one remarking on our absence. Chloe sat on the picnic table with a rapt circle of admirers at her feet as she sang and strummed chords on her ukulele—presumably some of her former co-op friends had arrived while we were racing in the woods. Louisa and Zelda lay on the picnic blanket staring up at the sky and whispering to each other. The two men who had come on the motorcycle were making out in the grass not far away. Fennel was sitting next to Jesse, talking to him in a steady stream that Jesse didn't seem very inclined to interrupt. He was watching Chloe. I grabbed a bottle of wine from the picnic table and took a giant slug, grinning happily at this scene. Argos bounded over to me and nuzzled my midriff with his big sweet head. I crouched down to tussle with him, and whispered in his ear:

"We're soulmates, buddy, you and me. Built to run." He poked his wet nose squarely into my mouth in response, and I hugged his scruffy neck. He smelled like he had been in the pond, but I didn't care.

We finally crashed around dawn, creeping back towards our cabins or cars feeling chemically depleted but strangely buoyant. Beau offered to drive the West Hill kids home, and for once, Louisa didn't seem particularly concerned about whether he was going to stay over or not; Fennel insisted on driving, in any case, which even Louisa had to admit was reasonable. She and Zelda had fallen asleep on the blanket, and when Zelda woke her up, Louisa beamed at her, and asked her if she wanted to stay.

"No, firebird. I've got things to do, I'm afraid. Busy day for me." She wore a sad smile as she said it, and turned to wave goodbye as she clambered back into her truck. Her friend Kayla had fallen asleep in the cab not too long after dark and looked like she was still unconscious, curled up in some sort of shawl. Louisa moseyed back to her cabin, waving at Chloe and me as she yawned. Chloe, Jack, and I had a cup of tea and watched the sun rise over the Homestead, feeling the calm settle over us before we dissipated, heading back to our own cabins. We wouldn't be making a dent in repairing the drying shed today, I guessed.

Chapter 14

We learned of Zelda's death two weeks later. Beau arrived home on his bicycle one afternoon after a visit to West Hill, his face drawn, and trailed by the blond waif Kayla, who struggled with an oversized bike. He called us all to the picnic table, and we sat in the full sunlight, expecting to hear something awful.

"It was a fire, in her barn. On the night of the solstice," he explained. "It's not official yet, but they're investigating. So far it looks like an accident, but they have to be sure. Her sister should be arriving at their house any minute."

"Ava. *That* fucking girl," spat Louisa. "What utter bullshit. I don't see how she can show her face in this town after leaving the way she did."

I assumed from this comment that she knew something more of Zelda's situation than the rest of us did, but I figured now was probably not the time for gossip.

"Ava'll be here soon, anyway. I mean, at her house," Kayla stated.

"Will there be a funeral?" Chloe asked gently, laying a hand on Louisa's arm. I could see Louisa fighting not to cry.

"They don't know yet. I don't know if you know much about her family," Beau said, glancing at Louisa's downturned face briefly, "but it's fairly chaotic at the vineyard, especially now."

"Fuck this," Louisa said, shaking her head. "I don't believe it."

"I saw her, that night," Kayla said, stuttering a little. "I went to the barn. She was strung out, Louisa."

"So what?"

"She was—I don't know, barely upright. She seemed totally out of it."

"So you think she accidentally lit herself on fire?" Louisa bristled.

I was surprised to see this demonstration of her attachment. Or perhaps I had flattered myself; I'd thought she took a shine to only a select few. That I was special. If she had so easily fallen for Zelda, what did that say about me? I felt selfish for thinking about it.

"Look, she hasn't been herself," Kayla explained. Louisa was glowering dangerously, and I could see the curve of Chloe's neck as she moved her entire self towards Louisa, to comfort. Jack looked unsure where to put his empathy and adopted a hangdog expression to communicate his general forlornness. I couldn't read Beau.

"I want to see her," Louisa announced. "I want to talk to the sister."

"I don't think you do," Kayla said. "She's a fucking piece of work."

"Give me her phone number. I need to speak with her."

"I don't know it! That bitch has been incommunicado for two years," Kayla said. "She lives in France. Zelda only talked about her when she got really drunk. Which I guess was kind of often," she admitted with a shrug.

Louisa strode off abruptly; it seemed like she might be crying.

"She's not used to feeling powerless," Chloe said, observing Louisa's posture, the squaring of her shoulders.

"We're all powerless," Jack said, with a note of bitterness. "Louisa has just been insulated from it her whole life by illusions of control. No thanks to her parents." His biting tone surprised me; Jack could be a sharp analyst, capable of summing a person up in a short, cold phrase, but only rarely would he be truly nasty. But he would counterbalance these moments of crotchetiness with pure, youthful joy: at a new idea, a sprouting scallion, a pregnant goat. I suspected he would be at his best when he was seventy: a fine wine, ripened to its proper age.

Seeing Louisa put the phone back in her pocket, Chloe went to her side, and I felt that eternal pang of exclusion, watching how they turned to each other. Louisa seemed so calmed by Chloe's presence at her side, even though her agitation at the phone call she had just ended was still visible. I envied Chloe's unerring ease, her infallible intuition for how to approach the skittish racehorse, as well as Louisa's willingness to turn to her, let Chloe comfort her. I knew I was capable of neither.

Jack decided to trail after the girls, and Beau wandered off to his cabin. But Kayla remained next to the picnic table, one foot scuffing the dust, alone as we all walked away.

I was shocked at the extent of Louisa's rage and sadness—it felt as though she were grieving, but as far as I knew, she had met Zelda only a few times, so her attachment seemed weirdly intense. I wondered if they'd known each other in different contexts, or if they had somehow spent more time together than I had been aware of. Louisa was too cranky for me to risk bringing this up with her, and Chloe appeared to know no more than I did.

We read Zelda's obituary—a rather bizarre one—in the newspaper, and when a Facebook event was created for her memorial service, Louisa insisted we all go. Jack and I balked; we both felt awkward, as though our presence would be not only unappreciated but somehow even gauche.

The truth is, though, that I felt Beau hovering, and I fantasized that perhaps, for the first time, he might in some way be within my grasp. With Louisa alternately fuming and moribund, Chloe was occupied with comforting her, making sure she didn't fly off the handle. This left Beau unoccupied. The morning of the memorial service, I caught myself giving him wry winks and the odd knowing glance with a sauciness that might have come off as manufactured, if I hadn't felt so newly and strangely confident. And it seemed to me that only Beau could see the change.

We weren't the first to arrive at Silenus, Zelda's family vineyard; the parking lot was already modestly filled with other battered pickups and a handful of tired Volvos. I quailed at the thought of arriving late; I had attended only two funerals—for each of my mother's parents—and both had been rather formal affairs, with visiting hours at a funeral home and a full liturgy at the church. Both had been remarkably dull. I had a feeling this one wouldn't be.

Kayla, who had hitched a ride with us, immediately hopped out of the truck and raced for the door of the tasting room, leaving us behind. We dawdled by the vehicle while Beau smoked a cigarillo, this the only indication that he felt on edge. His little cigars were props that masked any discomfort with an anachronistic puff of smoke. I wondered if Louisa and Chloe knew this about him, had observed him closely enough to notice the way he hooded his eyes when he lit the cigar tip, buying himself a moment of inscrutable contemplation of his shoes while he collected himself. I wanted to know if Louisa and Chloe had cataloged the different ways his eyes could squint: in mirth, in irritation, in an attempt at secrecy. I wanted these observations to be mine alone.

We wandered in three or four minutes after Kayla, and I was surprised by the scene. There were no elaborate bouquets of white hothouse flowers, no priest solemnly comforting each arrival, no cluster of hunched mourners who clearly belonged to the deceased. Instead, the tasting room at Silenus looked rather like a party, with wineglasses being handed around and a general social milling about. The view was spectacular; I had been driven up Route 414 along Seneca Lake a few times, but the vista still took my breath, even though it resembled the west shore of my own Cayuga Lake. The sprawl of the vineyards made it look like a different part of the world, the way I imagined maybe Lake Como, or some fantastically remote New Zealand panorama. I stood by the window to gawk and eavesdrop; I wanted a good view of the action, when it arrived. Jack brought me a glass of chardonnay, which he held up to the light appreciatively.

"It's a reserve, apparently," he said happily, and I couldn't help smiling. Jack loved to eat and drink, and he was an enthusiastic taster of anything put before him. But he had a more or less undiscerning palate—he enjoyed most wines with equal gusto. I'd noticed he liked to store up knowledge, and, for him, learning about the local wines was much like reading about different tomato irrigation methods. Information to be stored, then deployed at a later date. I sipped. Even my underdeveloped palate balked. Jack swished it around his glass and squinted knowledgeably.

"Not as oaky as I would expect," he concluded before sloshing at least a third of the glass into his mouth for a second try.

"Sure," I said. I was desperately curious to see Zelda's twin sister, whom I thought should be obvious but who seemed, bizarrely, not to be in attendance. I sidled along the balcony, looking out at the twinkly water and the plunge of grapes down to the shore. After a moment's contemplation of the view, I felt somebody at my side, and then saw Chloe's hand appear, bearing some sort of cracker.

"You should eat this," she said, holding out her gift. "Someone brought some really tasty Brie." I smiled, and let her pop it into my mouth. As I chewed, some crumbs tumbled from my lips.

"Good," I managed. "I like it."

"This is a really weird party," she said, shaking her head. She was wearing her hair up today, and the golden fuzz on the back of her neck caught the sunlight. Why didn't my skin look like that?

"Do you think Fennel and co will come?" I asked.

"I doubt it. Fennel wouldn't bother with the social graces."

"I suppose not." A frail woman in a wheelchair had just trundled out onto the balcony. In one hand, she clutched a full glass of white wine, which sloshed dangerously with each awkward maneuver. We were standing closest to her, and Chloe instinctively lurched to help her. Of course, Chloe never *actually* lurched; in a single movement, she curved her body towards the older woman, and in the graceful, clean way she always moved, she steadied the wheelchair and the woman's rickety arm. I saw Jack preparing to make the same adjustment, but instead he knocked his own wineglass onto a bystander's plate, and was forced to turn and deal with the damage.

"Did you want to get closer to the view?" Chloe asked, preparing to take the woman's glass to set on the edge of the balcony. The woman stubbornly hung on to it.

"Ha. I've seen enough of this view for three lifetimes. If this is the last time I have to stare at it, it will be enough." She snorted and took a serious slurp from her glass, her eyes going almost blank. "You two knew 'the deceased,' then?" she asked, turning back to us with a sharpness that surprised me.

"Not well," I said. "But we were acquaintances."

"Zelda had a hard time holding down real friends," the woman said with a cruel smile. "Still, nice to see a full house of gawkers." She drained the rest of her wine. Chloe glanced at me. The woman regarded her empty glass despairingly, and began the ungainly process of turning her chair around. "Should've stayed near the bar," she mumbled.

"Can I—can I get you a refill?" Chloe asked.

"That would be lovely," the woman said, handing off the glass. Chloe raised her eyebrows at me and disappeared inside. I stood, shrugging against the scratchiness of my shirt, trying to think of something to say.

"Pretty day," I attempted. Around the Finger Lakes, everyone is always happy to discuss the weather.

The woman said nothing. She looked down at her idle hand, which was trembling. When she noticed me looking, too, she met my eyes.

"A pretty day for a death?" she asked.

"That's not— I mean, I didn't mean—"

She waved away my stammering.

"You don't need to take me seriously. No one else does. What's your name, little thing?"

"Mack," I said, extending a hand. She reached out her shaky claw for my own. Her skin was soft; her hands seemed even older than she was.

"Mack," she repeated, looking at my face. "Not . . . Mackenzie?" Did she know my parents? I wondered. Remember me from childhood, maybe? "You're the one from that silly TV show? Who fucked up so badly?"

Her recognition caught me off guard—I suppose I had grown numb from living off-grid, in my little bubble. I saw with alarm that Chloe was standing behind her, a bottle tucked into the crook of her arm and two glasses in hand.

"I—it was a long time ago," I stuttered. "It was just on the air for a little while."

"Ha! I loved that show. *The Millennial Experiment*. Perfect. I watched it with my daughter." She waved a hand behind her head. "She thought it was hilarious. All you kids in Brooklyn, monkeying around. Great show. And then of course with you, and all that drama—excellent television! My God, Zelda would be so pleased that you're here. Mind you, she was generally not fully conscious when we watched your show, so who knows."

I looked up at Chloe, whose eyebrows were at her hairline.

"Wine for you, dear," she said, stooping down to hand over one of the glasses she had now filled.

"And aren't you a peach," the woman said. In the background, I could hear the sound of someone cuing up music, and I became aware of people congregating in the center of the room. We all turned to look. "I guess I'd better get back to my daughter's funeral. It wouldn't look good if I missed it. Hand me that bottle, would you, sweetheart? Or else my other ridiculous daughter will ration me half a glass every hour. Be a doll."

Chloe paused, then handed over the bottle. Emptying her glass, the woman put it in her lap and wheeled much more nimbly inside. I looked over at Chloe.

"I suppose you caught that," I said, pursing my lips.

"I did, though, I'm not sure—look, if you don't want to talk about it . . ."

I sighed. "I don't. But there's no point pretending it didn't happen anymore. The Internet is a horribly permanent thing."

Chloe reached out her hand and encircled my wrist with her two fingers. "You don't have to."

"Look, I really regret all of it," I began. "I never should have agreed to the show in the first place. But I thought it would help my research.

My dissertation work was on 'closed communities.' I'd originally thought I'd do fieldwork on prison culture, and then I was talking with my supervisor and we started discussing reality TV. As a joke, at first. Only after a while, it occurred to me that no one had really written much on the culture within these shows, like *Survivor* or *The Bachelor* or whatever. I got fascinated, and when I heard about this thing that was casting in Brooklyn, where I was living, I kind of couldn't resist."

"You were going to write about it?" Chloe asked, her blue eyes so open.

"Yes. Maybe. I knew methodologically it probably wouldn't fly, and my supervisor was pretty leery, but I just . . . I'd gotten so curious, you know? I figured it would be a jumping-off point. Maybe I could write an article about it, maybe it could be a chapter of my dissertation. Anyway. The show was called *The Millennial Experiment*, and it was a bunch of twenty-somethings who would have to live in this warehouse in Brooklyn and start up an urban farm and business. The challenges were like, who could make the best bathtub mozzarella or who could bottle the most kombucha and sell it to the local market. It was a bit self-mocking, you know, a bunch of hipsters doing the most hipster thing they could think of. But you could tell everyone was kind of into it, you know? And we all had to live in this weird, open-plan warehouse and everyone was sleeping together, of course. It was like a polyamory dating competition with homemade beer."

"I have no idea what that would be like," Chloe said with a huge smile, and I laughed.

"Yes, the irony isn't lost on me. Anyway, it was all drama and selling the roof-grown gladiolas at the farmers' market for the first couple of weeks. But eliminations started and people got weird and catty and it started to be a lot less . . . collaborative.

"There was one person who I just hadn't gotten along with from the beginning. We'd had this little competitive thing going, and it started to get a bit mean. Anyway, she was trans, but she wasn't out and uh . . . well, I got drunk on moonshine one night and during an interview, I outed her on camera, to the producers. I mean, they knew, of course, and I later found out she'd asked to not have it be part of the show until she could talk about it on her terms." I coughed to cover my discomfort. I'd spent months trying to repress what I'd said and done, desperate that my chance to start over would somehow undo this moment of colossal carelessness. "But *I* talked about it, at length, in my interview. I stayed on the show for a couple more weeks because no one really knew what I'd done, but of course the show aired, and the producers just . . . they played up that betrayal so that it was basically the central part of the show. Sara found out when the episode aired and . . . I mean, it was a social media shitshow. *Experiment* wasn't even all that popular—it aired on some off-brand channel. People tweeted just . . . awful things. But, of course, what I'd done was fucking horrible. I'd told someone else's story, without permission, on television. It was brutal, but . . . I kind of deserved it."

"You made a mistake, Mack," Chloe said, pulling me closer. "You don't deserve to be publicly pilloried for it."

"Well, I was. I got my own Twitter hashtag. #terfymackenzie. And when everyone found out where I was a grad student, my department got pressure to kick me out of the program. Which they did, of course. Even though I was probably going to drop out on my own. I had no desire to keep going with my research after all that."

"You kind of have, though, right?" Chloe asked.

"Not on TV," I said with a snort. "I guess my intellectual interests remain intact, but I . . . really, really like that we live off-grid."

"I would've thought you'd never try living with a group of people again."

"I didn't think so, either. But I met you guys, and then, I don't know, after that day at the waterfall . . . this just felt so *real*. That—the show—I mean, it was just that. A show, a performance. This"—I clutched her fingers—"we're—"

"I'm glad you didn't give up," she said. "And I'm really glad you deleted your Twitter account."

❦

Beau brought us to the first protest a few weeks later. He'd been attending demonstrations with Fennel and her friends, and Louisa had been pushing for an invitation since the very beginning.

"I realize it's a public protest, but I'm not going to just pitch up and stand around by myself. I want to go with you, I want to meet all the different groups and their respective spokespeople," she had said, verging on a whine.

"It's not like there are 'spokespeople,' Lou," Beau explained. "It's a protest. We're all just civilians demonstrating."

"I get that. But there's always an element of social organizing, and I want to understand that. Besides, I don't even know which interest groups are there."

"'Interest groups' sounds a little sinister," Jack pointed out.

"Whatever. I know there are different concerns. There are the people who care about natural gas storage, and the ones who care about fracking, and the ones who care about windmills—maybe your friend Fennel could talk me through it someday," she said.

"She would be *your* friend too," Beau said. "If you'd let her."

"Would she?" Louisa said in an arch tone. "We both know how Fennel feels about that, remember? I know exactly where her loyalties lie."

Beau wisely remained silent.

Jack went to a demonstration with Beau before we did—Jack rarely felt uncomfortable in social situations that would make most people squirm, and he apparently didn't share Louisa's compunction about securing proper introductions; he moved through crowds of strangers with easy joy. When he came back, he reported to us that it was "very chill" and we should all go together for the next one.

So, one week in July, we all piled into my pickup and headed towards Watkins Glen. The demonstration was to take place just out of town, at Lakeview, a company that was involved in—fracking? natural gas extraction? I was a little patchy on what, exactly, the precise purpose of the protest was, but in general I was comfortable protesting any corporate power.

When we got there, a small but vocal coterie of folks was blocking the driveway to a storage facility, holding up banners that exhorted us to PROTECT OUR WATERS and STOP GAS STORAGE and there were the requisite number of cardboard signs depicting two-color images of the earth, typically overlaid with peace signs. I immediately saw Fennel standing with Natasha and Jesse. Kayla stood there, too, her hair clumped and ratty, the bones of her arms poking out. She looked terrible. Next to her stood Sy, a gaunt and pallid young man who inhabited one of the Collective's yurts. Though I'd heard Fennel mention him, tetchily, I'd yet to meet him. His black hair was scraggly, and his beard grew in patches. I watched as Chloe walked directly to Kayla and gave her a long hug; Kayla's arms flapped momentarily around Chloe's torso before falling back to her sides. She barely met Chloe's eyes.

"You okay? You doing all right?" Chloe asked, stroking a jagged clump of hair that had fallen from Kayla's unkempt ponytail. Kayla nodded mutely and unconvincingly. "I know," Chloe said, and held on to her thin wrist. Beau had joined Fennel's side, and they were in conference over the developments of the protest so far.

"It's been quiet. Normally they've already arrested a few people by this point, but the cops have been weirdly quiet," Fennel explained, pointing to some officers in uniform hovering near cruisers. "So far it's just the usual suspects out today. The old-timers—and us."

"So what's the goal?" Louisa asked, scanning the crowd.

"Civil disobedience," Fennel said. From the tone of her voice, she might as well have tacked on a "no duh."

"But surely there's an ultimate goal to your civil disobedience?" Louisa asked with mock good nature. "A change in policy? An overturning of a court order?"

"Bill has pamphlets. There's a website," Fennel said, gesturing towards some of the other protesters.

Louisa stood a moment longer, clearly considering saying something, but after a glance from Beau she forced another smile. "Right. I guess I'll go talk to the organizers then. They'll probably be better informed, anyway." She flounced off towards the core group of people clustered behind the long WE ARE SENECA LAKE banner; most of them were middle-aged or older. The protest generation.

"Here," Natasha said to me, rummaging in her backpack. She held out a small sign that read NO FRACKING WAY. She added, "We always try to make some extras."

"For us newbies?" I asked, accepting the slice of heavyweight paper.

"Yeah, for people who are just starting to get involved. It's a tough thing. We're not necessarily raised or educated to practice dissent. There's a learning curve."

"The mass of men serve the state, not as men but as machines, with their bodies," I said flippantly.

"Is that Orwell?" Natasha asked.

"Oh, I don't think so." I laughed. "Probably just something I read in *The New Inquiry*." I don't know why I lied. Was I embarrassed about how many times I'd read Thoreau? Should I have been?

"Oh," she said with a shrug. "But yeah, in effect." We stood, shuffling side to side, both mildly uncomfortable.

"It's Thoreau," Beau said suddenly from behind my ear, making me jump.

"Jesus, do you have everything memorized?" I asked.

"Seems like you do."

"It just . . . came to me. I read a lot of him when we decided to . . . head out here. You know."

"Are you guys Thoreau fanboys?" Natasha asked, amused.

"No," I said, before Beau could agree. "I appreciate what he did and what he wrote but, I mean, the man was eating his mom's cucumber sandwiches the whole time. He went home to do laundry."

"But that's what made it possible for him to write," Beau said. "Which, granted, hasn't revolutionized the world but is still, you have to admit, damned influential."

"Sure, but doesn't his absolute position of privilege negate, I don't know, his sacrifices or his insistence on self-reliance? That whole 'Economy' section is basically just a tract hating on poor people."

"Not the most progressive stance, I grant you," Beau agreed. "But I still maintain that his beef was with capitalism, not the poor as such."

"Still, the fact remains that we can't all just withdraw from the world, like he did," Natasha insisted.

"That is absolutely true," Beau conceded, and he lapsed into a thoughtful silence. We stood, awkwardly.

"Would it be, like, an incredible faux pas to ask how you're feeling about the primaries?" I finally asked, not sure what else to say.

"Do not bring that up around Fennel," Natasha said with an alarmed expression. "Unless you want to start a blood feud."

"Or Louisa." Beau grinned. "There might be hair-pulling if those two girls get the chance to talk politics." As though reminded that Louisa was on the loose, he swirled off to be by her side.

"What's the deal with those two, anyway? Fennel and Louisa, I mean," I asked once Beau was out of hearing. "Do they have, like, a history?"

Natasha shrugged with exaggerated nonchalance. "I'm not exactly sure. You should ask Louisa."

I felt like I was carefully being redirected. "It just feels like there's a lot of rancor there—I don't quite get it," I said.

Natasha bobbed her head in agreement. "But what is democracy if not discord?" she asked with a deliberately wistful note.

"Emerson?"

"Who knows?" she said to me, and grinned.

A protest, as it turns out, can be fairly dull, especially if the police are treating it with a lack of interest. We chanted for a bit, sang a handful of Pete Seeger songs, and rocked back and forth on our increasingly aching feet. Finally, the cops asked us to move and arrested a handful of the older generation when they refused to disband.

"We have to space out our arrests," Fennel explained. "The Collective only budgets for so many bail hearings, and we're currently out of disposable cash for legal fees."

"Ah, the practical limitations of radicalism," Louisa said. Her smiles were distinctly passive-aggressive. "You know, my dad's a lawyer. I could ask him if he'd be willing to do some pro bono work during hearings or whatever. If you want."

"That would be really, really helpful," Natasha chimed in before Fennel could answer.

"Mack? Could you do me a favor?" Fennel asked. She was not in the habit of asking favors, and her voice sounded false.

"Sure," I said.

"Could you take a picture? Of me and Beau?"

"Oh . . . okay." What else could I say? Louisa glowered at me. I raised my phone to capture them.

"No, actually, let's stand over here. And use this." She held out a digital camera—I'd only seen her ancient flip phone, which didn't even have a camera. Frankly, I was surprised she didn't use an old-school device with film. She tugged Beau away from the group, so that they were directly in front of the gates the officers were attempting to clear. The drive up to the facility snaked away behind them. "Great, that's great," she said, giving me permission. I snapped a few images and offered her the camera to check my work.

"I don't know how—Beau, can you show me?" she asked, leaning towards Beau to look at the screen.

"You don't know how to use a digital camera?" Louisa asked.

"I don't like technology," Fennel said airily. "I borrowed this one."

Louisa rolled her eyes and turned away. Beau flipped through the photos I'd taken, and Fennel frowned.

"That one's good, but we need one where you can see the parking lot, where the trucks are," she said, holding the camera up for a selfie. Beau snaked his long arms up to push the button, adjusting the angle. They took a few shots, checking them each time.

"There," Fennel finally said. "Perfect."

"Let's get out of here and go get lit," Sy said. He'd been mostly silent during the demonstration, huddled next to an equally quiet Kayla. At his suggestion, Kayla bobbed her head enthusiastically. Fennel's face darkened, and irritation tautened her wiry frame.

"Not all of us need to get 'lit' to have fun," she said.

A long, awkward moment of silence followed. "You all should come back to the Collective," Natasha said to break the silence.

"Yeah, it'd be nice for you guys to show everyone the greenhouse," Beau said. "I've been bragging about it."

"Well, we haven't planned much for the community meal," Fennel said defensively. "The sprouts were only supposed to be for ten people, and Mike hasn't stopped by with the new bags of spelt, so we're running a little low."

"Oh, don't worry, Fennel," Chloe said. "We don't eat much." Louisa cracked an enormous smile and looped her arm through Chloe's. Fennel turned around to head to her van without comment, and Beau went with her.

"You know the way, Louisa," Natasha said, packing up her signs. "See you at the Collective?" As they walked away, I could hear Fennel talking to Beau, sotto voce:

"Can you get those photos to me? You know we need some more images, and of course, he wants to see them, too, before we move ahead."

Who could she mean? But I was too busy watching Louisa nibble Chloe's collarbone to register more than vague curiosity.

The Collective made the Homestead look amateurish and feral. I'd been so proud just days earlier, watching bunches of dill proliferate and tugging grubby radishes from the ground. But the Collective was significantly better organized, better manned, and better maintained than our little cluster of vegetables and rickety sheds.

The property was not entirely dissimilar to our own; there was a small farmhouse that served as the central structure, along with a number of smaller buildings radiating out from the house that functioned as housing and food storage and processing facilities. Fennel and Natasha each occupied a room upstairs in the farmhouse, where they held court, organized schedules, and monitored the kitchen. Sy and Jesse each had a small, functional yurt near the border of the clearing in which the Collective sat.

"Fennel was a founding member, I want to say, six years ago," explained Natasha, who was giving me, Chloe, and Jack a tour. Beau and Louisa had stayed behind in the kitchen. "Though none of the other founding members are in permanent residence anymore. Fennel's former partner, Mischa, still comes out once or twice a year to vote on new charter amendments. She's working on her dissertation on anarchic communities, and the Collective is one of her case studies. The founder, Matthew, stops in from time to time, though we never know when to expect him. Bit of a mystery man." Natasha led us through the low-ceilinged rooms of the farmhouse. The floors were a scuffed but sturdy wood. The molding, though chipped, was still intact and pleasantly rustic.

"Sy and Jesse came about three years ago, a little while before I did. They built their yurts at the same time. I came when they were finishing up construction, and took over Katie's bedroom. She was an original member who ended up moving back to California, where there's a satellite collective." She led us outside and pointed to the other buildings in quick succession. "That's the drying shed, the smokehouse, and the root cellar. The vegans live in that A-frame, that's Anjie and Jake, and that little cabin is for initiates, people who haven't been approved yet."

"Initiates?" I mumbled to Jack, who winked back at me.

"The greenhouse is probably our most important structure these days. The growing season is so short here that you have to be able to extend it a few months or you'll never manage to put enough up before the cold. You guys have a greenhouse yet?"

"Not exactly," I said, maybe a little defensively. "We did our seedlings in the kitchen window. Next winter we want to put in a small greenhouse, though."

"Yeah, until you do, you'll really struggle to get your tomatoes going in time, and you'll be waiting all summer for your cukes unless you get them started early. Fennel can share the seedling schedule she's been putting together for the last few years." We walked around the greenhouse, squinting through the cloudy plastic at the rows of tomatoes already turning a lovely blush.

"This is the garden," Natasha said, pointing to their much more substantial plot next to the greenhouse. Rows of squash and lettuce put our garden to shame, and their fences were much sturdier and taller than our own chicken-wire iterations. We walked to the edge of the woods and forged into the brush beneath the pines and oaks, sniffing the heady smell of deciduous and coniferous foliage in varying stages of budding and decay.

"And here's Fennel's pride and joy." Natasha swept one arm towards a series of logs arranged in straight lines under the thick shadow of a particularly dense cluster of trees.

"Stumps?" I asked with a frown.

"We've been calling it the mushroom factory." As I looked more closely at the logs, I could see pockets of fungi cropping up in soggy profusions, their dun color contrasting against the occasional swath of bright green moss. "Production's not quite where we want it yet, I'm afraid," Natasha explained, "but we're gearing up for a decent season in the autumn. We've had to experiment quite a bit with different species, to see what will grow well here."

"God, what if you could get truffles going?" Chloe speculated. "You could make a fortune at the farmers' market."

"I know, right? Locally produced forest gold." Natasha smiled. "Though I wouldn't mention it around Fennel. She hates that we still have to sell things."

We circled around the mushroom logs and headed back towards the farmhouse, our eyes filled with envy at the well with a pump, from which they gathered gallon after gallon of fresh water, at the shower stall with a much more efficient rain catchment than our own, at the large outdoor grill pit lined with brick.

"Well, you don't have a sauna," Jack said with equanimity. "So there."

In the kitchen, Fennel was boiling a vat of rice and a corresponding bucket of indeterminate beans. She declined offers of help, so we six found ourselves standing around the rugged kitchen table feeling unwanted and aimless. Finally too uncomfortable to continue loitering quietly, I grabbed a pot and said I would get some more water from the well and excused myself.

Outside, I breathed in the smells of manure and hay. We hadn't been shown the barn, and I knew there were animals because Natasha had brought us sheep's milk cheese and a few gallons of cow's milk. The atmosphere inside was so oddly hostile, I figured that livestock might make for better company. Leaving my water pot by the well, I struck off towards the only structure that could conceivably be a barn. The scent of warm animals confirmed my guess as I approached the doors and slung them open.

The pigs, sensing a human presence and suspecting snacks, barreled towards the edge of their stall. Two huge snouts poked through the rough beams, sniffing for any treats I might be carrying.

"Sorry, guys," I said. "I don't have anything for you." The sheep remained in the corner of their pen, escaping the heat of the day in the cool straw of their enclosure. One bleated companionably as I walked by. The enclosed part of the chicken coop was empty; everyone was out pecking at worms and insects in the dust of the yard, and they would come in only at dark, to roost and wait out the night in fear of foxes.

In the corner of the room sat a large metal cabinet that looked out of place; it was much newer than anything else in the barn, and there was a combination lock on its front door. I walked over to it, as curious as anyone when confronted with a barred door. I pulled on the combo lock, and to my surprise, it clicked open. Looking over my shoulder to see if I was being watched, I slid the lock from the clasp and opened the door.

Inside the metal closet hung two automatic weapons that I would guess were AK-47s—at least, these were the only type I had heard of. They looked military and menacing, hung on pegs against the back of the cabinet. There was also a shotgun slung less lovingly on a hook, and two handguns in holsters pegged to the wall. Shaken, I slammed the door shut and replaced the combo lock. I tried to lock it properly, but I realized a mechanism had jammed—the lock was unusable. Guilty and troubled, I slunk from the barn and headed back to the house, letting myself in through the kitchen's side door.

No one had missed me.

Chapter 15

As I'd read through William's journal and had gotten to know the West Hill Collective, something had begun to take shape in my mind: a Story. Because he broke his journal into seasons, I found that I could sense the slip and drag of time on this patch of land along with him. His entry about the child's death had reminded me of that cold day when Chloe and I had fallen through the ice in the pond, and I could feel our narratives twining and converging. I could sense them knitting together with the instinctual tug I'd been trained to obey, to sense the tremble of some truth and spin it into a fully formed thesis. And while I had left my schooling in my preferred vocation, I still fancied that I had something of that intuition. I was certain that there was more to be unearthed, and that I alone could knot together the disparate threads that would make a narrative. Maybe I couldn't redeem myself professionally, but I could perhaps remake myself, produce something of worth. The notes and writing I had been accumulating in my months at the Homestead began to line up, and through the messy veil of words I'd been amassing I could begin to see how to connect all of them.

I couldn't think too hard about what I would do with my story once I had written it, but I spent some time fantasizing about the possibilities. If I could publish it under a different name, maybe I could start over, without the tarnish of what had happened. Could I leave behind my shame? I could scarcely allow myself to think about the alternative: to publish with my own name, to write something so wonderful that it would annihilate the blemish on my identity and remake me as the teller of this new story. I was galvanized, envisioning, for the first time, a return to the future I had tried to secure for myself—perhaps no longer within academe, but maybe, possibly, within the larger world of letters?

I craved information. My project was currently anecdotal, a handful of recipes and copies of entries from Jack's planting almanac, little snippets of life here at the Homestead. The narrative I had in mind would collapse the past and the present, so that the historic attempts to carve out a life here would meld into the current one. I knew so little about the Collective—or, for that matter, the strange utopians who had set up shop here more than a century ago. I thought I would start with the company the Collective had been protesting; we'd been so woefully underinformed at the actual demonstration, I felt it was my responsibility to learn more.

Lakeview was a fracking company, basically. It was a local offshoot of a major Texas corporation that had investments all over the Marcellus and Utica shale, and it was trying to expand a facility on the eastern side of Seneca Lake, where we'd been protesting the other day. Not far from Silenus, Zelda's family vineyard, I saw. There had been some local outcry about this expansion, predictably, and a lawsuit had been brought against the company. I scanned through the entries I could find online: a few mentions in the local paper, a website for the Protect Our Waters group that we'd seen at the protest. I wondered why the Collective was so interested in thwarting this corporation. Obviously, they were anti-fracking and anti-corporation—perhaps this was just the most local opportunity for protest?

Google searches about the Collective itself yielded little information—a defunct Facebook page from 2014 featured a handful of pictures of sunflowers and compost, plus a photo that might have included Fennel, ropy and tan in the distance.

I resolved to interview someone and find out about these strange neighbors who were working themselves into our lives. I wanted an origin story, a tale of like-minded souls finding one another linked by a common purpose. Yet again, I'd forgotten a basic rule of research: you write the story you find, not the one you want to find. If I hadn't been so fixated on uncovering the narrative I wanted, would I have seen the one in front of me?

Louisa and Chloe had vanished together (in my truck) and had not bothered to tell me where they were going. I was miffed at yet another exclusion—their lamps had joined Beau's last night, and I had watched as all three streaked into the darkness, giggling quietly but without any sincere attempt at stealth. I had dozed propped by the window, sullenly reading Dickinson, until further sounds alerted me to their return sometime just before the early dawn of a hot summer day. Disgruntled, I had gone outside to sulk on my porch, childishly hoping to be noticed by one of the three, but only Argos had acknowledged my presence, and I had gone back inside and slept far too late.

I awoke sticky and thirsty, feeling guilty for my indulgence. Usually only Chloe lollygagged in bed, and I always took pride in being up early, already out in the field when the sun finally started heating the ground. I felt strong and capable in the morning, and today I had robbed myself of that feeling through my pointless jealousy. I harbored some self-contempt, disgust at my laziness.

I put on a pair of overalls and a bandeau top of Chloe's, since the temperature in my cabin already indicated a toasty day. The sun was baking our garden, and I hoped the mint wouldn't get cooked in the heat. Oddly, no one was in the garden or, I soon learned, in the big cabin. Standing on the porch with my hand shading my eyes, I scanned the property. A hearty halloo alerted me to Jack's presence on the dock.

I sidled over to the structure, where Jack lay stretched out, basking in the sun. He wore a battered straw hat and his underwear, nothing else. At my approach, he propped himself up on his elbows, a dog-eared copy of *The Republic* laid split open on his ribs.

"Mornin'," he said, smiling up at me.

"Where is everyone?" I sat next to him, dangling one foot over the dock to swing near the water.

"Chloe and Louisa are fetching more compost from Rudy's house—it seems we're running low, and she wants to put in a pumpkin patch?" He shrugged. "Pumpkins'll grow pretty much anywhere, so it's a shame to waste compost on them, but I guess Rudy has tons."

"And Beau?"

"Your guess is as good as mine," Jack said. "He was gone when I got up."

"Brushing up on your Greek?" I gestured to his book.

"Oh, I haven't got too much Greek. Very patchy—I stopped trying in my AP independent study. I just—oh, you were kidding," he said bashfully when he saw my amused smirk.

"I didn't realize you had any Greek at all. But I suppose it's good to revisit one's Plato."

"It's been a few years since I read it," Jack agreed. "I mean, of course I've got some objections—"

"Of course you do," I said. Jack had objections to nearly everything—tiny clarifications he insisted were necessary, subtle points of departure. Where exactly to plant dill, when to dig up a carrot, whether there would be thick fog at night. "I, for one, was never nuts about his gender politics," I said.

"No, you're probably thinking of Aristotle," Jack hurried to say. "Actually, I was just reading Book Five, which really deals with the question of gender in this 'ideal city' Socrates has been describing. Here, listen . . . where did it . . . here it is: 'But if it's apparent that they differ only in this respect, that the females bear children while the males beget them, we'll say that there has been *no* kind of proof that women are different from men with respect to what we're talking about, and we'll continue to believe that our guardians and their wives must have the *same* way of life.' "

"That's nice and egalitarian," I said. "There are people today who wouldn't be quite so willing to grant us womenfolk such parity."

"Well, there is the inevitable discussion of the 'weakness' of women," Jack pointed out. "That's what I struggle with in this book: sometimes Socrates—well, the character of Socrates—forces us to walk through minute steps just so we can agree on something like, say, 'the skills of a carpenter being carpentry,' and then he'll just say, 'and of course we all agree on the weakness of women,' and Glaucon is all like, 'yup, for sure, obvs.' "

"Well, Jack, some things are just self-evident," I said, flexing my biceps, which were rather small but were certainly not weak.

"In any case, Plato is trying to figure out the problem of sexual selection in this part of *The Republic*—"

" 'The best men must have sex with the best women as frequently as possible,' " a voice intoned from underneath us. I almost fell off the dock.

"Jesus, Beau!" I tugged my foot up away from the water as he slithered out from his hiding spot, treading water and giving his curly shoulder-length hair a shake in the sunlight.

"Howdy," he said.

"How long have you been lurking down there?" Jack asked.

"Long enough. Have you solved the problem of mating in the perfect state?"

"Hardly," I said, looking him directly in the eye with the quirk of an eyebrow. He grinned back and pulled himself almost effortlessly onto the dock. His skin, naturally, glistened—there is little else young skin can do in summer sunlight.

"Well, Plato thinks it's natural that men and women thrown together will inevitably find themselves attracted to each other—that's just how sex works," Jack plowed on, as usual somewhat oblivious to any subtext. Beau didn't stop looking at me while he answered Jack.

"What's the phrase Plato uses? Geometric versus erotic desire?" Beau asked.

Jack nodded enthusiastically. "Exactly. I really, really like that. Basically, you'll end up wanting to sleep with your coworkers and the people you went to high school with because, well, they're there."

"How romantic," I said.

"I'm not sure it's about romance," Beau responded.

"You would say that," I couldn't help adding churlishly. I broke eye contact and stared pointedly at the dock.

"Wee Mack, you seem bent out of shape," Beau said, grabbing my ankle firmly. I tried to pull it away from him, but he held fast. "Are you miffed?" He curled his neck downward to look up at me, and I had no choice but to meet his eyes.

"No," I said unconvincingly. He pulled my ankle closer to him, so that my leg extended into his lap. His skin was cool and wet, and my foot rested just an inch or two from the border of his underwear. My heel nestled in the strong meat of his thigh, and my calf quivered. I wanted very badly to point my toe and lay back on the dock, stretched out and vulnerable.

"Because," he said, folding my toes over and cupping my foot. "Just so you know. This is mine." He bent and bit my calf very lightly, then the inside of my knee, then my thigh. I couldn't look at Jack, but I knew that he was watching us intently. I imagined that he must surely be jealous, and while I felt some guilt, this realization of his want made me even more turned on. I closed my eyes, feeling Beau's mouth linger on my leg, his hands curling more possessively around my shin and cupping the back of my knee. My head fell back.

"Does anyone contest that?" I said, opening one eye to look at Jack, daring him to speak up.

"Is it really a contest?" he asked evenly. Jack could be more perceptive than I gave him credit for.

"Why don't we find out?" I pulled my leg from Beau and swung it out and away from him, careful not to accidentally knee him in the teeth. As I moved, I imagined Chloe making the same gesture and felt, for once, graceful—lovely even. I leapt daintily to my feet and un-clasped my overalls, letting them drop to the dock. Each of my move-ments felt choreographed. I imagined us as a realist pastoral, three nearly naked young bodies, caught in the sun with the glimmer of water and the swoop of a willow nearby. In the painting, Argos would romp in the foreground. And somewhere, hidden or conspicuous, there would be a memento mori, reminding the viewers, if not the subjects, of their mortality. Shivering, I turned and leapt into the pond.

"Always running away, that bloody nymph," I heard Beau say to Jack, and I waited for the twin splashes of their bodies to join me in the water.

Chapter 16

Chloe and I were trimming basil and fortifying the tomato stakes. She was eerily quiet—had barely spoken a word all morning. I wavered between trying to draw her out and letting her brood furiously next to me. Her silences had grown long and unpredictable, and sometimes, when I watched her surreptitiously, her eyes took on a blankness I didn't especially care for. She wore a large sunhat, but I could see that her forearms were getting freckled and pink.

"They look good," I observed as we trellised another tomato plant. I fondled the hard, green flesh of a beefsteak, imagining its slow swelling over the next few weeks. Louisa had insisted on a fantastic quantity of tomatoes, and a good third of our garden was committed to Cherokee Purples, Big Boys, Sungolds, Brandywines, pastes, Juliets. We would be swimming in tomatoes by the time August and September rolled around. Chloe said nothing, swatting at a horsefly that lurked near her shoulder blade. She had been withdrawn like this all week, and I was worried for her.

As I straightened up and dusted my knees off, a large truck pulled into the drive. It was a new Dodge pickup, sitting high off the ground, looming. The radio was playing something that sounded a lot like country, and the lights were on, even in the middle of this summer day. I glanced around the clearing, hoping to spot one of the boys or Louisa, but Beau was off on a mysterious errand and Louisa and Jack were in the woods, clearing a trail and collecting kindling for the woodpile.

Two large men swung out of the pickup from either side. From their dusty boots, grimy T-shirts, and noticeable tan lines, they appeared to be men who worked outside for much of the day. Chloe seemed to withdraw further, and for a moment I thought she might actually run wordlessly off into the woods. Where the hell was my damn dog?

"Which one of you's Louisa? Stein-Jackson?" the driver of the truck asked me.

"Who's asking?" I countered.

"You her?"

"She's not here now," I said. "I don't know where she is."

"Sure you don't. Listen, I need to talk to her before things get any more . . . out of hand." The driver moved towards me, closing the distance between us, and I tried not to flinch visibly.

"I don't know what you mean," I said cautiously.

"Right. I know her daddy's a lawyer, and you kids have been making quite the mess with all your paperwork and filings," he said, waving his hand dismissively. "But that's not how we do business out here. That's not how neighbors treat one another." He took another step towards me. "So I wanted to come out here and straighten things out. Make sure we all see eye to eye. As neighbors."

"Well, I'd be happy to leave a message," I said, realizing as the words left my mouth how sarcastic and unhelpful they sounded. Our neighbor picked up on this.

"I think you might want to suggest to your friend that she's meddling in over her head. I think you might want to remind her that this is a"—he paused—"tight-knit community, and that we all look out for each other. I wouldn't want her to end up on the outs with anyone."

"I'll be sure to mention it to her," I replied, as sincerely as I could manage.

"Good, that's a good idea. And I think we might stop by again, just to clear the air, like I said. Make sure she gets the message. It would be nice to keep things civilized."

"Sure," I said.

"You wouldn't happen to know anything about a little accident that happened out here a ways back, would you?" asked the other man, who hadn't said a word until now. His colleague glanced over at him with a flicker of censure, but then looked back at me.

"There was a fire. That's about all I know," I answered.

"How about you, sweetheart?" he asked Chloe. "You know anything about that little incident?" Chloe looked alarmed, her blue eyes big and blank. I didn't like the way he was looking at her.

"She doesn't know anything, either," I answered for her.

"That so. Where are the rest of your little friends today?"

"Errands," I answered. "The boys are due back soon, though," I added instinctively. Since childhood, I'd been warned always to behave as though a man were on the premises. Not that I'd want Jack or Beau starting a kerfuffle with either of these gentlemen. But it was Louisa who would be the most confrontational, and the most likely to cause an escalation. I hoped she stayed in the woods.

"Well, you pass it along to all your friends. I think we can do a better job . . . communicating in the future. Otherwise life out here is going to get downright unpleasant, am I right?" The driver of the truck tipped the brim of his baseball cap in my direction in a mocking salute, and they both swung themselves back up into the elevated truck. The giant engine revved aggressively, and they turned the truck around, gunning the engine so that its tires carved deep grooves into our drive. I could feel the hammer of adrenaline in the veins of my throat, my palms shaking slightly.

"Well, fuck," I said to Chloe. "I think we just got threatened."

Chloe just nodded, then walked towards her cabin as though nothing had happened. I watched her go, feeling a surge of anxiety as she shut her door, leaving me alone in the clearing to wonder how to interpret this unwelcome visit.

I went back to the garden, even though I couldn't think of any other tasks to do there. Finding the safety of the high chicken-wire fence reassuring, I pulled the simple door shut firmly behind myself, so that I was fully surrounded by the flimsy barrier. Then I walked up and down the rows of vegetables, looking idly at the irrigation furrows, occasionally checking the underside of a leaf for any bug that would signal an infestation. I finally sat in the back corner of the garden, near the potatoes and other root vegetables, waiting for someone to return.

Jack and Louisa got home first. I watched them for a moment before dragging myself upright. They were both bright red from exertion; Louisa's arms looked like she'd plunged them into a bed of poison ivy. They each carried a burlap bag slung over one shoulder, out of which poked twigs and small branches, all manner of green wood that would go in a corner of the woodshed to thoroughly dry out before the cold weather came.

I rotated the rough wooden latch that kept the garden gate closed and nudged it open with my hip, crossing the clearing to help them unload the kindling.

"Mack! How're the tomatoes? Where's Chloe?" Jack asked. He took a deep gulp of water from the thermos clipped to his belt.

"In her cabin. The tomatoes are fine, but we might have an issue with our neighbors."

"What neighbors?" he said. "The Collective?" Louisa maintained eye contact with the woodpile.

"Louisa, what happened to the back field? With the tractor?" I asked, trying to look her in the eye.

"I told you, we didn't have anything to do with that."

"I find that a little hard to believe, actually," I said. "And so, apparently, do some of the locals. We had a visit today."

"Who came?" Louisa whirled around to face me. "Someone came here?"

"Yep. Two fine gentlemen, of agricultural stock. They were not in a great mood."

"Did you document it? Did you have your phone? Oh, please tell me one of you recorded something with your phone!"

"No, Louisa, I didn't fucking record anything. I was too busy trying to decide whether or not to scream for help. They. Were not. Friendly," I explained.

"Are you both okay? They didn't touch you, did they?" Jack asked.

"No, but I'm pretty sure they meant to scare us. They're pissed about the lawsuit and whatever happened to the tractor. And whoever was involved," I added, with a nasty glance at Louisa.

"That's intimidation! It's completely illegal. It could make a huge difference with the lawsuit. I can't believe you didn't record anything. Fuck. Would you sign an affidavit, though? We can get my dad to interview you and Chloe, and we could report it, so there's a paper trail."

"Louisa, get a fucking grip. These guys just came to the house and threatened to make things, quote unquote, 'downright unpleasant' for us. I'm not especially interested in stirring shit up right now. I do not want my life to be 'unpleasant.' "

"Then they win, Mack! This is our chance to change how things get done out here. Agribusiness has been riding roughshod over what's good for the land, what's good for the community, what's actually sustainable, for decades, with zero accountability. If we can show that their practices aren't just unethical but are in fact doing real damage, we can turn—"

"Save it for the jury, Louisa. You'll get another chance to talk to them. They promised they'd be back." I spun around, not sure where I was planning to go but too irritated with Louisa to stay there listening to her. Did she really not understand? Or did she simply not care? "Oh, and Chloe has been locked in her cabin all afternoon. You might want to check on her," I called over my shoulder as I headed down the driveway to the dirt road.

I scuffed my way up and down the "shoulder" for at least an hour, pausing occasionally to observe life in the ditch. A few frogs, a couple of late-blooming tadpoles. The cattails had dissipated into fluff, and weeds grew thick along the banks. I felt suddenly unsafe at the Homestead, made vulnerable by these men who belonged in this county in a way I felt I did not. They had resources and sturdy bodies and a financial stake in the land I'd spent the day composting and coaxing into fertility. They had ownership.

But beyond my personal insecurity, I wondered about my friends, my comrades, the people with whom I'd undertaken this venture. I was sure Louisa was lying—maybe she hadn't personally sabotaged the tractor, but I felt certain she knew something about whatever had happened. Or maybe she *had* personally set fire to the tractor. Jack was fundamentally sweet, but he could be easily swayed, and I feared that Louisa and Beau's charisma could lure him into doing something he otherwise would never consider. And Chloe's blank stare today had rattled me; she had seemed completely non-present, and now I kept seeing her glazed expression, empty and cold. What would Chloe be capable of without her compassion, her deep feeling? And Beau himself. He walked so lightly, so carefree, as though nothing could touch him, or as though it wouldn't matter if it did—would he dare?

Finally, I saw Beau on his bicycle, spinning up the hill towards home. When he caught sight of me, he broke into a huge grin and hopped nimbly from his seat. There were bags hitched to the back of the bike, bearing what looked like comestibles.

"At the Collective again?" I asked, shooting for a casual tone.

"Yep. Their greenhouse is something else. Maybe next year we can rig a simple one, get a head start on seedlings. But, man, their stuff looks beautiful right now." He whistled appreciatively and showed me a head of lettuce that was indeed impressive. I stroked it.

"Beau. What do you know about what happened in the back field a while ago? With the tractor?" I asked, not meeting his eyes.

"Sweet Mack. Don't worry too much about it. It's done with, and none of us were there."

"The owners of the field came by today and threatened us," I said with a little more heat than I intended. "It's *not* done with." I looked up at him, trying to show that I was here, that I was listening, that I wouldn't judge if he told me the truth.

"Owners?" he scoffed. "Do any of us ever really own land? Seems like silliness to me." He laughed, and swung one leg back over the bike to cruise up the driveway to the Homestead. I watched him go, black-clad, and my heart sank as I stood there. Always watching. Lowering myself to the dusty ground, I took my shoes off and slid my feet into the ditch. The running water was bitterly cold, but I flicked my toes at tiny fish until I couldn't feel them anymore.

Death and Sex. It was all I could think about, the twin forces that drove every community, and every individual I was reading about. The desire to sculpt a worthy life seemed to be linked by two pressures: the certainty that the world as we know it would soon come to an end and the desire to have sex with people outside the traditional purview of marriage. I wrote and read, dragging home heaps of books from the public library each time I went into town. Whenever someone came to my cabin, they chuckled at the stacks of historical works piled high against my walls; I'd outgrown the bookshelves, and so the tomes climbed upward in wobbly stalagmites on my floor and sprawled across my bed.

Jack joined me one afternoon to flip through some of the drier academic texts in search of something that would underpin my thesis, and we giggled at the elaborate justifications concocted to let old men get involved with desirable young women. His quick brain was ideal for skimming dull pages and lifting out the paragraph that spoke to my work—he would tag the salient citation with a little colored sticker, a research organizational system he taught me and that became invaluable to my work. Though everyone seemed to respect my project, it was Jack who grew excited about it, and he would bring me morsels of information he'd stumbled across in his own voracious reading. My work allowed me a safe place to retreat to, so that I could withdraw into myself, and the more I read, the more I became convinced that it was my research that would ultimately help us succeed; if I could learn why these other communities had failed, I might uncover the secret that would permit us to remain, safe and happy, on our Homestead.

I traipsed over to Jack's cabin hoping to make use of his almanac—the little journal that contained the endless notes that chronicled his inventions. Always on the hunt for an innovation. I loved this about him, but I also found it to be a great hindrance to productivity. He did, however, keep excellent records, so he could determine when a cockamamie adventure actually worked out. I was fleshing out my project, writing down everything I could think of, and Jack was one of the best resources I had. Whenever the journal of our endeavors couldn't be located in the big cabin, it was likely to be found with Jack.

That day, I had a question about winter vegetables; it seemed to me that we had more than we should. Our root-vegetable cellar was oddly well stocked, given that we'd only begun planting in March. And Louisa had repeatedly mentioned a garlic harvest that we hadn't even put in yet, as far as I knew—garlic would go into the ground in autumn. We also had more potatoes listed there than seemed feasible, given our late start. I was hoping Jack could help me break down these seeming contradictions. I also, secretly, had other designs on that little book of his, filled with information and notes and his own strange brainy thoughts. I was hoping he'd let me copy more of it.

He called me in when I knocked, and I found him on his bed, reading a ragged copy of *Brideshead Revisited*.

"Beau lent it to me," he said as I entered. "He reminds me weirdly of Sebastian, if he were a bit more outgoing. Dashing and dissolute young gentleman, seduces all."

I laughed, then said, "I was hoping to pick your brain for a quick second. Had a few dull questions about vegetables."

"No prob. Shoot. Pick my brain."

"Well, Louisa said something the other day about the garlic harvest. She said we were going to have an epic harvest soon, and we'd be able to sell it and trade it for some of the veggies we haven't done yet."

"Okay, and?" Jack asked.

"Don't you plant garlic in the autumn?"

"Ah. Yes. You do." Jack frowned. I thought he could guess where I was headed.

"But we didn't start doing anything around here till March."

"You could get away with a March planting farther south, but here, I think it wouldn't be a great idea."

"And I don't remember planting any garlic," I said.

"Me neither." Jack rumpled his nose exaggeratedly; all his facial expressions seemed to be almost caricatures. His smile was always enormous, his guffaw too loud. He reached for his almanac and flipped quickly through the pages, each gesture large. "You're right," he said. "If there was garlic put in in the spring, I didn't write it down."

"No, that's what I thought. Also, potatoes."

"What about them?"

"Don't we seem to have a lot? I mean, we have almost nothing to barter with, but plenty of potatoes, always," I said.

"Louisa said she put in a crop earlier."

"Doesn't that seem weird? And where? I haven't seen any in the veggie garden."

"Um, yeah. Hm. That's all sort of strange," Jack agreed. "Should we ask her?"

"Of course you would go for the direct route," I said, smiling. "Never one to let things fester."

"What do you mean?" His expression was guileless.

"I mean that you can't stand secrets. You want to talk about everything, out in the open. You're a terrible gossip, you know."

Jack grinned. "Oh, Mack, you'd be surprised," he said. He paused, searching my face for something. "I guess, speaking of which . . ."

"Oh, goody. Here we go. Whose scrap of a secret are you about to reveal now?"

"Actually, I was wondering about yours."

I froze. "What do you mean."

"Mack, I mean, we live in the Information Age. The boundless digital and all. I totally understand why you don't want to talk about what happened before you came here. . . ."

I closed my eyes and breathed out slowly.

"I mean, if you don't want to talk about it, I get it. . . ."

I opened my eyes. "Did Chloe tell you?"

"She didn't have to. I Googled you way back, not long after we first met. Louisa said it would be mean to bring it up, though."

"She said that?" My eyes opened in surprise.

"She pointed it out, yeah. She said you'd come to it on your own. I've been waiting. . . ." He shrugged. "Just thought I'd clear the air."

"And here I thought I'd managed to get away from it."

"We've all got our reasons for being out here," Jack pointed out. "Frankly, yours makes a whole lot of sense. I mean, *you've* got a real reason to want to not participate in that world, in all that post-capitalist madness."

"Thanks," I said drily. "I thought we all had valid reasons for wanting something else."

"You know what I mean, though. That world really punished you. When you think about it, it's a much more authentic reason for wanting something else. We've elected to live out here, subsistence-style, when there are people all over the world who have no choice but to live day to day, hand to mouth. They don't do it out of high-minded idealism, they do it out of necessity."

"And we do it because . . . we're naïve?"

"We do it because that other world—the world of such huge injustice and cruelty—has become unlivable. And because we have the immense privilege to try something else."

Chapter 17

August brought with it bounty, even excess. We found ourselves wading through cucumbers, eggplants, basil, parsley, sweet corn, peppers, tomatillos, tomatoes, and mountains of zucchini. We ate zucchini twice a day, since it was difficult to preserve: raw zucchini salads, noodles made from zucchini, grilled zucchini, zucchini curries, zucchini on flatbread, zucchini fritters. After a while, I looked at every squash I picked with loathing and despair, heavy with the knowledge that I would later have to consume it. In desperation, Jack tried drying some, and Chloe put up a few jars of pickles that she was convinced would be "utter mush" by the time we got around to eating them. I tried to make a zucchini sauerkraut that turned to green goo after about three days, and, gagging, I was forced to chuck it into the compost. I later saw Argos munching away at the heap, and I shooed him off, nevertheless hoping it was the moldy zucchini he was eating rather than the sad little pond fish Jack had caught, which had turned out to be completely inedible. The dog's breath reeked for days, regardless, and I made him sleep on my porch, rather than flopped bonelessly in my bed.

I was writing more and more. Whatever I had begun was turning into something stranger, a bizarre mishmash of memoir and history. I chronicled the tedium of washboard laundry and jotted down the dates of which foods appeared when. I wrote cryptic notes about my friends and their foibles. I speculated wildly about the Collective. And I began to research William—or, more specifically, the community from which he had fled. I was fascinated to learn about their trap-making, complex marriage, and strange little eugenics project: stirpiculture, they called it. The ultimate failure of their experiment filled me with fond pity; how easily I could relate to good intentions gone awry! I scribbled my notes into a document that was interlaced with my own thoughts and observations, and the document began to metamorphose into a literary Minotaur of nonfiction, a hybrid beast caught in my maze. It gave me pleasure to flip through the pages, feeling as though the words gave weight to my life here, somehow made it more real. I wanted it to be perfect; my book should smell of pines and resound with the hum of insects.

The end of August and early September meant tomatoes. Per Louisa's requisition, we had planted twice what farms of a similar size would normally bother with, and our daily diet included about half a pound of Sungolds, snacked upon straight off the vine as we battled time to get their burnished flesh plucked before they fell to the ground and split open in seedy carnage. Louisa oversaw our haul with satisfaction, processing first those cheery yellow orbs, then all others as they rolled in. Paste tomatoes became sauce; Cherokee Purples, bright exotic chutney; beefsteaks were sun-dried and canned; and heirlooms got sliced and tossed into salads, laid on sandwiches, or eaten whole as snacks. We were drowning in lycopene. Louisa's ratatouille appeared on the menu at least twice a week.

Canning was tiresome and hot. Chloe and Jack had taken a community course about the process, so we could rest easy, confident that we wouldn't be stricken with midwinter botulism. With her ability to be detail-oriented to the point of myopia, Chloe boiled Ball jars and sterilized tongs and insisted on a completely sanitized workspace. Having accidentally set down unapproved vegetables in her sanitized area, Beau got chewed out with some thoroughness, and he joshed her gently for her precision. In a cranky tone, Louisa ordered him out of the kitchen, which he wisely departed.

In addition to the tomatoes, we were swamped with the rest of the canning and processing. Dilly beans, corn, and pickled beets: all to be canned. Sauerkraut to be started; potatoes to be buried in baskets of cheap rice in the root cellar. Onions to be stored; garlic to be braided and hung; herbs to be dried. Cabbages to be laid in their graves in the ground. We found a curtain of wild Concord grapes near the forest's edge, and we ate as many as we could before turning some into raisins and the rest into a cloudy grape juice. We filtered it with cheesecloth, but it still looked pretty damn murky; I think we all had our doubts about the advisability of fermenting it, though Jack thought maybe we could get a light fizz to it, like a *pétillant naturel.*

Each night we dropped into bed exhausted. The work of harvesting and prepping veggies took up the whole day, and that was in addition to any of our other obligations. Beau and Chloe still worked at least two days a week at the restaurant for cash; Louisa was still trying to haul in a bit of income from her online remote work, but since she had money anyway, it seemed half-hearted. Jack and I were dedicated full-time to our agricultural endeavors (it had been more than a month since I'd taken a catering shift), which meant we often ended up with the more unsavory tasks; I considered this a (mostly) fair trade, though we griped to each other when the composting toilet needed rotation, or later when we had to handle the painful task of garlic harvesting on our own.

We all had to dedicate time to splitting and stacking so the wood would be cured by the time the cold arrived. And as we harvested each vegetable, we had to deal with its plot in the garden, either tilling and replanting with late-autumn and winter veggies or letting it go fallow until the spring. Water had to be hauled, filthy overalls washed, chickens and goat fed, trails kept clear, honey harvested, buildings prevented from falling down. Our flock of chickens had multiplied alarmingly; a small brood was suddenly an intimidating flotilla of poultry, producing warm globes of protein that could be sold and traded. Argos followed me around as I moved about the Homestead and sometimes accompanied Jack or Chloe on their ventures into the woods. Beau and Louisa seemed to have no time for our leggy familiar.

The hot work of canning involved hours crouched over the stove with the water boiling. The main cabin was not especially well ventilated, and Chloe began using a spritzer filled with water, with which she would mist her face and the back of her neck to stay cool. After any canning session, whoever had been confined in the kitchen would leap off the dock into the pond; while it was slightly fetid and brackish as only late-summer ponds can be, this was still the best way to cool down. On the hottest days, I overcame my reservations and joined everyone in the pond, living for the feel of Beau's slick belly against mine underwater. Other days, I would dally in the woods, hoping to be waylaid by him while purporting to be hunting for wild strawberries (it was ludicrously late in the season for this) and (more plausibly) grapes, then sitting in dry pine needles beneath the deep shade of an old conifer, letting my aching muscles unclench while I dozed off, to wake with my short hair caught in sap.

My memories of that time are of being physically exhausted, of arms that ached whenever I lifted them, quads shivering from squatting in the squash patch, a sunburn on my nose making me feel sundrunk, groggy. But I was also content. We were all too tired and busy to fret about drama. The members of the West Hill Collective were, if possible, even busier with their more substantial harvest. They had neither the time nor the inclination to entertain us, even on the few evenings when we could have spared a few hours near dark. Instead, we would sit at the picnic table, eating ratatouille and grilled sweet corn and Caprese salad (the mozzarella made from unpasteurized milk we got from the Collective, this skill maybe the one benefit I retained from the *Experiment*) and sipping some of our bartered wine or Jack's improving honey mead. We skinny-dipped in the pond after dinner, all of us cavorting naked. I wanted the season to go on forever.

In early September, though, I realized that things had changed. I watched for the lights moving betwixt our various doors, sometimes thinking of William and his community, with their policy of free (but communally monitored) love. How could they ever have thought that would work? I waited for Beau to reprise his interest in me, but he stayed on the edges, giving me only the occasional kiss on the neck, a palm rested briefly in the small of my back. Enough, enough to keep me hungry. Chloe still sometimes crept in with Louisa, but she spent more and more time in her cabin, practicing her music. I wish I could have understood that she was withdrawing, drifting away from us.

When Beau went AWOL yet again, instead of Louisa's usual irritation and banging of pots, she was oddly casual. About a day after Beau's disappearance, she got a phone call from her father. After a few minutes of unusually sedate conversation, she came over to where I was standing, slicing cabbage into thin slivers.

"Can we take a quick ride over to the Glen?" she asked, dripping nonchalance. I saw Jack turn to glance at us, eyebrows raised. Louisa never drove; I wasn't even sure she had a license. She insisted on being chauffeured. Normally, though, Chloe brought her wherever she needed to go.

"Uh, sure," I answered. "Let me just finish up this cabbage."

"I'll wait for you outside."

I looked back at Jack, who shrugged a shoulder and returned to his pile of green beans and hot peppers.

"What do you think it's about?" I asked him.

"Look, I have an idea. But you should talk to Louisa. And Beau." This was circumspect for Jack, who always happily dished any shred of gossip he possessed. I shaved my way through the cabbage, tossed it quickly into a crock, dumped some salt on it, covered it with a plate and a cloth, and stepped outside. Upon seeing me, Louisa immediately headed for the truck.

As we drove, I waited as patiently as I could for an explanation. I had learned to let people reveal their stories as they wanted to—they rarely gave them up unless they wished to talk. Finally, as we were pulling into town, Louisa asked me to head for the police station. I bit my lip and resisted begging her for details.

I parked nearby and was coming around to the other side of the truck to go in with her when Louisa suggested that I wait at the nearby coffee shop. Affronted, I started to protest, but she shushed me.

"Look, I promise I'll tell you about it later," she assured me. "Right now, I just have to talk to my dad."

I glowered ineffectually before spinning on my heels and heading to the sandwich joint on the corner. I wasn't hungry, but I grabbed a bag of potato chips from the counter while I ordered an iced coffee. It had been a long time since I'd eaten processed foods or trans fats. I sat there sullenly, munching my bounty, which tasted almost unbearably salty, and waited for Louisa.

She and Beau and Rudy walked in the front door moments later. Beau was beaming, dressed in a black T-shirt and slim black jeans. His hair stuck up rakishly, and he clearly hadn't shaved in a few days. He looked beautiful, and more than a bit like an outlaw. In spite of myself, I could feel my pulse clamoring.

"Greetings," he said, and as I stood to give him a welcome-back hug, he gave me a kiss that fell half on my mouth and half on my cheek.

"Where've you been, sailor?" I inquired, looking from him over to Louisa.

"Listen, how about I stand you kids to some lunch and a beer across the road?" Rudy asked, his volume uncomfortably loud. The people working behind the counter glared at us over this blatant snub. Rudy was already a bright fuchsia in the midday heat, and he seemed unconcerned.

"Thanks, Daddy. I think that's a good idea," answered Louisa. Beau and I followed them out the door and across the quiet main street to the Wildflower Café. It was dark and air-conditioned, and we slid into the booths, Rudy sighing with relief and sliding his flesh across the rubbery seat. Having just eaten the chips, I was now definitively without appetite, but I ordered a beer and sweet potato fries, for the hell of it. Who knew when I would be granted such caloric bounty again? I slurped my beer, staring at my three dining companions and waiting for someone to explain. Finally, just as the food was arriving, Louisa cleared her throat.

"I imagine you're curious about what happened, Mack," she began. My expression, I hoped, was eloquent enough to express my irritation at being kept so persistently in the dark.

"Beau got arrested yesterday," she said.

"Ah," I said.

"For trespassing. And destruction of property."

"Okay. Whose?" I took another swallow of beer. I wasn't surprised, exactly.

"A fracking company," Beau said shortly.

"The one we were protesting? Lakeview?"

"The very same." He nodded.

"Were you alone?"

"No. I was with Fennel. And Jesse."

"I see." I looked around the table, unsure what to say. "Rudy?" I finally ventured. "What do you think of this?"

"He'll probably only get charged for the trespassing, and since it's young Beauregard's first offense, I don't think we need to worry too much. The hearing won't be for at least a month, in any case. He's out on a fairly moderate bail."

"And Fennel? And Jesse?" I asked.

"They have their own lawyer," Louisa answered quickly. "Part of what they raise money for is their legal fund. That's why they tolerate Sy, after all. He's the most financially solvent of all of them."

"Is this *their* first offense?" I said.

"No," Beau answered. I leaned back in the booth, my skin sticking to the plastic.

"I see. And . . . will we be bailing you out of jail again?" I asked.

"It's always possible," Beau said, breaking into another smile.

❦

After Beau's arrest, I was desperate to know what was going on at the Collective. It was clear that Fennel and Jesse at least were a little more civilly disobedient than I had expected. I angled for a visit, which bugged Louisa, but she could hardly forbid me to snoop around. I fussed at Beau, telling him I absolutely had to ask Natasha about her ferments, since my last two batches had ended up soggy—I thought she was the most likely one to talk to me about what they were up to there, and I figured if I could get her alone, she might say something. I claimed that I had made a special type of chutney for her, that I needed to speak with her before I ruined any more cabbages, and Beau finally relented; he invited me to come the next time he popped over to barter.

As the weather grew gradually colder, we wanted some of Fennel's precious mushrooms. I had prepared a big bag of raisins, several jars of chutney, and some apple rings so that I would be invited along for the trade. Driving the few miles to the Collective, I could tell that Beau was tempted to say something to me, but instead he smoked his cigarillo, exhaling out the window.

I was almost as excited to share my bounty as I was to corner Natasha and see if I could learn anything from her. Unlike nearly all my new friends, before I moved to the Homestead, I had never foraged for dinner, had never made chutney. This past year was the first time I had ever come near a farm animal or seen what a growing potato looked like or known how to identify a raspberry leaf. I was, in short, very pleased with myself.

When we arrived at the Collective, though, there was an air of frenzy, people flurrying around, trying to get very important things done. For the tail end of harvest season, this didn't seem too unusual, but it felt different in quality from some of my earlier visits. Beau appeared to notice it, too, though he again kept his mouth shut.

In the farmhouse's kitchen, we found Fennel, flustered and red, laboring over some type of brownish stew. This was what all of Fennel's food looked like, no matter what she was making, so it was difficult to identify this particular dish, but I guessed that it was a tomato-zucchini sludge. More zucchini. Fennel also didn't believe in salt or seasonings; she had spent some time dallying with macrobiotic diets and didn't approve of too much flavor. As we entered the kitchen, she seemed distracted and didn't even brighten when Beau stooped down to give her a kiss on the forehead. Indeed, as his lips met her salty brow, she glanced behind herself almost guiltily, and I thought I saw her flinch.

"We come to do trade," Beau announced. "Wee Mack has even brought some of her own contributions."

"That's great, Beau, but it's not really a good time. We've got a lot going on right now."

"It does seem busy. Are you guys harvesting something special? Anything we can help with?" I offered eagerly.

"No, no, it's not that." Fennel waved me away. "It's—"

"Where did the sheets on the line go?" Natasha interrupted, bursting into the kitchen. "I hung them out to dry hours ago and now they're gone, and I swear to God if they've blown off again I'm going to burn Sy's fucking DIY clothespins!" I'd never seen Natasha anything other than totally unflappable, and I barely recognized this manic incarnation.

"Do you think someone might have taken them down? The vegans were near the clothesline, digging up burdock, so maybe one of them . . . ?" Fennel suggested absently, turning back to her glop. "Shit, I think it's burning," she said. It was; I could smell it.

"Well, if they did, they could have told me," Natasha fumed, ducking back outside.

"Here, I'll help you look," I said hurriedly, plunking my goods down on the table and following her before she could tell me not to bother.

"Is everything okay out here?" I asked as we set off at a brisk trot towards the vegans' cabin.

"Yeah, yeah. It's just, we found out that Matthew's coming in, like, an hour. He's the original founder of the Collective," she continued. "So we're trying to get everything shipshape. It's something of a to-do."

"Really, just because he's a founding member? I thought Fennel was too."

"No, he's *the* founding member. He's the one who got everyone together out here—he bought the land, started the member charter. He recruited the first five girls. Fennel's the only one left now."

"First five girls?" I asked, my neck prickling a little. "They were all girls?"

"I mean, not by design." She waved away my alarmed expression. "The first five people who were ready to commit were just all women, that's it."

"And he lived out here with them by himself?"

"Look, it's nothing like that. We're not, like, a cult. We just all believe in the same principles of openness and sustainability."

This sounded a bit like a party line. "Okay," I said uneasily, thinking again of William's journal. "So he's coming soon?"

"He'll be here any minute. His room upstairs has mostly been left as is—we just need to tidy it up a bit. Clean sheets, you know."

Said sheets were located about two minutes later, having apparently blown off the clothesline and settled, luckily, on a bush. "I don't see why we can't just buy some actual clothespins. It would cost about two dollars," Natasha muttered, gathering the soft, worn cotton in her arms. I claimed the top sheet from the brambles and followed her back to the farmhouse.

I had never been upstairs in the farmhouse; Fennel was, unsurprisingly, territorial about her room, and we'd never been offered a tour up here. There were just the three bedrooms: Fennel's, Natasha's, and the one that sat empty. We'd heard it referred to as the guest room, but I'd had no idea that it was kept as a shrine for the Collective's glorious leader. I half-expected the room to be tricked out with creepy sex props (ropes hanging from the ceiling, mysteriously shaped furniture, a variety of leather), but it was instead a monastic chamber with a bare floor, a small double bed, and an empty nightstand.

"There's not even a lamp," I observed as Natasha and I hurried to dress the stripped bed. The mattress was striped and creaky; it reminded me of the mattresses at the sleepover camp I had been forced to attend as a kid because my parents worked in the summer. Those mattresses had always been redolent of urine and must, and I couldn't resist the urge to sniff this one; it simply smelled old.

"Matthew liked—likes—to keep time with the sun," Natasha explained, and I was surprised to hear her sound just like Fennel with her preachy admiration for this ultranatural practice. She normally kept a tone of removed irony in her voice when talking about "shared values"; it was one of the reasons I liked Natasha and found her, of all the members of the Collective, the easiest to talk to. She never sounded like she was in a cult.

"Is he coming alone?" I asked as we tried to fluff a single lackluster pillow, which nevertheless stayed persistently lumpy.

"I actually don't know." Natasha frowned. "Fennel spoke to him, and we've all been rushing around since."

"Seems like quite a bit of hullabaloo for one person," I said.

"I guess we're just trying to impress him, you know? To make sure he can see that we're still working hard, that we all still share his, well, vision." She glanced over at me as she said this, as though realizing what she sounded like. It occurred to me that I had yet to see the Collective's charter. Jesus, what if it was all hippie-dippie spiritual garble? Visions and revelations and energy work? I'd always assumed that it was a practical document to ensure that everyone was working towards the same goals, but for the first time I wondered if maybe the Collective had a different agenda than we had supposed.

"Well, I mean, no one could be unimpressed by the Collective," I said, genuinely meaning it. "It really is an amazing place, and you guys all manage to live almost completely without outside support. That's really something."

Natasha smiled. "It is. But you know how things go. It's like a high school reunion. When you see an old friend, you want to look your best."

"I totally get it," I reassured her. Having finished with the bed and wiped up some dust and crud from the windowsills, we returned downstairs. Fennel's culinary efforts seemed to be a disappointment, and she was fidgeting with her dreadlocks in an attempt to get them off her sweaty neck. It was hot in the kitchen, and I thought I could smell her, beneath the scent of tea tree oil that always hovered around her. Beau, I saw, had excused himself, and I went to join him and Jesse on the porch, while Natasha stayed to help Fennel.

Beau was smoking another cigarillo, and without asking, I plucked it from his fingers to take a drag. Though I was hoping for a quiet smile, he seemed not to notice. Jesse was talking about his plans to plant soy, so they could make their own tofu. I really couldn't see why anyone would bother; in spite of my all-natural lifestyle overhaul, I still hadn't developed a taste for the stuff. Beau asked a few questions about crop rotation and growing season, but I could tell that he was being polite, rather than storing the information for later use. Two or three people I didn't recognize had arrived at the farmhouse, and they greeted Jesse with a bob of the head without introducing themselves. Perhaps these were the ever-fleeting vegans?

"Is Sy here?" I asked Jesse, interrupting his description of tofu man-ufacturing.

"Think so, but he'll probably keep to his yurt. He and Matthew aren't entirely, you know, simpatico."

"Oh, really?" Beau asked, smelling gossip. He always tried to main-tain the sense that he was above such things, but I knew that he, like Jack, loved tidbits of social discord and interpersonal strife.

"Matthew is pretty firmly into the whole clean-living thing," Jesse explained. "Most of the founding members were. I mean, yeah, look at Fennel. But they didn't want to write that into the charter, because they felt that it's really a personal decision. Membership shouldn't be, you know, 'predicated on sobriety,' is how I think Matthew puts it."

"But I imagine he doesn't care for some of Sy's more blatant ex-cesses," I said.

"Not that you can blame him," Beau said. "Nobody really wants to live and work with a drug addict."

Jesse shrugged. "Really, it's not so bad. Sy keeps it together. He's smart. And, well, he does a lot to support the Collective. I mean financially." A black Prius coasted up the dusty way and came to its weirdly silent stop. The man who stepped out surprised me. I had expected, for some reason, someone older, more serious, dour-looking. But Matthew (I assumed that was who this was) was young, trim, and very good-looking. As he approached, I saw that he had scruff on his sharp jaw, and just a sprinkle of gray in his brown hair, and bright eyes that held my gaze. They were bluer than any eyes I had ever seen. He seemed to vibrate with energy.

"Jesse, my man," he said by way of greeting, pulling Jesse in for a surprisingly tender hug.

"Welcome, dude. So good to see you."

"Fuck, it's good to get out of the car," Matthew said, stretching his arms over his head. His button-down shirt lifted up to reveal a flat belly with a narrow line of hair that disappeared into his jeans.

"Hi," he said, turning to me. "I'm Matthew. You a new member?"

"We're neighbors, actually," I said. "We were just stopping by."

"And, Beau, hey," Matthew said, turning to address him. I was surprised. They knew each other? "We're neighbors now? No way. Where are you guys located these days?"

"About two miles north, northeast of here. Just this side of Mecklenburg. We're starting up our own little farm. A miniature collective," Beau said. I couldn't read his tone.

"Nice! And nice to meet you." Matthew turned back to me, a dazzling smile on his face. I couldn't stop looking at his eyes. "I didn't catch your name."

"Mack," I said, regretting this statement's lack of thrill value. I wanted to dazzle, but such was not my lot.

"You guys will stay a bit, right? I'd love to hear about what you're doing over there. And catch up," he added, with a nod to Beau. There was something dismissive in his treatment of Beau that I couldn't parse. Naturally, I was desperately curious.

"We'd love to stick around," I answered quickly, worried that Beau would make an excuse that would force me to leave. I heard the screen door open behind me, followed by a girlish yelp. Fennel flew past me and practically into Matthew's arms.

"Ay, it's good to see you," Matthew said into her dreadlocks, giving her a tight squeeze. I'd never seen Fennel so buoyant.

"It's been way too long," I heard Fennel admonish him, not relinquishing her grip.

"Totally agree. California is way too fucking far."

Fennel finally released Matthew and stood back to observe him. "You just drove all the way here?" she asked, preparing to censure him.

"Well, you know, I obviously had to stop for gas," Matthew said with a mischievous smile.

"Did you even get a proper night's sleep while you were on the road?"

"I pulled over a few places. Got my little tent." His smile broke further, as though he knew that this would frustrate Fennel.

"Matthew, you are going to get yourself killed. Seriously." But for once, Fennel couldn't seem to maintain her disapproval.

"Well, I did stop to visit some of our friends in Ohio."

"Oh my God! How are they? Did she have the baby? You have to tell me everything!"

"I will, I will. But first, let me come inside," he said.

Fennel blushed. "Silly me, come in. Dinner is on the stove. Do you have bags?" She fussed over him, seeming to fly off in all directions to see him comfortable. A canvas bag was fetched from the Prius, stew was stirred, Matthew was installed in the small room that had once been his. I hovered, Beau and I onlookers, outsiders to this little drama. We lurked until everyone had settled around the table and broken off hunks of Fennel's heavy, dark bread, dipping them into jars of pesto and licking their fingers with gusto.

"They can't be allowed to develop further here, that's all I'm saying," Fennel declared, clearly picking up a conversation she had begun with Matthew upstairs.

"I agree. We always considered Lakeview to be our primary target," Matthew said.

"I mean, they want to keep expanding in the area and to turn it into a hub for fracking and gas transportation. If they get their way, the whole lake could end up contaminated, and we'll wind up like Flint, with no drinking water."

"We're all on board, Fen. I know you guys have been getting stuff done out here. I've been working with the California group, and there's some consensus—they know that Lakeview is essential. Financing is the tricky bit—you know I don't agree with the methods—"

"I'm not happy about it, either," Fennel interrupted. "But we're not exactly going to sell enough cucumbers to pay for it. It's a question of which principles you're willing to compromise on for the greater good."

"Which is a *larger* question," Matthew acknowledged, digging a hunk of bread into a bowl of pesto and smacking olive oil from his lips. "And one with plenty of gray areas. As we know." He glanced over at Fennel, and they communicated something to each other using only their eyes. I thought I could see a flash of warning in Matthew's expression. What were they talking about? And what, for that matter, did California have to do with a natural gas company in upstate New York?

"But we don't want to leap straight into all of that," he added. "I've got plenty of time. We'll make a plan for a direct action with Lakeview that we can all live with."

"Beau's been pretty indispensable," Fennel said, apropos of what I wasn't sure. Everyone was momentarily quiet.

"It's always good to have . . . fresh blood," Matthew said. "And you, Mack? What's your story?"

"Mack's not really—" Fennel began.

"I've been to one of the protests," I said defensively. "I hate what they're trying to do. My dad worked for the power plant on Cayuga, and they fired him when he got sick. I hate those people. That industry."

"I didn't know that, Mack," Beau said.

"Well, he doesn't like to talk about it that much. Now he does maintenance for the county. He's not exactly proud of it."

"Well, we're happy to have you on our side," said Matthew, once again exchanging that mystifying wordless communiqué with Fennel. "But right now, I want to know: Who made this amazing pesto?"

"That was me," Natasha said. She had been watching our conversation silently and seemed strangely relieved to change the topic over to food.

"It's wonderful. Garlicky," Matthew said, mouth full and beaming. He dipped his bread for another bite and the oil nearly dribbled onto his shirt; just in time, he deftly positioned his mouth beneath the green bounty so that it spilled onto his outstretched tongue. "I could eat it with a spoon."

"Summer in a jar," Natasha agreed.

"I'm starving. What's for dinner?"

"We should really head out," Beau said before Fennel could describe her bland stew. I was disappointed; I wanted to know more about this Matthew. "Louisa's expecting these." He pushed back his chair and held up the mushrooms we had come for.

"Give her my regards," Matthew said, standing up, too, and holding Beau's eyes with his own while he held his forearm in a farewell shake.

"If it's all the same, I might not mention that you're here," Beau said. And he turned to leave without another word.

"Bye, guys," I said with an awkward wave, and hustled to follow him.

We found ourselves back in the truck and starting for home, me full of regret and wishing yet again that I had managed to impose my will on a plan.

"What was that about?" I asked, turning the ignition.

"Nothing. Louisa and Matthew don't really get along."

"Is that why she doesn't like Fennel, either?"

Beau glanced over at me, and with a knowing smile that held so much awareness of all my speculation, he said: "Well, that's part of it."

We were about to pull out of the driveway when Matthew bounded down the front steps and jogged to the truck. Beau rolled down his window.

"Listen, Beau," he said. "Let's maybe bury the hatchet. Why don't you guys stay for a criticism?"

Beau glanced over at me.

"A what?" I said.

"A criticism," Matthew said. "Beau knows all about them. Care to explain?"

Beau sighed before turning to me. "They're sessions where everyone gets to talk a bit about their feelings. If you feel like the work isn't being shared, or if someone's been doing something that gets under your skin. You sit in a room and, you know . . . bitch."

"It's supposed to keep interpersonal stuff from festering," Matthew explained. "Put everything out there. Align everyone's intentions."

Of course I wanted to stay. I'd read about similar sessions in other intentional communities, but I'd never thought I'd get to see one myself. Better still, I could write about it.

"I'd love to stay. If you think Louisa won't mind—"

"Oh, she will, no doubt," Matthew said. His grin was not entirely kind. "C'mon. We like to do it before dinner, so everyone has a clear heart when we sit down to break bread together."

"Honestly, Matt"—I saw Matthew flinch at Beau's abbreviation—"I think we might just skip it."

As I pulled out of the drive, I took my foot off the gas for a moment; I thought I could hear the sound of voices, singing together, eerily in tune.

Chapter 18

Tomatoes. When I closed my eyes, I saw a sea of red. I dug pulpy flesh from beneath my fingernails and wiped smears of crimson from my collar and cheekbones. Louisa looked like a *Braveheart* extra, with her bouncy red curls and swaths of ruby smeared across her face and forearms.

It was mid-September, and harvest was officially nearing its end. A few things would persist until the first hard frost, but this was our last chance, the final push before the cold.

A warm afternoon found us all (save Beau) gathered in the clearing, shucking corn and dicing tomatoes. Louisa wanted to try to make cornmeal, since we had already canned quite a lot of sweet corn, and we were all sick of fresh polenta, delicious though it was. After squabbling over tasks, we had settled into a happy quiet rhythm, broken only by Chloe's voice as she sang strange old folk songs from the British Isles. These dark tunes were an odd contrast to the brilliant sunny day, but I found them soothing. Her voice, unlike her hands and body, was untrained, and I liked the soft warble of her high notes and the falters when her throat caught. When her voice broke off in the midst of a line, I looked up from the silky husks I was so focused on stripping.

The same big truck Chloe and I had encountered earlier in the summer was in our driveway. I shot a quick look at Louisa, who appeared surprised but raring for a fight. I regretted her presence, even as I felt relieved that it would be her to confront them, rather than me. She already had her cellphone in her hand as she approached the pickup.

The same driver, who I'd since learned was Larson himself, emerged from the cab, though this time he was accompanied by a younger man, a guy I thought I had maybe seen around Ithaca. I sidled closer to Chloe, who had gone white and looked as though she wanted to retreat to her cabin.

"You don't have to stick around for this," I told her in a hushed tone.

"No, Louisa needs me," she answered, gamely trying to square her shoulders.

"Well, hello, ma'am," Larson purred. "I feel like I haven't seen you out of court in some time."

I was startled to overhear this; I didn't realize there had been any court hearings. I certainly hadn't been invited to them.

"Nice of you to drop by," Louisa said. "Would you like to taste a tomato? I think you'd be impressed by how flavorful and nonsynthetic they taste when you grow them organically. From heirloom seeds."

"That's very kind, but I'm partial to my wife's tomatoes. She's got a little patch in our front yard."

"I imagine you're much more careful not to dump toxic chemicals on the food *you* eat. After all, who would want to eat chemical sludge?"

"Actually, my wife uses pesticides on our garden patch, just like her great-grandmother did. Only you hippies have this newfangled notion that all chemicals are evil."

"Well, in that case, I expect our disagreement will be rather short-lived. Since you will be too."

Larson's face darkened. "Is that a threat, miss?"

"Just an observation on your health." Louisa smirked. "I hope you've got health insurance. Though if your Republican cronies have their way, I imagine you might find yourself out of luck. When they're done, they'll be the only ones in the country with insurance."

"Listen, I didn't come out here to talk politics with you," Larson said.

"I'm afraid these days everything seems to be political. Even, strangely enough, whether it should be legal to poison thousands of people, future generations, and destroy farmable land for the sake of one man's profit. Late-stage capitalism's a bitch."

"We're just protecting our livelihood," the younger man interjected. "This isn't about—capitalism or, or communism or anything. We're just trying to pay our mortgage."

"Your mortgage on your giant estate, safely situated fifty miles from here? I really do feel for you."

"My father worked hard for everything he has," protested the young guy. "No one gave us a red cent—"

"You mean no one other than the federal government that you feel so strongly should be eliminated? You've been accepting enormous subsidies from the feds for decades, and then you want to turn around and claim that it's all been fucking elbow grease. Your hypocrisy is disgusting." Louisa spat on the ground.

"Very ladylike," the young man sneered.

"Yes, that would be the very worst insult you can think of. That I'm not behaving enough like a lady. Keep talking, you sexist pig. The judge on our case is a staunch feminist, and I think she'll really be interested in how you came onto my property to launch chauvinist comments at me in a threatening way."

"Prove it, you psycho bitch—"

"Josh, that's enough," Larson the elder interrupted. "We're not here to argue, or to insult each other." He gave both Louisa and Josh a censorious look that I could only describe as paternal. "I came to discuss a settlement, as neighbors. This case is costing us both money, not to mention time and energy traveling to the court. It's in both our interests to come to an agreement."

"Then why aren't our lawyers here?"

"Like I said, I wanted to talk. As neighbors."

Louisa scowled at him.

"There's also something I think you should see," Larson continued, "and I thought you might appreciate it if we talked about it out of court."

Louisa paused. "Well, look, I'd invite you in, but as you can see, we're in the middle of harvest. I would've thought you'd be too," she couldn't help adding.

"We're on our lunch break," Larson said. He moved a little farther from his truck, and though Louisa looked hostile, she didn't object. I saw that under his arm he carried an envelope.

"It might surprise you to know," he said, "that we recently had a little incident at our cow barn. We went to milk the cows one morning only to discover that most of them had somehow gotten loose."

"Well, I imagine pasture-fed cows might be a nice change of pace for your usual consumers."

"The thing about cows, though, is they're not all that smart. And there were a number of calves in the herd. Unfortunately, they wandered off and got themselves in some trouble. When we couldn't find them, several of the babies were torn to pieces by coyotes." With a studied expression, he pulled what looked like a handful of photos from the envelope he carried and flipped through them thoughtfully. He passed a photo to Louisa. "Not a pretty sight, as you can see. A real shame."

Louisa looked uneasy, and handed him the photo back after a cursory glance.

"I guess you should mend your fences," she said. Her spunkiness seemed to have been deflated, though. "No pun," she added.

"See, that's the thing. It wasn't just one fence that failed. It musta been three, for these cows to get where they ended up. And cows, like I said, aren't that bright. They're creatures of habit. They tend to stick pretty close to their usual stomping grounds. No pun there, either."

"Maybe you have adventurous animals," Louisa said uneasily.

"I thought maybe so too. But then we figured we'd double-check the cameras, you know. See if anything maybe spooked them, in the night. A dog that got loose, maybe." Larson glanced casually over at Argos, and I resisted the urge to go stand in front of him.

"Wouldn't think you'd have security cameras to film cows," Louisa said.

"No, you wouldn't, right?" Larson smiled. "But we've had some security issues the last few months. As you know. And we had an attempted break-in at the dairy barns earlier in the summer, so we thought it might be a good investment. Just in case."

Though I could see only part of Louisa's face in profile, I caught the stiffening of her shoulders, and I knew that whatever was coming next wasn't good.

"And wouldn't you know it? It wasn't a dog spooked them cows and got them out. It was some kids. Maybe pranksters—what do you think?" Again with an exaggerated show of casualness, Larson pulled two more photos from his envelope.

"You recognize any of these kids? Maybe some of the ones you run around with?"

Louisa looked at each photo for a second or two before handing them back. "No, they don't look familiar. The quality of those photos isn't very good, though. I'd think you'd have a hard time proving an identity. You know, definitively. In court."

Though I couldn't see the smile she flashed at Larson, I knew exactly what her face looked like.

"Probably just some 'punks' on a dare," Louisa said. "Those darned kids, you know. Still, best of luck finding them. Wouldn't want any more baby cows to die unnecessarily. But then, what do you do with male calves again? They get slaughtered for veal, right?"

"Better than being eaten alive by a coyote," Josh said.

"That may be," Louisa said. "I wouldn't know. But I'm not quite sure what your cattle have to do with our disagreement."

"I think you have a pretty good idea," Larson said, straightening his photos. "Why don't you go call your daddy and ask him what he thinks. You've got my number. I'd be more than happy to talk it over, with either of you."

"And I'm sure we can catch up in court at the next hearing. Octo-ber, isn't it? I imagine you're very busy that time of year. Must be hard to carve out time for court. A real inconvenience."

"Yes, young lady, it is." Larson nodded once in goodbye, and he and his son churned off in a plume of dust, their Hemi engine revving all the while.

"I'll bet they don't even get fifteen miles to the gallon with that thing," Jack muttered.

After our neighbors' departure, Louisa was cagey and clearly wanted to be alone. Jack and I tried, unsuccessfully, to get her to divulge some information, but she was taciturn and unwilling to say much.

"Look, guys, it's classic intimidation tactics. They want to psych us out so that we'll settle and they can keep dumping toxins into our water. It's bullshit. I'd think you should be able to see that at least, Jack."

At this stage it was dawning on me how little I knew of Louisa's (and Rudy's) lawsuit, and I couldn't help needling her for information I should have requested months ago.

"Louisa, how far has the suit gone? It's, uh, civil, right? How much are you suing them for? Is there actually a precedent for this type of case?" I was suddenly impressed by the ballsy magnitude of what she was attempting, and how little I'd either cared about or contributed to this sector of our shared pursuit.

Louisa, however, wasn't fielding questions at this time, and an-swered me in what I considered to be her press secretary voice, each response couched in vaguely legalistic terms that committed her to nothing.

"That, I'm afraid, is privileged information," she said. Deflecting us, she returned to her cabin. Jack shook his head and went into the big cabin to sterilize some more Ball jars and start up a fresh batch of sauce. Though Louisa had been proprietary about her tomato sauce recipe in the beginning, she had since allowed anyone who was willing to replicate it to take a turn at the stove; the dullness of repetition had convinced her to relinquish her secrets. At least in that arena.

Chloe, I noted, had retreated back to her own bunk without saying a word. She was doing this more and more often; I frequently found her swaddled in her quilt in the middle of the day, conked out and damp with sweat. She would sleep through any jostling attempts to wake her. I occasionally wondered if she was taking tranquilizers or some other kind of downer; I knew very little about prescription medications, but her attitude and catatonic stare didn't seem appropriate to someone who wasn't stoned out of their mind. Surely not our Chloe, my Chloe?

She didn't answer her door. Though I knew she couldn't be asleep yet, I also understood that she wanted privacy. I reluctantly retreated back down the steps and scuffed my sandaled feet in the dust of the clearing. The wild grass we had attempted to cultivate had faded during that summer's drought; there was barely enough water for the vegetables, with nothing to spare for the extravagance of a lawn, something Beau liked to point out in a very pragmatic tone, as though we didn't realize it. It had been one of the driest summers ever, and nearly everything alive had been affected.

I was alone, so I gave in to my baser instincts. I went to spy on Louisa.

I sidled up as carefully as I could to her cabin, hoping that Jack wasn't peering from a kitchen window. What I was doing was very undignified, and I very badly didn't want to get caught snooping. I had, once or twice (or perhaps three or four times), in my lower moments, come skulking around these same sills, and I therefore knew that I was least likely to be observed and most likely to catch some helpful piece of dialogue by standing near the back, north-facing window. In broad daylight, I was too afraid to look directly into the frame; at night, the glimmers of light from within obscured my prowling face from any occupants. But if Louisa glanced outside right now, she would see me creeping near the tall grass she had inadvisably allowed to crop up near the base of her cabin.

I could hear her right away, because she was not making much of an effort to keep her voice quiet.

"Well, it was fucking dumb and irresponsible! I mean, Jesus. Fennel is supposed to be such a crackpot civil disobeyer, but none of you bothered to fucking, I don't know, wear a balaclava?" She paused in her tirade, presumably to listen for a response.

"Yeah, but why on earth didn't it occur to you that there might be surveillance? I mean, we know they've been careful after what happened with the tractor. It only stands to reason—" Here she was interrupted.

"No, you absolutely do not get to accuse me of having fucking less conviction than you, Beauregard. I play a longer game, and I'm not wasting my time—not to mention my criminal record—on doing something that won't have a long-term impact. I'm not just liberating a handful of veal calves so they can end up as aperitifs for the goddamn coyotes!" I could hear her pacing the boards of her cabin, and I thought I could also make out the rattle of glasses, the clink of the bottle of Scotch she kept on her shelf.

"Look, I did my best to throw them off. Did the whole 'see you in court' bit. But Larson isn't an idiot. He's suspicious, and he's got a lot at stake. I don't think it's a good idea to antagonize him over small potatoes, okay?" Another fretful pause.

"Look," she said again. "I don't need you to rationalize Fennel's genius plan. I see what she's getting at, but I also see that both her vision and her execution are maybe not ideal. You need to be careful about letting her call the shots." Louisa turned her head, and I missed some of her next rant.

"—their glorious leader's notion? Fucking Matthew? You trust him, after everything?"

Beau presumably answered, and I wished desperately that she had him on speaker.

"Well, it just seems a little impetuous to me, is all. And it's obviously a gigantic fuckup if Larson follows through and actually takes it to court. Am I supposed to swear before a judge that it's not you in the picture? Because I'll do it, but it's going to make me—and my dad— look like total assholes, Beau. . . . No, it's not that. I just wish you'd look at the bigger picture and, I don't know, fucking reflect before you do things. When did you turn into such a raging hothead? If I didn't know better, I would think it's Fennel goading you into this. . . . No, I'm not jealous." I could hear her smile as she said this, could feel her already forgiving him a little, already willing to be on the same side again. "Look, you just need to give her, and Jesse, and—actually, was that Sy in the picture?" She stopped pacing, and I could feel her head tilting back to lap Scotch from the glass. "Fuck. That is a much bigger problem. Fennel getting caught in this is bad, but if Sy ends up booked . . . I don't fucking want to think about it. I mean, the charges he might already be facing, he could say anything— Shit, hang on, I thought I heard something." I froze, like a guilty, busted deer. If she decided to walk the perimeter of her cabin, we would be having a very awkward conversation. Even if she decided to open her window . . . I crept towards the corner of the cabin, again hoping that Jack wasn't looking out a window.

"Look, I just wanted to call quickly and let you know. I need to call Rudy and tell him what's going on, before he gets blindsided by Larson's lawyer. Just, fucking keep Sy out of everything from here on out. You know we can't afford for him . . ." I didn't hear the end of her sentence, because I was dashing towards my cabin. Argos, seeing me run, greeted me happily, leaping up on his enormous haunches, and we pranced on the dry remnants of the lawn for a minute before I ducked inside to collect myself.

In spite of the intrigue, those late-summer evenings were my favorite. We would wash up late, in the gloaming, and converge on the big cabin for dinner. Some nights we opted for simplicity: big bowls of pasta primavera, green salads, bread, garlic. Some nights we spent hours cooking, each of us contributing dishes and condiments: pickled radishes, chèvre–squash blossom fritters, fresh whipped butter, tomatillo salsa. I'd never eaten so well.

After one such evening, we cleared the table and all, simultaneously, yawned. It had been a hard day of work; we'd bushwhacked and tilled an additional plot to put in winter veggies and had split stakes to encircle it. The chicken coop had needed cleaning out, too, and everyone was exhausted. Louisa gave us permission not to do the dishes, and everyone gratefully dispersed to their own cabins. Argos accompanied me, his tongue dangling. Every so often, he would nose my rib cage and run the length of his snout and face along my side, soliciting a pat on his head. When we got to my cabin, he entered before me and collapsed in a heap on the floor. Within moments he was napping, legs poking ridiculously up in the air.

In spite of my physical weariness, though, I couldn't sleep. Something niggled at me, some thought I couldn't let go, and I tugged out my research materials, hoping that whatever it was could be banished with some notes.

I flipped through my information on the Oneida Community, with whom I was growing bored; I felt I'd mined their odd little commune for what I could get. The sheaves of recipes and planting notes made me smile, remembering each day that corresponded to the entry in question. I had precious few notes on the Collective, still, and this bothered me—perhaps that was what was keeping me awake. Without last names, though, I had almost no information to go on, and I looked at the defunct Facebook page for the dozenth time, hoping to catch a subtle reference I hadn't seen before. But my battery was close to dead, and I didn't want to run the truck at this hour of the night to charge it.

Finally exasperated, I packed away all my papers in the box that lived beneath my bed. I'd made no progress tonight, and felt no closer to sleep. I slid down from the mezzanine and wrapped a scarf around my shoulders—the temperature was just beginning to dip in the evenings. I skirted Argos's sleeping body (his legs were now fully extended towards the sky, and every now and again he emitted a delicate "ruff") and went out to my porch, where I sat on the steps. I'd slipped a packet of cigarettes into my overalls, and though I rarely smoked, I wanted some sort of chemical relief. I lit one and sat, watching the fireflies winking in and out of the reeds near the pond. The whole clearing was dark, illuminated only by stars and those odd phosphorescent insects. The pond bullfrog croaked.

"Can I bum a drag?" a voice asked, and I startled.

"Jesus, is that you, Chloe?" I said, irritated to have been crept up on. "I didn't see you."

"I was just trying to clear my head. The thought of the dirty dishes was really bothering me, so I washed up, and then I was walking near the pond. Just trying to get some quiet." I tilted my head; though we tend to think of nature as peaceful, the clearing this evening was actually filled with all kinds of ruckus: the crickets, the frog, the occasional thrum of a mosquito, the splash of a fish. "I saw your lighter and thought I'd come say hi."

"Guess we're the night owls tonight," I said.

"I'm sure Louisa is still up. And probably Beau," Chloe said, interpreting my wounded comment correctly, as she always did.

"Not Jack, I bet. He sleeps like the dead."

"He doesn't have anything to worry over," she said.

"And Louisa and Beau? Do they? Have something to worry about?"

She looked sideways at me. "I imagine they do, and I'm betting you know more about it than I do. You're always hungry for information. I can't imagine much has slipped by you."

"On the contrary," I said with a snort. "I have no idea what those two are up to. They're secretive as hell about it, though."

"Beau is always like that, and Louisa . . . well, Louisa probably has a reason." Chloe sighed. "What do I know? It's always been the two of them."

"Really? I got the impression it was, um, the three of you, these days."

"That's the impression they like to give," she said. "I sometimes feel like, I guess, an accessory, though. Beau's attracted to me, and Louisa needs me, but there's always this sense that . . . I don't know, that I'm still outside it."

"Tell me about it," I said, hoping I didn't sound too self-pitying. Nevertheless, Chloe picked up on my tone.

"I know you understand. That's why I'm saying it. It's like . . . do you remember making shapes, in, like, geometry class? I remember drawing lines to complete isosceles triangles and hexagons and whatnot. And it makes you feel like the dots are necessarily connected, right? Like if there are five dots on the paper, well, then, you're making a pentagon. But that gives you the wrong impression. Sometimes you don't get to connect all those discrete points. Sometimes it's just a line between two of them, and those other dots just sit there, on a homework question that matters to no one. Pointless points," she said, smiling.

I wasn't sure how to respond. I wanted to speak in her metaphor so badly. "Well, we're not living in a homework assignment, right?"

"Don't you sometimes feel like we're living in some kind of assignment, though? Some task, some burden?"

"Haven't we chosen to take that on?" I asked.

"I don't know if I believe in choice," she said, attempting another smile. "Doesn't it sometimes just feel like repeating loops? Patterns?"

"Your brain has a very mathematical bent," I said.

"I suppose studying music changes your brain. Makes you look for repetition."

"I think you're right, though. Humans repeat too." I thought of the recurring generations of people who had tried to remake the world, here in this corner of it. Chloe accepted my cigarette and took a long drag on it before handing it back.

"I feel it pulling apart," she said. "Especially when it's quiet like this. I wonder if the strength of that one line—between those two, or the repeated line of music, whichever you like—I wonder if it's strong enough to hold us."

"I'm not sure what happens if it isn't."

"I don't like to think about it."

"I suppose we're supposed to make our own connections, then. Right?" I didn't dare look at her. She took my cigarette again and held on to my hand. She traced the lines of my fingers, and put the palm of her hand against mine. I could feel our calluses rub. She knit her fingers through mine and looked up.

"I trust you, you know," she said. "I trust you not to hurt me. Not to hurt any of us."

"That's all I want," I said. "To not do any damage."

"I know," she said, and leaned in to kiss me. Her mouth was unexpectedly soft, and I could feel her breath coming quickly. Could she possibly be nervous, to be kissing me? The notion made my belly swoop with pleasure. She seemed like she didn't want to open her eyes, and her heart was beating faster—I could feel it in the pulse of her hand that still held mine. I moved closer, leaning her back, until we both lay on the boards of my porch, afraid to speak and afraid to move except to angle ourselves towards each other. We reached for each other, giggling when we realized how impractically we were dressed for this.

"You know, whenever I imagined this, I didn't think I'd be wearing overalls," I mumbled. She laughed.

"Well, there's something we can do about *that*," she said. Argos slept on the porch that night.

Autumn

From the diary of William Fulsome

Autumn:

I begin to fear that we have over-reached ourselves. I always recognized my ambitions, our ambitions, to be lofty, nigh unachievable. After all, who can hope to attain Paradise? And yet. And yet I thought that if we lived close enough to God, if we dwelt fully within his Spirit, we would be welcomed into a Kingdom on Earth before we departed to that in the Afterlife. To live simply, to love one another, to worship, to father children who would go on to continue God's work. How modest, how attainable!

But the harvest season is drawing to an end. The flowers droop and molt, and it is the time of slaughter. I fear that we are insufficiently prepared. Wood we have, but Jeremiah informs me that our stores are inadequate for the long season ahead of us. We must pray for an early spring. The food stores are not what we hoped. But perhaps by practicing some abstemiousness and self-control we will make do and tighten our belt-buckles as the warm weather arrives!

Mary's condition weighs on me heavily. I never dreamt that our congress would lead to her conceiving—I practiced Male Continence dutifully, as I was taught to do as a young boy and have continued to do except for the occasion of the conception of my daughter with Elizabeth, an occasion that was planned and approved of by the elders in our former community. And yet Mary finds herself heavy with child, and I find myself heavy with Guilt and Apprehension. I cannot keep her safe from this child, from her own Flesh; I can do nothing but ensure that she gets food and rest.

I fear I cannot even comfort her. Still, I thought I saw her smile as she watched the chickens going to roost, and she put her hands on her belly and looked to the sky. Perhaps a child can heal her.

Jeremiah dotes on Mary, and I have seen him bring her a posy of autumn blooms. As leader, I feel I should comment, to each, on their impropriety. Due to her condition, Mary is unable to venture much into society, but in spite of our unconventional living here, she will likely have to answer for her morality eventually, once the child is born. I can insulate her from some of the outside world's cruelty, but it is evident that we can never hope to be truly self-sufficient and self-enclosed. The prudishness of society will require her to repent, sooner or later. My position, alas, prevents me from claiming the child as my own, of course, and therefore she will need to find the strength to support and defend it.

Annabelle grows nearer her time as well, and I can see the worry in Jeremiah's face as he watches her moving slowly around our farm; truly, she has grown enormous! I can scarce believe she carries but one child. We live so remotely here. If anything should go awry during childbirth . . .

Chapter 19

Summer collapses into autumn almost seamlessly in this part of the world. Hot days creep even into October, and everything is light and warmth, until, at some point, there's a crisp chill at dawn, perfect fruit, and the danger of frost. The overbearing monochrome of summer gives way to the flashy swoops of goldenrod, Queen Anne's lace, black-eyed Susans, and asters.

Beau and Chloe and I took a walk on one of those perfect fall days; it was just cool enough to wear a sweater, which you would strip off once you were out in the sun. We were going to look for raspberries, which were almost gone, but sometimes you could stumble on a patch that hadn't been ravished by the birds. Also, there was a peach tree up the road whose fruits had been dropping pointlessly to the ground for several weeks, and we wanted to fill our tote bags. Chloe was going to bake a pie, Louisa make preserves.

Beau was in an especially silly mood and was full of bizarre observations. He dangled from the branches of a tree, and then picked both me and Chloe up, one after the other, to hoist us over a ditch. It was an unnecessary gesture that made me quiver with pleasure; to allow myself to bend passively in his arms, to feel the muscle through his damp shirt, was easy joy, on a day that was too easily joyous.

The peaches were collecting around the base of the tree in spongy, insect-thronged heaps. It smelled pleasantly tangy, the scent of sugar more prominent than the undertone of rotten fruit. The tree sounded as though it itself were buzzing steadily, such was the drone of bugs beneath its boughs.

"This tree has clearly been cared for," Beau remarked, looking at a branch that had been trimmed. "Someone mowed this clearing sometime in the last month or two."

"Seems weird that they wouldn't harvest the fruit," Chloe said.

"Maybe they're out of town," I suggested. "In any case, it's a shame to let them go to waste."

"Agreed," Beau said. We gingerly avoided fallen globes on the ground, their pink skin bruised and punctured by the critters who had bored their way into the sweet innards. We plucked from the branches, trying to gauge which were ripest by their size. Chloe sniffed each one before she picked it, craning her neck to catch the whiff of fruit and looking as though she were about to kiss each of her fuzzy selections. Our bags were quickly filled, and I suspected we would come back before the first frost.

We strolled back home along the edges of the Larsons' fields. One field was planted with alfalfa rather than hay, and it smelled holy and clean. Beau ran through the green field, and Chloe and I followed; I stopped when my peaches began to pop out of the bag.

"Hard to remember that the Larsons are evil while you're walking in this field," Chloe mused. We looked for our raspberries along the borders, where agriculture gave way to woodland. Finally we found a cluster of berries, hidden from the hungry birds by a tree, and we fell upon the red fruit with starved glee. These berries tasted nothing like the plastic flats of Driscoll's my mother had brought home for special occasions when I was a kid; those had *looked* like raspberries, and contained the faint memory of their flavor, but these were the real deal. I liked the feeling of the seeds caught along my gums, freeing them with my tongue and gnawing on them as we walked, satisfied with the way it felt to grind them with my molars.

"Do you think about the jumper ever?" Chloe asked suddenly.

Beau glanced at me before looking back down at the ground.

"I have, on occasion," he finally said.

"Yeah, me too," I confirmed. I *had* thought of them from time to time, wondering, of course, why they had done it. The truth, though, was that that icy night felt very distant, not part of the same world as this field and this sunlight and the taste of fruit in my mouth.

"It's just always felt like an omen," she continued. "Sometimes I think about her at the oddest moments."

"Like right now?" Beau asked, looking around us at the field with a smile.

"Exactly," she said. "It's silly, I guess." She shook her head. "Let's go look in on my bees. I haven't been out there in a week, and we'll just have to cut around the second cornfield."

"Think how pleased Louisa will be if we bring some honey home," Beau said.

We circled around the corn, and I shifted the bag of peaches onto my hip; their weight had been digging uncomfortably into my collarbone. Argos bounded out of the woods, seeming to have located us by sheer doggy intuition. I offered him a peach, which he chomped on before racing off for a victory lap, fruit clutched in his jaws.

As we approached the boxes where Chloe's hive lived, she began to frown.

"I don't like the sound of that," she said, setting down her tote of fruit.

"Sound of what?" I asked.

"Exactly." She moved slowly and confidently towards the hive. I hung back, not sure what the protocol was for approaching a colony of bees. I hadn't been stung in years, but the memory of the bright heat of the bite and the cold chills that followed made me leery. Though I needn't have worried.

"They're gone," Chloe said in a desolate voice. "They're all gone."

"What do you mean?" I asked.

"Do you think it's a collapse?" Beau asked, looking over Chloe's shoulder.

"I'd have to check for the queen, but I imagine it is. Fuck!" She balled her fists and beat them twice against her thigh. Her voice was thick, and I thought she might be crying.

"Should we get in touch with Jesse?" Beau suggested.

"Yeah, I'll call him. But, I mean, there's nothing he can do. If it's a collapse, that's it. It's over."

"What's a collapse?" I asked.

"Colony collapse disorder. When all the bees just . . . disappear. They leave their queen behind and just . . . go," Chloe said.

"Why? I mean, what causes it?"

"No one knows," Beau said. "There are some theories. A popular one is pesticides." At this, he looked over his shoulder, back at the field we had just left.

"Louisa," I said, guessing at his train of thought. "She'll think it's because of the pesticides the Larsons use."

"It very well *could* be the pesticides they use. But that's definitely what she's going to think."

"God, she's going to flip," I said.

"Reckon so," Beau agreed. Chloe said nothing, just continued to stare at the silent boxes where her hive had been.

"Maybe—maybe we just don't tell her," I suggested slowly. "I mean, I don't like the idea of keeping secrets, but I just worry that she'll . . ." I trailed off. What exactly did I fear she would do?

"Let's just . . . not mention it for now," Beau proposed. "We'll talk to your man Jesse and see. No point getting that girl all riled up for nothing. You okay with that, Chloe?" He nudged her.

"What? Oh, sure. I guess." She waved a hand. "I want to see if I can salvage some of the honey. You guys go on home. I just . . . I think I'd like to be out here alone for a minute."

"Okay," Beau agreed. "I'll take your peaches, miss." He retrieved her tote bag and gestured with his head that I should follow him. We left Chloe there in the wildflower clearing, and I thought I could hear her begin to cry. As we walked home, the sun began to set. The disappearance of the bees made me feel anxious, and the beauty of the day seemed overshadowed by their loss. I knew that there was talk of honeybees disappearing, some fear of their extinction, but it had always seemed abstract.

"Do you think it's because of the pesticides?" I asked finally.

"I think it's because of the whole damn world, wee Mack. There's nowhere to get away from the poison."

The cold arrived gradually. The blowsy summer blossoms didn't get zapped by an unexpected frost but, instead, faded and drooped. The drought sapped color from the trees, denying us the usual flame of fall, but the chilled-out permutations of the thirsty trees' sienna and ocher were still undeniably beautiful, and the sunlight stayed with us well into October. One afternoon, Jack and I sat on the dock near dawn, watching furls of mist plume up from the surface of the still water. Everyone else was still asleep, while the two of us leaned against each other, sharing a blanket wrapped tight round our shoulders. We'd crept through the cold grass, snapping off frosty tips, trying not to disturb a heron that stood still at the far end of the water, its long legs disappearing into its own mirrored reflection. It had been startled by our movement and exploded up into the air in a display of avian power, rippling the pond. We continued to sit, feeling the warmth creep over us as the sun rose. A V of geese honked noisily overhead, flapping southward.

"Look, Jack. Geese podge home. To Florida, like your grandparents," I said. He nudged my shoulder with his and gave me a lazy smile.

Autumn is death. I had always forgotten this, or conveniently romanticized it. The brilliant demise of the leaves is such a gladiatorial spectacle that it's easy to see only the glory and delight of it. The harvest brings an overwhelming surplus of edibles, and the season's last cobs of corn and the sharp snap of apples feel anything but morbid.

But as I learned that year on the Homestead, autumn is the season of slaughter. Animals that will be too expensive to feed through the cold to come meet their ends on the chopping block in a harsh burst of gore. On our modest plot, we didn't have animals to spare; our chickens, whose egg production would taper off during the winter, would nevertheless be needed in the spring, and we hoped to breed Ferdinand when we got a she-goat. Our animal husbandry enterprises were as yet too modest to support our carnivorous diet.

Not so at the Collective. In addition to their bountiful stock of fowl (some of which would go to their deaths today or in the near future), they had a cow, three sheep, and two pigs. The cow's milk was crucial to them; not only did they rely on the milk for consumption, but Natasha's burrata business garnered a pretty penny from her sales to the local butcher. Early attempts to shear the sheep and transform their wool into yarn had met with laughably mixed results, but Fennel decreed they weren't done trying. This left the pigs. I had visited them in their sty (stereotypes being entirely true in this instance) and watched them inhaling food scraps in a cheerful frenzy. I had been repeatedly told that pigs were smart, but I found myself unable to look beyond their filth-encrusted snouts and indiscriminate hunger; whenever I stared into the pigs' eyes, I saw only appetite. The pigs weren't given names; rather, both were referred to as Wilbur. Not being good for much other than boundless consumption, they were always destined for bacon, shoulder, belly. This naturally didn't sit right with Chloe, and she avoided the pigpen as though their death sentence might be contagious. Or perhaps as though the moral weight of their slaughter was.

On the appointed day, Beau, Louisa, Chloe, and I trekked over to the Collective, having agreed to help. I was more curious than skilled; after a debate with Jack, I had been convinced that as a meat eater, I was ethically bound to take responsibility for the lives I consumed. Though I felt a wee bit squeamish about the prospect, I granted his point.

When we arrived, the pigs could tell something was up. They were rootling around their pen, making alarmed noises and pawing in the mud. Fennel greeted us as we crossed the clearing. She wore a large apron that showed clear signs of blood. Behind her, hanging from a tree, were the outstretched wings of a turkey suspended by its feet.

"Hi," Fennel called. "I've already started." She seemed already annoyed with us, even though we were barely late.

"Welcome to the bloodbath," Louisa said, moving closer to the turkey. Beneath its open neck was a carpet of hay, spattered and soaked with blood. The bird was entirely still.

"I wanted to get started. Get it over with. Normally I begin with the pigs, but it's better to have an extra hand." Meaning our tardy hands, I supposed.

"Doesn't anyone here help out with the slaughter?" I asked.

"Jesse usually does, but he's got other stuff that needs to be done today. That's why I asked Beau for help. The vegans are obviously out. And Sy's AWOL."

"Those pigs seem squirrelly," Beau said, glancing at the restless swine.

"That's why I usually start with them. Once they smell blood, they get antsy. And hard to deal with. The turkeys are too stupid to figure out what's happening right up until you slit their throats. But the pigs know."

I shivered.

"Well, put us to work, lord and master," Louisa said, mock-saluting Fennel.

Fennel took this literally and strode towards the pigpen, beckoning. We followed obediently ("like lambs to the slaughter," my mind treacherously completed).

"Let's start with the big guy," Fennel said, pointing to a massive hog. Both pigs were male; a female might have been spared to breed piglets later. "We'll put the other one in the barn while we work. He'll get panicky, and you don't want to be in the pen with a panicky pig." Luring the smaller pig back into the barn involved the bribery of tasty slop; while reluctant, the pig couldn't resist the temptation of corn-cobs and bread scraps and apples. Short-term thinking. He trotted inside, snuffling, while the larger pig tried to shoulder up to the slop bucket too. Fennel managed to get the pen door closed before Big Wilbur angled his way in.

"Don't worry, I saved you some," she said, patting Big Wilbur on his filthy skull. "It wouldn't be fair if only one of you got a last meal."

I looked at Fennel; she seemed unruffled, even happy. Her calm seemed unthinkable; I was vibrating with anxiety, afraid of how I would respond to seeing a living animal killed before me. Would the sight of blood make me vomit? Was I strong enough for this?

"Okay, Wilbur. You've had a nice little life. Thank you, buddy," Fennel said fondly, dropping the slop bucket in a corner of the pen and leaning over the fence to retrieve a gun that had been propped there.

I didn't know anything about guns, and so I couldn't determine what this one was. Fennel placed the barrel against the back of Wilbur's head; he continued grunting, unconcerned in his glutting, and she fired. Wilbur dropped, spilling the bucket and collapsing heavily into the mud, splattering filth onto Fennel's apron.

"Everyone should be so lucky as to go out while they're eating," Fennel said, wiping a fleck of blood from her face. It smeared across her cheekbone in a gory streak. She looked exhilarated. She pulled a long knife from her apron and bent to Wilbur's jowl, which she opened with a surprisingly athletic tug. The blood gushed from the wound, pumping in arterial bursts. "You have to do this while his heart's still beating," she explained.

I stared, unable to turn away from the prosaic carnage in the mud. Louisa was unusually silent, and Beau leaned against the fence, interested but distant. Fennel cracked her neck, then stretched her arms. "Once the blood is a bit drained, we'll drag him out of the pen and string him up on the hoist for cleaning. Pretty much like the turkeys. I've got the big water baths heating, and we'll wait until they get up to temp before we dunk him, to take off the hair and crud and all. You have to get the right temperature—otherwise you'll spend all day tearing away at dead animals. Not fun," she added, in case we were in any doubt.

Inside the barn, Little Wilbur began squealing in escalating grunts, pawing audibly at the stable floor. The sheep on the other side of the barn mewled in response, and the barn resonated with the sounds of troubled animals. Their dread infected me, and I began to feel my heart thudding anxiously in my ribs; I watched as Big Wilbur's spurting heart slowed, and my own raced even faster.

"I'm, uh, I think I need to take a minute," I said, not meeting any-one's eyes. "I'm just going to . . . take a walk." I couldn't bring myself to walk across the pen, the blood now pooling in a corner, so I clam-bered inelegantly over the fence. I fell to the ground and, too disturbed to feel silly, stumbled away from the barn. As I walked, I heard Fennel talking, still cheerful.

"It's always easier with the first one to the slaughter. The others know what's coming."

I wandered aimlessly about the Collective, wanting to clear my head (and nostrils) of blood and death. I hunted for Chloe's blond wisps, sure that she would have found a peaceful place full of life and beauty, rather than butchery.

And, indeed, she was in the flower garden, stroking the long stalk of a doomed sunflower while she talked to Matthew, who was crouched in the dirt before her. The sunflower had clung to life well longer than its peers—perhaps it had been a late bloomer, an ugly duckling? The carnage of the gladiolus plot lay around her, and Matthew was tidying up the remains. Chloe looked like a wild nymph, taking her tribute from the lowly male earthling kneeling in the grime before her. Mat-thew stared up at her, and the way her fingers closed around the heft of the plant seemed both sexual and menacing. When I'd acquired my

first Georgia O'Keeffe print, flowers became explicit, even porno-
graphic; watching Chloe in the garden, I was struck again by the car-
nality of petaled plants. I sidled up to them.

"Of course it's hard to keep things simple with sex," Matthew was
saying. So I hadn't imagined it. He tugged up a weed.

"It's not as though monogamy is simple," Chloe said with a shrug.

"No, not necessarily," Matthew agreed. "But group dynamics puts a
pressure on everyone to be really communicative and open. What's
hard with two is harder with four."

"Only if you find being open difficult," she said.

Matthew quirked his mouth flirtatiously. "Do you find being open
difficult?"

"It comes quite naturally to me," she said. After a pause, Chloe broke
the stalk of the sunflower, leaving its crowned head to droop, now to
regard the dirt for the rest of its tenure on the earth. With a smile, Matthew returned to his labors. Neither of them had yet acknowledged
my presence.

"Well, I've grown up a bit since I started with all this. I've had to
learn a few things the hard way."

"Oh, really?"

"I was the only man here, for a while," Matthew said. "I discovered
that that wasn't an ideal . . . balance of the sexes."

"Oh, you think so?" Chloe's knee tipped away, her foot perched on
the jut of her ankle.

"Since then, I've tried to be a little more gender diverse when setting up a colony."

"A colony?" I interrupted, not fully intending to. "Is that what you
call them?"

Matthew's gaze was forced from Chloe to me, and I came very near
to blushing. "Sometimes," he answered. "Sometimes we call them satellites."

"The Collective was the original, though, right? The first 'colony' or
whatever you started up?"

"Yep. It wasn't just me, of course. But it was the first one I was ever directly involved in establishing."

"And now? How many have you started?" I asked.

"A few more," he said coyly.

"Would you, I mean, would you be willing to talk to me a little bit about it? I mean, the process but also, like, the documents you draft in the beginning, how you decide who gets to participate, all of that?" I asked.

"Sure," Matthew said. "Do you mind if I ask why?"

I realized how strange my question had probably sounded. "It's— I'm working on a project, of sorts. I guess it's about intentional communities. I'm writing a bit about the Homestead, and some historical utopian communities. I'd just love to know more about the Collective, and some of your other . . . satellites."

"That's your little notebook, right?" Chloe asked. I dropped my eyes, feeling silly.

"I've just been putting together documents and notes. Recipes, short essays, stuff like that. It's very . . . amorphous," I explained.

"I think it's amazing," Chloe said.

"Yeah, I'd love to share some stuff with you. How about I give you my phone number?" Matthew suggested. "We could set up a time to talk it over, you can take notes, all that."

I nodded. I realized I was being dismissed, put off until some time when he wasn't . . . otherwise occupied. His eyes had already moved back to Chloe and the angle of her knee, softened by the curve of muscle and fat that supported the joint beneath. And over that, her pale skin. I took down his number and left them in the flower patch.

The election happened in November, casting a pall over the Homestead. The night of the Event, we went to Rudy's house to watch the coverage and, presumably, celebrate; Rudy had a television. By midnight, we were all staring at his screen in blank horror, our champagne flutes untouched, the liquid turning flat and sour, like our moods. We trudged back to my truck and returned to the Homestead, barely speaking. Jack was the only one who even tried.

"This just makes what we're trying to do even more important," he valiantly attempted. We all nodded, but it was sorry recompense for what felt like a fatal blow.

For the next week, we worked with grim determination, more certain than ever that the world was coming to an end. Chloe stayed in her cabin nearly the whole time, sometimes fiddling with her instruments but mostly sleeping, curled into a tight shell beneath her blanket. We all visited her to deliver tea and toast and bone broth, but she spoke only to Louisa, who emerged from the cabin each time with a worried knit to her brow. In all honesty, none of us really knew what to do, for Chloe or for ourselves.

Fittingly, the weather began to turn in mid-November: cold sheets of slushy rain and gray days. I was almost relieved when the first snow fell; it changed the muted landscape, at least temporarily, to a sparkly white, and we all tried to muster enthusiasm for a new season.

But, of course, we knew that the coming season would be the most difficult. Now we would learn whether we'd adequately prepared, whether we'd put up enough food, whether we had the stamina to do this. We were aware that we had safety nets; if we ran out of food, we wouldn't starve or freeze to death, we'd simply admit defeat and creep home to our parents. It wasn't appealing, but the stakes were somewhat lower than for the beleaguered family whose journal I read alone in my cabin. I thought of them often, wondering what it would feel like to stack firewood and know that if there wasn't enough or it was a hard winter, one of my children would likely die. *We are so removed from having to make decisions that really count*, I thought almost daily, even as I confronted the decision we had just made as a country. Surely the results of the election merely confirmed this growing conviction that nothing I did could ever possibly matter; hadn't I voted for someone else?

I mentioned these musings to Jack one day; Jack and I had grown closer, maybe out of default. Though he certainly could be cynical, he was by far the most positive of all of us, and I found myself wanting to be comforted.

"I just feel like there's literally no arena where the choices I make have any impact," I whined to him one day as we were yet again harvesting kindling that would dry in the shed all winter. "I mean, I can become a vegan, but does that affect the factory farmers? I can recycle, but what good does it do when most pollution and waste comes from corporations? I mean, I fucking voted, I was in the *majority*, and it *still* doesn't make a bit of difference." I threw up my hands in frustration, realizing that I was actually close to tears.

"Hey there," Jack said. "I know, it's easy to get a bit defeatist. But, I mean, we have to keep trying, right? We can't just hand over the keys and tell them, Fine, take it over the cliff."

"I sometimes wonder if maybe instead of trying to bring about change and battle these huge forces like 'the corporation' and 'the state,' it would be better to just let it happen. Let the state collapse, let capitalism have its way."

"Mack, you know who will bear the brunt of that sort of action. Or nonaction. It's not going to be the people who have benefited from these apparatuses for generations, it's not going to be those of us with safety nets. It's going to be the same people who are punished whenever there's any kind of geopolitical fallout." Jack shook his head, appealing to my sense of class.

I knew that Jack was aware of how keenly I felt my own class distinction, here at the Homestead. Chloe didn't come from the kind of money Beau and Louisa did, but she somehow managed to appear their socioeconomic equal, with her knowledge of arcane vintage cocktails and her bizarrely precise sense of European geography. Though I knew she'd had a scholarship and had taken out loans for her education, these mundane concerns seemed not to touch her; she floated, as ever. Whereas I blushed every time Beau made an allusion to something I didn't understand and flinched whenever Louisa teased me for my "peasant stock."

"I realize that," I told Jack. "But maybe the situation right now is worse for the global poor than a collapse would be. Maybe they have resources, an ability to live without that—"

"You can't really think that. There will be fewer resources for every-one, especially the global poor."

"At least there would be fewer people on the planet," I grumbled.

Jack turned his head slowly to look me in the eye. He arched an eyebrow, and I flushed. "You sound a little like Louisa there," he re-marked.

"Well, she's pragmatic," I said, not really wanting to defend either Louisa or what I had just said. I scuffed my feet along the trail, which was freezing into hard furrows. "I'm just out of ideas. And maybe run-ning out of juice."

"It's way too early for that, Mack my girl," Jack replied with one of his earsplitting grins. "The revolution starts today!" He gave a throaty whoop and raced deeper into the woods, running for pure joy. Argos happily bounded after him, with identical spirit.

Chapter 20

Frost and cold temperatures began to keep us indoors more and more often. In spite of the chill, we needed to do a few hours of tasks outdoors every day, but we would regularly be driven back inside with numb fingers and bright pink ears. We passed most of the day in the big cabin, braiding strings of garlic, sorting dried herbs, and playing cards. Jack tried to teach me to knit, but my fingers were clumsy, and I had yet to finish the monotone scarf I had begun, while Jack skillfully produced socks and shawls, the clacking of his needles a soft counterpoint to the quiet, almost like a clock ticking through the season. Beau had returned home one day with a chess set, and we all took turns playing him, though he typically won. Louisa didn't have the patience for either knitting or chess; she lolled anxiously by the window or spent time tapping out emails on her phone to her father. She had stopped speaking about her lawsuit, but I knew that she spent hours every week scratching out ideas and researching people who had had similar experiences. And staring out the window, as though she expected a truck to come cruising down the drive at any moment.

Chloe had reemerged, looking wan and thin, but she had begun to smile again, and was dancing a little, sometimes doing a recital for us in the big cabin. She hadn't been to class since spring, but she still worked part-time at the café where she had met Beau. I was glad to see her dressed and leaving the house, but I watched her for signs that she might want to resume hibernation. She had withdrawn from me since that night on the porch, and I wondered if she regretted it; I was too afraid of the answer to ask her directly. I'd tentatively tried to ask Beau about her mental health, but he had shrugged and raised his eyebrows, saying she was "a big girl," and I shouldn't worry so much. I had found this irritating, but arguing with Beau was more infuriating than just letting some of his more patronizing comments slide. There was no point fussing at him.

Stir-crazy and out of card games one evening, we found ourselves heading to the Collective for any kind of diversion. It was frosty out— not snowing properly yet, but forbidding with the serious nip of the late fall. Although normally opposed to these social calls, Louisa had brightened at the outing and put on one of her louder dresses and a swath of bright red lipstick—the latter, I thought, intended to piss Fennel off. We hadn't all gone as a group to visit since summer, and it felt almost formal to set out together. Chloe was wearing a white overcoat of dazzling impracticality, but she looked like a winter dryad, as though she could blow frost from her lips.

I had to drive slowly, for the roads were a bit slippery, and the mud had half-frozen in deep tracks that sent the truck swerving unexpectedly towards the ditch. I'd grown up driving in the snow, but it still made me nervous to tap the brakes and feel my wheels fishtailing behind me. I wished I'd put sandbags or logs in the back, but I just kept forgetting.

As I pulled into the driveway at the Collective, we all murmured appreciatively at the small colony; it looked like a cozy winter village, with lights burning warmly against the frosted backdrop. With a start, I realized that Christmas wasn't that far away. It was a holiday my mother loved with shameless, dorky enthusiasm, and I had learned to treat it with fond distance. But I realized that I missed my mother's cheap sugar cookies, garishly decorated with red and green sprinkles, and the fussy way she decorated the tree and lit fake electric candles in all the windows of our house, hanging a wreath on the door that would remain there until February. Maybe, I thought, I would go home for a week and let Mom feed me goulash and casseroles and other processed treats of the sort I had so recently disdained. The idea filled me with a warm, guilty pleasure.

We piled out of the truck, rubbing our hands together in anticipation, thinking how nice it would be to make mulled wine and talk to people who weren't the five of us, even if it was Fennel. We'd brought a few bottles of wine that, when uncorked, had proven to be cloyingly sweet, whether intentionally or not; our trades with local winemakers tended to involve a lot of product that was not exactly top notch. This wine was undrinkable on its own, but stewed with cinnamon and oranges and a dollop of rum it might make a nice toddy. Though I'm sure we were all thinking it, none of us commented that oranges most certainly did not grow locally; since Louisa had brought the citrus home, we all happily looked the other way.

We strode up to the farmhouse, chattering among ourselves. Jack had brought a bag of deer jerky, the product of a recent hunting party, and it really was quite good, peppery and moist. He'd done much of the drying in his cabin, and as a result, he had the permanent scent of smoked meat about him, venison in his hair and skin. His loosey-goosey commitment to vegetarianism was rather relaxed at this point. I knew he was proud of his contribution, and his pleasure made me glad. We knocked on the door, which Fennel opened.

"What are you doing here?" she asked before anyone was able to greet her. Though I'd grown used to her brusqueness, there was a sharp edge to her voice tonight that went beyond her usual rude baseline.

"We've come a-wassailing," Beau said.

"A-wassailing," Chloe echoed in her clear singing voice. "And Jack brought venison jerky."

"You can't be here," Fennel said, stepping outside and closing the door behind herself. She wrapped her arms tightly around her flat, rigid torso, hugging herself in the bite of the wind. "This isn't a good time."

"Oh, come now, Fennel. No one cares if your kitchen is a mess,"

Louisa teased. "It's cold out here, and we fancy some mulled wine." She held up the bottle she carried in illustration. "It's bad luck to turn away visitors."

"I'm serious. You guys should go. Now." She glanced involuntarily over her shoulder.

"Okay, okay," Beau said. "We should have called ahead. We'll head home." He seemed eager to usher us all back to the truck. Handing the car keys over to Beau, I lingered with Louisa a moment longer on the porch, waiting to see if Fennel would back down. She didn't.

"Come by the Homestead anytime!" Louisa sang out sarcastically as she descended the steps.

Fennel didn't open the door to go inside until after we had all gotten into the truck. I tried to catch a glimpse beyond her frame into the farmhouse but could see only the warm bustle of human bodies. As we pulled out of the driveway, I noticed that the black Prius was still parked there.

At the Homestead, we were unsure what to do with ourselves, or how much to say to one another. The awkwardness of the encounter seemed to make us all uncomfortable, and I didn't know who knew what about whom at this stage; somehow, the constellation of hidden information had grown complex. I wanted to ask questions, to speculate, but our days of uniting in gossip about the Collective were over, it seemed. We shuffled around the kitchen of the main cabin uncertainly, reluctant to return to canasta or mah-jongg (at which Beau tended to excel, as he did chess—it was less and less fun to play with him). I could see Louisa stewing, and I had conflicting desires to placate and provoke her. We made a listless dinner, eating the venison with our mulled wine aperitif. When it came time to clear the plates and do dishes and fetch water for the cabins, everyone was testy.

"Well, I do all the cooking. I don't see why I have to scrub pots every night of the week on top of it," Louisa bitched.

"I'm sure someone else would be happy to cook, Louisa dear," said Beau.

"Oh, are you volunteering? Because the only thing I've yet to see you cook is baked potatoes," she retorted.

"I like simplicity." Beau shrugged, refusing to be baited.

"I'll do some dishes," Chloe offered, unsurprisingly.

"It's fine, I'd rather do this than go back outside," Louisa snapped. "Jack, can you get more water?" Jack had been dozing off by the fire, and he looked startled at this request.

"I, uh, I'll go out in a second? I'm just . . ." He shook his head to wake up.

"Yes, of course, whenever it's convenient for all of you," Louisa said, slapping a wooden spoon unnecessarily against the walls of the sink. "Don't even worry about it."

"I'll get the water," Chloe offered, and the desperation with which she wanted things to be harmonious was slightly pitiful. She and Argos wore similar expressions of discomfort, eyes darting around the room.

"Naturally. You'll do anything, while the boys sit around, expecting to be waited on. And here I thought we were trying *not* to replicate the patriarchy."

"I'll get the fucking water," I said, and stamped irritably out the door before further comments could be lobbed about. It was crisp outside, and though I wore only a thin sweater, I paused to look up at the moon, hanging high over the pond. Since it was a clear night, I vainly tried to identify constellations. As usual, I found only the Big Dipper. I wanted to stay out here, breathing in woodsmoke and frost, but instead I dragged a bucket over to the hand pump, filled it, and lugged it back to the cabin, my core warm from the labor but extremities still cold.

Inside, the smells of dinner and human bodies felt claustrophobic. The bickering seemed to have stopped, and Chloe stood washing the dishes. While we chattered companionably for a while longer, I could tell we were all thinking of the Collective, wondering what was behind that door.

Not too many days later, I found myself more or less asking Louisa for permission to go home for Christmas. I felt silly, yet nevertheless obligated to, well, check in. Declare my intentions, but without wishing to seem too headstrong. Louisa, for her part, behaved like a college professor who has been asked for a hall pass by a grown student—she looked surprised, then made it clear that I really needn't have asked.

"Mack, if you want to spend the holidays with your people, that is entirely your call," she said as we reorganized the root cellar, making sure the oldest vegetables were within easy reach. "I didn't even realize it was Christmas. We don't celebrate it, obviously." I was, of course, aware that she would be unlikely to mark the holiday in any way, which added to my desire to be home, surrounded by familiar celebrations.

"I know, it's not that I'm asking permission," I clarified, though unconvincingly. "I just wanted to be sure there wasn't anything to be done around here or, I don't know, things happening that I should be here for."

"No, no, of course not. We'll manage just fine," she said, the unspoken "without you" ringing clearly in my ear.

I was hurt by her easy dismissal; I realized that I had wanted to be fussed over, begged to stay. Maybe I'd had some notion of doing Christmas here, at the Homestead. But the fantasy quickly dissipated with Louisa's uninterested wave of the hand, and instead of feeling truly disappointed, I discovered that the possibility of spending several days on the other side of the lake, with my own family, made me goofily happy.

When I told Jack that I was going home, he told me that he, too, would be heading back to his family, such as it was. I hadn't gotten too much detail from Jack about his parents and siblings; he tended to get very vague when pressed for details about his hometown or his upbringing. But once I was able to pin him down about his Christmas plans, he couldn't avoid answering direct questions without seeming ridiculous, and so I took the opportunity to grill him.

"They're from the Midwest?" I asked, meaning his parents.

"Not from, though that's where they've settled now. Actually, my mom's dad is originally from Missouri, near St. Louis—you don't actually care about this, do you?" Jack asked with a suspicious smirk.

"Of course I'm curious. I'm an anthropologist, after all. Or was."

He shook his head disbelievingly.

"You don't have to give me the full genealogy, if you don't want. But you're flying to St. Louis, in any case?"

"Yeah. My parents live a few hours from there now—that's their retirement house, I guess you'd call it—but my sister works in St. Louis. A lawyer. So we're going to her ridiculous suburban mansion, with her kids, and both my brothers are apparently flying in. Which makes it historic, for the Schumann family."

"When was the last time you were all together?"

"God, it must be before I went WWOOFing in France, because I haven't really been out there since then. So a few years at least."

"Are you looking forward to seeing them?"

"Yeah, I think I am," he said with a surprised smile. "I don't see them that often. But my grandparents were farmers, you know, and I actually want to ask my parents a little about growing up on a farm. I don't think I've ever really asked before." He shook his head again, seemingly at his own sentimentality. "What about you? Happy to see your folks?"

"I am. They're . . . I mean, they're not that far away, of course, but in some ways I feel like they really have no idea who I am. When I decided to move to New York, they all just shrugged, like it was whatever, but I know both my parents would rather give up instant coffee than live in the city. And that would be a real sacrifice, for them. They just accepted that it was what I wanted, like it was, I don't know, somehow the obvious course for me."

"I think that's a pretty common intergenerational experience," Jack said.

"Yeah, of course. But now I kind of just want to . . . let them make me dinner and not ask me too many questions, and I can hear about their daily routines and help my dad with the snowblower."

"Just a little slice of middle-class normalcy."

"Precisely," I said, thinking of the bulk jar of off-brand mayonnaise in my mother's pantry.

Winter

From the diary of William Fulsome

Winter:

Mary has lost the child. She is most understandably distraught. Annabelle, whose own child is growing heavy within her, sits with Mary and comforts her as best she can, but Mary is inconsolable. Annabelle, who is all too aware of the danger she and her own child face in the coming months, looks terribly wan, and though she continues to sit with Mary, it is damaging her spirit. No doubt Annabelle feels keenly the loss of her son, Josiah, several months ago, and remembers Mary's compassion. Observing their downturned, grief-stricken faces, I cannot help but feel that it is a terrible thing to be a woman. To carry always the imminent possibility of Life, so inextricably linked with that of Death. A woman takes a child's life in her hands to give birth, and once separated from that fragile umbilicus, forever tolerates the fear of that life being extinguished. What a strange, terrible burden. Male Continence is meant to mitigate this heavy encumbrance; by denying ourselves completion, we take upon ourselves some of that burden. In our failures, Jeremiah and I are both culpable. And yet, as men, we suffer very little from our failure.

Jeremiah behaved most strangely in the wake of the infant's death: he sat holding the child for hours after its early birth and short, suffering life. He grieves for the child as though it were his, and not mine.

∾

It is my fault. I have failed to live as Christ demanded. I have failed them. My vision—my Dreams, my Faith. I brought them here to live as I had been called to do, and my hubris may cost Annabelle her life. The loss of her child has turned Mary into a wraith; she scarce eats, and her Muteness has intensified. When I look at her face, I feel almost as if she is screaming, screaming at me, accusing. You! You did this! You must make it right!

And so I shall. I shall undo what I have done. I must do as the Lord asks me, so that we may all join him in the Paradise that has escaped us here. I will ready us for the Coming. I will cleanse us. They, at least, will be unpolluted. I will purify them before the Return.

Chapter 21

My childhood home reeked of cheap cinnamon candles bought from the Bath & Body Works at the mall just a few miles away, but I didn't care. I took my shoes off on the plastic mat by the door and let my feet sink into the grayish-beige carpet that my mother insisted was the most stain-resistant color available. Mom bustled around the kitchen, clearly in something of a tizzy over the fact that both my brother and I would be home for several days. Dad drank a can of beer and flipped through a tractor magazine that I suspected he had already pawed through several times; he wanted somewhere to focus his eyes while he tried to surreptitiously survey his children.

Ben had beaten me home and was full of stories about school. He was at SUNY Binghamton and seemed likely to outstrip me in every way. Academically, he was unimpeachable, and I could tell from Mom's approving nods that she felt his social achievements were much more satisfactory than my own questionable ones.

"You've clearly fallen in with the right sort," she said more than once during the next few days. My mother was unlikely to ever reproach me outright; this was as close to barbed criticism as she would come.

For my part, I was happy to sit back and let Ben brag about his classes, the track team he was on, his friends, the city. I remembered all too well my own smug tales when I was still in school. While I suspected that Ben's stories were more grounded in reality than my own had been, I didn't mind letting him bask in youthful enthusiasm. Here I was, just four years older than him but feeling jaded, like part of a different generation. As though I somehow lived in the "real world." It seemed undeniable that I lived in a different one.

Naturally, I couldn't remain quiet indefinitely; over dinner, the conversation finally turned, reluctantly but sharply, towards me.

"And how's life out on your hippie commune, big sis?" Ben asked after a particularly enthralling recounting of how he'd gotten his chem lab work finished *just in the nick of time*.

"Not really hippies," I said, chewing Mom's chicken à la king and trying not to think about where the chickens had come from. Mom always bought the cheapest family-size pack of everything (with a coupon), and I had narrowly prevented myself from being the obnoxious family member who asked whether the food was antibiotic- and cruelty-free. "We're just . . . we just grow most of our food." I let it go there. I realized I had no energy to explain our project, and that Ben probably had little interest in (or sympathy for) what we did at the Homestead. And, I realized with pleasure, this didn't bother me as much as it once might have.

"But you don't, like, use electricity, right?" Ben continued.

"Pretty much. For the most part, yeah, we stick to the hours of the sun." I realized with dismay that I was repeating something Fennel had said when we barely knew each other. It still sounded sanctimonious, but it was accurate.

"Cool. Isn't that hard, though? I mean, how do you get everything done?"

"Wake up early, I guess. There are five of us."

"Don't you get cold, honey?" Mom asked, nudging the bowl of iceberg lettuce in my direction, even though I had not asked for it. Though I could scarcely admit it to myself, I was enjoying the flavorless crunch of the pallid leaves, the sugary tang of the bottled Italian dressing. (Plentyofaddedpreservatives.)

"We have woodstoves in all the cabins, so we stay toasty warm. Really."

"But isn't that an awful lot of work?" she asked.

"I mean, sure. I guess. But you get used to it. It's really very cozy."

"Well, there's nothing quite so picturesque as a woodstove in winter," she agreed, happy to latch onto something about which she could be enthusiastic. "I always wanted one, you know. But in this house, it would just be so impractical."

"Not to mention expensive," Dad chimed in, not looking up from his plate. "Any idea how much those things cost?"

"Not to mention expensive," Mom agreed. "And I mean, with our schedules, who would have time to deal with the wood? All that splitting and stacking."

"When you can just turn up a thermostat? Yeah, ridiculous," Ben said.

"Well, it is a renewable energy source," I countered.

"You know what isn't a renewable energy source? Time," said Ben. "Specifically, my time. I mean, there are only so many hours in a day, and each one of those hours is worth something to me. Say I get paid twenty bucks an hour for my job—low estimate," he clarified, in case we thought he'd waste his time on such a paltry sum. "And then figure I end up spending an hour a day dealing with a woodstove. That's"—he paused to do some mental math—"over seven grand a year that I've wasted. Just thrown away."

"I used to think about that when I was doing housework," my mother mused softly. "When you kids were younger and I couldn't work."

"I don't want to crunch numbers with you, Ben. I'm not an economics major, as you regularly like to point out. But you don't actually get paid every hour of the day. And you haven't factored in the cost of traditional energy, like natural gas."

"Doesn't cost twenty bucks a day, I can tell you that," Ben snorted.

"The problem with you rationalists is that you think everything is so easily quantified," I said, hating the way my voice was rising in frustration. "Sure, natural gas and coal might be cheaper, monetarily, for now. But when we don't have air to breathe? When we've done so much fracking we can't drink the water? What's the price then? We'll be measuring prices in human lives."

"Oh, please. Did you go out and join a little Greenpeace cult or something?"

"Did you go out and turn into a Republican?"

"What if I did? It's not like the other side's got any real answers or unity at the moment. At least Trump stands for something," Ben retorted.

"Please tell me you didn't actually just say that," I said, my fork hovering in the air between my plate and my mouth.

"You liberals and your paper-thin skin," Ben teased. "You are exactly why this election went the way it did."

I put my fork down and pushed back my chair. "May I be excused?" I said, already rising.

"Mackenzie, we haven't even finished eating," my mother pleaded.

"Let her go," my father said, and I did.

"Fucking snowflake," I heard Ben mutter as I stalked to my room.

"Benjamin! Language, please," my mother chided.

In spite of my brother's frustrating presence, I *did* enjoy being home, with the thermostat cranked high; I wondered if the needle on that silent dial, fixed unusually high, was meant as a comment on my woodland lifestyle, but I found that it was relaxing to not worry about loading the stove or bringing in wood. I watched snow through the window, not fretting about whether I would have to shovel my way to the woodshed. Dad ran the snowblower with the same pointless regularity that he operated the lawn mower in the summer, carving unnecessary lanes through the yard. I spent time locked in my childhood bedroom, blankets heaped high around me and watching Netflix, which, with our hot spots and limited battery life, was not an option in the cabins. I would emerge to make a slice of toast (so blissfully easy with an electric toaster oven!) and a cup of tea before creeping back to my room. I sank into a motionless torpor of a sort I hadn't been able to indulge in since moving to the Homestead; there, it was unthinkable to spend a whole day without tackling a fresh task. I skulked around my house like a teenager, quite willing to let my mother do the dishes and prepare the food.

Christmas involved an excruciating visit to my mother's sister's house in Ithaca. She was older and more successful, professionally and matrimonially speaking, which made holidays at her house a display of riches as well as an uncomfortable performance of happiness by both my mother and my aunt. They never diverged from this competitive smiling and beaming, never acknowledged to each other when things might be hard or years might be a little lean. This year, I suspected, I would somewhat weaken my mother's position, since her children had for many years been her strong suit in the face of Aunt Marie's large city home and well-off husband. There was little I could do about it, other than drink too much punch or hide in my cousin's bedroom.

Marie lived in Belle Sherman, a posh neighborhood on the east side of Ithaca, and had a well-kept, four-bedroom home there. She was a therapist, as was her husband, and she had recently converted a downstairs room into a home office, where she now saw her patients. Within the first few minutes of our arrival, she was already telling us how delightful it was to work from home.

"What a privilege! I never thought I'd be the sort of person who can start their day in slippers and pajamas, but, oh my goodness, how I've enjoyed these last few months of not having to go into the office to do my notes and paperwork. I only see clients in the afternoon, because you know how I am, Jackie, with my sleep—I swear, I only get in one or two good nights a week, so being able to lie in a bit in the mornings has just made all the difference! I have no idea how you've managed to go in to work at seven all these years, bless you. I just can't imagine how you keep on doing it. Maurice, of course, still goes into his office, which is really for the best"—at this she winked conspiratorially at my mother, in the time-honored shorthand for "husbands are a real pest, aren't they." Mom smiled politely, though I knew that she herself would probably relish more time with my dad—their schedules had been so rigorously determined by work over the last twenty years that the waking hours they spent together were usually passed in front of a TV; they were both simply too tired to do much else.

Marie paraded us around the house, as she did every year, commenting on the updated fixtures, which sinks had new backsplashes, the new hardwood floors in Becky's bedroom, the laundry room, which now served as the dog's kennel. She patted their high-strung border collie on the head as she opened the door to this room, and Shep began barking madly at us, hoping to be liberated. I felt bad for the poor thing; he'd mellowed with age, but I had no idea what Marie wanted with a working dog. She had no patience for training, and Shep spent most of his day turning in circles here in the laundry room, shredding dryer sheets, or on a leash in the backyard. Maurice sometimes took him for a walk. Marie shut the door on the frantic dog, who whined pathetically. Maybe, I thought, I should offer to take him walking with Argos. Maybe I should steal him.

Neither of my cousins was home for Christmas dinner, which was a blessing, since they both loathed their mother and usually generated a tense atmosphere, if not an outright scene. They were now old enough that they could claim to be spending the holidays with their partners' families (or, in Portia's case, at a silent, nondenominational meditation retreat). Marie announced both excuses proudly; for once, she would not have the evidence of her unappreciated parenting on display. My mother, on the other hand, had me, trying my best to hide behind the obnoxious holly centerpiece. Ben, surly and hungover from a party the night before, barely looked up from his phone and might as well not have been at the table at all.

"Mackenzie, I must say, your hair is very bold these days."

"That's what I was going for," I answered, without real commitment.

"But then, you're very retro at the moment, I suppose. Living in a commune, like in the seventies! Do you remember, Jackie, my friend who lived at EcoVillage? Of course that's still going, but the commune lifestyle was very much in vogue when we were young too. What do you think of it, Andy?" she asked, addressing my father.

"I guess Mackenzie's old enough to be making decisions for herself. Not exactly the best climate for a dropout these days," he said.

"No, and I can't imagine that after that TV show—well, never mind. I'm sure it's very admirable, what you're doing out there. I can't imagine you have an easy time of it! Good for you, Mackenzie."

It seemed obvious that she meant the opposite, but there was no point rising to the bait. I poked at my food and hoped to go unnoticed for the rest of dinner.

Marie wasn't much of a natural cook, but she put an awful lot of effort into family meals, so that the food wasn't so much tasty as over-worked; this made it impossible to criticize. This year we all had our own individual Cornish game hens and an exotic display of the sorts of vegetables that did not typically grace the table at either my parents' home or the Homestead. Notwithstanding my mother's cream- and margarine-based cuisine, this was one of the richest meals I'd had in a while, and with the expensive zinfandel that circled around the table, I soon felt queasy and remorseful. Marie continued to pass various gratins and her salad of star fruit, mint, and feta back towards me, commenting that I seemed "very thin, don't you think, Jackie? All that healthy vegetarian living out in the woods, I bet you." I didn't bother to correct her but sullenly poked down as much food as I thought was polite. I resisted the urge to point out that not a single item on the table was locally in season. I wondered if this was how Fennel felt all the time.

By the time we reached dessert, my mother was grumpy, my father completely silent, and Maurice visibly drunk. Only Marie seemed in high spirits, and she regaled us with Portia's recent spiritual conquests even as we all pushed a soggy tiramisu around our plates. My father stood up as she was in midsentence.

"Going to make some coffee for the ride home," he announced, without asking permission.

"Andy, you should have said! Of course I don't typically drink coffee—it's not really very good for you—but I should have thought to offer. Maurice, dear, do you think you could help Andy in the kitchen?"

The two men gruffly excused themselves, both looking pleased to have escaped the table. I sat, trapped between my mother and aunt as they traded barbs over the ridiculous pursuits of their children.

"I happen to think that what Mackenzie is doing is actually quite something," I was surprised to hear my mother say as I concentrated on my roiling belly. "It takes real conviction to live the way she's been doing."

"I suppose that's one word for it," Marie answered. "But, I mean, surely it would be better for the world if she—if you maybe got a job, Mackenzie?" I shrugged in response.

"Well, I for one," my mother replied, "think it's unrealistic to expect every one of these, these young kids to find the sorts of jobs we've been lucky to have, you know. It's just not the same now. I think it's very brave to try something . . . alternative," she added, reaching for words that were uncomfortable for her.

"Yes, well, Mackenzie didn't really have that many options, did she? After what happened in New York."

My mother and I dropped our chins in near-identical gestures, cheeks darkening.

"Starting over is hard, too, Marie. As you know well, since your first marriage." This was unusually sharp for my mother, and I could see my aunt raise an eyebrow at her unexpected parry. I was absurdly pleased at Mom's attempts to defend me.

The men returned from the kitchen holding mugs of coffee. Maurice poured himself a large glass of port before sitting back in his chair at the head of the table, but my father remained standing, indicating that he intended to leave forthwith. I slipped into the kitchen and helped myself to a cup of coffee, and my father and I lurked conspicuously until Marie was forced to stop holding forth. Soon we left my aunt's house, breathing a sigh of relief at the crisp air outside. Back home, I folded myself into the twin bed in which I had spent my childhood nights, overwhelmed by unease and indigestion.

I've since wondered if I was looking for an out, that season; was my return home an attempt to reenter the world, to see if I could withstand it? If it was, I got a definitive answer. The week I spent with my family left me feeling sick and miserable. Just the sight of my brother filled me with rage, and when we encountered each other in the kitchen (he drinking bottle after bottle of off-brand cola, me poking around the fridge, increasingly hankering for something homegrown, nutritious) we invariably degenerated into churlish middle schoolers, bickering aimlessly but with a lot of heat. When he finally left, he lorded his sense of purpose over me, repeating his plans to graduate and get a job again and again, relishing my father's occasional grunts of approval. I wanted my woodstove, my project, my people, my braids of garlic, my cup of bone broth, my kombucha scoby, my dog, my dim gas lamp.

It would make more sense if something had happened: If my father had finally snapped, tossed me out in frustration at my refusal "to grow up." If my mother had said something cruel, something I couldn't forget. If I had been poisoned by the baloney sandwich I inadvisably ate, standing in front of the open fridge at two A.M., a portrait of insomniac modernity. But I was simply bored, anxious, beleaguered by dozens of tiny small things that made this world feel uninhabitable now. Now that I knew it could be different.

If I had been testing myself, to see if I could return to this life, I had failed. So I went back to the Homestead, to see how that would play out.

Chapter 22

My return was hopeful and excited, much as my departure had been. That week with my family had reminded me of the suburban desperation I so longed to escape and had thrown the dramas of the Homestead into pleasant relief. Leaving Lansing reassured me, made me feel as though I was once again on the right path. I played the tape deck in my ancient truck loudly and cracked the windows so that I could sniff the mud and snow and even the faintest hints of grass as I drove down the hill, then through Ithaca, then over West Hill and towards the Homestead. I took a detour so that I could cruise by the Collective on my way, slowing down as much as I could without risking becoming trapped in the slush and ice; I could see hardly anything from the dirt road, and though I was tempted to go knock on the door, our last visit had made me feel somewhat unwelcome. Instead, I continued on, heading for that familiar plot of land.

I expected to see someone in the clearing when I pulled up—Argos, at the very least—but the whole place was eerily quiet. At first glance, the cabins seemed to be empty, and I noticed that the tree we had felled and dragged back towards the woodshed with the tractor still sat there, uncut, unsplit, unstacked. Even though I knew Jack was the most diligent about the firewood, I thought that Beau and Louisa would at least have attempted to make a start on it, since there was so little to do in the gardens this time of year.

After parking the truck, I poked my head into the main cabin, which was frigid and smelled stale; I noticed that a batch of sauerkraut had been left uncovered on the counter, and a thick film of scuzz had accumulated on the surface. I thought about skimming off the frothy skin and submerging the cabbage beneath the plate and jar of water that should have been protecting it all along, but Louisa would murder me if I interfered with one of her in-progress ferments. I placed my hand on the stovetop, which was stone cold—there hadn't been a fire here for at least twelve hours, probably longer. There was no smoke coming from Beau's, Chloe's, or Jack's chimneys, either.

This left only Louisa, who was in her cabin, wearing a large sweatshirt, thick socks, and nothing else. Her stove was pumping out BTUs, and she looked flushed and sleepy, as though she had recently been napping. Her head was nestled on a book.

"Thought I heard you pull in," she said, rasping. "I would've come out to say hi, but I've got this miserable flu. Don't come too close," she warned. I perched on her small table.

"Where is everyone?"

"Jack is still with his family. Chloe is in the hospital, and Beau is doing whatever he sees fit."

"The hospital? What the hell happened?"

"I think she's got what I have, just maybe a little worse," Louisa said, burying her nose in her blanket for a massive sneeze. "You know she hasn't exactly been chipper the last little while. I think her immune system is depressed too."

"I wish you'd told me," I said, sulking. "I could have gone to visit her."

"I thought Beau texted you." Louisa shrugged. "She said she doesn't really want to see anyone anyway. She should be home within a day or two."

"Don't you think you should maybe go to the doctor?" I asked, scrutinizing her. "You don't look entirely shipshape yourself."

"I'm fine. I never get sick. I'll be back on my feet any second. I'm drinking fluids and sleeping lots, which is all the doctors would have me do anyhow."

"Still, you've been out here all on your own? What if you'd gotten worse?"

"Honestly, Mack, you sometimes act like a maiden aunt from the eighteenth century. It's just the flu. Rudy's checked in on me a few times, and I'm perfectly comfortable. I've been drinking gallons of hot honey water." She gestured to the copper kettle that sat on her stovetop, which was steaming lightly. "Would you make me another cup, actually?"

I busied myself with her mug, drizzling honey into the slightly cloudy water, then handed it to her.

She thanked me, adding, "It would be better with lemon, obviously, but I think it'll be a few decades yet before we're able to grow lemons in our orchard. Global warming will get us there, though, never fear."

"How's it been, otherwise, this last week?" I asked.

"Quiet, really. We spent some time with the lovely Fennel, who deigned to let us in the front door earlier this week. Other than that, not much. Chloe and I got sick, Beau had to borrow a car, and I've been quarantined. Nothing to report, General." She gave me a lazy salute.

"You really should have called me," I said again, hurt. "I wasn't that far away. I would've come in a second if I'd known."

"It was clear you needed a little break," Louisa said as airily as she could with her croaky throat. "I wanted you to have some time with your family. The winter can get long and weird. How was your lovely bourgeois home?" she asked. I had underplayed my blue-collar background, and because I had been to NYU, Louisa was under the impression that I was fancier than I actually was, an impression I was in no hurry to correct.

"Full of questions they didn't really know how to ask. Polite. Unsure. I think my brother is turning into a conservative."

Louisa laughed. "A youthful blunder, let's hope. But your salt-of-the-earth parents? Still drudging along?"

I was a little offended by this characterization of their working-class grind, which Louisa believed involved more desks than manual labor, but I supposed it wasn't inaccurate. "They're fine. The big development in my dad's life is his new snowblower, which he likes more than either of his kids. My mom spent three days on the Atkins diet and has pronounced it—I think the word she used was 'codswallop.'"

Louisa smiled. "Yes, please, bring me tales of the great outside world. I've had nothing but my own busy, frothing head to entertain me, and I'd love to hear what the real people are doing out there." She waved in the direction of the driveway. "Really, I am glad that you're back," she said with a quirk of her mouth, reaching out to give my hand a brief but forceful squeeze.

We expected Beau later that evening, but he didn't show, and while Louisa tried to be flippant, I could see that she was both irritated and worried. I was myself concerned about Argos's absence—normally, I would have already had ample opportunity to stroke his wiggling rump and fend off kisses (Argos booping my face with his wet snout), but though I'd called for him several times, he was nowhere to be found. Louisa admitted that she hadn't seen him for at least two days, and I fretted, despite knowing he was more than capable of fending for himself, even in the chilly late-December weather. I made a couple of hot toddies, and Louisa and I sat on her bed, talking until her bleary eyes closed. When I moved to creep back to my own cabin, she caught my hand, and I slept, perhaps inadvisably, against her feverish back, sinking into the warm flush of whiskey and wood fire.

Our three comrades all arrived together a day later, on New Year's Eve. Beau drove a borrowed car that I thought might be Jesse's ragged Honda Civic. He'd picked Jack up from the tiny regional airport and Chloe from the medical center. Everyone seemed in high spirits, even

Chloe, and I was pleased to think that the celebration Louisa and I had planned for the New Year's festivities would be enjoyed by all. While we had hoped for a wild turkey, I'd been unsuccessful in snaring or shooting one. Louisa had stashed some venison steaks from Jack's earlier exploit in Rudy's freezer, and she was going to make a big pot of cacciatore, though she lamented the lack of olives. I convinced her to substitute some dried mushrooms, and she had the dish on the stove, beginning to bubble, when everyone pulled into the drive.

I was strangely relieved to see them all; a part of me had been thinking that maybe they just wouldn't return, that our little dalliance here in the woods had simply come to an end. It seemed inevitable. But here they were, Jack regaling us with a humorous diatribe on unchecked airline corporations, cheeks bright from the cold outside. Chloe complained energetically about the lighting, food, and routine at the hospital. I was happy to see that she looked perfectly healthy, if still on the thin side. Beau loafed on a stool, watching our little group with a distant smile. Once, he stood behind me as I kneaded some dough for a loaf of bread and rested his hand on my hip as his lips grazed the short hair at the back of my head. In my distraction after this contact, I pulled too many rosemary leaves from their stems and absently kneaded all of it into the bread dough, instead of adding it to the stew. I pretended this was fully intentional.

That evening, everything briefly seemed as it had been; we avoided talking of the lawsuit or even mentioning the Collective. Jack was full of tales of his boisterous clan. I transformed my brother into a comical lout for the amusement of my friends. We ate the venison cacciatore. We drank wine. Chloe fetched her ukulele and played us anything we requested, making up lyrics when she didn't know the song. Jack crooned along, tipsy, in his confident but off-key warble. Louisa sat in Beau's lap, and they exchanged no recriminations or taut silences. All of the tension of the last few weeks and months seemed to have dissipated. When we all said good night, I didn't feel the need to monitor who went to which bed; I followed Jack to his, without a glance backward.

We fumbled in the dark, unbuttoning clothes and giggling uncertainly. Several times our lips found each other's, and his latched onto my clavicle at one point, a sensation that was both erotic and ticklish. We raked our hands through each other's short hair, and our similarly bony hips met, a startling collision of our skeletons, separated by two sheaths of skin. When we finally stumbled up onto his bed, more or less naked, we were both sleepy and delirious, and instead of letting this classical dance escalate the way we both expected it to, we were surprised to find ourselves content to snuggle deeper into the down blanket and fall asleep, limbs cozily entangled.

As light seeped across the sill, I stirred against Jack, who was a sturdy sleeper. He didn't wake up when I straddled him to dismount the bed, a posture that was crudely imitative of the act we had failed to consummate the night before. He rolled over as I tugged on my jeans and flannel shirt. My boots were warm, nestled close to the dying fire, and I put a log into his stove before I headed outside, zipping my parka tight across my chest.

I walked a few feet across the clearing before allowing my eyes to focus on the scene before me, too wrong to fully take in. Stopping in my tracks, I was unable to breathe as I observed the animal that lay stretched out near the picnic table. I dragged my feet until I stood a few feet from the creature, then dropped to my knees in front of Argos. His head was tilted at a troubling angle and one of his front legs was bent in an unnatural position, although neither appeared to be broken; he was strangely floppy. He looked dead, though when I leaned in to check his breathing, he mewled. The relief and fear in that one sound broke me in half: I desperately wanted him to live, but his suffering hurt me somewhere I'd never been aware of.

"Hey, buddy. Hey, I'm here," I murmured. I stroked his sweet head and he whined again—I didn't know exactly where he was injured, so I withdrew my hand, feeling horribly impotent.

"Louisa!" I called. "Please! Wake up!" I waited, tense and frightened, until she appeared from her door a moment later, tugging a robe around her body. Beau wasn't far behind her.

"Here! Over here!" I called. "Hey, sweet guy, hey there. We're going to help you. I got you, sweet pup." My breath hitched—I had no idea whether we could help, whether he was beyond helping, but I wanted only to reassure my dog, to let him know that I was here, that I would do what I could.

"Oh God, is that Argos?" Louisa crouched down next to me, her pajamas muddied by the cold dirt. "Ah, fuck. Hi, big guy." She, too, tried to stroke him, as delicately as she could, and though Argos whined, his tail thumped the ground. I had begun to cry, choked tears spilling across my cheeks. Beau stood, surveying the scene.

"Damn" was all he said.

"Probably got hit by a car," Louisa said, shaking her head. "And those assholes didn't have the decency to come tell us."

"Help me get him up in the truck," I begged. "We can take him up to Cornell. They'll be able to help him." Again, I hoped madly that this was true. Argos didn't look good, though; if we were going to help him, it would have to be now.

"Mack . . . are you . . . I mean, do you want to put him through that?" Beau asked gently.

"What?" I screeched. "What do you mean? We have to get him to a vet!"

"Do you think he'll make it to the vet?" Beau said.

"We have to try!" I wanted to claw Beau. How could he be saying this?

"Let's get him in the truck," Louisa said, making the decision without batting a lash, as usual. She gave Beau a sharply censorious glare; he merely tilted his head. "We have to try," Louisa repeated. Beau shrugged and knelt down to help.

"I'll pull the truck over," I said, already racing to my cabin for my keys. I snatched them up and flew out the door, skipping the steps and sprinting to the truck.

In the cold air, the engine chugged in protest, and wouldn't turn over at first. I thought seriously about weeping, but when the engine flipped, I cackled with sobbing relief. I pulled the truck across the lawn, grateful for the frost that had hardened the soil. Beau and Louisa lifted Argos into the cab as carefully as they could, and his big head nestled against my thigh.

"We're gonna take care of you," I said, leaning down to plant an awkward kiss on his snout. His tail thumped again, hitting the door of the cab.

"There's not really space for either of us," Louisa said, and I looked up at her in panic.

"No, come with me!" I said. "I might need help navigating and getting him out of the truck." Neither of these possibilities was likely, but I understood that I couldn't face this alone: if I was going to have to say goodbye to my friend, I wanted her there with me. Louisa's no-nonsense competence would help me feel grounded—without her, I feared I might fly entirely off the handle.

"Okay," she said, relenting. "I guess I can maybe squeeze in here, on the floor. . . ." She wedged herself into the passenger-side floor space, folded into an uncomfortable pretzel. Argos's long legs poked at her head; in different circumstances, it would have been comical. As we pulled out, I saw Chloe appear in her doorway, a white-clad ghost. Beau went to her side.

The ride to the Cornell vet school was tense and silent. I knew perfectly well how to get there, and made each turn with a grim sense of progress. Argos whined at the beginning but soon quieted entirely. I could feel his breathing slow, and I thought maybe he was unconscious. When I glanced down at him, I noticed a few flecks of blood at the edges of his lips. I drove faster. Louisa called ahead to let them know we were coming; as the school was always open and filled with aspiring young veterinarians, whoever was on duty would be waiting at the door.

When we reached the school, a few vet techs helped us lift Argos's massive body, which was now disturbingly limp. I hoped that at least he wasn't in pain. They immediately began to wheel him off to be examined and I panicked.

"Wait!" I said. "I have to— I mean I haven't said goodbye." The words felt terrible, inconceivable, but I realized that I needed to smell the top of his head before they took him away. I leaned over the gurney, kissing him where I always did, on the bridge of his nose.

"I love you, pupper," I whispered, giving his ear a soft stroke. They took him away from me, and I sat down on the cold cement of the entrance and began to sob into my knees. It was at least two minutes before Louisa could get me back on my feet and outside for fresh air; by then, the other pet owners had begun to glance at me in alarm, and to clutch the warm bodies of their own creatures closer to them. I wailed outside and Louisa wrapped her arms around me. She was gentle, and I clung to her while she did her best to console me. Finally, she pulled her head back and held my face in her hands, looking into my blurred eyes.

"This is life, Mack," she said, and kissed me firmly on the lips. It surprised me so much that I stopped carrying on, and after she held me a moment longer, we walked back inside to wait in the lobby for news.

"He didn't survive," the vet was explaining. She seemed impossibly young, younger than me, maybe. "There was quite a bit of internal bleeding, and most likely what I suspect is kidney failure. You said you don't know exactly what happened?"

"We weren't there," Louisa explained. "This is how we found him. We figured it was a car."

"Well, I'd say that was unlikely," she said slowly. "We can't say for sure without an autopsy, but I'd be more inclined to think he'd been poisoned."

"Poisoned? With what?" I asked.

"Again, there's no way to know until we get the blood work and other tests back. The most common accidental poisons are antifreeze or pest control substances, like rat poison. Do you folks store anything like that where he could have gotten into it?"

"Absolutely not," snapped Louisa. "We don't have anything like that at the Homestead."

"Maybe it could have come from a neighbor's property," the vet suggested. "Non–pet owners aren't always as careful about toxic substances." At the word "neighbor's," Louisa flinched.

"We'll get the results back in a few days. In any case, it was pretty quick and he didn't suffer too much," the vet added.

"You have to say that whether or not it's true," I said tonelessly.

"No, I meant that—"

"It's okay," I interrupted. "It's a nice fiction, and I appreciate it. I really want him not to have suffered."

"I'm so sorry. He was a lovely, healthy guy. He seemed really special." Neither Louisa nor I responded, and the vet shifted uncomfortably. "Right, so can I just confirm the info on the microchip?"

"He doesn't have a microchip," I said, frowning. "At least, not that I know of. We found him. He was . . . a stray." I wanted to say "wild, brave, full of the woods," but I didn't have it in me.

"Well, his previous owner must have had it inserted, then. There's a chip with contact details right on the back of his neck. His name's T-Rex?"

"Ugh, that's terrible," Louisa said. "No, we called him Argos."

"Oh," I said, not sure what else to say. "Um, can I see the number?" The vet looked unsure, but then handed me the clipboard.

"He belonged to someone named Lisa Robertson," the vet noted. "Do you know her?"

I looked at Louisa, who shook her head, though she wore a hooded expression. I told the vet no.

"Well, I guess if you got him as a stray, it's not that surprising. Maybe she was vacationing around here and T-Rex got loose."

"I guess." I shrugged, finding it difficult to care. I didn't like her calling him that. "Can I write this number down?" I asked. "I might try to get in touch with her, to let her know what happened." Louisa watched as I copied the number into my phone, saying nothing.

"That would be kind of you," the vet agreed. We bumbled through more formalities: she gave us the highlights from the examination notes, mentioned that she'd found a tick on his chest, and we discussed how to deal with Argos's body. Both Louisa and the vet seemed to think that cremation was the obvious option, but I, for some reason, balked. I wanted his body to stay at the Homestead, his bones to be in the ground near my own feet. Though Louisa clearly thought me silly, she agreed to take Argos's body home with us after he had been "prepared." Thankfully, there was no bill; this was fortunate, since neither Louisa nor I had thought to bring our wallets. We were told to return in a few days, to collect his corpse and the results of the autopsy, which had been offered gratis for "teaching purposes." We drove back through Ithaca, over West Hill, just a few hours after we had come from the other side. It was a bright cold winter day, and Louisa held my knee as I drove.

Chapter 23

Argos's death removed the emotional cushion that had allowed me to pretend all was well at the Homestead. I had let my attention slip from what was truly happening, let my gaze dawdle on the story I desired. I had watched my four friends as we'd tilled and stacked and fermented, refusing to see anything that didn't coincide with my vision of rural perfection. It took the death of the only creature that had wholeheartedly given me all he had to make me snap open my eyelids and look around. His death could have been accidental, but in my bones I felt that it wasn't. I was forced out of my shell, the sleepy place I had inhabited while I'd waited for everyone around me to act. Without the insulation of Argos's cozy body, and after the trauma of his death, I realized what I had been ignoring. Something was happening around me. And I became convinced that I was the only person with the ability to change our course; if I could solve the mysteries of the past, I could save us.

I took to lurking around Louisa's cabin whenever I thought I could do so unnoticed. I waited in particular for her phone calls to Rudy, which offered summaries of what she had been working on. Lurking beneath the sill yet again one snowy January afternoon, I learned that the lawsuit had not been going well at all—they'd encountered an unsympathetic judge who tended to rule in the Larsons' favor for important motions. Rudy and Louisa were generally failing to make much headway in the case. It seemed likely that it would, in fact, be thrown out soon, in the next few months, if not weeks. Louisa's voice rose in panic.

"Daddy, look, I get that we're the Davids and they're the Goliaths in this scenario, but we can't just concede that point. If they're able to establish that there is not necessarily a link between their groundwater and our own—which is flagrantly ridiculous, of course— No, I know the surveyors' reports are problematic. . . . Yes, I realize you're aware of that. I'm just trying to be sure that we both have a handle on, you know, the stakes— No, of course you're taking this seriously— Goddamn it, this isn't about my mother, or about you and me! Can't you just for one minute focus on the details of— Okay, well fine, I'm going to call the guy from the cooperative extension and see if he'd be willing to do another affidavit, or get a colleague to. . . . Yeah, fine, call me back." I heard an exasperated curse from inside Louisa's cabin, followed by a more committed scream of fury. I slunk away from her window, wondering exactly what she might do if she didn't get her way in this particular instance.

I had put off calling Lisa Robertson, Argos's presumed former owner. I couldn't bring myself to tell her what had happened. I had no desire to think about his death, and shied away from any memory or thought of him. Instead, I curled up in my bed and tried not to remember the feel of his warm fur as he leaned against me, the way he had of puffing his lips and emitting little explosions of air when he dreamed. The way his legs would roach upward, transforming him from poised hunting hound to endearing fool, all four paws in the air. I still slept against the wall, as though he were next to me in the bed.

But the niggling sensation that there was something to be learned from his death bothered me, and I finally steeled myself to make the call.

I phoned repeatedly, but no one answered. This didn't surprise me; I never picked up calls from unrecognized numbers. Finally, I left a voicemail, hoping she would ring me back.

When she did, I was outside turning over the compost; both my skin and the heap of rotting food scraps steamed in the cold air. We'd been running low on compost ever since we'd expanded our flock of chickens; the round, scampering poultry consumed many of the veggie scraps we would otherwise have used to create nutrients for next year's garden. I managed to slough off my gloves in time to answer my phone, looking around myself. I didn't especially want to be overheard, though I wasn't sure why.

"Hi, is this Mack?" a voice asked.

"Yeah, hi. Lisa? Lisa Robertson?"

"Listen, I'm not sure why you called me, but it's a pretty shitty thing to joke about," she said. She was audibly upset.

"Umm," I said. "I'm not trying to joke about anything. Maybe you misunderstood? I called about your dog?" I couldn't bring myself to call him T-Rex.

"Look, it's taken me months to say goodbye and I just— Did Fennel ask you to call?"

"Fennel? What? No, I'm . . . hang on, I feel like we're not totally on the same page. Can I just explain, for a second?"

"If this is one of her fucking manipulative tricks to get me back out there, you can tell her I'm not interested."

"Look, I have nothing to do with Fennel," I said. "We're acquaintances, but that's not why I called." I heard silence on the other end, and suspected she was considering. I took a deep breath and kept going.

"Okay, so a few months ago, a dog turned up at my cabin. He didn't have a collar, and there was nobody around, so we figured he must be a stray."

"Where was this? Where are you?"

"I'm in Hector, near Mecklenburg," I said.

"And you're telling me you're not involved with the Collective?"

"Like I said, they're acquaintances. But no, there are just five of us here on our property. We call it the Homestead," I added sheepishly, unsure how else to explain. "Look, we found the dog and we thought he'd been abandoned. He'd been living with us since last spring. But he was—I'm really sorry to be telling you this—but he was killed a few days ago. We're not sure exactly what happened, but we think he might have been poisoned."

"Jesus. Oh fuck." I could hear her crying, her breath huffing as she tried to catch it.

"Was he your dog? T-Rex?"

"I called him Rex," she said brokenly. "He—he disappeared about a year ago."

"Were you living out at the Collective then?"

"I was in the process of leaving the Collective," she said, composing herself. "It was, well, a little messy. Fennel was pretty upset that I was going, but after everything that happened, I just couldn't stay anymore, and she was so resentful—"

"What happened?" I asked.

"You know, that whole thing with Matthew. I'm sure everybody has moved on, because everyone always forgives him, but I just couldn't stay anymore. Not with the way he pulls everyone's strings, and I mean, it just got creepy."

"Okay, so, I'm new to this whole thing. How about you pretend I don't know anything."

"You don't know about Matthew? The rumors? I mean, I guess they're not actually rumors in every case."

"I have no idea what you're talking about," I said.

"Listen, I feel weird talking about this on the phone," Lisa said. I feared she would hang up.

"Do you want to maybe meet for coffee?" I asked.

She paused. Then: "I guess. I guess so. I feel sort of obligated to explain, since you're a woman and they clearly haven't kept to the 'transparency agreement' we made during my last criticism. Do you have a car?" I checked the drive. Yes, the truck was there.

"I do. Where do you want to meet?"

"The coffee shop in Trumansburg? Can you get there in an hour or so? I live just a few blocks away," she said.

I eyed the compost pile, then glanced around. I didn't think anyone would notice me leaving.

"I'll be there in an hour."

Though I'd tried to clean myself up, I felt grubby as I sat in the coffee shop, waiting for Lisa. My short hair stuck up in the back, and I was wearing a Carhartt jumpsuit that was perfect for working outdoors in the winter but was uncomfortably hot inside. I sipped my coffee; it tasted wildly bitter after months without anything nearly so tannic.

A girl about my age came inside and looked around, scanning the faces in the café. When her eyes rested on me, she tilted her head, and I nodded mine. She came over to me.

"You Mack?"

"How could you tell?" I asked.

"Your overalls. The farmer's uniform."

I smiled.

"Listen," she said, "let's talk outside. This town's too small." She glanced around the coffee shop at the other silent patrons. "If you don't mind?"

I readily agreed, hot as I was. "You don't want a coffee first?" I asked.

"I sort of lost my taste for it, after the Collective," Lisa explained. "That, and a lot of other things."

We walked outside and sat on the benches there. I could hear the rush of the creek to my right; the snowmelt was coursing through the creek bed and under the bridge where we sat.

"Sorry to make you go out of your way," Lisa said. "I just—I feel pretty weird talking about the Collective in general, and I haven't gotten used to phones again, even during the last year. You know how Fennel is, about the phones. She gets so pissy whenever anyone uses them, but she knows she can't entirely forbid them."

"Her disapproval can be very motivating," I said, rolling my eyes.

"Even long after the fact. Anyway, thanks for coming."

"It's fine. I was happy to leave the compost behind. At least for a little while."

Lisa laughed. "I hear you. That's something I don't miss. Though there are plenty of things that I do." Her smile twisted sadly.

"So, you were a member?" I asked.

Lisa took a deep breath. "I joined when I was really young. I was a runaway from my family in Buffalo, and I had an aunt here in Trumansburg. Have an aunt. She let me crash with her while I was supposed to be sorting things out with my parents but . . . instead I met Matthew. You've met him?"

I nodded.

"Then you know how . . . unnerving he can be. You never quite know where you stand with him, but you really want to find out. I was fifteen. I had no sense. I actually met him over there, in the bar. I snuck in with a fake ID." She pointed across the road to a bar whose windows were shuttered. "He was charming, and compelling, and he just believed in things so intensely. He invited me out to the Collective, which was just a run-down house and a few tents at that point. My whole life was such a shitshow, and there he was, explaining to me how I could start a different one. I met Fennel, and I just . . . I don't know, everything seemed to click into place for me. I packed a duffel bag full of jeans and moved out to the Collective with the rest of the girls. And Matthew." She took another deep breath.

"I was definitely in love with him. Like I said, I was fifteen. I believed in him, and he had, I thought, kind of saved my life. It didn't matter that he was twenty-seven, it didn't matter that he also seemed to have a thing with Fennel, who was twenty. We were all in it together, working for the same thing. We were going to save the world." She snorted.

"You don't have to explain to me," I said. "I know what it's like."

"And it was good, for a long time. Years, even. Matthew made me get my GED, Fennel taught me carpentry. The Collective grew. I got a dog. That would be Rex," she said, closing her eyes momentarily. "But the more vegetables we grew, the more members we seemed to acquire. What had started off so small turned into a much bigger venture, and

I didn't always like the people who showed up. You've met the vegans?"

"Sort of," I said. "I mean, I've been introduced to them."

"Yeah, they were doing a vow of silence when they joined. And they were spooky as fuck, I'm telling you. Just wandering around with their dead eyes, never communicating. But Fennel thought they were fantastic additions, because they'd both done a lot of farm work. And she liked, quote unquote, 'the integrity of their vision.'" Lisa snorted again. "It sounds so silly now, I can't believe how into it I was.

"Anyway, the politics started to get weird. We had started formally doing the criticisms, and those can get really nasty. Have you been to one?"

"We didn't stay," I said.

"Well. Everyone has all this pent-up frustration, and that's the only place to let it out. I hated the criticisms. And I hated a lot of the new initiates. And I hated that I was losing Fennel to this, I don't know, sort of fundamentalism. I loved her too. And there was Matthew, who was kind of my life for a while there.

"But then there was Allison." Lisa paused, and covered her eyes with her hands for a moment.

"Who was Allison?" I asked.

"Allison was another young woman. She showed up at the Collective with Matthew one day, and she was just immediately welcomed. When I joined, it was all women except for Matthew, but now there were the guys too. Jesse and Sy had put up their yurts, and we had maybe two or three other male initiates. Matthew was pretty selective about which guys he let stick around, if you know what I mean.

"Allison was really beautiful, and easy to be around. And it was clear from the beginning that there was something between her and Matthew. We weren't delighted about it, but the whole point of the Collective has always been free love and open doors and all that. No one said anything. Until we found out her age."

"How old was she?"

"She was seventeen. So, older than I was when I arrived. But I was twenty-one by then, pretty much over the hill. Allison was fresh blood. Things turned south pretty quick. Allison's parents showed up one day and basically held a deprogramming intervention, where they accused us of being a cult and of sexually exploiting minors. Matthew was who they really meant, but we were all accused of collectively seducing a teenage girl and forcing her into slave labor. It was pretty disruptive."

"I bet," I said, imagining the scene.

"Allison went home with them, and even though Fennel tried to get in touch, we didn't hear from her. Then, one day the cops showed up and arrested Matthew."

"For what?"

"Statutory rape," Lisa said. "I didn't really even know what that was then, and when I found out, I was pretty freaked out. That was me, too, after all."

"Did you identify with Allison?" I asked.

"She had parents who came to get her," Lisa answered softly. "Anyway, things felt pretty toxic after the arrest, even when the charges were eventually dropped. I think Matthew settled; his family has money and they just made it disappear.

"But I didn't feel at home anymore, and I wanted to leave. Fennel tried and tried to persuade me to stay. She promised me my own cabin, that I could get a job off-site, that I could go to community college and the Collective would pay. But I was starting to understand that I just didn't want to be owned.

"Then, right before I was going to move out for good, Rex went missing."

"Christ," I said.

"It could've been coincidental, I suppose. But Rex never disappeared for too long. He always came home. I went calling for him in the woods, looking everywhere. But he wouldn't come back. I stuck around a few weeks longer, looking for him."

"Do you think . . ." I didn't finish the thought.

"Do I think Fennel took him? Yeah, I think she might have," Lisa said. "I've thought about this almost every day for the last year, whether she would do that. And I've decided that I think she probably did."

"I mean, did you think she killed him?"

"I did wonder, when he never turned up. But I figured she took him out in the woods, maybe over to the national forest, and just set him loose. Which I guess she probably did, since he showed up on your property."

"That's pretty fucked-up," I said.

"You have to understand how deeply Fennel believes they're doing the right thing. My defection was symbolically and practically really bad news for the Collective, especially after Matthew's scandal. Scandal, ha. Rape accusations. My leaving made those rumors look true, and it made the Collective weaker. She would do what it took to keep me there. Especially since there were a couple of new recruits she was trying to get to commit right around then. They'd arrived after Matthew's arrest and right around when Rex went missing, so I don't think they knew anything about it, and since the charges got dropped, it's not like Matthew was on a database or anything. She wanted it minimized. But my leaving was a big statement. No full member of the Collective had left them yet."

"Do you . . . do you remember who the new members were?" I wondered if they were any of the people I'd since come to know.

"Oh yeah. The redhead is hard to forget, and so is her dark and mysterious sidekick."

"Wait, do you mean . . . ?" To my mind, this could describe only two particular people.

"Fennel really wanted them. She had a bit of money, and he had, I don't know, this thoughtful intensity. Their names were Louisa and Beau."

I lost the thread of the questions I knew I should be asking.

"I heard she killed herself, actually," Lisa said.

"What? Who?"

"Allison. I heard that she took a nosedive off Ithaca Falls last March."

———

I drove home processing what I'd heard: Matthew's transgressions, Fennel's ruthless commitment, Louisa and Beau's proposed membership in the Collective. Why had they never said? Why conceal it from all of us?

And could Allison have been the jumper we saw at the waterfall? Was that the name Beau had screamed up at the gorge?

Though I maybe should have thought of the implications of all these revelations, I thought first of my project. I couldn't help noting the parallels with what I'd been writing about—Oneida, and William, and the other communities that had collapsed for a simple reason: sex. Who gets to have sex with whom, and who controls that decisionmaking. I mulled over instance after instance, running through the list of utopian communities I had researched, considering which of them had tried to redefine marriage and sex as a central way of reordering society. It seemed the key to me, this one central question that everything orbited around, the very thing I had spent so much time fretting over.

As I navigated the slushy roads, I mentally organized the communities into categories of how they had dealt with the problem of sex and marriage. There were those who'd proposed complete celibacy and separation of the sexes, like the Shakers and the Rappites. The Icarians had opted for mandatory marriage, insisting on its centrality. The Mormons had gone for their version of polygamy. And, of course, there were those who'd wanted something like free love, like at Modern Times, or the so-called complex marriage that the Oneidans favored. Louisa May Alcott's family had ultimately left Fruitlands because other participants felt that Bronson's loyalty to his wife and child threatened the unity of the community. Even Beau's beloved Thoreau had hightailed it into the woods to commit himself to his celibate musings after being rejected by the woman he loved. What happened, what was happening, at the Collective was almost a perfect case study, with the high-minded ideals being compromised yet again by a man who wanted to fuck all the young women. If I could write it all down, if I could make a coherent narrative about it, maybe I could change something, show us the error of our ways. If I could just ferret out enough information, and find the right words, I could solve this problem, and maybe we would be spared these same pitfalls at the Homestead. And maybe, at last, we could find a way to not let it ruin our experiment.

When I pulled into the drive at the Homestead, I was prepared if not to confront Beau and Louisa, at least to sit down with them and try to get the story of their involvement with the Collective. It bothered me immensely that this had been hidden from us, and I couldn't understand why.

But Beau wasn't home. He didn't return home in the hours before sunset, and when I woke up the next morning, he was still gone. I didn't want to pitch a fit if he was just staying over at the Collective, so I drove by to check, pulling up to the farmhouse to see who was around. But it seemed that no one was; there were no cars parked there, and when I knocked on the farmhouse door, no one answered. The only chimney emitting hints of habitation belonged to the vegans, and I was hardly about to go visit them. I looked at the property differently, in light of my conversation with Lisa, and I wondered at everything that had happened here that I still knew nothing about. I wanted to find out, to solve the riddle. Glancing around to make sure I hadn't missed anyone, I tried to open the door. Oddly, though, it was locked; I hadn't even realized there was a lock. It was unusual to encounter a barred door here in Hector, and I wondered why they had bothered.

At home, Louisa seemed supremely unconcerned. She strolled around the garden, checking to see that the hay was spread evenly on the raised beds. She spent an absurdly long time with the chickens, talking to each of them and trying to coax winter eggs from their reluctant cloacae. She cheerily made cup after cup of nettle tea for Chloe, who shadowed her closely, leaning her blond head on Louisa's shoulder while they stood, looking out at the field. Frustrated with her insouciance, I finally cornered Jack while he was repairing the fence around the main garden; some desperate young deer had made an attempt on its borders.

"Where the fuck is Beau, and why doesn't Louisa care?" I asked him. "He doesn't have family, so where else could he be?"

"Where do you think?" Jack said with a shrug.

"He's not at the Collective. No one is."

"What do you mean? How do you know?"

"I went there. No one's there."

"Oh." Jack wrinkled his forehead; he looked puzzled, then worried. "I assumed that's where he was. That's where he usually disappears to."

"I know. But Louisa's not even worried." I glanced towards her cabin. "It just seems off to me. Normally she's seething whenever Beau disappears. But she's totally calm. After Argos, and with the lawsuit . . . doesn't it seem weird to you?" Jack nodded slowly. "Should we do something?" I asked. "I don't have Fennel's phone number, and Beau's obviously not answering his. I've tried him three times."

"Have you called Rudy?" Jack asked.

"Louisa's dad? No, of course not, why would he—"

"Listen, I have a hunch where Beau is. Let's just give Rudy a ring and see if he knows anything."

"I don't have his number." I paused, reflecting. "But Louisa sometimes leaves her phone in her cabin. And I could probably peek at it when she's cooking, if it's not password-protected. . . ." I started to spin through other possible techniques, ways to lift Rudy's phone number from her.

"Mack, he's a lawyer," Jack said, shaking his head in amusement.

"So?" I responded.

"Let's just look up his office phone number online."

Beau was in jail, again. And Louisa, apparently, had refused to bail him out and had forbidden Rudy to get involved. He'd been arrested more than two days ago, and as far as Rudy knew, no one else had yet posted bail for him. When we asked about Fennel and company, he claimed not to know. Jack and I hung up the phone, entirely unsure what to do.

"Maybe if we could talk to Natasha," I finally suggested. "She's the sanest one of all of them, and she might give us some straight answers."

Jack and I got in the truck, not even bothering to make up an excuse for Louisa and Chloe. Hopefully they'd assume we'd just gone to town. How had it come to this? We swung into the driveway at the Collective, prepared to find it still empty. But I halted the truck at the sight of not just Jesse's Honda but the black Prius in the drive. I glanced over at Jack; I'd told him that the Collective was deserted.

"Well, maybe they'll have some answers for us," Jack said, lurching from the cab. "Straight from the horse's mouth." Because, for whatever reason, we both felt certain that Fennel was involved in this, and that she would know about Beau's arrest.

She greeted us at the door with a wide smile.

"I thought some of you kids would show up sooner or later. Thought it might be Chloe, though," she said. "Come in. We're just trying to make a plan for Beau." She beckoned us inside, where Matthew, Natasha, Jesse, and two others sat around the table.

"Reinforcements," Matthew said, standing up to greet us. He gave me a kiss on my cheek that felt warm and sincere, but I still couldn't help cringing. "Sit down with us. We're trying to fix this."

"Tea?" asked Natasha, hopping up to get us cups. I declined, but Jack said yes.

"Is he still in jail?" I said, not sitting.

"For the moment," Natasha answered, pushing a cup of tea into my hands even though I had said no. "He got picked up all on his own this time. We used up everything in our legal fund with the last arrest, so no one's been able to post bail for him."

"How much is bail?" Jack asked.

"What the hell were you doing?" I asked.

"Five grand," Fennel said. "It's a bit steeper for your second offense. The hearing could be a little rough too. They might try to make an example of him, and Mr. Stein"—she bit his name off acerbically—"has declined to help. Presumably because of Louisa. Who has washed her hands of this. So we're trying to think of how to scrape together bail, and then what our best defense will be, to help him out. We've got about five hundred dollars that we can spare, but that leaves us a little short." She glanced at Matthew and Natasha.

"We were just putting together a list of people and organizations that might be able to help," Natasha added, for our benefit. "Matthew has some friends who do this sort of work, and it will take a little bit of time to pull it all together, but we think—"

"You're just going to leave him in jail while you figure it out?"

"We don't really have many options," Fennel said pointedly. "They don't just let him out because we promise to pony up."

"Yes, Fennel, we realize that," I snapped. "Why is he alone, though? Weren't you with him? What *were you doing?*" I tried to quell the hysteria creeping into my voice, but was not entirely successful.

"We cut open the fence of the company we've been protesting," Natasha said. "It was just the three of us." She gestured at herself and Jesse. "It was supposed to be reconnaissance, so we could get a feeling for the site, but they've hired full-time security guards since the last time we were there. Beau ran directly towards the guy so that Jesse and I could get out."

"So he took the fall for you," I said accusingly.

"That was the plan we'd agreed on," Fennel said. "Beau has the fewest arrests, except for Natasha. And since she's black, we generally try to keep her from having any interactions with law enforcement. For obvious reasons."

"Oh," I said meekly. "Still. You can't just . . . leave him."

"We're not planning to, Mack," Matthew said, putting a hand on my shoulder. "We're going to get him out, and we're going to do everything we can to make sure he doesn't serve time for anything. But he did enter into this knowingly. Knowing the possible consequences."

"Unfortunately, those fucking corporate goons have their fingers in everything. They probably have a super PAC to elect judges," Fennel spat. "Along with those agro-trolls your little orphan Annie has been picking a fight with. You can bet they'll be more than happy to testify about Beau's 'hostility' if it ever comes to that."

"The Larsons are involved?" I raised my eyebrows and looked at Jack in real alarm. "Does Louisa know?"

"We don't know if they're involved or not, but it's reasonable to guess they might be. They sold off mineral rights to a big parcel of land just a few weeks ago—had you heard that? Those assholes realized where the real profit is, so they're taking the fracking money and getting out of Dodge. Going to start over farther south."

"We're worried that Louisa doesn't want to implicate herself with Beau's current legal trouble because of the lawsuit with the Larsons," Natasha explained. "Which is understandable, given how much she's put into fighting them." She looked over at Fennel, who rolled her eyes.

"I can't believe Louisa would just . . . leave Beau in the lurch like that," I said.

"You don't think so?" Fennel snapped. "She cares about controlling Beau, not about protecting him. She hates that he's found his own interests, and she wants to punish him for acting on his own principles. Just like last time." Her face was dark with anger.

Now that I knew she was referring to last year, Louisa and Fennel's mutual antipathy made much more sense.

"I think it's important that we're all on the same side," Matthew interjected calmly. "We're here to protect our Mother, the Earth. And while we all might take different tacks in achieving that goal, ultimately what we all want is a safe and healthy planet."

"Which is fine," I said. "But what about Beau?"

"I have an idea to help Beau," Jack said. "Why don't you guys let me deal with it?"

I looked at him in surprise. "What sort of idea?"

"Look, I need to make some phone calls. How about I check in with you guys in a few hours?"

Fennel and Natasha both nodded at Jack's suggestion, and they all swapped phone numbers.

"Can we at least visit him? Let him know we're trying to help?" I asked shrilly, feeling that I was about to be shut out of whatever would come next.

"I'm sure he already knows," Matthew said, in a tone that was meant to be reassuring. We were shuffled out the door moments later.

Jack returned home with Beau the following day, looking pleased with himself. Beau merely shrugged when asked how he was, and Louisa made a point not to ask any questions at all. Jack wouldn't tell me what he'd done to get Beau out. But I knew that he must have gotten his hands on over four thousand dollars in less than a day, and I upwardly revised my impression of Jack's bank account. I'd had no idea that he was so well-off, and I asked myself, yet again, whether I knew any of these people with whom I lived.

Chapter 24

It was sap season, finally. It wasn't terribly cold when the three of us walked out into the woods, Jack and Beau and I, bearing our sawed-off plastic milk jugs, tree bores, and the spigots we would ram into the maple wood to harvest the sap. There hadn't been very many hard frosts, so we weren't expecting a prodigious output, but Louisa was determined, naturally, and I found myself in my ragged parka and fingerless gloves as Beau showed me first how to identify the maple trees ("Canadian flag," he said, holding out a leaf that had clung to the tree branch for my inspection and describing the tree's trunk) and then how to dig the tap into the flaking bark and attach the gallon jug to the whole arrangement with some wire.

Since Beau's arrest, we had all avoided discussing anything contentious or related to the Collective. We could all feel the tension, and it was as though no one was willing to disrupt the delicate balance of the household. It seemed that we were all afraid of being the one to topple our castle in the air; I knew that I didn't want to be the person who kicked out the foundation, and so I bit my tongue, and prevented myself from asking for clarification. This didn't stop me from enumerating every speculation that crossed my mind in the file that constituted my project—I stayed up late into the night, obsessively scribbling, composing half-fictions from the few facts I had.

"We'll check on them every other day," Beau was explaining. "I don't expect very much this year, but we'll see. Worth a try." Jack was bounding around in excitement, pointing out every maple tree he saw.

"Take it easy, old sport." Beau chuckled. "We only have twenty gallons and twenty taps to work with here."

"Surely that's a massive amount of syrup," Jack said.

"Not really. I don't remember the exact proportions, but you have to boil the shit out of this sap to get syrup." Beau stood up from where he had been affixing another tap to the base of a thick maple. "My mom used to do this with me, when I was a kid. She really liked being out in the woods."

Jack and I exchanged glances; I couldn't remember Beau ever having independently mentioned his mother before, and I was afraid of startling him off the subject. I was, of course, morbidly curious.

"Once, when I was six or seven, she woke me up in the middle of the night. It was winter, bitterly cold, but I got into my snowsuit and followed her outside. She had me get in my sled and tugged me out into the woods. There was a moon, but it was so dark—I'd never been outside at that time of night, in the woods, and I was a little scared. She pulled me into this grove of trees and got into the sled with me, right behind me, and held me. She told me to listen. And after twenty or thirty minutes, we heard this owl, hooting right near us, and I could see its wings in the dark as it hunted a mouse." Beau shook his head; he wasn't prone to monologues. "I finally fell asleep, and she must have pulled me back to the house before dawn. But sometimes I wonder if she didn't plan for us both to die out there. In the woods. Listening to the owls."

I looked at Beau's face, unreadable as he gazed up into the canopy, as though that owl might appear to him now. I could feel his hurt and his sadness as he remembered his mother. So used to his easy demeanor of distance, I couldn't stand to see him vulnerable.

"I rejoice in owls," I cried, spinning in a circle and gazing up at the trees. Beau smiled and Jack joined me in a fast twirl, spinning me around. We eventually both tumbled onto the hard ground, cackling. Beau watched us until I reached up my hand and tugged him to the ground between us. I snuggled into the crook of his arm, aware of the chilled, stiff mud beneath me. I could sense Jack tentatively leaning in closer on Beau's other side. I suppose we were very silly.

Though I badly wanted to speak to Beau and Louisa about their year at the Collective, they never seemed to be in a room together, and I knew I wouldn't be able to bear it if I asked and they dismissed me. I figured that if I asked Beau outright, he would write it off casually and make me feel as though I were creating drama where there was none to be had. So it would have to be Louisa.

The phone call from the vet school provided the excuse I needed to approach her. While I was in the field, someone left a voicemail letting me know that I could come claim Argos's body, along with the autopsy results. I found Louisa in her cabin, where she was clattering away at her laptop.

"Do you want to go with me to the vet school?" I asked. "Argos is ready."

She glanced up from her typing, her forehead furrowed. She was wearing glasses, and I tried to remember if I had ever seen her in them before.

"Um, sure. If you need me. Do you need me?"

"I wouldn't mind the company," I said. Quite frankly, I would have preferred Chloe's compassion to Louisa's brusque competence, but I needed to speak with her, and she would grant me this boon, would help me fetch my dead dog—she could hardly not.

"Gimme fifteen," she said. "I'm almost out of juice with this thing—maybe we can do a power stop, charge some devices."

She met me in the truck, and we were nearly in town before I summoned the courage to mention what had been on my mind.

"I spoke to Lisa Robertson," I told her.

"Ah," she said after a moment. "I thought you might."

"Why didn't you tell me?"

"Christ. I don't know. Beau and I talked about it. You know him, though; he was all for being cryptic. But I suppose it had a lot to do with the fact that we didn't want you three to feel excluded. As though you were somehow the second string."

"What do you mean?"

"Like we'd failed with the Collective, and you all were take two."

"Well, weren't we?"

"No!" she answered fiercely. "See, that's why I didn't say anything. I didn't want there to be suspicions and questions hanging over it. We were starting for real, with the Homestead. The Collective was just a—I don't know, an experiment. I was mostly humoring Beau. He was curious, he'd been going to the anarchist meetings. He dragged me along to the Collective and suggested we try it out. It was half-assed from start to finish. I wasn't even living out there full-time."

"And why did you leave? Because of the stuff with Lisa?"

"Well, Fennel did try to keep that all hush-hush, but we all knew something was happening. We just didn't know what. As you can probably guess, Fennel and I weren't exactly best friends.

"But I guess we really left because of Matthew. He—ugh, I hate talking about it. Anyway, we were all drunk, Beau was off with Fennel, and I was irritated. Matthew was by the stove in the living room, and he started flirting . . . let's just say he propositioned me. Repeatedly. Aggressively. I was pissed but also pretty incoherent and I made Beau take me home. Afterward, I brought it up during criticism and Fennel just flipped out. She protected him, said I was lying, said I was too drunk. Basically, she said it was my fault." Louisa paused to take a deep breath. "And, honestly, I thought it might have been too. But we found out about Lisa and Allison a few weeks later, and that was that for me. I told Beau he could stay but that if he didn't leave with me, I wasn't sure I wanted to see him again. So he left with me."

"But he stayed friends with Fennel," I pointed out. "And even Matthew, sort of."

"The thing about Beau is that he hates the idea of being owned. I shouldn't have given him the ultimatum; he would've come with me anyway. But because I did, because I put down my foot, he balked. I think he stayed friends with Fennel out of defiance, to prove that he was his own man. And maybe, partly, to punish me."

"For what?"

"For Matthew, maybe. For years of tiny slights and injustices. To see if I would stay, even as he did something that made me furious."

"As what? Proof of you caring about him?" I asked.

"You have to understand, he's lost everyone. His father left him, and then his mother really left him. I'm the only person who hasn't. I think he pushes everyone away to see if they come back, because he can't bear it if they're the one to walk."

"Well, that makes some of his behavior a little more comprehensible," I conceded, thinking of how he could be so present in one moment and then unattainable the next. Louisa chuckled.

"I know it can feel cruel," she said. "But he's like that because he's vulnerable. If he cares enough to avoid you, he really cares." She patted my knee, and I laughed.

"Well, I'm not sure that makes me feel better, but thanks."

"What do you mean you cremated him?" I heard myself yelping at a petite vet tech. "We're here to pick up his body."

"I'm really sorry, but that's the standard procedure. Most people can't safely bury an animal at home."

"Well, I can," I insisted.

"I'm really sorry," she repeated. I fumed for another moment, but there wasn't anything to be done. "Do you want the autopsy report?" she asked. I nodded, reaching out my hand. She gave it to me and mutely scuttled away to fetch Argos's box of dust.

Louisa looked over my shoulder as I read the words "cholecalciferol" and "anticoagulant rodenticide" and "renal failure." Argos was now just a list of clinical terms and a container of ash.

"Rat poison," Louisa said.

"What?"

"He was poisoned, Mack. Both of those are rat poison," she explained, pointing to the salient words. "Not just one poison but two."

"Who has two different kinds of rat poison?" I asked, bewildered.

Louisa's face looked dark. "Someone who might be trying to kill something a little bigger than a rat," she said.

We drove home in silence. I had no idea what to say, and I felt the weight of the box against my pelvis every time we took a curve in the road, the chalky remains of my pup just a soft knock at my hip as the road twisted up the hill.

Chloe was waiting for us in the driveway, and she came to me instantly as I hopped down from the truck.

"I am so sorry," Chloe said, taking my face in her hands and pressing her forehead to mine. "He was—" She didn't finish her sentence, and through my own clotted lashes, I could see her wet cheeks, her petal skin salted. She held me a moment longer, her frame shaking a little, the way it did whenever she was moved. It felt like she knew, that she felt it too.

She took my elbow, and we walked towards the clearing opposite the pond. Beau and Jack emerged from the big cabin, followed by Louisa, who had summoned them, and we made a gloomy processional towards the spot we had chosen for Argos's burial. Louisa had one arm wrapped around Argos and the other around a whiskey bottle.

In the back field, where I had run so often with the dog, we stopped and formed a loose circle. There were several inches of snow on the ground, and the day was weakly lit by an anemic sun that refused to break through the low cloud cover. We stood twenty yards from the tepee made by the low-hanging branches of a huge pine tree; I could smell its sap. A hungry doe watched us from the edge of the trees, and countless other animals observed our progress, unseen.

"He was an excellent fellow," Beau began. "I respected him."

"Hear, hear," said Jack, shifting uncomfortably. Not knowing what to say, he might say the wrong thing, something awkward, so I cut him off, unable to bear a parade of platitudes.

"He was a creature without words," I said, "and that's how we should say goodbye to him. He had no use for language and its lies and cruelties and failures." There had been no gradations of truth with Argos, nothing left unsaid. These months, wrapped in words and ideas as I had been, I'd wanted only the simplicity of his deep breath after a long run, the genuine affection he showed when we had been apart.

Wordlessly, as I had asked, Louisa opened the box and slit the plastic bag inside with a Swiss Army knife. I was momentarily furious that she would assume the responsibility of scattering his ashes (it was my right!), but I realized I wanted nothing to do with that cold container. It could mean nothing to Argos, and it was nothing to me; I had said my goodbye in the cab of my truck, as his kidneys failed.

Louisa tossed the ashes into the air, and there was thankfully enough wind to carry them up and away from us; she had timed it well. A final dollop of dog remained, and these she emptied gently towards the ground; they skittered just above the snow, racing away from us, much as Argos had done. She replaced the lid and put the box between her feet, notched into the snow, and picked up the whiskey bottle. It was from the distillery on Seneca Lake, and the label was stamped with the image of the Finger Lakes. She poured out a driblet onto the ground, and I saw the amber liquid collide with the dusty gray of the ashes on the snow before it melted. Taking a hefty glug, she passed the bottle around until we had each tasted it. Silent, we turned and walked back to the cabin.

We sat around the table, not bothering to fetch down cups for the whiskey, just handing it around. Louisa's cheeks were already bright red, and they deepened as she stirred the coals in the wood oven; she had been perfecting a method for baking bread in the stove, and that's what we would be eating for dinner, with some garlic preserves. I had no real appetite, anyway.

"He was poisoned," she finally said, breaking the grieving silence. "I think you all should know that."

"Poisoned?" Chloe echoed. "What do you mean?"

"I mean that he ingested at least two different kinds of rat poison before he died of kidney failure," Louisa said. "He wasn't hit by a car. He was killed."

"We don't actually know that," I corrected. "It still could have been an accident."

"With two different kinds of poison? And a dog that size?" Louisa asked.

"I mean, if one of our neighbors keeps two different kinds of poison and Argos maybe got into the garage or something," I suggested.

"Argos wasn't a stupid dog," Beau said. "Have you ever known him to eat anything that was bad for him? Remember, he was half feral when we found him. He wasn't a fool."

"He was just a dog!" I said.

"Mack, I know it's alarming," Louisa said. "But we have to get real. Things are getting intense."

"What are you talking about?"

Louisa glanced at Beau. "I think it's retaliation," she said.

Beau raised his eyebrows. "You think they're that upset?"

"I think they could be," she answered.

"What the fuck are you guys talking about?" I asked.

"I have a notion," Jack said. He had been quiet, and I could see he had been thinking. "At least, I know what you're thinking." Louisa looked at him expectantly. "You think it's the Larsons."

"Yes, I do," she agreed. "I think they're pissed about . . . some of the things that happened recently." She glanced again at Beau, who met her gaze without blinking.

"What exactly is going on with the Larsons, Louisa?" Jack asked.

"Why don't you ask Beau?" she said.

"We all know about Beau's little breaking and entering. And the destruction of property charges. *I* was the one to bail him out, if you recall," he said testily. "What's going on in court?"

"I don't even know," Louisa said with an exasperated sigh. "But this— I think they're trying to intimidate us. Make us panic and withdraw."

"Clearly they don't know you all that well," Chloe said. Louisa stuck out her tongue.

"They want us scared so we'll back off?" I asked.

"Well, it's not going to work," Louisa said.

I spent the next few days in my room writing and rereading my own writing, as though I would find the truth of Argos's death inscribed somewhere in the history of the Oneida Community or in my transcription of our chutney recipe. Could I predetermine the end of our story if I fully understood the stories before us? And always, I found myself with a missing piece of the puzzle when I flipped through my notes on the Collective. I knew virtually nothing about them, even after nearly a year. I still had no real answers about Lisa, or Allison, or even Louisa—just accumulating anecdotes. I knew that I needed to speak to Matthew, though I dreaded it.

I drove over to the Collective alone; it was too cold and slushy to walk, a forty-five-degree sleet coating everything around us with the wet. The sun hadn't even bothered to try coming up this morning, and the sky had been frozen in a predawn gray. Everyone else was battened down in their cabins, I assumed, flipping through philosophy books. Or keeping each other company. Distracted as I was by my work, I had less space for my own jealousy.

I climbed the steps to the farmhouse and knocked on the door. Natasha answered.

"Mack! What a surprise! Are you alone?" She looked over my shoulder, expecting to see my people, no doubt, but I shrugged in assent. "It's cold out there, did you walk? Come on in," she said, ushering me inside. "We were just starting dinner. Let me check with Fennel, but I'm sure you can stay."

I smiled in thanks and peeled off my gloves, looking around myself. Maybe if I could get Natasha alone, she would open up.

"Come to the kitchen," I heard Natasha call, and I shucked off my soggy boots into the heap of footwear by the door, abandoning my parka to a chair. I clung to my phone, though, ready to record.

The kitchen smelled of food, and there were six people inside: Natasha, Fennel, Jesse, the vegans, and Matthew. I was the seventh.

Fennel glanced up at me from the onions she was chopping, her expression neither friendly nor unfriendly. Jesse waved hello, though he was in the midst of what looked like a heated debate with the vegans. Matthew stood up and moved towards me, giving me a half hug. I flinched, but he felt so warm and genuine that I found myself softening towards him, all at once uncertain. Could Louisa have gotten it wrong? I was angry with him, and angry with myself for doubting what I had heard. Righteous indignation faded to uncertainty as I had to confront him.

"Mack, right?" he said, smiling, those intensely blue eyes meeting mine.

"I guess that's me," I agreed, wary.

"Look, I'm not sure we have enough for another plate at dinner," Fennel explained, setting her knife down on the cutting board. "You know we have a pretty careful menu schedule for the winter, right? I mean, you have to know how many turnips and onions you're going to need, and that involves planning. Something not everyone manages to get right."

"I wouldn't dream of depleting the winter stores," I said, rolling my eyes. I was hoping to get a sympathetic roll from Natasha, but she was looking at the counter. "Actually, I need to talk to you," I said, turning back to Matthew, hoping he could hear the chilliness in my voice. "Could we?" I cocked my head in the direction of the living room, which was empty.

"I hope I can make up for our ungenerous hosting in any way I can," he said graciously, with a quick look towards Fennel. She blushed at the recrimination, something I had never seen her do, and I instantly felt allied towards Matthew. I wondered if this was his strategy: let Fennel alienate people, and leave him to apologize. It worked pretty well; I felt less on guard.

The living room was warm and smelled of pine. There was one tattered couch and several cushions on the floor. I didn't know where to sit, so I sidled close to the stove, making a show of warming my cold fingers and hoping Matthew wouldn't invite me to take a seat.

"Listen, I'm here to talk about something uncomfortable." I wasn't sure how to even begin.

"Lisa?" he asked.

I blinked in surprise. "Yeah, actually. How did you know?"

"Doesn't matter." He waved his hand. "Listen, it's no secret. What happened with me and Lisa was a really important part of my life. I'm not ashamed of it."

"So you guys were together?"

"Of course! I was in love with her for years. She's really special— have you met her?"

"Yes," I said.

"Then you know. You know she's just got this . . . integrity." He smiled widely.

"Yeah, but she didn't exactly leave here on the best terms."

"I do blame myself for that. Things with Allison . . . well, let's just say that was a stupid, naïve mistake."

"What exactly happened with you and her? Allison?"

"I didn't know her age. If I'd had any idea, nothing would ever have happened. But she said she was nineteen, and I think I was . . . God, I was probably just blinded by lust and didn't question that, because it was what I wanted to hear."

"And you're, what? Thirty?"

"Something like that, thanks," he said with a smile. "But I get your point. Too old for her. Look, Allison was just a fling. I liked her, and she was so beautiful. But if I'd thought for a second it would jeopardize our life here, or her life, I wouldn't have looked at her twice. So what can I say? I'm weak."

"Okay, so you were in a relationship with Lisa, even though she was, what, fifteen?"

"Christ, is that what she told you? No, no, I never even touched her until she was eighteen. She was just a fucked-up kid when she got here. It took her a couple of years to find herself and grow into this really incredible woman. That's when our relationship started, and we were really happy for a while."

"And Fennel?"

"Fennel's always been part of my life," he said with a soft smile. "And don't worry, Fennel's twenty-seven." He arched his back, stretching. "Look, Lisa was jealous. Of Fennel and, later, of Allison. So when things kind of blew up in that arena, it wasn't surprising that she got upset. She could be really possessive, and it was something we were working on."

"Working on?"

"Part of our mission is to not try to own anything. And that includes people," Matthew said. "From the very beginning, we've tried to let everyone make their choices as independently as they can. Choice is, you know, kind of our thing."

"What about Louisa, then?"

"She's still pissed, huh?" He ruffled his hair with both hands, and it poked up fetchingly.

"Yeah, a bit." I leaned against the beam behind me, my hands stroking the soft old wood.

"Well, the thing is, I don't totally remember that night," he said, looking genuinely embarrassed. "Does she?"

"You should ask her," I said, trying to maintain a hostility that was fading. "So you don't actually know what happened?"

"If anything happened, I don't remember it. I remember having a conversation with her that got pretty silly—we were actually right over there"—he pointed at the cushions closest to the stove—"and then I woke up in my bed. I even had coffee with her the next day. We were hungover, and we started the day later than everyone else," he added with a rueful smile. "She didn't say anything to me then, and it was only a few days later that she mentioned that she was upset. I felt terrible, but I really just didn't know what had happened."

"So 'she said, he said.'"

"I mean, that's the tricky thing, right? Everyone has different memories of what happened, and it's easy to interpret things so differently. Do I wish I'd done some of it differently? Absolutely. But I'm not a monster. I never wanted anyone to feel unsafe. And the fact that Allison died—"

"She killed herself."

"Yes," he answered, burying his head in his hands. If this was a performance, it was convincing.

When he looked up again, I studied his face, which seemed honest and open. Could I trust him? Did I? I didn't know what to do with what he'd told me, or with the feeling I had that he was sincere. I turned my face away from him and leaned my cheek against the flesh of the beam, cooling my skin from the heat of the fire. My cheek rubbed against something jagged, and I pulled away in surprise, to see what it was. The word ARCADIA was notched deep into the wood and looked as though it had been charred.

"What's that?" I asked. Matthew looked where I was pointing, startled, then shook his head to clear it.

"Oh, that's from our utopians. A family named Fulsome. They carved that—or, I should say, William did—while they were living here, back in the late nineteenth century."

"Actually, they lived on our property," I said, correcting him. "We think they were the ones who planted our orchard. Such as it is."

"That's strange. There can't have been too many utopian communes in these five square miles. Our Fulsomes? Are you sure you've fact-checked?" Matthew waggled a finger at me. I flinched. "Here, follow me. I've got some photos that came with the farmhouse." He walked over to the modest bookshelf, which held mostly ragged cookbooks and moth-nibbled classics. From the top shelf he produced a slender handful of old daguerreotypes—is that what they were called?—very old-looking photos mounted on stiff black paper.

"This is William Fulsome and his family," he said, handing me the top photograph. "Or, I guess, his family and fellow laborers towards a perfect society."

I looked at the image of two couples, three children, and a teenage girl. Of course I had no way of knowing what William looked like, but this could easily be him, Elizabeth, Jeremiah, Annabelle, and the silent Mary, with their combined brood of offspring.

"I didn't realize," I said. "So, wait, they lived here?"

"In this very farmhouse," Matthew said. "It's one of the reasons I wanted to buy the place. I loved the idea of these people having been here before, trying a similar thing. That beam was originally right by the front door, but the farmhouse has been renovated a few times since they lived here. Now the reminder has moved from entrance to hearth, which I think fitting. A little grandiose, maybe," he acknowledged. "But we have to aim high."

"I thought they lived on our property. I found—" I stopped myself before revealing the existence of the journal. I didn't want to share it, not before I had completed my project. "Do you know about what happened to them? Whether they found their Arcadia?"

"I don't know for sure. I turned up some old documents, records of their spending, and I don't think they stayed here for too long. I called the historical society in Trumansburg, though, and apparently they have a few scraps of paper on the Fulsomes. I meant to go over and check it out, but I ended up getting distracted. Fennel says that's my major character flaw," he added with a smile. I wondered if Fennel was counting his sexual predation. "Always starting the next big project before I've finished with the last."

"I've been accused of that myself." I was wary of him, but still drawn to him. I found the conflicting feelings unsettling.

"What have you two been discussing this whole time?" Fennel said from the doorway.

Matthew and I both straightened, as though we had been interrupted doing something we shouldn't have. I felt guilty, even though I couldn't have said why—perhaps because I was warming to Matthew, believing his story.

"History," he answered lightly. "But what's past is past."

No, it's not, I thought. That is completely inaccurate. We are living in it now.

"Actually, I have one more question, and then I'll get out of your hair," I said. "What happened to Lisa's dog?"

"That mangy old thing? Wolfhound or something, right?" Matthew asked. I watched Fennel's face. "He took off into the woods, didn't he?"

"Right as Lisa was planning to leave," I said.

"Dogs don't like stress." Matthew shrugged. "Those were a bad few days to be here at the Collective."

"You've met Argos," I said to Fennel. "Why didn't you say anything?"

"Lisa's dog was named Rex," she said breezily.

"Yes, but we didn't know that when he turned up as a stray at the Homestead. Didn't you recognize him?"

"I guess not. I've never really been an animal person." She shrugged.

"How long was he out in the woods? Before we found him?"

"Oh, not that long. A month or two maybe? Nothing could kill that dog."

"Well, something did," I said.

Fennel looked me in the eye.

"Rex was never a cautious dog," she said.

Chapter 25

At the Homestead, in my little cabin, I raced through William's journal, poring again over the few entries I had already read. How much did I know of this man? I had researched his family for my project, of course, and knew that the original community, Oneida, had begun to collapse after the leader was threatened with charges of statutory rape (uncomfortable associations with Matthew's legal trouble crossed my mind). He had decided to abandon his noble project, leaving behind several dozen disciples to fend for themselves as he snuck across the Canadian border. It was a flighty, romantic tale, and I'd consumed the scant number of books and journals that detailed his doomed colony.

Though William's journal wasn't dated, I had guessed it to be from the late 1800s, so well over one hundred years old. His recounting of their time in Oneida suggested that he and his family had left sometime around the start of its decline as the community became embroiled in infighting and a collapse of leadership. And sexual jealousy, of course.

But I knew nothing of what had become of William. I had, indeed, incorrectly surmised that he had lived on our own small property, basing my suppositions on Rudy's apocryphal claim that a utopian society had dwelt there. I hadn't fact-checked at all, merely indulged in my own romantic fantasy, pretending that the righteous William or the creepily quiet Mary had maybe slept in my own little cabin, fantasies that made me feel connected with the past, and perhaps a little less alienated from my own confused present. The photographs Matthew had shown me were not irrefutable, but they strongly suggested that William and his friends had resided at the Collective's farmhouse; it seemed unlikely they would have expended the time and finances to take a picture in front of a home that wasn't their own. I had seen no evidence of any time on the Homestead in that handful of photos, and judging from the condition of the wood, our cabins didn't seem to be more than a hundred years old, when I considered it objectively. The farmhouse had been at the Collective since the early nineteenth century. Yet again, I'd gotten it wrong.

I'd never heard of the historical society that Matthew had mentioned, but I headed to Trumansburg as soon as I could, chomping at the bit to unearth more documents. The petite woman who manned the desk proved to be indispensable, showing me how to navigate the deeds and some of the frayed documents that were the centerpiece of the institution. As she helped me dig deeper, I was distracted by a poor reproduction of a life-sized dapple-gray mare; the statue dominated the museum's insubstantial square footage. Said horse had a hoof in the air and a postal bag affixed to her hindquarters; her display was meant to signify the importance of the postal system to this region and, in particular, to this small village in its fledgling days.

"She used to have a rider. A U.S. government worker in uniform," explained the woman, whose name was Pat. "But we had some teenagers who thought it would be cute to vandalize it, and I don't know if we can repair him. Poor Chuck," she said, shaking her head fondly. "I'm afraid it doesn't seem entirely believable that a lone horse would trek through the wilderness delivering mail. But that's what happens when the municipality cuts your funding." She clucked disapprovingly and turned back to the matter at hand. "What's the address again, dear?" I repeated my request.

"Of course, of course. You mean the utopians. We won't be able to find the property marked on any of the contemporary maps from the period, since the cartography was so basic then. And, of course, the place they were living was so remote. Not like now. But I think it's on the next survey—yep, here we go. Does this look about right to you?" She held out a county map and pointed to a small cluster of properties. "This would have been after they left, of course, but from what I understand, several properties are still there. And the pond, of course, which is distinctive." Her long fingernails circled the almost figure-eight-shaped pond. Likely not ours, then.

"That solves it, I guess," I said.

"You know the place?" she said, brightening.

"Quite well, actually."

"Then you know the whole gruesome tale?"

"The what? What tale?"

"Of how their little adventure ended? I suppose it's a bit of a ghost story, rather apocryphal, but it was an old favorite."

"Do you have any relatives who knew them?" I asked.

"I'm old, missy, but not quite that old. My grandfather lived out in Hector, though, and he had a soft spot for scary stories." Pat paused, raising her eyebrow at me, seeming to know that she had me on tenterhooks. I wondered when she had last had a captive audience.

"Would you mind telling me about it? I'd love to be able to personalize William's story a little more. For my project."

"Well. Sure. But now, I can't promise the whole thing is one hundred percent true. Grandpa was one for tall tales, so he may have embellished a bit."

"I'd still love to hear it," I pressed. I could see Pat settling in; she sat back into a chair. I felt like she should have knitting, or some other useful activity with which to keep her hands busy. "Do you mind if I record?"

She looked at my phone a little suspiciously but nodded. "Well. I don't know how much you know about our Mr. Fulsome."

"Assume I don't know anything."

"Well. He was a fairly young man when he came here—to Hector, in any case—in his thirties, I believe. He was one of the descendants of the leader of a utopian community that was founded north of here, in the Burned-Over District. Our friend William had grown tired of the community, and had, I guess you could say, lost faith. He wanted to marry, and the community forbade monogamy. So he left, taking with him two young women and their children, to join other members of the community who had left before them.

"Jeremiah Winthrop owned a parcel of land out here that had been handed down in his family for a few generations. An ancestor of his had fought in the Revolutionary War, and it was common to give distinguished veterans some land after the end of the war. The land, of course, originally belonged to the Native Americans, but the federal government didn't much care about those details, so they divided up everything into homestead plots. The Winthrop plot was a valuable one, nice and big. Jeremiah, though, was an idealist. Instead of working the land his father had left him, he went off to join that commune. When he decided, after a few years, that it wasn't right for him, he took off and headed back home to Hector. He offered the property to his friend Fulsome, when William wanted to leave not too long after. Their goal, they decided, was to continue with their vision of utopia, but without the complications that had plagued their last attempt. Smaller scale, they thought. Monogamy. Raising their own children. See, they believed that Christ was about to come back any day, and they just had to keep on living right until he showed up, and then they would ascend right up to heaven with him." Pat leaned back into her chair, and her story. She seemed to be enjoying herself.

"Problem is, they knew almost nothing about farming, certainly not about subsistence farming; jobs were divided up at Oneida, and the more educated folk did clerical work and the like. Our friends knew how to harvest strawberries but not how to grow a cucumber or put up enough food for the winter. And they were living in a remote place, remember. They would've had one horse, and not many neighbors. The closest town was almost a day's ride away.

"The story goes that the winter came on hard and fast, and things went south for our perfectionists, so to speak. The babies got sick, and two of them died. One of the women was pregnant—the unmarried woman, I think it was—and lost the infant. They were running out of food way too fast and everyone was getting squirrelly, stuck in their cabins and watching the babies die. You know how winter can be." Pat smiled incongruously. As though my experience of winter typically involved watching babies die.

"Winthrop's wife, I think her name was Anna, well, she and her one surviving kid got sick sometime in late winter. Winthrop put them on a sled and decided to drag them into town—he couldn't watch another child die, and he loved his wife. So he headed for the city on a horse and sleigh, leaving behind William and the two women, both sorta mad with grief, you know. They were running out of food, like I said, and one of the women got sick and William just sort of cracked, I guess. He wrote a letter about how he'd seen Christ's return and he was ready to take his wives into the afterlife to meet him in the kingdom of heaven. 'Our attempt at Paradise has been so successful that two of our little ones have gone before us to prepare the way, perfect beings,' he's supposed to have written in a letter, or some such thing. He went out onto the pond and cracked a hole in the ice, and then he dragged the two women and the little boy and little girl one by one out onto the ice and dropped them in. The women likely sank to the bottom, but he must have held the little ones down. Then he walked back to the cabin and hanged himself from the rafters. Winthrop found him a few days later, when he came back to tell them that Anna was recovering in town."

I must have looked sufficiently horrified at this story, because Pat laughed, sharp and barking. "I agree, it's a dark little story, isn't it?" I just stared at her, and stopped recording on my phone.

"Mind you, it could just be an old wives' tale," she continued. "My grandfather said the story came from a letter Winthrop wrote back home to the community, to let them know what had happened to Fulsome and his family. I guess the letter is with the community documents over at Syracuse. The university.

"My grandpa believed the place was haunted, of course. That the ghosts lived in the pond there and dragged people below the surface, preparing them for Christ's coming. You can guess that we stopped swimming in ponds for a bit."

"I can imagine," I agreed.

"Well, I hope that's helpful to you," Pat said. "Like I said, it might just be an old ghost story. But I have a feeling some of it's true. You might be able to fact-check at the university archive, if you want to. See if they have Winthrop's letters."

"What archive?" I asked.

"At Syracuse. They have some papers to do with the Oneida Community; they might have something from our locals stashed in there. Should be interesting, anyway."

"Thank you for telling me all of this. And, yes, I might follow up with the archives, see if I can track it down. Depends what my project ends up looking like, though."

"That's up to you," she said congenially, if dismissively. "I leave here at four, and still have to put away one or two more pieces of paper."

"I'll get out of your hair," I promised, standing to leave with my treasure.

"Pieces of paper. That's all it really comes down to, isn't it? So many accumulated scraps of words, and that's what we build our lives on." She shuffled the papers on her desk, looking around the room, which was indeed simply accumulated stacks of paper.

"Better than nothing," I said and left.

I stared at the pond from my cabin window, wondering if there were skeletons in the frozen silt, whether blue corpses waved their tattered arms towards the surface, willing living beings into the water as their heavy petticoats drag them ever downward. I found myself giving the pond a wide berth.

The days were filled with pale sap, sticky but almost clear. We would lug the gallon jugs back to the clearing near the big cabin and dump them into a large pot that sat suspended over a quiet flame, reducing the liquid within to dark syrup. The pot gave off a perpetual cloud of sweet steam, and I liked to stand near the fire, letting my hair and clothes become drenched in the scent of firewood and boiling maple. Walking in the woods between the trees was soothing and quiet—the birds were active for a few hours a day, but the summer cacophony of activity was virtually silenced in these winter months.

We started to talk about spring, cautiously. We didn't want to wish for it too hard, almost as though thinking about it, fantasizing about it, would delay its arrival. We limited ourselves to practical consider-ations: when to till the beds, when to put in peas, whether the seed-lings we planned to start in the big cabin's windows would have enough time and light to grow. Louisa spoke enviously of the West Hill Collec-tive's greenhouse, and she and Jack began to design a very simple one of our own, to be built mostly with plastic sheeting and jugs of water painted black and stacked in the sun to keep the temperature up. Maybe we could get it built sometime in March, Louisa mused. Start the seedlings in the kitchen and transfer them outside once the green-house was in good shape.

One evening, as Louisa and I were washing dishes in the kitchen, I asked her the question that had been on my mind.

"Louisa?"

She paused in her drying. "What?"

"When you asked me to join the Homestead. Did you want me here because of what I did? I mean, because of why I left New York? *The Millennial Experiment?*"

She set down the plate she was holding. She took a deep breath.

"Yes. That is a part of why I picked you. Your shame, the publicity of your embarrassment . . . When I found out, I knew that it would . . . that you would care about all this that much more deeply. And that you would . . . maintain privacy. Discretion," she said.

And though I'd thought this answer would hurt me, I found myself instead pleased: I had, indeed, been chosen.

———

Beau continued to head off on his missions, but he was around the Homestead more often than he had been before Christmas. Whether this was to pacify Louisa or a result of his legal troubles, I wasn't sure, but his presence had a stabilizing effect on everyone. Exasperating as he could be, it felt good to be around him; his laughter made one feel especially clever, and he had a way of pausing thoughtfully before speaking that lent all his comments gravitas. During his absences, I noticed that Louisa was unconcerned, and even seemed supportive of his friendship with our neighbors. Once, she went with him on a visit, without duress or protest, and I wondered at her strange new acceptance. I asked Jack about it, thinking he might have some insight, and he paused before answering me.

"She didn't say anything to you about it?"

"About what?"

Jack bit his lip, debating whether to continue. "The lawsuit," he said after a pause. "It was dismissed."

"What? I can't believe she didn't completely fly off the handle! When did this happen?"

"Not long after Beau's arrest. It had been sort of inevitable for a while, but I think it was still a blow when it happened."

"Huh." I reflected on this. She hadn't told me, so I was hurt. And she'd told Jack? But without worrying about the lawsuit with the Larsons, she seemed to be less upset with Beau's connection to the Collective. Surely she hadn't come around to their belief in direct action? But as I thought about it, that seemed to be exactly the sort of thing that might appeal to her; without a legal win, she might feel that triumph by any means was now a legitimate option. To my eternal regret, I didn't ask Jack that day if he knew anything more. Simply because he, too, felt further away from me. Those final days at the Homestead, we were all withdrawing, each into our own preoccupations and manias.

My fascination with the Collective translated into a fever of writing; my document grew, and I added speculation, details on the satellite in California, and any information about Matthew and Fennel I could track down online. My narrative was beginning to split and twine back into itself; I was weaving a story about us, about our comrades a couple of miles away, about the perfectionist community that had settled here. In grander moments, it seemed I was writing about everyone who had undertaken a project like ours: to start over and remake the social contract. Those few of us with the means and the desire to begin again, better. I felt like I was in the middle of a complicated braid, and each strand had to be carefully plaited into the others or the whole thing would dissolve between my inexperienced fingers.

I was eager to continue my research on William's tragedy. I'd emailed two people at Syracuse University, trying to set up a time to visit and have a look through their archives. They seemed willing to let me come, though distracted, and our correspondence moved at a sluggish pace. In the gray winter light, I was desperate for something to do, something with momentum that would relieve the tedium of winter days spent largely indoors. I could only lose to Beau at mah-jongg so many times before I stabbed him in the eye.

Finally, we set a date in early March, for a Monday. I would be allowed to poke through the documents to find the letter that would corroborate the gothic tale related to me by Pat at the historical society. Did it matter to me whether or not the story was a fiction? I knew it should. But in all honesty, I'm not sure that it did. At least not enough.

Chapter 26

The drive to Syracuse is a bleak and dull stretch along the interstate, and I contemplated it with reluctance, particularly in light of a sinister weather forecast that predicted snow. Still, I reasoned, if I were to change my plans every time the winter interfered, I would be static until May, and I hopped into my truck nonetheless. My decrepit old rust bucket had no jack in which to plug my phone, and I owned only one tape, a tinny old Neil Young, which, like the truck, I had inherited from my dad. I couldn't stand advertising anymore, and therefore found the radio intrusive. So I drove in silence, watching the gray carpet of slush encroach on the shoulder of the highway, musing, sometimes aloud.

I hadn't told anyone where I was going. I felt emboldened by my solitary project, imagining how I would present it to my comrades once I finished writing everything down: A tale of nineteenth-century utopian dreams, and the interwoven story of our own contemporary attempts. The truth about William, and perhaps about Matthew. The truth about us. Caught up in the flush, the near mania of fresh fantasy, I pictured my triumphant return to writing. Hell, maybe I could even publish after all—?

My visit to the archives was not, however, as revelatory as I had hoped. A librarian showed me where to hunt, took my bag, and gave me instructions. She seemed annoyed when I mentioned my specific interests—William Fulsome and Jeremiah Winthrop—and she pointed out that this was my own research, and everything was alphabetically organized. Thus, I was left to my own devices. Much good it did me.

After hours, I had located a log that mentioned William and a roster that recorded Winthrop's financial assets when he joined the community, but I had found no trace of the apocryphal letter that recounted William's breakdown. The heater in the archive was cranked up unforgivably high; after a season of woodstoves, sweaters, and perpetual shivering outside, the forced air felt stuffy and unbreathable. I wished that I weren't wearing my long johns beneath my overalls. After pawing through letters that spelled out a lot of tedium and some heartache, I felt defeated. Without confirmation, how could I hope to write this story? Did it work as well without its macabre end?

The librarian poked her head back into the room where I sat.

"Oh, you're still here? I thought you must have left."

"Nope, still combing through history," I said, trying to smile and cracking my neck.

"Haven't you looked outside? You said you came from down eighty-one?"

"Near Ithaca. There aren't any windows in here. What's going on outside?"

"The weather's starting. I would have left hours ago, if I was you."

"But the blizzard isn't supposed to roll in until tonight," I said, standing up.

"Well, lake effect and all. The roads might stay clear for another hour, but unless you want to spend the night here, you'd better get going," she chided. She clearly thought me a fool, and I wondered if she wasn't right. In a vague panic, I tidied the documents I'd been looking at. I didn't have enough money in my bank account to pay for a hotel room, and I certainly didn't want to get stuck on the highway overnight. My heater didn't really work.

"Don't worry about all that—I have to reorganize it anyway," the librarian scolded. "Go get your things and head home, while you can." I bobbed my head in thanks and scooped up my bag and coat in the entryway. Struggling to force my arms into my parka while simultaneously fishing for my keys and my phone, I stepped outside into the parking lot.

It wasn't a full-scale blizzard yet, but the weather had indeed started. Gusts of icy air were swooping down from the Great Lakes, and I fumbled for my zipper. Although the snow was falling delicately, the wind turned everything I could see into a pixelated gray as I walked through the fine dusting already on the asphalt to my truck. I turned it on and cranked the heat as high as it would go, though I knew it would generate little more than a gust of air in the cab. I was already nostalgic for the claustrophobic atmosphere in the archive.

My phone had a worrying six missed calls. One from my mother, four from Chloe, and one from Louisa. My mother was the only one who had left a voicemail, and I skimmed the transcription without listening to her voice; she wanted to make sure I wasn't driving anywhere. Oops. Chloe had texted follow-ups to her call:

> Where are you?
> I'm worried for Beau.
> I think something's happening with him and Louisa and Fennel.
>
> Mack??? I think you should get back here.

My heart started skittering and I stabbed at my phone, trying to call her back. No answer. I tried Louisa and Jack next; Beau didn't have his cellphone on, of course. No one answered. I tried to calm my breath. Absent my truck, they had probably just walked to the Collective for something and decided not to trek back in the snow. Maybe Chloe had gone after them. Now they were all likely drinking wine and laughing, preparing to hunker down for a snowstorm. Louisa would make the atmosphere festive. I felt a stab of envy at the thought of them already huddled around a stove. I put my truck in drive and started to head for home.

The highways weren't bad; the plows were out in force, salting the road prodigiously, and the visibility was still fine. I fussed at the radio until I found a local station, and learned that what I had flippantly been treating as a small storm was likely to be a major blizzard; feet of snow were predicted to fall on our roofs in the next two days, and people were advised not to travel unless it was an emergency. Feeling adrenaline begin to course through me, I tapped my hands on the steering wheel, keeping the car at a clean fifty miles an hour. There weren't too many other cars on the road, and I forced myself to sing along to Neil Young until I turned off the interstate.

The back roads were a bit dicier, but still not bad, and my truck fishtailed only once or twice, when I braked on a decline. Yet again I cursed myself for failing to put sandbags in the back. I pulled over at two gas stations to call my friends, who still weren't answering. It was chilly inside the truck, and without gloves, my fingers felt wooden on the steering wheel. I needed to warm them up. I called my mother as an afterthought.

"Sweetie? Oh, I've been worried about you. Are you all ready for the storm?"

"Yeah, you bet, Mom. We've got plenty of food, and we're going to make a little party out of it."

"Oh, good, that's such a relief. I've just been picturing you cold and hungry out there in the woods, and it's been driving me to distraction. You don't have to drive anywhere, do you?"

"Nope, all settled in," I lied. "It sounds like we'll be doing some shoveling, but otherwise we're planning a few days of cozy reading next to the fire."

"Well, that sounds nice. What a relief. You've got enough fire? I mean wood, or whatever?"

"Yes, Mom, we're totally fine. Don't worry about us."

"Maybe tomorrow I'll have your father come and plow you out?

He'll probably be picking up some shifts with the city, so he could probably make it out there to Hector. . . ."

"Let's talk the day after tomorrow. If we're not dug out by then, maybe I'll take you up on that," I said.

"Okay, sweetie. Just wanted to check in. Thanks for calling. And stay off the roads!"

"You too, Mom. Love you."

"Love you too."

I hung up the phone feeling guilty, but I could hardly tell her that I was still a good twenty minutes from home and all my friends were apparently missing. No sense in worrying her. A part of me wanted to turn right before Ithaca, go north up the lake, and pull into the driveway at my parents' house, instead of continuing around the curve of Cayuga and heading west, towards the next lake.

Finally unable to listen to another second of Neil Young or the radio stations, which had all become impossibly loud, booming advertisements and aggressive jingles (had they always been that way, or was it living in the woods that had so sensitized me?), I drove the rest of the way in silence. And it was silent, except for the sound of my truck. The roads were mostly deserted, and the snow muted any noise or light, so that I felt like I was totally alone. As I turned onto our road, the snow seemed to fall more heavily, and the pines that lined the dirt track curved in on me, adding to my sense of insulation. I had a memory of being young, driving with my father through heavy snow, high up in the seat of his truck, which sported a snowplow. He used to drive me around in snowstorms, shoveling heaps of snow and gray slush off the roads, and we had driven quietly, with just the sound of his noisy heater and the scrape of the blade that carved up the country roads. I had felt safe then, very unlike the disquieting hum of anxiety that now vibrated to my fingertips.

The Homestead looked empty, and I didn't pull my truck all the way up the drive, wary of getting stuck in the soft snowfall. I again wished I had gloves as I slammed my door; the cold metal bit my fingers. I checked the cabins, which were all empty, unsurprisingly. Swear-

ing, I got back in the pickup and tried Chloe and Louisa again. Chloe
answered.

"Jesus, Mack. Where have you been?"

"It's a long story. What the hell is going on?" I struggled to keep from
yelling at Chloe; if I got aggressive, she would shut down on me.

"I don't know," she said, sounding almost teary. "It's—they left, this
morning. I didn't realize, but Louisa left a note and I found it and now
I'm not sure where they are but it's not good and now the snow—"

"Where are you right now?" I interrupted.

"At the Collective. I called Natasha once I realized, and she's here."

"Okay, I'm on my way there. Just stay put, we'll figure this out in a
minute."

I churned out of the driveway; for one panicky moment my wheels
spun ineffectually, searching for purchase on the slick ground. I realized I had gunned the engine and let up on the gas. The truck jolted
out of the rut, back onto the road.

The lights of the farmhouse were on at the Collective, and I made
for the front door in relief, pulling up the hood of my parka to shield
my cheeks from the burn of cold. I entered without knocking and
barely paused to kick off my boots on the way to the kitchen. Natasha
and Chloe sat at the table, cups of tea in front of them. Natasha was on
the phone but not speaking. She shook her head and hung up.

"Matthew's off-grid too. Fuck," she said. Chloe gripped her mug,
gazing out the window with that worrying blank stare of hers.

"What is going on?" I implored.

"They're doing it. Today," Natasha answered.

"Doing what?" I asked.

She looked at me in surprise. "Oh. You didn't know?" When I stared
at her with raised eyebrows that indicated I most certainly didn't fucking know anything, she continued: "I thought you might be looped in,
but I guess not. It probably won't come as a surprise to you that Beau
and Fennel have been . . . branching out from their, uh, traditional ac-
tivist roles."

"I had gathered that there might be some not-strictly-legal interventions, yeah," I said. "But I was under the impression that they were going to knock it off for a bit. After their arrests, et cetera."

"Well, that was the idea. But then Matthew showed up." Natasha said his name with surprising bitterness, and I speculated that she might not be overjoyed to share Fennel with the man her friend so clearly idolized. "He's got a habit of stirring things up. He's always felt that the West Hill Collective lacked . . . ambition."

"What did they have planned?"

"Well, I don't exactly know. At a certain point, I asked Fennel to not give me too many details. It became rather clear that things were headed in a direction I wasn't totally comfortable with. I'm all for a little civil disobedience, but . . . my mom is sort of a public intellectual, and I don't know that I really want to get arrested. I apparently don't have that Black Panther streak in me." She shrugged.

"But you think they're doing something today?"

"Here's what I know: They want to do something to the natural gas company, something that can't be ignored. Fennel has been wanting to make, I don't know, some sort of big statement, and then Louisa showed up a few weeks ago, saying that all this 'guerilla shit' is pointless. For the first time, she and Fennel seemed to have found some common ground, because they both liked the idea of something 'big.' But they don't want anyone to get hurt. When they heard about the snowstorm, they got excited. The whole facility will likely be deserted. No employees, and probably almost no security guards."

"So they're going to, what, set the place on fire?"

"Look, like I said, I don't know exactly what they're planning. They might just be going in to break some windows or something." I stared at Natasha. "I agree," she said, "not likely. But I stopped asking questions."

"What car did they take?"

"Fennel's, I think. Matthew left yesterday, naturally. Set his plan in motion and then he's off."

"Well, given his record, I'm not surprised he doesn't want to get his hands dirty here," I said. "But Fennel's van isn't exactly the most reliable getaway vehicle. Christ, they'll be lucky if it even starts."

"I know. She doesn't even have snow tires," Natasha fretted, looking out the window at the darkening sky. Chloe, who had said nothing since I got back, just sat there blank and silent, fingers wrapped tightly around her mug. "They've been gone hours."

"What do we do?" I finally said.

"I guess we wait," Natasha said, looking out the window, as though she might see our friends come straggling home through the snowy woods. I texted Louisa:

> I know (more or less) what you guys are up to and
> I don't care. Please just let me know you're OK.

Then I sat down to wait.

Chapter 27

We couldn't have waited more than thirty minutes before my phone buzzed, but it felt like we'd been holding our grim vigil around that table for hours. I knocked over Chloe's mug in my fervor to get to my phone. On my screen, a text from Louisa:

> Shit went south. F's van is stuck and we had to book it
> on foot. Headed to the picnic spot in Hector Forest.
> Chloe knows where it is. Come get us. It's fucking cold.

I read the message aloud to Chloe and Natasha, and Chloe jerked her head up at the mention of her name.

"It's not really a good day for a picnic," she said. I couldn't tell whether this was a joke or just a product of her increasingly dissociative state.

"Do you know what they mean? Chloe?"

"Blueberry Patch, I think. Beau brought me over there in the summer. We ate strawberries, though, not blueberries," she answered.

"Can you get me there? We need to go fast."

"I guess, probably." She shrugged. "They picked a bad day for this."

"Couldn't agree more. But we should go, before the snow gets worse." Even as I said this, the wind gusted outside, and I realized we were starting too late. "Natasha? What are you going to do?"

She bit her lip. "I don't know. I want to come, too, but how will everyone fit into your truck? We can't exactly sit in the back in this weather."

"Fuck. Good point. I hadn't thought of that." I looked over at Chloe. "Maybe I should leave her here too."

"How will you find the right spot?" Natasha asked.

"We've got Google Maps. Here, show me where to go, Chlo." I nudged Chloe, and she gave me some directions to a spot in the national forest about seven miles from the Collective. She pointed to a small country road in the middle of the green, then a dot labeled "Blueberry Patch Campground."

"Just drive there, park, and call Louisa," Natasha suggested. "Or text her, I guess; reception isn't great out there. They won't be far into the woods, and you can pick them up at the trailhead."

I nodded, trying to memorize the curl of roads that would take me closer to Seneca Lake, into the woods. I would have my phone, though. I dropped a pin.

> OK, I'm headed towards Blueberry Patch in my truck.
> I'll text when I get there.

Louisa responded immediately:

> Phew. Thx. See you in a bit!

"She seems pretty damn cheerful," I muttered. "Glad to see she's taking it seriously."

"Do you have a hat?" Natasha asked. "You should layer up, in case you have to walk in to find them."

The thought filled me with dread. I had the primal instinct to bolt the door and inch closer to the fire. Not go careening around in the storm. Still, there were a few hours before the worst of it hit. I was an experienced snow driver. As long as I went slowly and braked carefully, I would probably be okay. The fact that I would be on remote country roads might even work in my favor; I'd be less likely to encounter the stupidity of panicky drivers, and the salt from the county plows wouldn't have turned the snow into slippery slush yet.

I let Natasha bundle me in an extra sweater and a silly-looking deerstalker hat.

"I feel like a penguin," I complained, waddling comically back and forth. Chloe laughed, and the sound of it calmed me. I smiled at her gratefully.

"Well, practicality over vanity," Natasha said in a perfect imitation of Fennel.

I snorted. "If ever there was a time. Okay, I'm off. I'll try to check in when I have them. Stay inside," I admonished, though it hardly needed saying.

On the stoop, I said, "I feel like an Arctic explorer, heading out for a dangerous mission," aware that I was stalling for time. Chloe smiled sympathetically, obviously understanding, and suddenly she gave me a fierce hug.

"Bring them back, okay? I need you all to come back."

"I will. I promise," I said. Fool.

The roads were clearly worsening as I headed out yet again. Any residual memory of the safety I had felt driving with my father evaporated as the wheels of my truck slid out from under me, then kept doing this every few hundred feet. I clung to the steering wheel, my head nearly poking over it, as though being closer to the windshield would help me see better. After passing through Mecklenburg, I turned off the highway and was soon driving through uneven drifts of snow. I had to anticipate the depths of each drift and accelerate my truck through it or risk the truck bed getting caught in a dune. This nearly happened twice, and I fought panic as the wheels spun for one second, two seconds, three before releasing me.

The seven-mile drive, which should normally take about fifteen minutes, dragged on for almost an hour at my creeping cautious pace. As I made the final turn onto Picnic Area Road, my driving anxiety began to shift towards worry for my friends. What on earth had they done? What if they weren't at the meeting spot? Would we all be able to fit in the truck? I crept up the final hill scanning every tree, rock, and snowdrift for a flash of movement, a surge of color—anything to indicate a human presence.

At the top of the hill, I coasted to a stop, dark woods on either side of me. I realized that I had been here before, over the summer; we had indeed come for a picnic near a pond, and had napped lazily in the sun after a sweaty hike. There was a pull-off area that was used for trail parking in the summer, but I couldn't risk leaving the road. I put on my blinkers—a pointless gesture, since I'd yet to see another vehicle—and texted Louisa. My fingers were freezing, and I wondered why I hadn't gotten a pair of gloves from Natasha.

Parked on Picnic Area. Don't see you guys. In the woods?

I stared impatiently at my phone, waiting for a response. After three or four minutes, I called her. It went straight to voicemail. This was not encouraging. I called Jack's phone, with the same response. I didn't know Fennel's number, so I texted Natasha, asking for it. She responded quickly, and I dialed the contact she'd forwarded me. Again, straight to voicemail. I remembered Natasha's comment about the cold; if they'd used their phones in this weather for more than a minute or two, they had likely run out of battery. On a cold day in Ithaca while I was looking up directions, my own phone had dropped from a sixty percent charge to being completely unresponsive, only to go back to being nearly fully charged as soon as I plugged it in inside. Steeling myself, I prepared to leave my truck. I debated pulling it off the road, but it would almost certainly become mired in the snow. I also considered leaving the keys in and the hazards on . . . but what if I was in the woods long enough to drain the battery? I leaned on the horn for a good ten seconds, the noise muffled by the falling snow, hoping someone might materialize.

Stepping out of the truck cab was alarming, not just because of the wind and the drop in temperature; I realized that I would have to walk around in this, possibly even lose sight of my vehicle. This whole thing was obviously a terrible idea. I was taking a stupid risk, and I had no idea if my friends were even anywhere near here. But what if they were just beyond the tree line, with dead cellphones, unsure of where to go? I couldn't drive away, nor could I just get back in my truck and wait.

I began calling into the woods, hoping for a hint of a voice. Reluctantly, I trudged through the snow away from the road, towards the break in trees that I thought might be the trail. I called each of their names, one after the other. I walked as far as I dared, then turned back towards the road, afraid to let it disappear entirely, zigzagging to cross the trail and cover as much ground as I could. The sun, already obscured by the storm, was setting fast, and visibility was going to be a problem really soon. My hands and feet were numb. When I reached the truck, I hopped inside for a minute to try Louisa again, without much optimism. In the digital silence that followed my texted plea, I girded my loins to head out to the trail on the other side of the road.

Six inches of snow had fallen now, though in the dusky gloom of the woods it seemed lighter, and the wind wasn't as sudden or as harsh. If not for my fear, and the knowledge that what I was doing was colossally stupid, this solitary wander in the forest might have been beautiful, almost spiritual. I was the only animal afoot, no doubt watched by the other creatures from their snug perches and warrens. An unseen owl followed me with a skeptical eye; a creeping fox popped a head up from her den to track my clumsy progress. With my miserable human senses, all I could see or hear was myself: the damp edges of my hood rustling in my periphery, the uneven crush of my own feet through the soft powder, the heavy panting of my lungs as they alone burned and warmed. In my dazzled glaze, I almost forgot to keep shouting for my friends. Deciding to risk another phone call, I freed my hands from my sleeves, where they were bunched into balls. Strangely, I felt unconcerned by their stiffness, or by the repetition of Louisa's voicemail. I wondered how long I had been out here in the forest, searching—it seemed that it could be just a minute or two, or maybe hours. And when I tripped into a half-frozen ditch and sprawled over a log that collided with my head, it was almost as though I didn't mind, such was my abstracted joy in the woods.

"Mack get the fuck up I need you to show me where the truck is and I won't let you just fucking sleep so just get the fuck up."

I cracked my eyes (which, I was surprised to discover, I had at some point closed) to see a puce Louisa glowering at me, her fur-lined parka rendering her an incongruously redheaded Inuit.

"I tried to call you," I said accusatorially, not stirring from my position on the ground. I didn't feel very cold anymore, which was, I dimly recalled from childhood lectures on hypothermia, not a great sign. My right arm was soaked through with freezing water.

"My phone is dead. The cold. Obviously," Louisa said. As though this were somehow my fault.

When she answered, I realized I had spoken aloud.

"No, it's not your fault. I have a few ideas of who I'd like to blame, but that doesn't feel constructive at the moment. Will you please, as I have asked a few times, get the fuck up?"

Begrudgingly, I complied. "Where's the truck?" I looked around myself and, for a few unsettling moments, wasn't sure what direction I had come from. But I could make out the vague impression of my boots in the snow. It wouldn't be long before they disappeared, though, since snow was clearly falling faster.

"Should have brought bread crumbs," I said. "I'm a shitty Hansel and Gretel."

"Agreed, entirely. This is extremely not good, Mack."

I looked at her, and something occurred to me. "Where's Beau and Jack? And Fennel?"

"You've hit upon my central concern," Louisa sniped, and her pursed lips and scared rabbit eyes finally registered through my fuzz. She was terrified. "We got separated. I'll tell you the story once we're in the truck. I hope you have a phone that works," she added, pulling me along.

We began trudging back to the road, which, it turned out, was not that far away; it was certainly closer than I had thought while I'd stared up at the pine trees swaying over my head. I clumsily located my keys (Why had I locked the truck? How stupid, I thought. What if someone had gotten to it and been unable to get in? What if I had dropped my keys in the snow?) and we piled into the cab. Louisa demanded my phone, and I handed it over before turning on the engine so it could charge.

"They're all dead," I said, explaining.

"Jesus, what the fuck, Mack!" Louisa said, turning to look at me in horror.

"No, no, the phones," I corrected. "I've been trying for hours. All the batteries must be dead."

"Shit. And you spoke to Natasha? She hasn't heard from anyone?"

"She's home with Chloe. They wanted to come, but, you know, space." I gestured at the truck's cab.

"Fuck."

"What happened, Louisa?" I finally said.

"It just went wrong," she answered, shaking her head. "We thought the snowstorm would be the perfect time, because everything is shutting down. We were sure no one would be there, and we could just go in and get out and it would be a day or two before someone caught on. We knew the trucks couldn't do their usual run in this weather, and they'd be stuck there. We figured it would be empty. So we broke into the property. Beau had figured out a way in, the last time he was there, before he got pinched. Once we were inside, it was easy. We torched some paperwork in the office—files and names and the like. We made digital copies of everything that seemed useful, to put online. Home addresses, that sort of thing. Then we fucked up the trucks, so that they'd have to pay attention. Sugar in the tanks, slashed tires, broken windshields, the works. It felt amazing." Louisa smiled softly to herself, with a quiet glow that was incongruous with our current circumstances.

"And we thought we'd done it. We were pumped—I've never seen Fennel look so happy. I mean, we know we can't hope to really change things, but you have to start somewhere, right? The sight of those trucks, absolutely annihilated. It'll cost them hundreds of thousands of dollars. Anyway, we got back to Fennel's van, which scared the shit out of us for about two minutes because it didn't start. But we got it going, and we took off. Thought we were fine.

"But a mile or so on, we see this SUV come up behind us, and it keeps flashing its lights at us. We figured it was a security guard, because most of the Lakeview rent-a-cops drive those fucking gas-guzzling Suburbans. Jack and I wanted to pull over, but Fennel was . . . I don't know, she was so determined that we get away. It's like she was just . . ." Louisa shrugged and shook her head. I'd seen Fennel in her stubborn moods, and I could imagine the terrier-like fixation that would cause her to do something stupid.

"We maybe could have talked her down, but Beau has a gun, and he pulls it out, takes a shot at the guy's tires."

"Why on earth would he do something that stupid?" I asked, stunned.

Louisa shook her head. "Heat of the moment? Male idiocy? His abiding sense of anarchy? Who knows. You may have noticed he's been coming off the rails a bit. Anyway, the guy follows us. So Fennel is essentially now in a car chase in the middle of a blizzard on country roads, and some guy in an SUV is trying to ram us off the road, and Jack keeps begging her to just stop, pull over. But she was convinced she could get some distance or—I don't know what she thought, actu-

ally. I mean, he had our plates. Who knows what *he* was thinking, for
that matter, chasing us in this weather.

"This only went on for about a mile or two, but we'd made it a ways
up Mathews Road when Fennel, in her infinite wisdom, tried to take a
sharp turn onto, I forget what it's called. Burnt Road or something. Her
van flies out of control, and the SUV that's been on our ass cruises
right into us, then into a ditch and flips over."

"Fuck me," I breathed. As I warmed, some sense of reality was steal-
ing back over me, and Louisa's words began to register. She seemed
bizarrely calm—perhaps she, too, was hypothermic?

"Then we made a tough call," Louisa continued. "Fennel was unconscious, since the other guy had hit her side of the car. Jack's shoulder
was dislocated, but he was okay to move. The guy in the SUV didn't
look like he was in great shape, but he was still breathing. So I used
Fennel's phone and called 911. I said that I was her and I'd just been in
a car accident. I gave them the location, and we decided to go."

"Jesus, Louisa! You just left them? Isn't that a fucking crime?"

"It is. So is breaking and entering, destruction of property, and man-
slaughter. For Beau it would be his third arrest this year." She bit her
lip. "Look, I don't know how I feel about it. But we panicked, and it
just seemed like our best shot. Otherwise we could stick around and
get arrested, and there would be no more decisions to make. I don't
know. I don't know."

"Okay, but then . . . where are Beau and Jack?"

"We were all together at first, and Beau knew his way through the
woods—he spent a lot of time out here as a kid, and if we went through
the woods, we could pretend just to be stupid hikers if we got picked
up. Dumb survivalist kids." Louisa laughed at this. "Not inappropriate,
as it were."

"But where are they?" I pressed.

"One minute they were right behind me," she said softly. "And then
they weren't."

We were essentially paralyzed; we couldn't leave, with Beau and Jack still in the woods. Nor could we get ahold of them or see them through the wintry screen that obscured anything more than a few yards away. Louisa and I both made brief forays to both sides of the road to call for the boys, but the futility of this gesture was more alarming than reassuring. They could be a scant five hundred feet from us and would neither see nor hear us. Meanwhile, it was clear that the storm was only going to intensify. Plugging my phone into the charger, I scanned weather apps with mounting anxiety—the Finger Lakes were preparing to have more than two feet of snow dumped upon them over the course of a storm that would last at least another forty-eight hours. We were genuinely fucked.

After hours of pointless attempts to locate Beau and Jack, Louisa turned to me.

"I don't think we can find them alone," she said, stating what had been obvious for some time. "We need to call someone."

I nodded. "What do we say happened, though?" I asked.

"We'll say that we were out hiking and got turned around in the snow. They'll think we're idiots, but hopefully they won't connect us with what happened at Lakeview. I mean, they probably will. But at this point . . ." She didn't finish the thought.

I handed her my phone, and after a pause, she took it. She made the call, calmly summarizing our situation: we had gotten separated from our friends, and we now feared that they were lost in the national forest in the midst of a historic blizzard. We would sit tight and wait to be rescued. In reality, we had no choice; the drifts that had accumulated across the road made it abundantly clear that we were going nowhere under our own steam. We sat silently in the cab, shivering. I dreaded the arrival of our rescuers—having to lie, looking deeply foolish, answering questions I wasn't sure how to answer. This anxiety allowed me to subsume the much larger fear that Beau and Jack might not be found. Not in time.

A fire truck came whirring over the top of the hill, kicking up plumes of snow as it plowed its way towards us. I glanced over at

Louisa, who sat grim and tight-lipped next to me. We hopped down from the pickup to greet our knights in shining armor.

"You the kids who lost your friends in the woods?" one of the young men asked, naturally addressing himself to Louisa.

"Yes. They've been out there a few hours now. I think they're through there"—she gestured towards one side of the road—"and must have gotten off the trail somehow."

"Not somehow. This is no weather to be hiking in," the man scolded. "Do they have any survival gear on them? Are they dressed for this?"

"More or less," Louisa answered. "But now that it's dark . . ." She trailed off, and I felt a panicked thud of my stomach surging up towards my rib cage.

"What about you two? How long were you exposed?" The firefighter looked at us carefully.

"Not too long," Louisa answered. "We're okay."

"I'm not sure you are. Your friend looks like she might have some hypothermia. How long were you outside, hon?" He peered at me closely.

"I'm not sure. A few hours?" I said. The firefighter gestured to one of his colleagues, who had been busying himself with equipment. "Can we check her out, maybe get a heat blanket?" He directed me towards the truck and his solicitous fellow hero, who had me hop up inside. I stumbled slightly hoisting myself into the vehicle.

"Have you been experiencing any disorientation? Sleepiness?" this new man asked me.

"I guess? I'm not really sure," I answered.

"Confusion? Slurred speech?"

"I don't know? Maybe?"

The firefighter peered at me, and I felt weirdly unwilling to meet his eyes. My stupidity had brought this man out here. He rooted around behind himself for something, and when he turned back he held a thermometer, which he placed in my mouth.

"How about you move your hands for me, tap your fingers in order."

I obliged, but we both paused when we looked at the two outer fingers of my right hand. They were stiff and vaguely bluish. The firefighter reached out to touch them, and the warmth of his hand made me jerk. The skin on those two fingers was hard. "Was this hand exposed to the weather?" he asked.

"I tripped into a stream a few hours ago, and my hand got wet. But I didn't notice anything," I tried to explain. Really, who could be bothered with two numb fingers when I'd lost two friends in the cold?

"You've got some pretty bad frostbite here, and you're hypothermic. I think we need to get you straight to the hospital."

"But I need to stay here and find Beau and Jack," I argued feebly. "I need to help find them."

"You need to take care of yourself," the firefighter said firmly, and turned away from me to call an ambulance.

Chapter 28

I slept on the ride to the hospital, and nodded in and out once I arrived there. I felt unspeakably tired and just wanted to curl up in the fetal position and shiver beneath the blankets until Jack and Beau were found. In my disaffected delirium, I apparently furnished someone with my parents' phone number, because my mother and father soon appeared at my bedside, looking quite reasonably distraught. I tried to apologize to them, but my mother shushed me through a veil of tears and a clearly fraudulent mask of stoic bravery. My father looked both pissed and worried, which seemed about right. I thought about my lack of health insurance with detached horror, and rolled over to fall back asleep.

At some point, a doctor came in to inspect my bandaged fingers. As he peeled back the gauze, he openly frowned at them. I tried to catch a glimpse of my hand and saw two darkened digits.

"Let's just monitor how they do over the next couple of days before we make any decisions," the doctor said. This was not comforting, but I shrugged and tried to go back to sleep.

Finally, I had the presence of mind to ask about my friends.

Louisa was apparently here at the hospital, being treated for exposure, though she was fine and would likely be released in a few hours. No one knew about Beau and Jack; they weren't, in any case, at this hospital. I wanted to call Natasha and Chloe, but I realized dimly that Louisa still had my phone. So I fell back asleep.

I woke again to find Louisa by my bed, looking down at me.

"Hey, you," she said. "How are you doing?"

I waved my gauzy mitt at her and felt the sharp stab of pain there. "Oh, you know."

"Fuck, Mack. I'm so sorry."

"Not your fault," I said. "What's the word on Beau and Jack?"

She met my eyes, and I saw the fear in hers as she shook her head. "No one has found them yet. But the storm . . ."

I glanced out the window, where it was apparently daytime, though the sky was darkened by the whiteout. "How many inches have fallen?"

"A foot, at least. The storm is supposed to go through tonight and most of tomorrow."

"Jesus," I said. We didn't need to say what that meant. "Jesus."

"The searchers are going to keep looking, though," Louisa said, trying to smother the note of despair. "It's possible they could have stumbled out of the woods and found a house. Or been picked up on the road."

"Wouldn't they have tried to call us?"

"Probably. But, you know, maybe they're trying to lay low," Louisa said, dropping her voice.

"God, what about Fennel?" I said with a jolt, realizing that she had completely disappeared from my mind in my worry about the boys. "Was she okay? What the hell happened?"

"She was airlifted. She's okay. Concussion, so they're keeping her a little longer, and I think a broken arm, but mostly all right."

"Has she said anything?"

"I really don't know," Louisa answered. She paused. "I hope not. The security guard who followed us is dead."

"Oh God."

"So it's only a matter of time before they charge Fennel with what happened at Lakeview. Then it all depends on what she says."

I stared mutely down at my hand. How had all of this happened?

"Listen," Louisa said, "I'll let you sleep some more. Chloe and Natasha want to visit, but you know, with the snow . . ."

"No, they should absolutely stay put. We don't need any more of us out in this," I said, watching the snow pile up on my window.

My fingers were amputated a few days later. This felt too surreal for me to process in my numbed state, so I simply nodded at the doctor's explanations. Normally he'd wait longer, he said, possibly even weeks, but I was developing symptoms of septicemia. Okay, I said. My mother wept; she, clearly, was in a more emotionally attuned state. When I woke up from the surgery, I felt faraway and relaxed. I surveyed my swaddled hand for several minutes; encased in a baseball mitt of gauze, it didn't really seem different. I couldn't feel it at all.

I was released from the hospital after my recovery. The storm had ended that Wednesday night, as predicted, and the town was gradually shoveling out driveways, dealing with downed power lines, and returning itself to business as usual. For us, usual had disappeared beneath the snow.

Jack and Beau were still missing, which was a tactful way to avoid saying that they had almost certainly died of exposure during the storm. Louisa was still stubbornly insisting that they might be holed up somewhere, avoiding questions. In moments of optimism, I clung to this absurd notion too. But the fantasy was folly; I knew they were dead.

Fennel was released the same day I was, and while she had so far avoided arrest for what had happened at Lakeview, it was clear that the cops suspected her. Sitting with Louisa in our kitchen, I was trying to learn how to drink tea (and, indeed, do everything) with my left hand when she told me that Sy had been arrested that morning on a varied bouquet of drug charges.

"I talked with Rudy about it, and he says they likely put pressure on him to come clean and tell the whole story, give one of us up. Rudy says they'll threaten him with trumped-up charges to see if he'll talk."

"Do you think he will?" I asked.

"No idea. And I don't know what Fennel will say, either. They're throwing the word 'terrorism' around."

After Louisa had fetched Chloe from the Collective and the three of us had briefly conferred with Natasha, we'd all agreed that the two communes would maintain some distance from each other until things settled down. I had no desire to see or speak to Fennel; I was glad she was okay, but I harbored a deep sense that none of this would have happened without her. And Matthew.

"Louisa?" I finally asked when my addled wits began to return. "You said you made copies of things? In the Lakeview office?"

"Yeah, I don't really know exactly what all we managed to get, but the idea was to put some shit up online. Personal info about the head honchos, anything that seems at all incriminating. In the interest of transparency, of course." She rumpled her nose and shrugged. "I'm not sure what the plan was, exactly. I think Beau might have intended to go terrorize the higher-ups personally, once he had their addresses. Something extreme, no doubt. In any case, he had all the information on him when he . . ." Louisa trailed off, her mouth tightening.

"How did you get inside?" I asked. "To access the offices? I mean, you can't have just walked in there."

"Well, you're not entirely a fool, I guess," she acknowledged wryly. "That's what a lot of the money got used for. We had an inside guy."

"Seriously? You paid someone off?"

"Low-level office flunky, from what I understand. All Fennel's purview, of course. Matthew put them in touch. I don't know too much about it."

"And the, uh, gun?"

"Ditto. Matthew"—she said his name contemptuously—"showed up with the firearms. We are not to be trusted with the nitty-gritty. Not that getting a gun is at all difficult."

We sat in silence, contemplating the gray bleakness outside.

"What will we do about Chloe?" I finally asked, for the third or fourth time since arriving home. It was evident that Chloe was not well; she was just short of catatonic. Louisa told me that Chloe had lethargically sipped some soup she'd brought her. When I'd gone to visit her, she had been in bed. She'd raised her head and given me a wan smile, then turned back towards the wall. Although I'd stroked her back through the thick comforter, I may as well not have been there.

"I don't know what to do for her. I know she has depressive spells, especially in the winter, but this . . ." Louisa shook her head. "This is more on a scale of a proper breakdown. Which worries me. Obviously."

"Me too."

"It's happened before, you know," Louisa said after a pause. "She was hospitalized in her first year of school. She's bipolar, maybe. She's been on meds as long as I've known her. I'm worried that she may have stopped taking them." I watched Louisa's wide forehead contort, etched with concern, and suddenly, unable to help myself, I started laughing. Louisa squinted at me with suspicion until I was able to speak.

"We are one sorry bunch," I finally said. "I'm an eight-fingered dropout with massive debt, you're a terrorist, Chloe is a bona fide nutjob, and two of us are popsicles out in the woods!"

"Well, when you put it that way," Louisa said drily. "Want some more tea?"

We sat around the Homestead for several days, unsure what to do. The local news had a lot of coverage about the blizzard's aftermath—power outages, a dead homeless woman, salt shortages, etc. There were also a few mentions of the vandalism at Lakeview, linked with the nearby car accident involving a security guard and a possible suspect. In spite of our agreement not to contact anyone at the Collective, I was itching to text Natasha to see if Fennel had been arrested or was being questioned. The cops interviewed Louisa and me twice, trying to figure out if we knew anything about the Lakeview attack; security footage had shown that there was more than one person involved, and Fennel would have to give someone up eventually.

When the cops pulled up the drive a third time, I had my suspicions about what they were coming to tell us. Louisa met them at the door of the big cabin, where I joined her. We left Chloe in her cabin. The cops were gentle when they told us about the body they had found. From their description, it seemed evident that it was Jack. I pictured his clear blue eyes frozen shut, his lips colorless, his sandy hair immobilized in ice. I felt a desperate stab as I remembered running my hands through that hair on a New Year's Eve that seemed like it was part of a different millennium. As I sat listening to a bland recital of his "painless" final moments, all I could think of was regret, frantic regret that I hadn't fucked him that night. This seemed like an unforgivable error, something I would never have the chance to correct. The strangeness of this thought, this one particular regret, anchored me and prevented me from considering the vastness of what really had been lost: the life he would have had, all that was held in his brain, watching his hair grow gray. Louisa leaned over and squeezed my good hand, and I realized I had been sitting there utterly unresponsive.

Louisa and I went together, full of dread, to Chloe's cabin. I was barely able to speak and had no idea how we would tell Chloe—Chloe who had wandered around like a ghost these past few days and who gave the impression that she might simply evaporate. Louisa, grim-faced, seemed to realize that she would have to do the talking, and I could see her marshaling her words. In the end, when we sat on the edge of Chloe's bed and Chloe turned to us with her wide-set eyes, blond hair clinging to her damp forehead, Louisa said simply: "It was Jack. They found Jack."

Chloe rolled over wordlessly and wept into the mattress, the blanket pulled over her head. Louisa and I stroked her, trying to soothe her quaking, but she didn't stop. I looked over at Louisa after ten minutes, and saw that she was weeping, too, her pink cheeks glistening. She said nothing. Realizing that I was about to lose my composure, I stumbled from the cabin, shaking freezing tears from my lashes as I headed towards my own bed. Inside, I could only ball myself up on the bed and sob. I wept for Jack, and for Beau, who was certainly dead as well, but in that moment, I most wanted Argos, his sweet, sympathetic nose buried in my neck. And so I mourned the dog, because the loss of my friends felt too big.

I was awakened by the bright lights of an ambulance later that night, and in a sleepy delirium, I thought maybe they'd found Beau, and they were just dropping him off at home. I stumbled down the ladder and was pulling on my boots before I realized the impossibility of this fantasy. Outside my window, the ambulance was stopped next to Chloe's cabin. Flinging a shawl around my shoulders, I raced across the clearing, where Louisa stood, shivering and watching a team of paramedics carry Chloe from her bed.

"She's okay," Louisa immediately reassured me. "I don't think she actually meant to die. She said she just lost track of how many she'd taken."

"Jesus, she overdosed? On what?"

"Mostly her anti-anxiety meds. But apparently she got her hands on some of Sy's oxy, which didn't help."

I shut my eyes. Maybe it was time to leave.

But the next morning, I couldn't bring myself to abandon Louisa, who clearly hadn't slept, and who was fluttering around the big cabin in a fit of activity. She couldn't settle. I watched her burn oatmeal, make three consecutive cups of tea that she didn't drink, and then just stand there, staring out the kitchen window. When she reached for her heavy coat to go outside, I was afraid to ask her what she was doing.

"Going to look for Beau, of course," she said. "Can you give me a ride?"

So I found myself setting out towards the national forest again, Louisa staring pensively out the window. I realized that I couldn't really drive with my damaged hand; shifting was deeply painful, and I tried unsafely to do it with my left, wincing.

Louisa noticed my difficulty by the time I was getting the truck into third gear, and after a pause, she said, "Pull over. I think you'd better let me drive."

I was hesitant but in too much pain to protest. "What's a ticket for driving without a license at this stage?" she said, so I let her maneuver my truck over the still-snowy roads to the forest. For someone who categorically refused to drive, she seemed capable enough, and only her white-knuckled grip on the wheel revealed her nerves.

Our search in the forest was, unsurprisingly, fruitless. It was a clear day, but we had difficulty walking in the deep snow. I fell once and managed to resist decades of conditioning to avoid landing on my injured hand. Louisa called for Beau for nearly two hours as we circled the area around the trail where she'd last seen him. I couldn't bring myself to tell her that this was madness, that if Beau was still out here, in the woods, he would be frozen. But I understood her need to do something, however pointless.

After our antics in the snow, we drove around to a few of the houses near the forest. Louisa knocked on doors and asked strangers if they had seen Beau. She even peered into a few chicken coops, hoping to find him curled up and surrounded by a warm flock of poultry. As it grew dark, we headed home.

"I'll try again tomorrow. And maybe I'll post something on Craigslist."

"What? Craigslist?"

"Beau loved to read the Missed Connections section. It was sort of a hobby of his," she said with a private smile. "It was silly, but I think it appealed to his inner romantic." She shook her head, clearly remembering a younger version of Beau. "Anyway, if he's hiding out somewhere, he might try to contact me—us—that way. You know, if he managed to get out of the woods and somewhere safe."

"Louisa—" I began.

"I know. But I keep thinking Matthew could have gotten to Beau. He couldn't come with us to Lakeview, but we called him when things went wrong. I keep wondering if maybe, I don't know, maybe if he came back to look for us and Beau was near the road . . ." She didn't finish. It was the desperate reasoning of denial, and we both knew it. Yet even though I found it an implausible scenario, I clung to it, hoping that Louisa might be right. Her pursuit had a sad, frantic quality, and I didn't have the heart to dissuade her from roaming the forest looking for her lost love, the Heathcliff to Beau's Cathy.

Later that day, Chuck Larson appeared at the Homestead. I was alarmed—surely he hadn't come here to continue the dispute?—and Louisa immediately stiffened. But he stepped out of his truck with an armful of flowers and walked slowly towards the front door; we watched through a window until he reached the steps.

"I came to offer my condolences. We heard about your friends," he began stiffly. "I was sorry to hear about it. These are from my wife."

"Sustainably grown, no doubt," Louisa said. I jabbed her in the ribs with my elbow.

"Thank you," I said. "It's nice of you to stop by."

"That's how we are around here. You look out for your neighbors." It was tense out here on the stoop, and I looked down at my feet, clad in the socks Jack had knit for me. If I wasn't careful, I would lose some toes too.

"I appreciate you stopping by," Louisa finally said. "You didn't have to do that."

"Look, I'm not a bad guy. I'm sorry about how things went down here, but I'm just trying to make an honest living."

"And my dog?" I couldn't help asking. "What about Argos?"

"That wolf thing? What—what are you talking about?"

"Are you sorry about him too?"

"Look, I don't know what you're talking about. I just wanted to come over and tell you I'm real sorry for your friends. It's hard when someone that young goes, and I know you folks must be having a rough time. If there's something you need, well, you can ask. We're still your neighbors."

"I thought you sold off your rights," Louisa said.

"We're still your neighbors," Chuck Larson repeated. "And here in Hector that counts for something. My best wishes." He tapped the brim of his John Deere baseball cap and turned to leave.

After Jack's body was found, neither Louisa nor I had any desire to stay at the Homestead. Chloe remained in the hospital, on a seventy-two-hour suicide watch. We didn't believe that she had truly tried to die, but she'd come close nevertheless. After those three days, Chloe voluntarily committed herself for a six-month inpatient treatment.

Fennel was arrested first, and Louisa followed shortly afterward. It was obvious that Fennel had given her up—possibly out of spite, possibly because she was too tired to lie—but Louisa seemed almost relieved. She'd been wandering around in such a cloud of guilt that she seemed grateful to be punished. She and Fennel both pleaded guilty. Louisa was sentenced to nine months, Fennel to three years because she had been driving and had the subsequent charge of reckless endangerment. She and Louisa were both lucky that bullets were never found; either Beau had missed, or they were overlooked. I glimpsed Fennel once, waiting for Louisa's hearing; her dreads had been shaved off, and I hoped for her sake she was still adhering to her no-mirror policy. I considered her jail time inadequate—I still suspected her of murdering our dog, in order to protect Matthew and conceal the charges against him. Perhaps she thought that by erasing Argos, she could somehow erase what happened between Matthew and Lisa, or erase the trail that would connect the two. She was not, I believe, entirely sane. She hadn't given up Matthew, and I heard nothing of him; he had effectively vanished.

I ask myself, from time to time, who is responsible. Who bears the burden for what we did and failed to do? Fennel and her cold machinations, Louisa with her heated rage? Beau, probably, should shoulder the most blame, but, as ever, I can't seem to hold him fully responsible. I blame myself, who did nothing, nothing but write and get the story wrong. My project lurks like a spider, waiting to entrap me again. I know better now, though, than to navigate that web.

I visited Louisa only once before departing for South Africa. Still defiant and sharp-tongued, she seemed okay in prison, and I left knowing that I would worry about her but she would be fine. Chloe wouldn't be allowed to see visitors for several more weeks, so I had no way to say goodbye. The decision to go was easy and sudden: I stumbled across an online article about voluntourism in Africa, and half a day of Internet research led me to Cape Town and JobsNow. I was so desperate to leave I didn't even consider other options.

And so I have sat here, doing penance. Filling my days with tasks. The sheer folly of what we tried to do is stark from this perspective. To grow our own vegetables and bathe in a pond? I've seen hardship now, seen those who live hand to mouth. Looking at these townships, I understand that our venture was just a silly little game. The vanity of it! But what could we do? I've done no good here, just sought a salve for my mewling conscience.

The last letter I receive in Cape Town haunts me, like many of those early ones I received after heading home to Ithaca. This one, though, doesn't come from pissed-off viewers; nor does it come from Auburn Correctional. She's out.

I recognize Louisa's handwriting, unfurling madly across the page. I skim at first, trying to ascertain with a quick glance why she has written me, my stomach flipping with possibility and dread. Has she written to say that Beau has been found? Dead, alive? That Chloe has succeeded in her bid to end it? That the Homestead has burned to the ground and the Collective has disbanded and the apocalypse has finally come to the whole Burned-Over District?

No. She writes none of this. The seedlings are starting slow this year; it has been rainy and cold so far. She is sick of another winter, sick of firewood. Her new year, she says, has been like Thoreau's, solitude in the woods—Beau would be pleased. But she feels she has been doing penance, rather than seeking the good life. And in some ways, she writes, this is easier. You don't have to aspire, to live fully, you simply have to *endure* penance. There are fewer choices. It has been lonely on the Homestead, though the solitude is better than having to face other people.

She is expecting Chloe, who has been slowly climbing out of her chemical hole. It has been a long year for her, too, but Chloe is stronger than we gave her credit for. Louisa has been sprucing up her cabin in preparation, hanging conifer branches near the door, stacking wood in case of spring squalls. I can almost see her hesitation in writing those words, "spring squalls." She doesn't mention my cabin, but it hovers there, ghostly. They are all filled with ghosts, each of those buildings. Though she doesn't say it, I know there will be pine boughs at my threshold and a stack of wood by my door. Do I dare face those ghosts? Can I live side by side with them?

But, of course, I already do. My old delicious burdens. It is time to carry them home.

Acknowledgments

Thank you to Molly Atlas, who has shepherded this manuscript from vague notion to actual, existing book. Thanks to Kara Cesare, who, as always, sees into these characters and patiently draws them out of hiding. To all the people at Random House involved in editing, design, and production—particularly Bonnie Thompson and Loren Noveck, who catch errors both micro and macro and spare me vast embarrassment. Thank you to everyone at ICM and Curtis Brown who has read, commented, and nudged this book into the world.

Thank you to my family: Em, for reading this book several times and insisting that there *is* actually something there and that I really should finish it. To my dad, Mike, who helped with my "research garden" and made maple syrup with me as a kid, and taught me the names of local flora and fauna out in his woods. To my mom, who listened to me rant about this novel for years. To my dad's neighbors, the Benfords, who let me assist in the annual turkey slaughter and plunder their amazing garden. To the various people in the Ithaca/Trumansburg/Mecklenburg food community who answered questions about cheeses and curing meat and crunchy sauerkraut—chances are that if you spoke to me in the last two or three years, I asked you about sprouts or compost. To my South African cohort, who have read, discussed, and given me insights: Christopher Honey, and my Steyn family, Lauren, Elbert, and Marinda. To my friends Katy Schoedel, Erik Hillman, and Joanna Cerro, for reading and reminding me of our misspent youths and pond swims and nights spent prowling outdoors. To the friends we have lost, Collin Anderson and Xeno Taylor-Fontana, who are there in every word.

I also owe thanks to Erik Reece, for writing *Utopia Drive*, which was enormously informative and let me think about American attempts at perfection much more clearly. To the folks at the Oneida Community, and their efforts to keep the history of that project alive; I apologize for liberties I've taken in portraying the Community, which is more complicated in fact than I've allowed it to be in this book.

Thanks to Legs the whippet, who kept me company and lent emotional support through almost every page of this book, often with his head almost obscuring the keyboard. And always, to Jan, who is reader, editor, co-conspirator, sympathetic ear, problem-solver, first opinion, second opinion, font of literary knowledge, and egger-on—you make all this possible.

About the Author

Caite Dolan-Leach is the author of *Dead Letters;* she is also a literary translator. Born in the Finger Lakes region, she is a graduate of Trinity College Dublin and the American University in Paris. *We Went to the Woods* is her second novel.

Caitedolanleach.com
Facebook.com/caitedolanleachauthor
Instagram: @caitedolanleach

About the Type

This book was set in Berling. Designed in 1951 by Karl-Erik Forsberg (1914–95) for the type foundry Berlingska Stilgjuteri AB in Lund, Sweden, it was released the same year in foundry type by H. Berthold AG. A classic old-face design, its generous proportions and inclined serifs make it highly legible.